About the Author

Chris Bonnello is an author, speaker and special needs tutor based in Nottingham. Following a career in mainstream primary school teaching, since 2015 he has been an autism advocate through his website, Autistic Not Weird (https://autisticnotweird.com). He has won multiple awards for his work, and delivered speeches as far away as India and the Sydney Opera House. The *Underdogs* series, which began in 2019, is his first published venture as a novelist.

Underdogs:
Tooth and Nail

Chris Bonnello

unbound

This edition first published in 2020

Unbound
6th Floor Mutual House, 70 Conduit Street, London W1S 2GF
www.unbound.com

ISBN (eBook): 978-1-78965-096-9
ISBN (Paperback): 978-1-78965-095-2

Cover design by Mecob

Printed and bound in Great Britain by Clays Ltd, Elcograf S.p.A.

To the memory of my adopted godparents,
Ted and Mary Ward, who taught an
autistic child to lead people.

And to my adopted godson Morgan,
who I am eternally proud of.

Super Patrons

Vicky Allen
Saffron Allen Scott
Samantha Allen-Turner
Sarah Ashley
Autistic Not Weird Patreon supporters collective
Christopher Bates
Jenny Bates
Bradlei Binns
Dionne Booth
N Brannon
Colin Broderick
Fiona Broderick
Ash Brooks
Carrick Brooks
Darren Brunton
Richard Buck
Suzy Burnett
Ruth Byrne
Kristen Callow
Jaxon Campbell
Megan Campbell

Lyn Campos Navarro
Bart Ceelen
Beau Ceelen
Daphne Ceelen
Fleur Ceelen
Tom Chappelle
Rachel Chavez
Valkyrie Childs
Ysgol Cilgerran
Billie Clarke
Eliza Clarke
Noah Clarke
Nick Collins
Tanja Collins
Andrew Combs
Lara Conner
Sarah Cooper
Anita Coulson
Dawn Louise Cox
Brendan Cueva
Heather Cueva
Sandra Cunningham
Vic Cutting
Jim Darby
Tegan Davis
Carly Day
Robyn DeCourcy
Alex Diviney
Linda Dolman
Sam Dooley
Linda Douglas
Ilja Drost
Laurens Drost

Lucca Drost

Penelope J. Dugan

Samuel R. Dugan

Helen England

Josh Erickson

Sarah Erickson

Finley Evans

Simon Everaerts

Elijah Farris

Caitlin Ferrence

Kirsty Finn

Matthew Fleming

Andie Fox

Toby Fox

Joel Francis

Lewis James Fretwell-Smith

Indie and Joshua Frost

Jackie Giles

Sam and Claire Giroux

Benjamin Giroux #oddtoo

Jess Gomersall

Finley Greenfield

Zoë Grey

Clare Griffiths

Christie Groves

Miriam Gwynne

Paul Hallybone

Shona Hancock

Carl Harding

Ciara Harris

Dylan Harris

Robynn Harris

D. Hartman

Abi Harvey

James Harvey

Nicole Hastie

Robynne Hawthorne

Charlotte Hester-Chong

Jaime Hodgson

Harry Howarth

Justin Howarth

Kristiaana Humble

Izzy

Katie Jean-Louis

Alexander Jenks

Amanda Renee Johnson

Kendra Johnson

Theresa Johnson

Bethan Jones

Melina Kacoyannakis

Belladonna Frida Kahlo

Dorina Kasapi

Keepa Family Angela Ren Jacob Dylan Keisha

Charlotte-Ann Kelly

Corwin Testarossa Kimberley

Jennifer Knab

Gabriel Knight Laurin

Jessica Lambert

Barbara Leaf

Jemma Lee

Julie Lehrman

Claus Liberg Rasmussen

Gary Lloyd

LondonGaymers (A. Rider's Second Family)

Theo Lote

Jess Lupton

Poppy Lupton
Jodi Lynn
Emma Maher
Making Momentum
Leo Marson
Lucas Marson
Emma Martin
Paula Mathewson
Alison Matthews
Kayla Matthews
Lindzi Mayann
Sarah McCarthy
Julie McCarvel
Mary McCormick
Christy McDonald
Jasper McDonald
B A McGilvray
Blake McMahon
Lauren McMahon
Shilo McManus
Wayne McManus
Hoi Ming Lee McVey
Paul Micallef
Andy Milligan
Fiona Moncur
Artemis Moon
Wendi Moore
Wyatt Moore
Kelly Morris
Rachel Moseley
Kris Mosqueda
Scott Murdoch
Colin Murphy

Misty N
National Autistic Society South Bucks
Jodie Norman
Alexandra Nudds
Linda Nudds
Sebastian Nuñez
Adam Oliver
Martin Ollier
Barbara Paier
Aaron Parker
Mary Parker
James Craig Paterson
Phillip Perry-Walden
Melissa Phillips
Dylan Phipps
Stephanie Poole
Cassandra Prucha
Pukehohe High School
Pukekohe High School Library
Jayden Rafique
Rebel Rebel
Henry & Oscar Reid
Angela Reynolds
Cian Reynolds
E C Rickett
Alex Rider (The Aspie, Not A Spy)
Brian Rodewald
Lorraine Ross
Luca Rossi
Jean Sando
Mary Anne Savage
Dora Schmora
Tara Segrave-Daly

Clara Seow
Callie Shackleton
Ben Sharp
Jo Sharp
Oliver Sharp
Zoe Sharp
Nicola Sheldon
Heather Sheppard
Eilidh Skinner
Bruce George Smith
Chad Smith
Morgan Smith
Sophie Smith
Charlie Smitsdorff
Helen Souter
Niav South
Christel Ursula Sparks
Tina St Ruth
Ziggy Stardust
Lucas Stephens
Jennie Strong
Victoria Strudwick
Troy Stuart
Arran Swinscoe
Stephanie Tarnutzer
Marcel V. Taylor
Rachael Moon Taylor
Zuzu Taylor
Michael Teegarden
Aidan Thornley
J Toohey
Su Underwood
Irene Valdez

Sheila van Nie
Frank van Sebille
Remedios Varo
Martin Versteegen
Will Versteegen
Andrew Walden
Barry John Walden
Julie Walden
Mark Walden
Gavin Walker
Kay Ward
Juliana Watson
Rosalind Weinstock
Kristine Weiskopf
Amanda Wheeler
William Stephen White
Sarah Whiting
Sandy Wild
Kat Williams
Steven Wilson
Vicki Wingrove
John Wofford
Susan Wolfe
Ana Maria Young

The Underdogs of Spitfire's Rise as of May 16th, Year One

First name	Last name	Age	Notes
Kate	Arrowsmith	16	Secondary student, Oakenfold Special School, Harpenden. Diagnoses: Autism, Severe Anxiety.
~~Charlie~~	~~Coleman~~	~~15~~	~~Secondary student, Oakenfold Special School, Harpenden. Diagnosis: ADHD.~~
Gracie	Freeman	15	Secondary student, Oakenfold Special School, Harpenden. Diagnosis: Global Development Delay.
Alex	Ginelli	22	Deputy store manager, Fixit hardware store, Bancroft Road, Brighton.
Mark	Gunnarsson	18	Post-16 student, Oakenfold Special School, Harpenden. Diagnosis: unclear.
Jack	Hopper	17	Post-16 student, Oakenfold Special School, Harpenden. Diagnosis: Asperger Syndrome.
Joseph	McCormick	64	Lecturer in Mathematical Sciences, Greenwich University.

First name	Last name	Age	Notes
Thomas	Foster	9	Year 4 pupil, St David's Primary School, St Alban's.
Lorraine	Shepherd	52	Nurse, Queen's Hospital stroke unit, Luton.
Raj	Singh	15	Secondary student, Oakenfold Special School, Harpenden. Diagnosis: Dyslexia.
Ewan	West	16	Secondary student, Oakenfold Special School, Harpenden. Diagnosis: Autism (PDA profile).
Simon	Young	14	Secondary student, Oakenfold Special School, Harpenden. Diagnosis: Down's Syndrome.
Shannon	Grant	17	Daughter of Great Britain's autocratic dictator, Nicholas Grant.

And the highest-ranking staff of New London Citadel:

First name	Last name	Age	Notes
Nicholas	Grant	55	Undisputed ruler of Great Britain.
Iain	Marshall	43	Head of Military Division.
Nathaniel	Pearce	42	Chief of Scientific Research.
Oliver	Roth	14	Primary assassin.

Prologue

Oliver Roth never felt like words on a screen did him justice. He sat at his workstation, browsing the clone factory incident report, and wished it had been written with a little more flair – with him being recognised as more heroic. He had earned it.

He grabbed his last slice of pizza and ate it in two mouthfuls. Life in New London's upper floors, with literally only three people in the country who outranked him, came with its fair share of luxuries. Among them was the opportunity for pizza on demand, even for breakfast. Yes, as a growing boy and a professional assassin, healthy eating was important. But only when his bosses were looking.

Besides, they'd forced a fourteen-year-old out of his bed at half six in the morning. So him eating pizza for breakfast was their fault, really.

Executive Summary Report: New London Clone
Factory Destruction

Roth huffed. Nicholas Grant, dictator and master of Great Britain, had chosen such a stale and wooden title for such an exciting few days.

Updates in progress: May 16th, Year One

On April 23rd, <u>Shannon Grant</u> fled New London with her associate, <u>Lt Anthony Lambourne (deceased)</u>. They hid in a disused NHS health centre with a small group of Takeover Day escapees. There they were found and killed by <u>Keith Tylor (deceased)</u> within twenty-four hours, with the exception of Shannon. As commanded by Nicholas Grant, Shannon was transported by Tylor back towards New London. However, she was able to kill him and escape.

Wow Nick, could you have made this sound any more boring? This is your estranged daughter you're writing about!
    But Roth smiled. That was the great thing about being asked to proofread. He could make whatever edits he wanted.

She was able to stab Tylor more than fifty times and leave him dead in somebody's back garden,

the edited sentence said. Roth had never liked Tylor anyway. Smiling, he read on.

Before their escape, Shannon and Lambourne produced a computer virus which would shut down and destroy New London's clone factory, which ultimately made its way into the hands of <u>Terrorist Faction 001</u> (known among themselves as the 'Underdogs'). It is assumed that Shannon

remains sheltered with them in their
countryside hideout (which they have named
'Spitfire's Rise').

OK, let's make the next bits more interesting.

The ~~insurgents~~ Underdogs invaded New
London on April 25th, with a team
comprised of <u>Ewan West</u>, <u>Kate Arrowsmith</u>,
<u>Jack Hopper</u>, <u>Alex Ginelli</u> and <u>Charlie
Coleman (deceased)</u>. Their intention was to
~~neutralise~~ annihilate the clone factory,
although they were ~~forced to evacuate~~
chased by Oliver Roth into the Inner City
prison. The exception being Alex Ginelli,
who was separated from his group (see
also: <u>The Ginelli Project</u>).

'Oliver,' came the gruff voice of Iain Marshall through his
radio.

'Nearly done, calm yourself.'

He knew his tone would annoy his boss. But Marshall was
the kind of man who deserved to be annoyed whenever
possible. Anyone who would willingly choose to be New
London's Head of Military Division was never going to be a
barrel of laughs.

'We're waiting for you in the Experiment Chamber right
now. You don't want to miss the fireworks, do you?'

'You perform the AME experiment without me and I'll
break your pretty little jaw. Now wait a second.'

Marshall huffed and fell silent. Roth continued his edits.

The ~~insurgents~~ Underdogs were able to

utilise ~~a weakness in the Inner City walls~~
staff incompetence, and escaped the prison
on the morning of April 28th. They were
able to destroy the clone factory as
planned (in addition to seizing intel on
the AME project from an officers' sector),
and escaped with Alex Ginelli. The
exception being Charlie Coleman, who was
~~apprehended and killed~~ shot repeatedly in
the chest by Oliver Roth, bringing his
Underdog kill count to eight of the morons.

Roth smiled. It was an improvement at the very least. He read
the final paragraph as he rose to his feet.

To date, the surviving Underdogs remain at
Spitfire's Rise. They are assumed to be
planning their next move against the AME
project. As a result of their raid,
research regarding AME has been sped up
dramatically.

Talking of AME, it was time for those fireworks. Roth jogged
towards the door: Grant, Marshall and Pearce would wait for
him even if he walked, but he couldn't wait to see the
experiment for himself.

With a swipe of his keycard and the flicker of a green LED,
Oliver Roth was granted access to the Experiment Chamber.
The teenage assassin found himself in the same room as Iain
Marshall, New London's Head of Military, and Nathaniel
Pearce, its Chief of Scientific Research. Only Grant himself was
missing.

'Evening, Oliver,' said Nathaniel Pearce with shallow sarcasm. It was barely seven in the morning, but Pearce took every opportunity to point out his colleagues' faults, including lateness.

Roth smirked, and said nothing. Part of being fearsome meant knowing when *not* to step into arguments.

'Is the subject ready?' Roth asked, spotting the figure behind the glass.

'He doesn't look it,' replied Pearce, taking a sip of coffee from a mug which read 'smart-arse and proud of it' in big bold letters. 'Not that it matters.'

Roth took a closer look at the clone inside the chamber. He may have been a manufactured collection of factory-grown flesh and organs, but the emotions on his face seemed very real. He showed signs of nervousness and suspicion, clueless as to why he was armed to the teeth with an assault rifle, holstered handguns, grenades and a belt full of hunting knives. Especially since the Experiment Chamber around him was almost empty, hosting little more than a pair of stone pillars that stretched to the ceiling, positioned a metre apart in the centre of the room.

Roth glanced to his left. Iain Marshall was predictably impatient, his hands in his pockets and his top lip beginning to quiver. Nathaniel Pearce wore his usual creepy smile, perhaps a little too entertained by his own work.

'Are we nearly there yet?' Roth asked.

'AME is four months ahead of schedule,' Pearce replied. 'You can wait another minute.'

Don't say that like you're proud, Roth thought. *If it weren't for Ewan West stealing our plans from that officers' sector, Nick wouldn't have made you speed up the research. McCormick and his special needs kids have had three weeks to plan their next move.*

Special needs kids. It may have been true, but Roth used the phrase to insult his enemies rather than underestimate them. Thanks to their efforts in April, New London's glorious clone factory had become a burned-out ash pit which hadn't grown a soldier in three weeks. Those 'special needs kids' were the reason why the ageing clone population was in steep decline, only propped up by imported soldiers from other Citadels.

The phone rang at the side of the desk, and Marshall picked up the handset. Without seeking permission, Roth pushed the speakerphone button to allow himself and Pearce into the discussion too.

'Experiment Chamber,' Marshall said.

'Iain,' came a lively voice through the speakerphone.

It was the voice of Nicholas Grant.

'Morning, sir.'

'Looks to me like you're ready. Commence the experiment, gentlemen.'

'You're not coming down?'

'Floor F's too low for me. The view on my screen is perfect.'

Roth leaned over the desk.

'Hey Nick,' he said, 'I bet you wish Shannon were here for this!'

'My daughter made her decisions,' Grant answered. 'Now she can live with them.'

Roth looked to his left. Pearce's face wore an entertained grin, and one corner of his lips perked at Grant's last sentence. Roth could not interpret what that particular grin meant, and Pearce did not elaborate.

Roth had not spoken to Shannon much during their time together in the Citadel. As far as he remembered, the girl had spent most of her days locked away in some far corner of Floor A like a fairy-tale princess. Whether this was through her own choice or through her father's overprotection, Roth had never known; he just knew that Shannon Grant had been a private neurotic failure of a person, and she was probably still her private neurotic failing self in Spitfire's Rise too.

'*Now*, if you please,' Grant finished. Roth brought his attention back to the Experiment Chamber and the clone who stood inside, and he remembered how excited he was to witness the proceedings about to take place.

Pearce nodded and pushed a button. The CCTV cameras around them began to record.

'Eight minutes past seven,' announced Pearce, 'May sixteenth, Year One. Final phase of practical experimentation underway. Atmospheric Metallurgic Excitation, research trial twenty-six. Commencing.'

Marshall retrieved the radio from his belt, and spoke to the clone behind the glass.

'Soldier,' he began, 'move to the other end of the room. At jogging speed, passing between the pillars.'

Roth watched in amusement as the clone gave a frightened stare towards the shielded humans, perhaps trying to ask his superiors why. When none of them gave any reaction, the clone turned his head forward again.

He knows his only option is obedience. Poor guy.

The clone ran for about ten metres, weighed down by his excessive array of weaponry, before passing between the two stone pillars.

He didn't live long enough to notice what happened next.

The slow-motion replay would later show the air rippling around him, as if he had run through a vertical surface of water. The previously blank space between the pillars turned crimson and wavy when touched. The clone's head, the first part of him through, was unaffected by the waves. But his fate was sealed as his metal equipment followed.

The space between the stone pillars burst into action. Tiny lightning shards attacked the metal in the clone's grasp: his assault rifle and handguns, his grenades, the belt buckle and hunting knives, and the fronts of his steel-capped boots.

But at that moment, Oliver Roth could only watch at regular viewing speed. To him the dozens of explosions seemed instantaneous, as every metallic item around the clone's body was detonated by the red barrier. The shrapnel from the firearms and blades ripped through his limbs, sending his extremities across the room and his artificial blood splattering across the chamber floor. His right hand slapped the bullet-resistant glass in front of Iain Marshall, causing hysterical laughter from Roth. As the clone's torn remains fell to the ground, nothing more than visceral chunks of carved meat, the rippling red curtain faded back into invisibility as if nothing had happened.

Bloody hell, thought Roth, grudgingly impressed. As much as he despised Nathaniel Pearce, the Chief Scientist had surpassed himself this time. Atmospheric Metallurgic Excitation had once been a crackpot idea from the depths of Nicholas Grant's imagination, but somehow Nathaniel Pearce had brought it into the realm of reality: an invisible wall of energised air that destroyed anything forged from metal.

'Sir,' Pearce asked into the phone, 'are you happy?'

Nicholas Grant's discreet laughter answered the question for him. As Roth started to bounce on his toes with an excited smile, he looked to his side and found even Marshall smiling. Pearce rested his *smart-arse* mug at the side of the control panel and started to applaud himself.

'Happy is one word for it, certainly,' Grant said. 'Nat, can you confirm that AME can be reproduced on a much larger scale?'

'Everything we understand about the laws of physics tells me it is now possible,' Pearce replied. 'If it works for a square metre, it'll work for a square mile. And if it works for a square mile—'

'And are we still on target to achieve this within four days?'

Grant's attachment to May 20th continues to make his decisions for him, Roth thought to himself.

'Yes,' finished Pearce. 'It'll be done within four days. Happy anniversary, sir.'

Chapter 1

The underground tunnel from Spitfire's Rise was too small for Kate to stand up inside. Whenever she tried, the soil would scrape off the ceiling into her hair. It wasn't the effect on her appearance that bothered her, but rather the sensory chaos of a mud massage against her head.

There were another twenty-ish metres before the trapdoor to the grassy hill. Raj was nearly there, barely patient enough to wait for his girlfriend.

'Come on,' he whispered in the darkness.

Kate took a deep breath. Normally she only broke the rules on Sundays, but today she and Raj had a special reason for sneaking outside. Raj reached the trapdoor, pushed it open, and natural light flooded into the tunnel. He barely gave himself a moment to acclimatise before hauling himself up onto the grass.

Kate dipped her head a little further and walked along the last wooden planks before the exit. Last year, McCormick's idea of an underground tunnel had sounded great: an opportunity to enter and leave Spitfire's Rise without using a visible entrance that might give away its location. But it had taken a long time to dig for a hundred metres, and the claustrophobia of those months had stayed with her.

'Before we do this,' Kate said as she approached the grass-covered trapdoor, 'are you *sure* today is the 16th?'

'Yep. And even if it's not, let's celebrate him anyway.'

May 16th. Her brother's birthday. James Arrowsmith, autistic like Kate but in a completely different region of the spectrum, had turned nineteen just four days before Takeover Day. His profound disabilities were so complex, and his reliance on routine so strong, that nothing at all was allowed to change for his birthday. Wrapped presents and birthday songs would have been intimidating to him, but he had spent the day happy with how people had treated him.

He *had* eaten his dinner with a birthday candle. But he had done that every day for the previous eight years. On his eleventh birthday Mum and Dad had placed a battery-powered candle on his plate (not wanting to scare him with actual fire, of course), hoping he would tolerate it without becoming anxious. Even as a seven-year-old, Kate had wondered whether the candle had truly been for James' sake or their parents'. But James had *loved* the flashing light, so much so that he had demanded it the next day. The day after, too. Before the family knew it, every single dinnertime, all year round, needed to feature a battery-powered flashing birthday candle on James' dinner plate.

On his nineteenth birthday the candle was used accurately once again, just like how a broken clock was correct twice a day. And Kate remembered spending the day looking at James with beaming smiles. Even during her time at Oakenfold Special School, after her escape from mainstream, smiles had been hard to come by. So that day with her brother must have been wonderful.

Wow, the world had changed. James was now twenty years

old, celebrating with whatever routine he had established in the depths of New London's Inner City prison. He had been in there for almost a year, assuming he was still…

Maybe he really is alive.

But maybe he's not.

Maybe he found Mum and Dad.

But maybe he didn't.

As was always the case, the worst part was not knowing. Even after almost a year apart, Kate's co-dependency with her brother remained strong to the point of causing enormous anxiety. And with no facts to guide her, every possibility could float around her mind. Especially the worst ones.

Kate shook the thoughts out of her head, and climbed through the trapdoor. She gripped the overgrown grass and used it to pull herself up. The wind was soft, but cold. The sky had probably been clear all night, judging by the temperature.

'Never stops being beautiful, does it?' said Raj.

Kate looked up. Raj had already stopped searching for clone patrols: they were almost unheard of in the countryside now, twelve months after the end of the purges. Instead he sat himself at the top of the hill and admired the view, waiting for Kate to join him, and then closed his eyes to pray in silence.

Kate sat on the grass next to him, thinking about how curious it was that she and Raj Singh had ended up together: two Oakenfold Special School students who had never spoken back in the old days, largely because Raj was in a class specifically for dyslexic students who could barely read their own names. There were some great thinkers in that class, but none who would be able to complete a formal written exam. Raj himself had been a genius at anything that required visual-spatial thinking, and could come up with bright ideas that would never have crossed Kate's mind, but his inability to record his brilliance on paper had left him in a class on the other side of the school to her. But here they were a year later, the autistic girl and the dyslexic boy, going out after however many years of not noticing each other's existence.

She sat herself on the grass and found that Raj was right: the Hertfordshire countryside was a fine place to spend a war. Not all soldiers had picturesque villages and winding rivers outside their living quarters.

The Citadel of New London was somewhere on the horizon, a grey line only visible on a clear day. Many of Kate's fellow Underdogs (and classmates from Oakenfold) had died in that grey line somewhere, and almost everyone she loved was somewhere inside the prison at its centre.

She dropped her head, her gaze landing on the village before her. A year without humans had not done much to dent its beauty. The church looked old anyway, as did most of the houses. The village looked antiquated rather than abandoned.

She looked at Raj, whose eyes were open again. Whichever god he worshipped, he had finished praying to them.

'You know what feels really weird?' she asked.

'Hm?'

'We're four days away from a whole year in Spitfire's Rise. And I still don't know the name of our street.'

'Be thankful,' said Raj. 'McCormick played a smart move, getting Ewan to rip up road signs so nobody could give our location away.'

Then making him rip some up from other villages too, so Grant couldn't just look for the place without road signs.

Kate smiled, as if the memory had been a good one. In reality it had been terrifying whenever Ewan invited her along. Destroying road signs whilst trying not to read them, since the less they remembered the better. Trying to remain unobservant, whilst looking for the clone patrols that were still scouring the countryside. Knocking down every village sign within half a day's walk to the east, and then a *full* day's walk to the west so that Spitfire's Rise couldn't be located in the middle. Every village's name and identity lost for the safety of thirty-two people, most of whom had since…

'What would you call this village?' she asked to distract herself. 'If you could name it for yourself?'

'Some things are too beautiful for words,' answered Raj.

'Stop avoiding the question,' Kate said with a laugh. 'I think it should have some kind of posh name… something-borough or something-ington. What about you?'

There was a noticeable pause before Raj gave his answer.

'It wouldn't be right for me to try.'

'Oh, come on.'

A much longer pause.

Is that nervousness? He's looking at his feet… that means he's worrying, doesn't it?

'…My taxi to Oakenfold took me through this village every day,' Raj said. 'And I could read the sign well enough, so, yeah.'

Kate's heart stopped. Or at the very least, she could no longer feel it.

'You know…'

'Yeah.'

'All along, you've always known—'

'Yes, Kate. I know the name of this village. But nothing more than that.'

Nothing more was needed. Kate's arms and legs began to lighten, as if somebody had switched the gravity off beneath her.

For all my years of fighting anxiety, it still doesn't take much. Even the smallest thing.

No, this is not the smallest thing. My boyfriend just told me our lives are in real danger. He only needs to screw up once, and, and…

'McCormick knows,' Raj continued. 'I was honest with him about it. That's why he's not sent me anywhere for a while. Nowhere I could get captured, anyway…'

Raj fell silent. Kate heard it too. A creak came from the grass-covered trapdoor, and by the time they turned their heads around Mark was halfway out.

'Back inside,' he grunted. 'Now.'

'Oh come on!' said Raj, as if he had just lost a life in a videogame. 'We've only just come out!'

'And now you're coming back in. Move.'

Mark Gunnarsson, by far the fiercest student in Oakenfold – even more so after his year in a youth offenders' institution – spoke with a surprisingly calm voice. With a reputation like his, he never needed to shout. His stony face and piercing eyes were enough of a substitute for raw volume.

'Three minutes, mate,' offered Raj. 'It's her brother's birthday.'

'It's his birthday inside too,' Mark answered, standing himself upright on the grass. 'Now, McCormick's woken up the whole bloody house and got us searching the place like you're properly missing. And I already lost an hour to Ewan getting ready for his precious raid. Get inside so I can go back to sleep.'

He held an open hand towards the trapdoor, his shoulders hunched and his face humourless.

Kate rose to her feet, as did Raj at her side. As their heads came close on the way up, she whispered into his ear: 'How did they know we were gone?'

'Don't know,' she replied. 'We did the same as every Sunday.'

It didn't take her long to work it out.

'It's not Sunday,' she said. 'All the other days Jack wakes up early to power the generator, so he must have…'

When she turned to the trapdoor, Mark was gazing at the sky with widened eyes. Something was wrong.

The sound was distinctive enough. Maybe because there was nothing else in the countryside. Or maybe because a year had passed since they had last heard an aeroplane.

Somewhere to the east, a fleet of them were heading for the grey line in the distance. But Kate had never seen aeroplanes that fast. They weren't usually that shape either, but it was difficult to tell from so far away.

'Missiles,' Mark whispered.

Kate gasped. It would explain why there were so many of them, flying in no particular formation, and at a steep downward angle. Someone, somewhere, had launched an enormous missile attack on New London Citadel.

Her stomach plunged, and a sense of absolute powerlessness overcame her as she realised the truth: that however fast she could run, however many bullets she could shoot, however much she could worry for the citizens of New London who would die as collateral damage, the events before her would unfold the same way regardless. There was nothing in this world she could do to change the outcome.

Nicholas Grant, however, had the whole event covered. Or at least the Cerberus system did.

There were explosions – lots of explosions, but they were all tame. Grant's near-impenetrable network of defence missiles rose from the corners of the Citadel, giving it the appearance of a giant birthday cake, and intercepted the threat with a series of detonations.

Once upon a time, the Cerberus system had been Grant's way of persuading the British government to trust him with their country's safety. His promise of almost futuristic security

– in exchange for limitless funding and influence – had been the catalyst for everything that had been allowed to happen since. That morning Cerberus had been used to repel a foreign attack for the first time, but not in a way the government could ever have predicted.

By the time the smoke started to clear, it was obvious that nothing remained in the sky. A couple of seconds passed in silence, and then the soundwave reached Spitfire's Rise. The explosions had lost their volume over the many miles in between, and sounded little louder than tame fireworks. But those inside the Inner City prison must have been in a state of utter panic. (Although from Kate's experience on the inside, perhaps some were already harvesting the fallen metal debris to reinforce their fragile shelters.)

'Well,' muttered Mark, 'looks like Grant's safe.'

The internal conflict gave Kate a heavy heart. The world may have been a better place if Nicholas Grant and the rest of New London had died in a horrifying missile strike, but at least James would survive his twentieth birthday.

'What the hell was that about?' Raj asked at her side.

Kate had no idea how to respond.

'Something big,' she eventually said.

Chapter 2

Ewan had hated shopping centres for as long as he could remember. The crowds, the noise, the pressure on all five senses and the constant onslaught of *everything* demanding his attention. His mother had tried her best when it got too much for him, but she couldn't control the inside of his overloaded brain. Ewan's childhood memories of Luton Retail Centre consisted of him not meeting the public's expectations, their frowns of disapproval and their lack of sympathy whenever he had a meltdown.

I guess those memories apply to my whole life, really.

Luton Retail Centre felt much more pleasant nowadays. Ewan had the whole place to himself, except for one trustworthy friend by his side.

'I hope you know your way around,' Shannon said to him, 'I spent my school years avoiding places like this, thanks to all the popular girls.'

'You and me both,' said Ewan. 'Well, replace "popular girls" with "humans in general". OK, it's round the next corner. I think.'

He was revealed to be right: the catalogue store had neither moved nor closed down since whenever his last visit had been, and hopefully it was still well-stocked. Other Takeover Day escapees would have looted it before the clones hunted them all down, but nobody would have thought to steal the GPS devices for hikers.

Whatever they stole, they wouldn't have held on to it for long. We probably only survived the purges because of the thermal blocker my dad stole from his barracks, keeping our body heat off Grant's scanning equipment.

Ewan entered the store and headed straight for the warehouse at the back. Shannon paused and grabbed the nearest catalogue.

'No point in searching before you know its serial number, Ewan.'

Ewan saw her point, turned around and headed back to her. It was one of Shannon's interesting abilities (and he was seeing more of them week by week): she could point out Ewan's mistakes and misjudgements without him feeling uncomfortable. He wasn't sure how she managed it; maybe it was some kind of unspoken empathy. With a father like Nicholas Grant, her own childhood may not have been much better than Ewan's.

'So how's this for your first mission?' he asked as she flicked through the catalogue's faded pages. 'It's a boring one I know, but boring is good. Trust me.'

'The first time you met me I stabbed a man to death,' Shannon answered without looking up from the page, 'after he slaughtered my ex and a load of innocent people. I know that boring is good, thanks. Besides, this mission doesn't really begin until we know where the test centre is.'

Ewan gave an understanding nod. Even though it was her first outing as an official Underdog (leaving aside that first night and her deadly attack on Grant's number two assassin),

Shannon had already proven her worth. Since their last victory – which could never have happened without her providing them the technology to destroy the clone factory – Shannon had spent three weeks analysing her father's plans, the scariest of which was AME. Atmospheric Metal-something-or-other: an anti-metal shield over the whole of New London, and presumably one for each of his other Citadels, which would render Grant and his allies utterly indestructible.

The stolen plans had mentioned an AME test centre: a building outside New London where a smaller shield could be launched and examined before the real version went live. The centre was reportedly half-complete, but they had most likely sped up production after their plans had been stolen.

But other than the words 'test centre' and some GPS coordinates, the paperwork had contained no useful clues. The time had come for Ewan and Shannon's final piece of research: finding where those coordinates led to.

Shannon found the technology section, and ran through the item list with a finger which brushed away the dust as it went. Ewan glanced too, and saw the prices on some of the items.

'Three hundred quid?!' he asked. 'People paid that much for a GPS thing? They could have just downloaded an app.'

'There are always people who want quality,' Shannon answered. 'Photographers didn't stop buying professional equipment just because their phone could take a few snaps. Right, how about this one? "Purpose built for the great outdoors, accurate to within one metre, contains 1:50,000 Ordnance Survey maps—"'

'Can you use it to search for coordinates?'

'Only one way to find out. Ewan, grab me some batteries.'

She ran for the warehouse, leaving Ewan to turn and head for the pound shop next door.

She just commanded me, the Underdogs' head soldier, to obey her.

Why aren't I uncomfortable? Shouldn't my PDA kick in or something?

As Ewan walked into the pound shop, he wondered how much Shannon knew about his pathological demand avoidance. She must have seen the diagnosis on the list of names she had first brought to Spitfire's Rise, but a three-word diagnosis was no description of lived experience. The words 'pathological demand avoidance' weren't enough to summarise a childhood of being frightened by other people telling him to do things, or the loss of self-control that came when people's demands made him uncomfortable. A year ago, a command as blatant as 'Ewan, get me some batteries' would have switched on his defiant instincts as an act of self-defence, but somehow it was different when the command came from Shannon.

Shannon had done a good job of climbing up his friendship rankings during her time at Spitfire's Rise. McCormick would always hold the number one spot thanks to his life-changing compassion and influence, and ever since Charlie Coleman had been gunned down by a red-haired assassin, the runner-up spot had been occupied by Kate. But Shannon was now in third, which wasn't bad for three weeks of friendship.

There was something else though: something which numbers and rankings couldn't account for. Shannon was fiery and determined. Uncompromising yet vulnerable. There was too much common ground for Ewan to ignore. For most of his life he hadn't liked people who were similar to him, and he wondered what that told him about his opinion of himself. But at that moment he was met with a young woman whose anger and passion pointed in the same direction as his own, whose fiery nature aligned with him rather than fought against him.

Ewan grabbed the nearest pack of batteries and headed back for the warehouse. He had been right about the looters; with so many boxes strewn across the aisles it was difficult to find

Shannon. By the time he did, she was ripping open the cardboard packet. She removed the GPS tracker and tossed it over to him, and he got to work with the batteries.

'Bloody hell, I miss the internet,' he muttered. 'In the old days this whole trip could have been avoided by using a search engine.'

He took a moment to feel grateful that the Underdogs still had phones even though the internet was gone. Nicholas Grant could have knocked out their communications just by destroying a few phone masts, and the simple reason he hadn't was because *he* had needed telephones too. His Citadels' secure intranet system, however, had enabled him to safely cut off internet access for the whole of Britain without impacting himself.

'Yeah,' answered Shannon, 'well, here are the numbers when you're ready for them.'

'One second... go.'

'Fifty-one point eight one two—'

'Wait wait, slow down. Let me process what you're saying.'

Shannon sighed sympathetically.

'Sorry, Ewan,' she said. 'I still keep forgetting. You just don't—'

'I don't look like I have learning difficulties. Yeah, heard it before.'

'Well, you just seem really capable...'

'Wow, autistic guy with PDA and anger issues is capable of doing stuff. Stop the bloody press. Now just go slowly. Fifty-one...'

Shannon read out the rest of the numbers with a saddened look on her face, which may have meant guilt. It made Ewan feel sad too. Normally it was nice and satisfying when he made someone realise just how little they understood his needs, but there was no satisfaction when it happened to Shannon.

'Seven five eight eight,' Ewan repeated as he typed in the final numbers. 'And our mystery location is...'

He pushed the search button, and waited for the map to load. When it did, it revealed a large building the outskirts of Harpenden.

'Where is it?' asked Shannon.

'Not far at all. About half a day's walk from Spitfire's Rise. In fact, pretty close to...'

Ewan looked closer, and his eyes widened.

'Ewan, what is it?'

The device shook in Ewan's hand. He was trembling from a mix of fear and rage, which must have been what Nicholas Grant had wanted when he had chosen the location.

He threw the GPS tracker against the nearest wall, where it smashed to pieces. Unsatisfied, he took a short run-up and booted an empty box down the warehouse aisle. It didn't go as far as he wanted, thudding to a quick stop like it was trying to insult him, so Ewan ran again with a scream and stamped it into the ground as if it were personal.

'Ewan?'

He took steady breaths and tried to ground himself. He rested both of his feet flat on the ground, one hand against his hip, and the other gripped against the nearest shelf.

'Your father's after a fight,' he snarled, 'with me and my friends, personally. You want to know the *real* name of the "AME test centre"?'

'It's not...'

'It is. *Oakenfold Special School.*'

Half an hour had passed. Ewan had barely stopped running since they had escaped Luton, and it was difficult to run and talk at the same time.

'Alex,' he barked into the phone, 'you know what Oakenfold means to us, right? The guys at home won't like the news.'

Ewan knew he was using the other students' fears to mask his own. The very thought of breaking such sensitive news terrified him. But he didn't need Alex to know he was terrified.

'Mate, they're already struggling with the missile attack on New London. Losing an already-abandoned school isn't going to add much stress.'

'Is that meant to be some kind of comfort?'

'It's meant to be the truth.'

Alex Ginelli was hardly a sensitive guy, and he had no empathy for teenagers with special ed backgrounds. The twenty-two-year-old from Brighton had been brought up in a different world, where places like Oakenfold Special School were safely hidden away from the rest of society. And even in the world he inhabited, he kept himself far away from most people emotionally. Alex put on a distinct lone wolf persona, and it showed so strongly that it was probably a part of his real personality too. But it meant he had an outside perspective in most situations, and Ewan reluctantly admitted it was useful at times. Alex had certainly been in his element during their last mission, sheltering alone in a bungalow until the others were ready to escape. Without his self-isolating approach to combat, perhaps he would never have been able to help Ewan, Kate and Jack escape New London alive.

'Look mate,' Alex continued, 'I'll head home and pass on the news to McCormick. If you're sure I can abandon comms.'

'We're only an hour away, and the hard bit's over. Go and tell him.'

'Got it. You've probably used up your three minutes of untraceable time, so I'm hanging up before Grant ends up finding you. Interrogate Shannon about the attack, though. She may know what's going on in Daddy's world.'

Without another word, Alex was gone. Ewan removed his phone battery, and slowed himself down.

'You OK?' Shannon asked from behind.

'Alex is passing on the news.'

'So we can stop running now?'

'If you like.'

Once he was at walking speed, Ewan looked at his surroundings for the first time. His vision had been fixed to the road like a blinkered racehorse, and he had relied on Shannon to watch out for patrols. The countryside was as pretty as always, and that annoyed him. His own world was in a mess, full of missile attacks and school invasions, and the rest of the world had the audacity to act as if nothing was wrong.

'So what do we know about the missiles?' Shannon asked.

'Basically nothing,' Ewan gasped. 'Could have been an attack by one country or a bunch of countries. The question is why they'd bother.'

'Because my dad's a megalomaniacal dictator who destroyed Britain as we know it?'

'I'm talking about the Cerberus system. Your dad promised the British government that it would make Britain almost invincible to long-range attacks. That's how he got them to go along with whatever he wanted.'

'*Almost* invincible,' said Shannon. 'I guess that explains it.'

Ewan rested a hand against the nearest road sign. He was more tired than he wanted to admit.

'What?' he asked.

'With Cerberus, he's almost invincible,' Shannon explained. 'Missiles can't touch him, and any planes dropping bombs would just get shot down. The only way he could lose is by a land invasion.'

'A land invasion with enough soldiers to scale Citadel walls and fight back a million clones on their way to Floor A?'

'Technically possible, I guess,' answered Shannon with a shrug. 'But with AME, he'll be *actually* invincible. The world believes this is the last opportunity they'll ever have to bring him down, and a one in a million chance is better than a zero in a million chance. Maybe somewhere right now, someone's trying a land invasion that's failing just as badly.'

Ewan wiped the sweat from his forehead.

'And they chose today because…'

'Because my father must be close. He'll have sped everything up after your break-in.'

'And we've no idea how long we have,' Ewan whispered. 'Weeks, days, hours—'

'Four days,' interrupted Shannon. 'We'll have until midnight on the twentieth.'

Ewan stared into Shannon's face, and found her as worried as him.

'One year from Takeover Day,' he muttered. 'I didn't think your father was the sentimental type.'

'May twentieth is his birthday. It's pride, not sentiment.'

Ewan rolled his eyes, and restarted his walk home.

The rest of the journey passed in silence. The less they talked the faster they could move, and the more time Ewan could spend with his thoughts.

He had hoped they would be productive thoughts, but they weren't. They were chaotic ones that cycled through his brain, growing bigger and bigger as they went. The thoughts themselves never changed: his brain repeated the exact same phrases, but said them louder each time until they became his whole universe. Grant took Oakenfold. *Grant took Oakenfold.* *GRANT TOOK OAKENFOLD.*

Over the course of his life, Ewan had tried numerous strategies to break the cycle and set his brain back on track, and the most effective one had been finding a distraction. After a childhood of being told distractions were bad, it seemed strange that they worked so well for him in times of anxiety. (Of course, adults commanding him to avoid them had only forced him to do the opposite.)

Ewan found a suitable distraction, in the form of his mentor's face pictured in his mind's eye. Dr Joseph McCormick, the anchoring figure of stability for Ewan and the rest of the Underdogs, who had turned him little by little from an impulse-driven violent child to someone vaguely capable of doing things well. Ewan pictured everything about McCormick: his glasses that magnified the calmness in his eyes, the hair that wore thinner on his scalp, and that warm smile that he seemed to wear no matter what mood Ewan was in. The mere image of that face in Ewan's mind helped him to steady his breathing, and before long he could start to refocus on his long march home.

It was almost midday when he and Shannon got to the trapdoor, and a short walk through a narrow tunnel led them to the cellar entrance to Spitfire's Rise.

Ewan let Shannon through the door first. Partly out of respect, and partly so she would not see him glancing at the Memorial Wall on his way past. The name of Charlie Coleman still looked out of place: Ewan's old classmate and Temper Twin, with whom he had shared troubled times at Oakenfold and heroic adventures at Spitfire's Rise, now reduced to two words on a slab of dead people's names.

Gazing at his best friend's name felt like staring at the sun, so Ewan distracted himself with the cellar's other contents. Namely the weapons and combat tools on their respective shelves, and the doors to the other two underground tunnels to neighbouring houses: one which led to the room where they kept their electricity generator, and the other which led to their makeshift farm where they grew their freshest food.

As Ewan and Shannon climbed the stairs, they began to hear gasps and high-pitched voices from inside the house. Ewan had predicted his friends' reactions well; the news about Oakenfold must have been painful for them too. But their shouts were even more panicked than he had imagined. It was not worried conversation coming from the Underdogs: it was mass hysteria. He and Shannon scrambled to the top of the stairs, and burst through the door to the living room.

The collapsed body of Dr Joseph McCormick lay on the carpet, unmoving.

Chapter 3

Throughout Ewan's life, his first reaction to emotional hurt had always been anger. Whether it had been students setting him off, or idiot teachers asserting their authority with pointing and loud voices, anger had always been his go-to state of mind.

But with McCormick out of sight in the clinic, his anger was nowhere to be found. All he felt was *fear*, and lots of it.

It was barely midday, but the boys' bedroom was packed. A crowd of people had found various excuses to be there; nobody mentioned the little fact that McCormick and Lorraine could be heard arguing through the walls of the clinic, but each person had sat themselves as close to that side of the room as possible. Presumably, on the other side of the clinic, Kate, Shannon and Gracie were doing the same in the girls' bedroom.

'*No*, Joseph,' came a muffled yell, 'I will *not* do that to you!'

Well, he's still awake at least.

The relief when McCormick had woken up on the living room floor had nearly reduced Ewan to tears. The man had tried to get to his feet too early, and a flurry of hands had struggled to keep him upright as he stood. Ewan's memories of what had happened next were a blur, but Lorraine had sat

McCormick on the sofa and asked a bunch of questions. Most of his answers had been along the lines of 'don't worry, I'm fine'. At some point he had been helped up the stairs to the clinic, with a full pint of water in his hand.

McCormick did not appear to be in immediate danger, but people didn't collapse without reason. And as Kate so often said, the worst part of any worry was not knowing the truth.

'I don't care about the chain of command,' Lorraine continued, 'and you bloody well know it. *I'm* the woman with the scalpel, *I* decide where it goes!'

Ewan was used to Lorraine being blunt and uncompromising. But this wasn't defiance. It was fear, just like his own.

'What's she talking about?' asked Thomas at his side, his little nose pushed against the wall and his voice unusually wavy by his regular chirpy standards.

Ewan shushed him. The nine-year-old's anxiety may have been more visible, but it was no more severe than Ewan's. Ewan was just better at pretending not to be frightened.

'Scalpel?' asked Raj. 'She's not thinking of operating, is she?'

'I don't know,' answered Ewan, 'because people keep bloody talking.'

That shut everyone up.

Of all the people in the room, the lad with the Asperger's diagnosis was the only one who knew what to do. Jack Hopper was as quiet as a dead church mouse, with one hand cupping his ear against the wall and his eyes forming their strongest expression of concentration. Once in a while he even brushed his dishevelled hair away from his ear. Every sound wave mattered.

Ewan imitated Jack's pose, and hoped it would reveal some extra words.

'What you're asking is terrifying,' Lorraine continued. 'I

can't put it any... *no*, it's *not* my personal fears getting in the way of the greater good! I'm not that selfish! The greatest good is keeping you alive, and cutting you open would...'

A pause, and inaudible words from McCormick.

'Then go out there and see what *they* think!' Lorraine yelled. 'If this goes like I think it will, they'll lose the most important figure in their lives!'

McCormick spoke again. He muttered something about 'defeating the object'.

'Is McCormick going to die?!' wailed Thomas. Ewan decided it was the wrong time to shush him.

'I don't think so,' he replied. Hardly the reassurance the boy would have wanted, but it was against Ewan's nature to make false promises.

'He'll be fine, don't worry,' said Raj with a smile. Ewan bit his lip, but said nothing.

Whatever else McCormick said, nobody had heard it, not even Jack. Even in moments of intense emotion, even with a friend as close as Lorraine losing herself in front of him, his voice never rose. The only clue that he had finished was that Lorraine started to talk again.

'Of course I'm afraid,' she said. 'I've had friends die in this room. I watched Callum die when his insulin ran out, and Roy with his cancer. I'm not cutting you up for *anything*, and especially not for you to go and get yourself killed in battle!'

The last couple of words distracted Ewan from remembering thirteen-year-old Callum Turner's existence. It had been a long year, and even at Oakenfold they hadn't talked much.

Battle? He's not...

'Lorraine can operate, right?' asked Thomas. 'Wasn't that her job in the old days?'

'She was a nurse, not a surgeon,' said Raj. 'Massive difference.'

'…Do operations hurt?'

'Not really. They put you to sleep first. I had an operation on my spine when I was twelve, and I didn't feel a—'

'*Shh.*'

Silence fell again, but it was too late. Lorraine had started to sob, and her voice became a whisper.

Ewan had never seen Lorraine cry, but had heard her a couple of times. Most recently when Roy had passed away, from a type of stomach cancer that could have been dealt with easily in a real hospital. She had not been seen outside the clinic for two or three days after that.

But she never really talked about her troubles. Ewan wondered whether this habit came from the fact that her housemates were often her patients too. Lorraine had gone for so many years hiding her emotions while on the wards that perhaps she naturally hid them at Spitfire's Rise.

But it must have been more complicated than that. Emotions always were.

Because Roy had been her friend. Just about the only man her age to have made it to Spitfire's Rise. And underneath her bossy exterior, she probably cared about the teenagers a great deal. She had certainly cared about Shannon when they first met.

Maybe she sees herself as more than 'the nurse'. She has responsibility over who lives and who dies here. The pressure on her is enormous, and she's probably already crushed by the memories of people she couldn't save.

No wonder she doesn't want to operate on McCormick.

*

According to Ewan's watch, only two hours had passed. He had to check Kate's watch at his side to make sure his batteries weren't dying.

Lorraine had surfaced long enough to shout the words 'meeting, downstairs' into the boys' bedroom, and allowed the news to spread by itself. The living room was full now: ten people in total. All the surviving residents of Spitfire's Rise minus the two in the clinic.

Ewan looked across the remaining Underdogs. It was rare to see all of them in the same room at the same time, and with so many Oakenfold students together it almost felt like being in a classroom again. Alex was perhaps the least comfortable person present, the only twenty-something in a room where nobody else had reached eighteen.

Suddenly, the unexpected happened. Dr McCormick, who had been face-down and unconscious on the same carpet hours earlier, walked into the living room with a broad smile. Perhaps he had misjudged the atmosphere, or maybe he was trying to reassure people. Either way, the rest of the Underdogs had no idea how to react. Thomas had his hands up as if ready to applaud. Silent Simon had his jaw gaped open, his breathing audible. Raj shifted forwards to the edge of his seat as if being closer would help him to hear. Lazy Gracie gave the most generic reaction possible, trying to blend in with everyone else. Mark looked up in vague curiosity, either unaffected by the day's events or pretending to be.

'Afternoon,' McCormick said softly. 'First things first, I'm feeling much better and you don't need to worry.'

'Cough-cough-*load-of-rubbish*-cough,' said Jack. A ruder set of words had crossed Ewan's mind, but he chose not to say them.

'But you obviously deserve an explanation,' McCormick continued, without offering Jack any response. 'My cyst has been acting up. I've had it in my abdomen for the last thirty years, and normally the pain is bearable. That said, my lifestyle hasn't exactly been healthy this last year, and something-or-other must have changed in there.'

'Is there a… more scientific explanation?' asked Alex.

'I'm a mathematician, not a biologist. Even Lorraine is struggling, but we both agree I'm better off without it inside me.'

Concerned faces in the crowd began to look at each other. A couple looked at Ewan, as if he could do anything. They only reminded him of his own powerlessness, and as with everything else in life that lay beyond his control, it grated horribly against his nerves.

'Didn't sound like you were agreeing,' said Raj.

'We didn't agree on how to get it out, as I'm assuming you heard. Lorraine's idea was to hold out until the end of the war, and leave it to a real surgeon once we have hospitals again. But I think that's just avoiding the issue. In the end, we came to an agreement. Anyway, this meeting isn't about me. There are more urgent matters at hand.'

Ewan blinked himself back to reality. For several minutes, he had forgotten anything existed outside of McCormick and his health issues. The man leaned back against the nearest wall, the way he sometimes did when yielding the floor to another speaker.

'Kate,' he said, 'could you describe what you saw this morning?'

'We've been told already,' muttered Gracie.

'In multiple conversations, with varying details, from different people. Let's all be told the same thing. Go on, Kate.'

Kate shuffled forward to the front of her sofa, hands clasped as if in prayer.

'Raj and I saw a bunch of missiles flying towards New

34

London. The Cerberus system destroyed them before they got there. But it means—'

'If they wanted to wipe out Grant,' Alex interrupted, 'they should have just detonated a nuclear device in the upper atmosphere and caused an electromagnetic pulse. Would have fried all their circuits forever.'

'You watched too many movies in the old world,' Jack interrupted, flicking his fingers together to aid his thinking – 'stimming', as he called it. 'If an EMP attack were close enough to affect their circuits, it'd be close enough to just wipe out—'

'Alex, Jack, let her finish,' Ewan said. He noticed a little smile of gratitude on Kate's face.

'So none of the missiles got through,' she continued, 'but it means someone's declared war on Grant. Might be more than one country, we don't know. That's it, really.'

The room fell quiet, until Ewan noticed McCormick nodding at someone behind him. When he turned, Shannon had lifted a finger to speak.

She repeated everything she had told Ewan on their journey home: how nobody with any sense would attack her father unless the task would become literally impossible later. With AME just days from being operational, the world had launched a last-gasp attack on her father. And they had failed.

Naturally, the conversation led to the test centre at Oakenfold. The other teenagers – Ewan's last surviving free schoolmates – looked understandably emotional. For some of them, that building had been the one place in the world where life had made sense. Where Silent Simon had been treated as more than just 'the Down's kid', and recognised for the pleasant, nonverbally sociable person he was. Where Gracie had been more than the girl with Global Development Delay, and people tried to meet her halfway rather than judge her. The place that had accommodated Jack after his suicide attempts. The reactions on their faces reflected the love they had all had for Oakenfold Special School.

Going by the lack of surprise on his face, McCormick still remembered everything he had been told about the matter that morning. That surprised Ewan. His collapse could only have been an hour or so after Alex had broken the news to him.

When Shannon ran out of words, McCormick took centre stage again.

'If Shannon is right about the deadline being midnight on the twentieth, this doesn't leave us much time. So make no mistake – this will be an intense few days, involving *two* missions. The first will be a visit to Oakenfold, to learn as much as we can about Atmospheric Metallurgic Excitation. How it works, how the shield is activated, and most importantly how to destroy it. The strike team will consist of—'

'No,' said Mark. 'You don't get to decide this one.'

Most of the room shot surprised glances at Mark, who sat in his usual pose but with his hands noticeably tense. Ewan wasn't surprised at the interruption at all: if Mark hadn't done it, he would have spoken up himself.

'This is *our* school they've taken over,' Mark continued. 'It's *us* who should take it back. Besides, we're the ones who know the place. We know its layout and its weak points better than any of Grant's people. There's only one strike team that can possibly do this.' He pointed his index finger at each former student in clockwise order. 'Raj, Gracie, Simon, Jack, Kate, Ewan, and me. *We'll* be doing this one.'

The room looked back at McCormick who, in true McCormick fashion, was smiling.

'I absolutely agree,' he said. 'You've named the exact line-up I had in mind. My suggestion is that you all get some rest now, because you'll be setting out tonight and striking in the early hours of tomorrow morning. This leaves Alex and Shannon on comms, as Lorraine and I will be, er, unavailable. She'll start her operation as soon as you leave, so by the time you're home tomorrow I should be awake again. And on the night of the nineteenth I'll be ready for action.'

McCormick had said his final sentence with an air of optimism, but it was met with a deathly silence.

He'd better not be saying what I think he's saying...

'Ready for action?' asked Raj.

'Yes, on the nineteenth we'll need to find a way into New London, then raid the upper floors and wipe out every trace of AME we find. It's a tall order, I know, and it'll take place higher up in New London than we've ever reached before. But if we don't manage it, we lose the war.'

'But *you?*' asked Raj again. '*You*, ready for action? No disrespect but... how old are you, seventy?'

'Sixty-four.'

'Oh, that's OK then.'

'I've been to New London before,' said McCormick. 'Just once, but I've been. Besides, the kings of old were always on the battlefield for the conflicts that won or lost their wars. It was expected of them. Even in World War Two, the generals joined their privates on the D-Day beaches. It wasn't like the leaders of today who watch drones on TV from thousands of miles away.'

Ewan could feel rage and helplessness creeping into his mind, and his eyes began to twitch as if tempted to cry. Thomas, who must have been daydreaming through McCormick's words, laughed about something to do with generals and their privates.

'Sorry,' said Alex, clearly not sorry at all, 'but there's a reason kings and generals don't go into combat now. By the time they're sixty-four they know they're past it.'

'Lorraine thinks so too, unless I have my cyst removed. I was lucky enough to get through that mission in December without it bothering me inside the Citadel, but I haven't risked going back since. And it's touch and go whether I'll even be better in time, so the sooner it's taken out, the better.'

Ewan had no idea what 'touch and go' was supposed to mean, but he found himself hoping that McCormick would have a very, very slow recovery. A whole week in the clinic would be worth it to keep the old man away from New London, from the thousands of clones that would try to kill him, and from Oliver Roth. Half a year in bed would be worth it.

He had not thought about that December mission since it had happened, but it had been bloody scary at the time. McCormick had left the house with Mark, Sally and Rachael, all of whom had been Oakenfold students, and none of whom Ewan had trusted to keep him safe. (As if to prove Ewan's point, to date McCormick had outlived two of them.) Since Ewan himself was still recovering from an ammo raid, he had been left at Spitfire's Rise with nothing but his fears to keep him company. McCormick *had* eventually returned, unharmed against the odds but in tremendous pain thanks to that cyst. And once he had arrived home, he had returned to the sight of Ewan smashing up the boys' bedroom from anxiety.

Ewan brought himself back to the present. He had spent so much time dealing with his own reaction that he had not thought to look at his friends. When he lifted his head from his knees, he found Simon even shakier than normal, Raj's hands clasped as if in prayer, Jack's fingers buried in his dishevelled hair and Lazy Gracie actually giving a damn. No wonder Lorraine hadn't turned up to the meeting.

'What the hell makes you think Lorraine's qualified to perform operations?' asked Mark.

'What makes any of us qualified soldiers? In these times, we take what we can get. Lorraine's surgical performance may make the difference between us destroying the AME project and us losing the war, and I can't think of anyone I'd trust with the task more than her. So on the nineteenth, barring any unexpected injuries, the strike team will consist of myself, Ewan, and at least two others... who I'll decide later.'

Depending on who's still alive after Oakenfold...

'If I can bring more than four of us I will,' McCormick continued, 'but it looks doubtful given my entry plan. We can hardly use the water treatment centre again, so I've had to think outside the box. Any questions?'

Nobody asked a question. Not even about his entry plan. Ewan suspected nobody felt able to, and they were all as stunned as him.

'Then I'm calling this meeting to a close,' McCormick finished. 'Oakenfold students, I know you'll have a lot on your minds, but try to spend today in the most relaxed way you can.'

McCormick's smile was warm and sympathetic as the room's population started to gradually shift. Ewan sat still the longest, and was the only one to notice McCormick's changing expression as his teammates left. The warm smile dropped, and his eyes grew wide.

McCormick was as scared as everyone else.

Chapter 4

McCormick opened the door to the cellar and descended the steps with a hand on the bannister. His feet were trembling too much for him to trust his balance. When he arrived in the cellar, which doubled as the Underdogs' armoury, he saw Ewan already prepared. Clothes, weapons, everything. The assembly time was ten o'clock that night, another five minutes away. But knowing Ewan, he must have wanted some time away from the others. For a leader, he needed a lot of moments to himself.

McCormick could not see Ewan's face as it fixated on the Memorial Wall, now twenty-one names long. The dead Underdogs had outnumbered the living for a while.

'What was that thing you used to say to Thomas?' Ewan asked without turning around. 'You kept saying it to him after Beth died.'

'I said plenty of things to that boy after he lost his mum. Could you—'

'It was something about how missing her would be painful but not a bad thing...'

McCormick nodded, and made his way to Ewan's side. Before he spoke, he took a look around the cellar for Ewan's sake to make sure they were alone. No doubt the lad had established that nobody was in the farm next door or the generator room, but it was best to double-check. Finding nobody, McCormick repeated the words as he joined his lead soldier in staring at the Memorial Wall.

'The pain of missing someone is always worth it for the joy of having known them. Always.'

'Yeah… that was it. Where did you hear that?'

'I have to admit,' McCormick said with a smile, 'I made it up myself. It was a lesson I learned after Barbara died. As much as it hurt to lose her, I'd take that pain all over again. If mourning is the natural cost of love, then it's a cost worth paying.'

When he looked towards Ewan, he saw his disengaged expression. Maybe the lad couldn't apply positive thought to the deaths of his family. Or Charlie.

'Why,' McCormick asked, 'what are you thinking?'

'Right now I've reached Ben Christie,' Ewan answered. 'I need to remember something about him.'

McCormick gazed at the Memorial Wall, and found Ben towards the bottom of the list. Only Rachael Watts, Daniel Amopoulos and Charlie Coleman had died after him.

'How come?' he asked.

'Because a few weeks ago I watched my best friend become nothing more than a chiselled name in a slab of rock,' Ewan said, pointing a twitching finger at Charlie's name. 'And once I saw it, I realised how easy it'd be to forget who these people really were. So now, every time I look at this, I read down the list and try to remember something about each person.'

McCormick knew that smiling wouldn't be the reaction Ewan wanted, but he found his young friend's attitude touching. He hid the smile as well as he could, as Ewan pointed to the top of the wall and reeled off some memories.

'Sarah Best used to help Kate when she got anxious in

French. They weren't even friends but she helped anyway. Callum Turner came up with the Oakenfold Code... "the problems are not the person". We all adopted it, and the teachers were proud of him for coming up with it at the age of twelve. Joe Horn always joked about being best in the school at chess club, even though he never reached a semi-final. Then there's Elaine, Arian and Teymour... they deserve to be remembered for more than just dying on Jack's generator mission.'

Ewan turned to McCormick, revealing the redness in his face.

'Remember a few weeks ago,' he snarled, 'when I yelled at you for not adding the Rowlands? Three good people died in New London helping us get out of the Inner City, and they didn't even become chisel marks. They didn't become bloody anything. And I don't want to forget them either.'

'If they mean that much to you—'

'It's too late now. You've already added Charlie, and he died after them. I'm scared about what's going to happen next.'

Scared. Have I ever heard him use that word before?

'You're taking a stupid risk,' Ewan said with watery eyes, anger and love blending in his voice. 'If Lorraine's hand twitches at the wrong time, your name's next on this list. Whether you die on the operating table, or somewhere in New London with your stitches ripped open. If you meet a clone that's faster than you, your name's next on the list. If...'

Ewan's sentence collapsed. McCormick tried to take advantage of the silence, but couldn't find anything to say. His lead soldier was absolutely right.

'Don't you dare become just a chiselled name in a bloody rock,' Ewan managed to continue. 'Other than my dad, you're the only man I've ever trusted. You're not allowed to mean that much to someone just to die on them. Don't you *dare* do that to me.'

McCormick closed his eyes. As a mathematician, he knew the logical response. As a human, he didn't want to hurt a young man who meant so much to him. But as a leader, he knew there were some situations that were impossible to get right. He chose to be honest.

'Ewan, I will keep myself on this planet as long as I can, for you *and* the others. But if it ever came down to a choice between staying alive for you or dying for millions of prisoners, you understand that I have to choose the greater good. That's why we're fighting this war.'

Ewan turned back to the wall with a cold expression on his face. McCormick heard other people's footsteps at the top of the stairs, and realised how little time he had.

'Ben Christie was a terrible singer,' he said. 'He used to randomly burst into song, and whenever Thomas told him to shut up he'd smile and sing louder.'

Ewan gave a barely-visible smirk, and nodded. McCormick watched as Ewan's gaze dropped to the last three names – Rachael, Daniel then Charlie – and then relaxed himself.

Truth be told, Ewan seemed more relaxed than McCormick.

How do we know this wall won't have all of our names on it one day? McCormick thought to himself. *Is there truly a chance of anyone here becoming more than 'a chiselled name in a bloody rock'?*

No, this war won't end like that. We won't let it. One way or another, this Memorial Wall will never be full.

The voice of defiance buoyed him, but McCormick knew it was only guaranteed to be true because there would be nobody left to chisel the final name.

The Oakenfold crew came down the stairs. It didn't take long for all seven students to ready themselves, with everything from assault rifles and knives to radios and lighters. It may have been a mission that impacted them personally, but it was encouraging to see them driven by vengeful enthusiasm rather than fear. The comms team, Alex and Shannon, joined them in the crowded circle, and they all linked hands around the Memorial Wall.

'To honour those who gave everything they had,' said McCormick, 'we will give everything *we* have. To honour the dead we will free the living, united by our differences.'

'United,' came the response. But it sounded different to normal.

Some of the students, including Mark and Raj, had said it emphatically. Like they were preparing for a fight to take their whole world back. Ewan and Kate had barely whispered, and McCormick noticed that their eyes had glanced towards him. They were afraid of what would happen to him once they left.

It was an unusual feeling, having his worries reciprocated. Normally when his soldiers left, he would hope and pray that he was not saying a final goodbye to any of them. This time his young fighters feared the same for him too.

Nine Underdogs went into the exit tunnel, with not one word spoken between them. Simon gave a worried look towards McCormick, and Raj gave a hopeful thumbs up. Gracie looked like she was trying to avoid the sight of him altogether. They were gone a moment later, leaving McCormick in a Spitfire's Rise he did not recognise: one that lay completely silent.

In order to break that silence, the first place he visited was the living room. Thomas was there, spread out on the empty sofa with his face buried into the backrest. He should have been in bed an hour earlier, but McCormick didn't mind. The boy had spent the entire day processing the news of the operation, and still needed more time.

'Thomas,' he said.

'What?' came the nine-year-old's whisper.

'I'm going to the clinic in a few minutes. I just thought I'd say good night.'

'Good night.'

There was no expression in Thomas' voice. He was giving the response expected of him; the next line in the script.

Once in a while, he would leap at McCormick and cling onto him like some kind of cuddly leech, keeping his thin arms wrapped around his chest until he had been told to let go at least three times. It was problematic for an ageing man, but on principle McCormick never objected. At that moment, a hug attack from Thomas would have been most welcome. McCormick was frightened. More frightened than he wanted any of his Underdogs to know.

But there would be no hugs that day. Thomas, like most of the crowd in the cellar, despised him that day. McCormick sighed, and walked to the foot of the stairs.

'I love you, Thomas. And I'll see you tomorrow.'

'Mum used to say that.'

It wasn't worth pushing the issue. McCormick left the living room and made his way up the stairs.

If only to delay the inevitable, he opened the trapdoor to the attic and pulled down the ladder. There must have been enough time to see Barbara.

He would forever be thankful to his old friend Polly for letting him lodge in her house after Barbara's death. She couldn't possibly have predicted her home would become a place like Spitfire's Rise. McCormick's most treasured possessions had been in Polly's attic long before Takeover Day, just metres above a houseful of people who had no idea he had any prior link to the house at all.

He found the cardboard box in its place next to the boiler

and, as always, picked out the Anglesey honeymoon photo first.

When he knelt down to grab it, his arm brushed past a second cardboard box. Momentarily distracted, he checked inside it to see if the envelopes were still there, and counted eleven as expected. He wondered how many would remain when the time came to hand them out.

He brought his attention back to his late wife. There was surprisingly little to say to her. On the brink of going under the knife, in a house where all the occupants were angry with him, only one topic came to mind.

'That's the worst thing about leadership, Barb,' he began. 'They can train you to teach, and they can train you to guide people. But they can never train you to deal with the loneliness.'

He kissed the part of the photo which held Barbara's face, and returned it to the cardboard box. Once it was back in place, he had run out of excuses. It was time to face Lorraine.

Lorraine could be an intimidating person, but never more so than now. McCormick lay flat on the clinic bed wearing nothing but his underwear, as the Underdogs' nurse marched to and fro across the clinic in an understandably foul mood.

She opened the top drawer of a dulled filing cabinet that had once held McCormick's student assessment data. Now it held Lorraine's emergency medical supplies, some of it in sealed jars that had dusted over from months of idle storage. Lorraine's hand emerged with an unused bottle of clear liquid, and she readied her syringe.

'I never thought I'd use expired drugs on a patient,' she mumbled with a weak tremor.

McCormick had a couple of humorous comebacks in mind,

mainly about how he never paid attention to use-by dates on food. But he knew the process would be more tolerable if he only spoke when asked a question.

'So how much do you weigh?' she asked.

'Still eighty-four kilograms.'

'Not eighty-three or eighty-five?'

'Well, we might have all weakened the springs on the scales by weighing ourselves too much,' he said with a chuckle.

'Do you definitely weigh eighty-four kilograms?'

'Yes. I do. So one kilogram makes a difference, does it?'

'If you give the wrong amount of anaesthetic to a patient, you could kill them. If you give a child an adult's dose they won't wake up. I have to calculate how much to give you based on your age, height, weight, body mass index and general state of health, and I can't afford to get it wrong. A teaspoon too much will cause permanent brain damage.'

She poked the syringe through the bottle's foil cap, and spent nearly a whole minute measuring the correct amount, tapping the syringe to get any bubbles to the top, then squirting and re-measuring. Eventually she seemed satisfied, and turned to McCormick with the loaded syringe.

'And all of this,' she continued, 'so you can go running around in New London and probably get yourself *killed*!'

'If I get killed and we destroy the AME project... I know you don't want to hear this, but that's a win. An extremely good one.'

'It'll be a better win if the shield dies and you don't.'

'Obviously,' said McCormick, suppressing the nerves in his voice. 'And that's the result I'm aiming for. I don't want to die, Lorraine. I want to go out on the nineteenth, run around and shoot clones, get out alive and make it home again. But that involves risk, as war always does.'

'Has it occurred to you that you'll be under the same roof

as Nicholas Grant? Marshall and Pearce? *Oliver Roth*? And just days after an operation?'

'It's crossed my mind,' McCormick answered, staring up to the ceiling to avoid Lorraine's glare. 'But have you read the AME report? It's terrifying. I have to be there for this, Lorraine. I can't just sit at comms while the young ones do the dying. That's what cowards and presidents do.'

'There's no shame in recognising your limits.'

'No, but there's shame in accepting them.'

Lorraine did not reply, and McCormick breathed a sigh of relief. Tired of conversation, and fatigued from debating the issue, he stretched out his right arm and invited the needle towards his skin. The inside of his lower arm was still dotted with miniscule scars from forty years of blood donations. He was no stranger to needles.

'Just... promise me you're not looking for trouble,' said Lorraine.

'I promise I'm doing the right thing. That's enough.'

'No, it's not. If I do this, you have a *duty* to keep yourself alive and uncaptured!'

McCormick gave a warm smile. Their two principled minds had done nothing but clash ever since his collapse, but beneath their differences they were the closest of friends.

'I'll do everything I can to stay out of trouble,' he said. 'And believe me, I won't just be doing it for you. I've got my own vested interest in staying alive!'

Lorraine took a deep breath, and in the seconds it took to find a vein and insert the needle, McCormick tried to forget the enormity of the operation. His friend was using expired anaesthetics to send him to sleep, and then she was going to carve him open with a sharpened kitchen knife. All this without any surgical training, and a selection of memories that remained from her nursing years. And at the end of it all, there was the soldering iron that lay at the back of the room. The very sight of it made him shudder. When the time came…

A prick in his arm caught his attention, and he turned his head just in time to see the last of the colourless fluid vanishing into him. McCormick's nervous system began to numb itself, and his last conscious sight was of Lorraine's eyes as she began to cry.

Chapter 5

A year and a half ago, during one of his worse meltdowns, Ewan had found a way to escape Oakenfold. It had been a ridiculous strategy: in his unthinking rage he had run outside, lumbered up to the gate and just pressed the buzzer – an idea which the rational Ewan would never have considered. The receptionist assumed it was a class heading out for a PE lesson, and had buzzed him out without checking the CCTV screen.

It had taken the rest of the day for anyone to find him. Maybe they had assumed he had run into Harpenden to take a bus somewhere, but Ewan hadn't been stupid enough to surround himself with the general public. All he needed to do – all he had the mental strength to do – was find a hiding spot on a nearby hill that overlooked the school, and stay there until transport home arrived at the end of the day. It had seemed like a good idea at the time.

Once he had calmed down and realised how much trouble he had got himself into, he had spent the afternoon searching for the perfect vantage point: one where he could watch the panicked staff running in and out of the gates, the entertained students looking on from the windows, the police cars coming and going, and his mother's arrival when the school finally called and admitted they'd lost her son.

It had taken long enough, but that day's troubles were finally worth it. Ewan and his team knew exactly where to hide outside Grant's AME test centre.

He hadn't liked the prospect of walking the whole way around Harpenden rather than through it, as it added miles to his team's journey. But it wasn't like they were short on time. They had about ten minutes' walking left to do, and several hours of waiting would follow.

Ewan turned around to look at his friends, expecting them to be weary and exhausted. It was nearly midnight, after all. Instead, he found them just as determined as they had been at Spitfire's Rise, but without the additional layer of worry that McCormick had given them. Out of sight really was out of mind.

Raj and Kate were at the back of the group, whispering to each other. Ewan decided to keep away from them when he noticed their hands were joined. Mark was towards the front, overtaking Ewan whenever he got the chance. Whether he was hurrying the group or trying some kind of power play, Ewan neither knew nor cared.

In the middle was the trio Ewan almost didn't notice: Silent Simon being straight-faced and apprehensive – a world apart from the smiling humorous boy he had been at Oakenfold. Lazy Gracie, who did and said as little as possible, allowing herself to be led by people she considered superior to herself. And Jack, who was stimming his fingers and most likely daydreaming again. Or planning for all possible outcomes. Sometimes the line between the two was blurry for him.

'Ewan,' came a whisper from Raj, audible from a distance in the silent countryside.

Ewan turned around to find Raj holding up his mobile

phone and battery. He nodded, and Raj prepared to phone comms.

'Mark,' he said, 'time Raj. Three minutes.'

It got rid of the icy giant breathing down his neck. Mark huffed, but did as he was told. Once the phone was switched on, Grant's technology would take a minimum of three minutes to detect its location. Calls to the comms unit were never long.

With Mark at the back of the group timing her boyfriend, Kate ran up to Ewan.

'How are you doing?' Ewan asked.

'Me? I'm an expert at conquering my demons. I'm fine. I was wondering how *you* were.'

There was a clear waviness in her voice. Kate was nervous, but rushing in headlong. Life experience had taught her that the only way of destroying her fears was to do the things she was scared of, so the mission was right up her street. She'd be fine.

'Ewan?' she said. 'How *are* you feeling?'

'Kind of conflicted, to be honest,' he answered. 'Back at home, it was obvious why Grant took Oakenfold. He wanted to make us feel pressured into taking the school back, but also scared of doing it. Logically we just need to tell ourselves to not be sentimental, and use our knowledge of the school to our advantage. But… it's different now we're this close.'

'Oakenfold meant something to us,' said Kate. 'There's no shame in feeling emotional about going back.'

'Yes there is. Emotional distractions could mean death.'

Ewan looked behind him. Raj was deep in conversation with either Alex or Shannon, and Mark held up two fingers to represent two minutes left.

'I'll be fine once we've stopped hiding,' he said. 'It's just this particular hiding place. It—'

'Was this where you hid the day you escaped school?'

'...Yeah. And wow, that backfired. Still can't shake Mum's reaction from my head. When we got home...'

He shook his head, unwilling to continue. Kate seemed surprised.

'You lived with your mum?'

'Um, yeah. Don't most people?'

'I just assumed it was you and your dad. I mean, you talk about your dad all the time, but... I've never heard you mention her.'

Ewan shuddered. Bloody hell, that hurt! As if the pressure of approaching an occupied Oakenfold wasn't enough, a girl he had lived with for almost a year had opened his eyes to something awful: one of the worst results of his avoidance habit.

Please tell me I haven't gone a whole year without mentioning my mother. I must have at least thought of her.

'Dad got us our weapons. That's the main reason I've talked about him, I guess.'

'What were they like?'

Kate, you're my friend and everything, but please just shut up.

'Complete opposites of each other. You couldn't imagine two people being so different. They say opposites attract, but maybe their opposite genes mixed so badly they gave birth to the ultimate screw-up.'

Kate opened her mouth, but Raj cut in before she could protest.

'I told them we're striking at three,' said Raj. 'That's still true, right?'

'Yeah. Thanks.'

Raj fell to the back of the group, and Kate went with him. Ewan had just enough time to breathe half a sigh of relief before someone else picked up the conversation.

'You want some advice?' asked Jack. 'From someone else with a dead mum?'

Ewan hadn't even known Jack was listening. In most conversations, it was difficult to tell the difference between when he was concentrating and when he was daydreaming. In both cases, he looked away from people and flicked his fingers. As a child, it had led to adults talking about Jack as if he weren't in the room. Apparently, non-autistic people thought his ears only ever worked in conjunction with his eyes.

Ewan's mouth opened, but he reigned in his impulses and stopped himself before telling Jack to mind his own damned business. In all fairness, his thoughts were always worth a listen.

'I was twelve when Mum died,' said Jack. 'I didn't talk about it for a long time. Surprised I even told *you* when I did, to be honest.'

'A cancer death's different to being sprayed with bullets, Jack. You didn't see the moment she turned into a corpse.'

'I'm not competing with you, Ewan. If I were, I'd tell you how long and drawn out my mum's pain was compared to yours. I'm talking about the aftermath. Maybe you don't mention her because the memory of her death is too painful. But I've heard you mention everyone else who died that day, including little Alfie. So I'm going to guess your relationship with your mum was a little complicated.'

'You mentioned *advice*, Jack?'

'Yeah. Don't let things rot.'

Ewan threw a glance at Jack, looking as confused as his face would let him, although he suspected Jack wouldn't see his confusion in the dark.

'When I was about fifteen,' Jack continued, 'I realised I couldn't remember her voice. You know my memory, Ewan, it's spectacular – every fact about dinosaurs I learned as a child

I can still regurgitate now – but I can't remember stuff when I spend years shutting it out.'

Ewan took a moment to see if he could remember his own mother's voice. He was afraid Jack might be right.

'I didn't want to deal with the hurt,' Jack continued. 'But when I realised what I was forgetting, I changed. I decided the hurt was worthwhile. Bring on the pain, if it keeps her alive in my head.'

Ewan nodded, and gave an answer that didn't reference his mother.

'McCormick says something similar,' he said. 'One of his little catchphrases. The pain of missing someone is always worth it—'

'For the joy of having known them,' finished Jack. 'And he's right. I don't know what kind of relationship you had with her, but keep it alive. Even if it means—'

'Have to stop you, Jack. We've arrived.'

The hiding spot was still in the distance, but it was a convenient excuse to withdraw from the conversation. Their vantage point was a crater next to the hill's peak, surrounded by trees. An elevated view with excellent cover. Ewan approached, knowing what sight would await them once they reached the brow of the hill.

And there it was. Oakenfold Special School.

Oakenfold, where the world had made just a little more sense. Where people either knew how to accommodate students with special needs, or at least gave a crap about trying.

Oakenfold, where the problems were not the person.

In order to cope with his own reaction, Ewan looked at his friends' faces for theirs. But each of them echoed his own feelings: complete and utter confusion.

He had expected Oakenfold to look like a military compound, lit up with floodlights, with armed checkpoints and vehicle barriers and so on. What they found was just their old school, with no extra construction work and the lights turned out. It was like Grant's employees had gone home for the night.

'This place can't possibly be unguarded,' said Mark.

'Maybe they want us to think it is,' answered Gracie. It was a clever comment, coming from her.

'There'll be a least a minimal guard somewhere,' Ewan said. 'Maybe even inside. So let's be stealthy. Go as long as you can without firing a shot.'

'Do we even have to wait until three?' asked Raj. 'Doesn't look like it's getting any quieter, and we're giving them three hours to spot us up here.'

'We stick to the plan. In New London the watches start and end every six hours – three and nine in the morning, three and nine at night. They'll do the same here too. Consistency and all that.'

'Bit of a leap of faith, isn't it? I didn't think you liked those.'

'We stick to the plan,' Ewan repeated impatiently. 'We wait till three, sneak in while the guard changes, and we grab all the information on AME we can get our hands on. After we learn what we'll be up against in New London, we wipe out every physical trace of the technology from Oakenfold…'

He hesitated before finishing his sentence.

'…Even if it means burning our school to the ground.'

Bloody hell, comms is boring. Especially when your partner's silent.

When it came to missions, Alex preferred being on the comms end of the phone. He was less likely to die that way. And Mark had been right: the Oakenfold mission belonged to the students and them alone.

Still, a little action would have been appreciated. Or at least *something* happening, even if were just a conversation with Shannon.

It was the early hours of the morning and she was sitting upright in her chair, dutiful and focused. As if she had restructured her sleeping pattern specifically for that night. It made Alex feel ashamed of his own tiredness.

I wonder if McCormick's still alive? He thought. *If the operation were going to go wrong, it would have happened by now.*

Alex shook his head, and tried to think optimistic thoughts. In all probability, Lorraine had already sealed him up with that soldering iron and cried herself to sleep.

He needed something to distract himself. With nothing to do, his mind would start to mull over all the worst possibilities. He had once heard someone say that's how it worked for Kate, except it seemed more painful for her.

There was only one distraction available, and she didn't seem in the mood for talking. Especially not about the subject Alex had in mind. But it was worth a try.

'So Shannon…'

'Hm?'

Already Alex was wondering whether it was a good idea. It struck him how little he and Shannon had in common. In fact, he knew so little about her that he didn't even *know* whether they had anything in common. He wasn't sociable in the getting-to-know-you sense – more in the take-the-mick sense – and Shannon hardly spoke to him unless the conversation was necessary.

Better ask, then.

'I've been wondering for a while. Hope you don't mind me asking, but… what was he like?'

Shannon looked piercingly into his eyes.

Ouch, no wonder the autistic lot find that painful.

'Who?'

'Your father. The great Nicholas Grant.'

She didn't answer at first. She just let the question hang in the air like the smell of a carcass.

'Does it matter?' she eventually asked.

In a rare display of shyness, Alex backed down.

'I suppose it doesn't.'

'He was a monster,' she said. 'I never heard him talk, because he only shouted. He smashed up my room whenever he got drunk. He only fed me when I obeyed him. He once had a barbecue with all my childhood toys, and performed a ritual to our overlord Satan while rocking out to death metal and stealing candy from puppies. Is that what you want to hear?'

Alex was ashamed to admit that for the first few sentences, he had actually believed her.

'I didn't see that much of him,' Shannon said, 'that's the truth. Around the time I left primary school he got into Marshall–Pearce, and spent his days building up his takeover project.'

'So he didn't... abuse you or—'

'Bloody hell Alex, you're crap with social boundaries.'

Alex looked away, pretending to have heard something. Shannon didn't fall for it.

'It was neglect, I guess. Which is a type of abuse. There was a big empty hole where my father should have been. And everything he did after Takeover Day, all the luxuries he showered me with to get me back... it made no difference. Gifts mean nothing if they come from an invisible man.'

She rested back in her chair, and let out an enormous huff.

'If it makes you feel better,' said Alex, 'my dad was an arse. He was more my taekwondo coach than my dad. I think I'd rather have had a guy who wasn't there, instead of a guy who thought comfort zones were something I wasn't allowed to have.'

Shannon didn't answer.

'Then again, I'm kind of glad he pushed me. Without the drive he gave me, I wouldn't have lasted long in this war. He's probably the reason I prefer doing things alone, but maybe he's also the reason I'm still alive.'

'Maybe *my* dad's the reason...'

She trailed off, and Alex decided not to chase the other half of the sentence. He had poked around enough for one night.

The phone rang, and Shannon's hand shot to it first. Perhaps she wanted to leave the conversation more urgently than Alex did. Ewan's face appeared on the smartphone screen, but he spoke so quietly that Alex couldn't decipher his words.

'Yeah,' replied Shannon. 'OK, good luck.'

They're going in. Must be three o'clock already.

Ewan said something else.

'Fine, Ewan, I know it's never luck. Just keep yourselves safe.'

Chapter 6

Kate had gone silent, but her brain was loud with anxiety. Ewan's orders were received by her ears but the meaning of his words washed over her.

'Kate,' he said, 'you and Mark go for the staff areas. Simon and I will go from classroom to classroom.'

'Which leaves the function rooms like soft play and the speech therapy place for me and Gracie,' said Raj. 'You want us in the least likely places to see action, since we're the least effective soldiers.'

'Shut up, Raj.'

'It's true though, isn't it? I can read you like a book.'

'Raj, you can't even read an actual book.'

Kate took a deep breath. Her wits were returning. Maybe it was the casual insults thrown at her boyfriend that woke her up. She looked around the group, back on their feet at the brow of the hill and sheltered behind the tree line.

'So... what about me?' asked Jack.

'Keep guard here.'

'What, so I have to miss out?'

'You get to protect us. Alert us if you see—'

'Is this because I talked to you about—'

'—*alert us* if you see anything approaching. Or any activity that's not us.'

Kate did not understand why Ewan was so irritated with Jack, or what they had talked about that could have caused the tension between them. Jack shook his head, the hair beneath his helmet waving across his face in messy protest.

'Just do yourself a favour, yeah?' he asked.

'What?' said Ewan.

'If this place is abandoned, they've probably finished the testing already. When you're close to the entrance, throw a bullet first and see if it blows up. Don't walk gun-first into a shield that detonates metal.'

Ewan nodded, and Kate heard him whisper something to himself under his breath. Then, with no words of encouragement for his team, without even repeating the mission criteria, he started his walk down the hill, followed by Kate and the rest of the students.

This has got to him. Already.

The emotional impact of the night was probably compounded by the fact that there had been no changing of the guard at three o'clock. Ewan had relied on the enemies' routine for his strategy, and the rug had been pulled from underneath his plans. More than that, it suggested that the building had not been guarded in the first place, and they had wasted three hours of their time outside an empty building.

Kate understood his frustration. When one thing bothered her, it bothered her. When several things bothered her at once, she lost her capacity to think. Both she and Ewan reaped the benefits *and* suffered the consequences of autistic single-mindedness, and were unable to focus on two different sources of anxiety. Ewan could have coped with the emotional strain of seeing Oakenfold, or the sudden change of circumstances, but not both.

Ewan left the bottom of the hill, and led the march across the car park towards the school entrance. As Kate followed, she noticed how neatly the abandoned cars were parked alongside each other. When the clones had come, nobody had been given a chance to escape in their own vehicles. She even recognised a couple of the cars as belonging to specific staff members.

Part way across the car park, Ewan removed a bullet from his pistol and lobbed it towards the school. The bullet glided through the air and smacked against the wall without complaint. Oakenfold was unshielded.

By the time they reached the front entrance, Kate was first in line. She lay a hand on the door to her old school, took a deep breath, then paused as Simon started frantically jumping up and down, pointing towards something inside.

'Simon?' she asked.

Then they all saw it. In the corner of the entrance hall, a door-shaped shadow fell on the wall opposite the toilets. And where there was shadow, there was light.

'Well spotted,' said Raj. 'Someone's left the light on in the loos.'

'So?' asked Gracie.

'Well if Jack were here,' said Raj, in an obvious protest against Ewan's team selection, 'he'd tell you that's proof that the clones have been here. Because all the *other* lights have been switched off since... since we last saw this place.'

Since Takeover Day, Raj. You can say it.

'You know what else I'd say?' came a voice from the radio that made Kate jump. 'I'd say it's proof that *this place has electricity*. By the way, watch the controls on your radios. Make sure you know whether they're transmitting or not. And only use them if it's absolutely urgent, or you're sure there's nobody around to hear. While I'm at it, don't use your torches inside until you know you're alone. Not even lighters. You can't afford to give yourselves away, even from a distance.'

There was annoyance in Jack's voice, which he was trying but failing to hide. Kate understood why. He must have wanted to see the inside of the school that had saved him from suicide in his worst years. But Jack of all people knew the importance of duty and following commands, even if it hurt him.

'Right,' muttered Ewan, 'thanks Jack.'

'Oh, and if they've got electricity, they might have set the alarms. Be careful, and remember the code's 1989.'

'How the hell do you kn—'

'Because I spent years looking at the faded one, eight and nine digits every time I walked past the alarm. And the school was founded in 1989, so it doesn't take a genius.'

Kate looked back at Ewan's hands. Even in the dark, she could see their tightening, determined grip.

'I hope the alarm *is* set,' he said. 'It'd mean there's no clones inside. Kate, open the door.'

It was harder than Kate had thought. The inside of Oakenfold would be where her ugly past met her ugly present. It had been the place where she'd tried to recover from her years of bullying – and only partially succeeded. Now, the best school on Earth would showcase the horrors of a post-Takeover Britain.

She pulled the door open, and the last free students of Oakenfold Special School crept back into the building they had escaped from together. After almost a whole year, it could perhaps have been a sentimental moment. But Nicholas Grant was days away from launching an invincible protective shield that might have been perfected in that same building, so it hardly felt magical.

The alarm didn't sound. Ewan looked disappointed, as far as Kate could tell. It wasn't proof that clones were in the building, but it kept the possibility open.

'Nothing above a whisper,' Ewan said, following his own instruction. Before splitting up, the group of six stood together for a brief moment of shared empathy. Raj said it first.

'United by our differences, guys.'

'United,' whispered everyone else.

Ewan wasted no time in heading for the classroom nearest to the entrance – the one for the profoundly disabled students, who had needed rolling in and out of school in specialised wheelchairs. Simon followed him with a nervous huff.

Raj and Gracie headed straight for the sensory room, already resigned to not finding anything interesting.

'Shall we?' asked Mark.

'Yeah, sure,' replied Kate.

'This way first. Head teacher's office.'

The reception was right next to them, but Mark had made his decision to inspect the most important room first. Kate started to follow him as he set off, but a thought struck her.

'Wait… isn't this the long way round?'

'Yeah. There's something I need to grab from my locker. Assuming they haven't raided it.'

I was at my locker when it started…

Kate's brain faded into autopilot as she followed Mark, her eyes fixed on his feet as they trod before her. It was the least appropriate time to retrace the past, but perhaps Nicholas Grant had chosen the school for that exact reason.

And to be fair, it was working.

It had been between English and maths, and she had been exchanging her exercise books in her locker. Chloe and Sally had complained about not getting a signal on their phones. In the background, Charlie was shouting about his human rights being taken away because he couldn't access social media.

The staff had looked worried, but said nothing. Rule number one in times of crisis – hide everything from the students, even news that might help them.

With Chloe and Sally equally clueless, Kate had walked down the corridor and noticed Raj talking to his friend Callum.

'I overheard two of them,' said the dyslexic kid who would one day become her boyfriend, 'saying something about a fire in town. But not just one. Loads of buildings are on fire. There were gunshots too. Maybe it's a riot.'

Kate had not believed the bit about gunshots. She had learned a lot from the false rumours people had spread about her in mainstream. Exaggerations and blatant lies were unquestioningly believed in schools, while the truth was ignored for not being entertaining enough. But *something* was worrying their teachers…

'OK,' said Mark, returning Kate to the present. 'Here we are.'

Kate realised how lucky she was that some sneaky clone hadn't opened fire from around a corridor corner while she had been daydreaming. She'd have been dead before noticing any attackers. Of course, Ewan would have called it lack of due care and attention on Kate's part, rather than luck.

Mark opened his locker in near-total silence, the clicks of his combination lock the loudest noise in the corridor except for Kate's erratic breathing.

'Can't even see the numbers,' Mark muttered. 'I just know I put them to triple-zero whenever I locked it, so I know how many… here we go.'

The pained scrape of the metal locker sounded deafening to Kate's sensitive ears. But the faint expression on Mark's face showed his indifference to it.

'Single malt,' he said. 'Scottish, twelve years old. Well, thirteen now.'

'Malt?' whispered Kate. 'Isn't that vinegar?'

'Whisky.'

'You brought alcohol into school?!'

'Kate, I spent a year away from lessons after stabbing my dad in the leg. I was already set up to fail my exams, and my adulthood was screwed before it had even begun. When Grant took over I was about a month from leaving this graveyard. Thought I'd do some celebrating on my last day, in front of as many people as possible. What were they going to do, expel me?'

Kate could barely contain her disbelief. She looked at the walls, if only to make her face less visible to Mark. She could have sworn one of the pieces of artwork on the corridor wall was Simon's, since it was as bright and vivid as his personality had been back then.

It was odd how the little things stuck in her head. Kate had also been looking at Simon's artwork when the rumoured gunfire had reached Oakenfold Special School. Everyone was late for maths but none of the staff cared. They were all too busy with this mystery crisis that the students must not know about.

Until Judit Ciskal, one of the reception staff, broke the news. She was wounded, bleeding from her shoulder, and running full pelt down the corridor yelling at the students to hide. There had been screams and meltdowns and panic attacks at the sight of real blood and the promise of something dangerous in the school.

Kate remembered the sight of her first clone: the tall bald model, which she had seen a hundred times since in a hundred other clone soldiers. She had believed him to be a real human at the time. He had run around the distant corner in navy blue uniform, with an *actual assault rifle* in his hands. It had been a sight Kate had never seen before, and would never have expected in a school.

And wow, this clone had been angry. The type of angry she would later learn was built into their neurology, as Nathaniel Pearce had built his soldiers with 'peace' and 'war' settings. She had seen angry people before, but nobody with that kind of face…

Judit had stopped to bend over and help a frozen student to his feet. When the clone had got too close, she drew out a cutlery knife and went for him. And that was when the clone had shot her to death.

'Besides,' said Mark, 'I'm eighteen now, so I can legally drink this even by old world standards. This is coming back with me tonight, and I'll still use it to celebrate leaving Oakenfold. Just leaving in a different way.'

Kate jumped at the sound of Mark closing his locker, and followed him further down the corridor. He reached for his radio.

'Anything yet, guys?' he asked.

A short pause, which Kate used to collect herself.

'Nothing in the classrooms,' came Ewan's voice. 'But they give a good view of the outside. Simon mentioned a bunch of metal shapes he saw around the school's perimeter.'

'Mentioned them?'

'He does talk, you know. Around people he actually trusts. He saw these little shapes outside dotted around the place. They look like land mines.'

'Better be careful on the way out then. Raj, how's things?'

A short pause, although long enough for Kate to hear Mark's voice echo off the walls. It had risen above a whisper, and that worried her. Mark's complacency could spell trouble, but she didn't dare to tell him with words.

'I'm here too, you know,' said Gracie. 'Raj found the sports hall, and he's looking through it right now. It's packed with these huge things.'

'What kind of things?' asked Mark, impatiently.

'He said something about power. He thinks they generate electricity or something. They're big whirring things that reach halfway to the ceiling.'

'So that's how they're powering the school, huh.'

Kate took out her own radio.

'No,' she gasped into it, 'this is something else. We can power the whole of Spitfire's Rise with a small petrol generator. Those things in the sports hall are for powering the AME shield.'

'It'd make sense,' came another voice, which she recognised as Jack's. 'The energy needed to maintain a shield over the school would be massive. Oh, and I'm fine out here, by the way.'

'Have you seen anything?' asked Ewan.

'I'd have told you if I'd spotted movement,' said Jack. 'But now you mention it, I can see those little land-miney things too. But I don't think they're actual mines.'

'How come?'

'Because they've made no effort to hide them. They must be for something else.'

There was a momentary silence. Neither Kate nor any of the other students came up with any ideas.

'We'll keep searching,' Kate said. 'We're almost at Paul's office.'

Even after a year it still felt good to call the head teacher 'Paul' instead of 'Mr Dale'. Special education had always been less formal in those ways, and it had been the ideal refuge for teenagers who had been traumatised in schools full of Misses and Misters in posh suits.

'Speaking of Paul,' said Mark, 'I wonder if we've found him.'

Kate looked around, and saw nothing. Then she looked down and noticed the skeleton a metre from her toes.

She shuddered, but held herself together and kept silent.

It was the remains of an adult. Presumably a staff member. Or perhaps an adult student, since Oakenfold catered for nineteen-year-olds too. But Kate didn't like to think of people in James' year dying in their school.

I know your birthday ended three hours ago, she thought, *but happy birthday, James. I hope it was one that you liked.*

'I don't even know what happened to Paul,' she whispered. 'He might have survived. I... I know who this is.'

A cutlery knife lay next to the wall, less than a metre from the skeleton. Judit had made the mistake of threatening a clone with a weapon, so she had been executed instead of captured. But Kate hadn't hung around to watch. She just ran.

At the other end of the school, a small group of staff members had shepherded the students through the back exit into the outdoor play area. It was normally reserved for the Block One students – those who were profoundly disabled – but that morning it was open to everyone. Kate had followed, looking for her friends in the crowd, finding only Chloe and Sally. She made it through the exit doors, and her heart leapt with relief at seeing James rocking himself next to the swings. When he saw her, his rocking and grunting had not stopped. But he had reached out towards her with a nervous stimming hand. It was love, in the kind of way only James could show, and that nervous stimming hand had been etched into Kate's memory ever since.

Mark and Joe Horn were already attacking the fence. It was a sturdy fence, deliberately designed to keep people like them inside, but when half a dozen others joined in it didn't take longer than a minute.

The staff members didn't follow. Presumably they had got themselves captured trying to save more students.

When the fence came down, only some of the students fled. Some didn't want to risk getting shot. Some were frozen in panic. Some of the Block One students simply thought they weren't allowed to leave school, because it wasn't home time.

Kate had watched as James had frozen himself to the swing, too deep in his routine-based comfort zone. But eventually he had relented and taken his younger sister's hand. Maybe the fear of losing Kate had been worse than the fear of breaking his routine.

In what she remembered as Oakenfold's proudest moment, each Block Two student chose someone with a more noticeable disability, and brought them along on their escape. Even Silent Simon had found another student with Down's Syndrome and helped her along.

In what she remembered as Oakenfold's most shameful moment, it had taken five minutes for them all to realise the difficulty of guiding profoundly disabled teenagers through the countryside with a literal army giving chase. Even Ewan – who had been absent that day, but met them in a field on his way to Oakenfold after something dreadful had happened at his house – had been in no position to come up with bright ideas. When a row of soldiers appeared at the end of the field, Mark had shouted 'get bloody running, they're not worth it!' and everyone had obeyed.

Everyone except Kate, who had tried. But two minutes later...

She had evaded the oncoming army, and James had followed his captors as instructed. Within a few minutes, she had found the group again and joined them in their confused chaos.

So there they were: the last free students of Oakenfold. Kate, Mark, Ewan, Raj, Simon, Jack, Gracie, Sarah, Callum,

Joe, Chloe, Sally, Rachael, Daniel and Charlie. (Kate raised an eyebrow when she realised she had thought of the dead students in Memorial Wall order.) They had wandered across the fields in a clueless daze, until Ewan had run ahead to find a place to shelter. He had later returned – with bloodied hands – and guided them all to the place he'd found. Inside, an ageing man with tears in his eyes had welcomed them…

'Judit Ciskal?' asked Mark. 'Receptionist extraordinaire?'

Kate nodded.

'Looks about her height. I remember her running around as well. So maybe Paul Dale's still alive… guess we'll never know. Let's get to his office.'

Kate followed, hiding her contempt for the young man who had – rightly or wrongly – forced her away from her brother.

One thing was certain, though. Whether the skeleton had been Judit or someone else, Kate had known them personally.

The arrival at Spitfire's Rise was the end of Kate's personal story of Takeover Day, but as time went by she had pieced together a nationwide picture based on the accounts of other survivors. The very first place Grant had attacked were the barracks and RAF bases, disabling any military force on British soil that had not belonged to him. (Even Ewan's dad had only narrowly escaped with his life.) After that, his armies had focused on places where children could be found – schools, nurseries, theme parks and so on – because once he had the children, he had the parents too. All it had taken was a television broadcast with the words 'your children will be waiting for you in your local habitation complex', and resistance among half the adult population was gone.

Not long later the National Grid had been taken down, Grant using his own power sources to run his Citadels, and the invasion of city centres had begun. Rural villages had come afterwards, and places with immobile populations – mainly hospitals and care homes – had been saved for last. Kate imagined that Oakenfold had been pushed further down the priority list because of the disability levels of some of their students, allowing them to hear the news of Grant's armies before they arrived.

It was another thirty metres or so to Paul's office. When they arrived, Mark poked his head around the glass built into the door, and leapt back as if from an electric shock.

He had seen something inside.

Without a word or anything beyond a finger held out to silence Kate, he whispered into his radio. *Really* whispered.

'We've found someone,' he said.

'Where?' came Ewan's immediate answer.

'Paul's office. One clone in front of a laptop... bloody fast asleep.'

'Actually asleep or just pretending?' asked Raj.

'His radio's at the other end of the desk. He'd have to climb to reach it. If he were pretending, he'd have it in his hand.'

So this was their trap, thought Kate. *One clone in the head teacher's office with a panic button. Once he presses it, a whole clone army descends on Oakenfold and makes sure we never get out.*

But if that's true, what's the laptop for?

'So,' she asked, 'what do we do?'

Mark had already drawn out his knife.

Before Kate could breathe another word, Mark had silenced his radio and pressed against the door.

For a huge figure, Mark was stealthy when he needed to be. He crept through the door, holding it open for Kate behind him, and took tentative steps across Paul's old carpet. He positioned the knife in his hand with the blade facing inwards.

He's going to slash the clone's throat.

The sleeping figure's face was clear in the glow of the laptop screen. Mark stepped around the other side of him so he would not cast a shadow across his face, and in the blink of an eye his left hand had gripped a batch of hair.

Kate wished she had closed her eyes: by the time the victim had opened his own, the knife had done its work. Mark had cut deep enough for the creature in the chair to be beyond saving, and the sheer panic in his face showed that he knew it. There was enough energy left in him for a gargled groan, and then he was dead.

Kate started to breathe again. Mark's attention went straight to the laptop.

'This technology's pretty complicated by clone standards,' he said. 'It's not the usual numpty-proof system they use in New London.'

Kate had noticed. She had also noticed the lack of a panic button on the man's radio, and the fact that he had used his vocal cords to let out his final groan. She chose to say nothing. Mark would put the clues together by himself, and react in his own way.

'Now this is really weird,' he said. His voice quivered, suggesting to Kate that he had worked out what he had truly done. As predicted, he was trying to ignore it.

'What's weird?' she asked, trying to ignore it too.

'The AME shield is ready. Just a tap of this button and it goes up.'

Kate walked over to look, careful where she stepped. The carpet beneath grew redder, stickier and more soaked with every heartbeat. There was a progress bar on the laptop screen, 100 per cent complete, waiting for someone to click 'OK' and raise a metal-proof shield over Oakenfold Special School. They were one click away from achieving a feat never before seen in the realm of science, and proving that Nathaniel Pearce's technology could make Grant invincible forever.

But its controller had fallen asleep. In fact, the progress bar said the task had been finished at 12:09 a.m., so he must have been asleep for the last three hours.

It can't be that simple, can it? She thought. *Heroes don't just win because villains fall asleep, right?*

'I won't lie,' said Mark, reaching for the laptop's power button. 'I thought this one would be harder.'

'Don't switch it off,' snapped Kate. 'We need to take a look. This might tell us what we'll find in New London.'

Mark grunted, and stepped aside. Kate minimised the progress bar – checking, double-checking and triple-checking she was not about to press 'OK' – and started to search.

There was surprisingly little to search through. The most interesting result was a list of coordinates – about fifty of them – in a program that clearly had something to do with the AME controls. Curiously enough, the GPS coordinates were all nearly identical, with just a few differing numbers at the end of each one. Whatever these things were, they were in almost exactly the same place.

'Guys,' she whispered into the radio. Mark saw her, and turned his own radio back on. 'I think I know what those land-mine-shaped objects are for.'

'Oh,' added Mark, 'and the guy we mentioned is now dead. Good job he fell asleep on duty – the shield was one button away from going up.'

The others expressed surprise, but Kate stopped listening. She scanned through the contents of the man's laptop, and found nothing more of use. In the background, Raj said something about an interesting find in the library.

'Can't see anything useful here,' she whispered.

'Right then,' said Mark, raising the butt of his assault rifle, 'if you'll allow me...'

'No, don't just smash it. They'll be clever enough to put

the pieces back together. This needs to be *really* destroyed… whisky's flammable, right?'

'What, so I should pour my precious single malt over a computer and set it alight? Besides, we'd have no way of putting out the fire once it starts. Let's get some acid.'

He headed for the exit, not bothering to check the corridors as he walked into them.

'Acid?' asked Kate.

'Yeah, from chemistry.'

'They never had anything that could melt a computer…'

'No, they didn't. But if you do your research, you can combine the boring stuff to make a corrosive solution. And it's *corroding*, not melting.'

Kate followed Mark around the next corner, wondering what kind of person Mark could have been in a different life. He was capable, intelligent, determined and had no diagnoses that she knew of. Oakenfold wasn't designed for people like him, even though life had led him there.

'The lab's the other way,' said Kate.

'Staff room first,' Mark replied, pointing at the next door down.

'Looking for more drink?'

'Looking for keys. They never kept chemistry stuff in unlocked cupboards.'

He opened the door to the staff room. It was windowless, and pitch black. Mark, without a moment's thought, switched on the light.

The room lit up to reveal a dusty, lifeless room. Empty mugs of tea rested on tables full of teachers' marking, the writing on the staff whiteboard had faded away, and a collection box for school pantomime tickets had collected a year's worth of dust.

But Mark was worried.

'Someone else is here,' he whispered. 'That other guy had a friend.'

Kate scanned the room for clues, and found literally nothing. If someone were to try designing a room to look as dull and boring as possible, they could not have done better than the sight in front of her.

'How do you—'

'Guys,' Mark said into his radio, 'there's at least one more of them. Be careful.'

He looked into Kate's eyes, the fear in his face clear and obvious.

'We need to get back to the office. Before someone else finds the computer still on.'

There was a noise. Kate turned round just in time to see a uniformed figure run past the staff room, straight towards Paul's office.

Mark opened fire, and missed.

Chapter 7

When Kate fired her own bullet, it struck the man in his lower leg. It didn't appear to slow him down; he stumbled and shrieked, but hopped around the corner of the corridor as fast as he would have done anyway, perhaps carried by his own momentum.

'Get him!' Mark yelled, the expected ferocity in his voice replaced with worry. Kate did not need telling twice, and charged with all her energy towards the corner. She knew the risk of the man lying in wait behind the wall with a pistol pointed in her direction, but she ran anyway. Something told her the man would be more interested in reaching Paul's office than winning a gunfight.

When she and Mark turned the corner, she was proven correct. They were just in time to see the door to the office slam shut, and heard the locking mechanism as they approached. The door was sturdy – thick and secure enough to keep any staff member safe from a violent student or an ambitious burglar. This would not be easy.

There was an electric scream of '*Pete!!*' from behind the door. The man in the chair with the carved throat now had a name: one that would stick in Kate's memory until the day she died.

Mark got to the door first, and smashed the little square window with the butt of his rifle. He was answered by a short burst of pistol fire, and jerked his head away from the spray of wooden splinters that spat from the empty window frame. Kate reached the door and poked her rifle through the window just in time to see the man grab the laptop in both hands and haul it to the floor, before her own bullets shredded the surface of the desk where the laptop had been.

Crap, he only needs to push one button.

But I can't hear a shield going up outside. Or even anything being pressed in here. Why hasn't he just done it?

She looked at Mark's disgusted face. His eyes were pointed at a bullet wound in his upper arm, most likely from return fire after he had smashed the window. Reaching through and opening the door with the inside handle would not be an option.

'You made a big mistake, mate,' Mark yelled to the sheltering figure. 'Back when you used the staff room.'

'Really?' replied the man. 'I didn't touch anything in there except the kettle…'

Does he really care, or is he playing for time?

Mark Gunnarsson is stood outside the door planning to kill him. Of course he's playing for time.

'You touched the light switch,' said Mark. 'Oakenfold's full of those crap energy-saving bulbs that need three minutes to warm up. I walked in, switched them on and the place lit up in a split-second. The bulbs were still warm, and your mate was asleep. Someone else must have used them earlier.'

'Huh, how clever of you. Are you sure you were a student here? You're not nearly stupid enough. What a way to live your life.'

'Yeah, well you're about to get killed by a retard. Proud way to go.'

Kate bit her lip. The confrontation would have to end sooner rather than later. But the door was firmly locked, and the man was hidden behind Paul's desk where bullets could not reach him.

Then she remembered the other weapons they were carrying. She pointed to Mark's belt, and he nodded.

'Back in a bit,' he whispered. 'Keep him busy.'

Mark turned and fled, clutching his reddening upper arm, and left Kate to face the bullets alone. How she was supposed to prevent the man in the office from raising the shield, she had no idea. His laptop was right in front of him, and he was one button away from success.

And again… why hasn't he done it already?

'Raj, we need to go!'

'Why?' asked Raj, thumbing through the paperwork balanced on the library shelves. 'The gunfight's over there, we're over here. The others can handle it. What's going on here is important.'

'No,' yelled Gracie, 'we have to get outside! Back to Jack!'

'He'll never be your boyfriend, Gracie. Come here, I need you to help me read this.'

By the time Raj had looked up Gracie had fled, leaving nothing but the sound of her running footsteps. Raj breathed a sigh in the most irritated tone he could manage, and refocused on his work.

The school library had been turned into a miniature archive for the AME project. The original contents of the bookshelves had been thrown to the corners of the room – everything from the children's encyclopaedias to the advice books for young adults applying for work – and replaced by binders of paperwork that must have been important to the team that had worked here.

Wow, Ewan picked the wrong Underdogs to search these rooms, Raj thought. *God, if you're going to bless me with the sudden ability to read, now would be a good time.*

A thought struck Raj which made him stand bolt upright. Divine intervention or not, it saved a lot of time.

Raj's mother had spent most of his childhood calling him 'my little detective', since he could see straight to the root of any problem without being distracted by the extra details that got in everyone else's way. With or without the ability to read, Detective Raj Singh had the perfect brain for this task. He didn't *need* to learn the entire dictionary to find the information worth stealing. He just needed to find the documents with the right key words.

We're here to work out what to do in New London… so those are the two words I need to look for. I just need to find a capital N followed by a capital L. And look for 'AME' too. Even I can spell that one.

Raj grabbed the first file that came within reach. A quick browse revealed none of the magic words. The next file revealed none of them either. Raj wondered whether this was what browsing foreign language books felt like for the average person.

The third file contained 'N– L——' and 'AME' in the same paragraph. It was hopeful. He opened it up, and smiled at the sight of diagrams.

One of them was a map of the Outer City.

My little detective, said his mother's voice in his head.

*

Kate poked her face through the smashed window to the office. The dead body of Pete stared back at her, his frightened expression stuck to his face like a horrible waxwork sculpture. There were shuffling sounds from the carpet behind the desk, and Kate shuddered. The man's hands and knees must have been dragging through his colleague's blood as he crawled. Perhaps the blood from his lower leg was mixing with it too…

'Phone, on!' he called out. On her head teacher's desk, Kate saw the sudden rectangular shine of a smartphone screen. It let out a little ping, which the man barely waited to hear before shouting again.

'Call Nathaniel Pearce, speaker!'

Kate sighed. Voice-activated technology meant her enemy would not have to break cover in order to call for reinforcements, or even be close to his phone to communicate.

The phone was answered within one ring.

'Talk to me, Hargreaves.'

It was definitely Pearce. Kate had heard his voice back in New London, the day they destroyed the clone factory.

'Pearce!' Hargreaves screamed. 'They're here, and they've killed Simmonds!'

'Is the shield up yet?'

Pete Simmonds. And now Hargreaves. Now I'm going to have two names burned in my memory through guilt. If I live.

Hang on, Pearce, you were just told one of your staff was dead! Do you even care?

It was obvious he didn't. Kate wasn't much of a logician, but it must have meant that Pearce had a priority for the night that outweighed the well-being of his staff. No competent villain would throw their minions away as if they didn't matter… unless there was something else that mattered more.

She also knew that the longer she let Pearce talk on the

phone, the worse off she would be. She leapt in front of the window and fired bullets at the desk, none of which struck the tiny smartphone. A hand popped over the desk and returned fire, forcing her to shelter. Once the bullets stopped, she peered again and saw the phone in the corner of the room. In his panic to grab it, Hargreaves must have sent it flying across the office. Unfortunately, it lay out of range for Kate as well.

'Well?' Pearce asked, his volume unaffected by his phone's new location. '*Is* it on yet?'

'No,' Hargreaves shouted from behind the desk, 'it's not.'

Kate sighed with relief.

'Simmonds told me it was ready for launch three hours ago,' said Pearce. 'What are you wai—'

'And if you'd have let us launch it at midnight, the dead body next to me would still be al—'

'Hargreaves, calm down. If the shield's ready, it's your duty to raise it. Trap them all inside.'

That was the plan all along... lure us here and make it impossible for us to escape.

'Just send in the Harpenden squad!' the voice behind the desk began to wail. 'They're only a mile away!'

'And give the rebels time to destroy the shield? It needs testing. Raise it *now*.'

Kate fired a couple more bullets at the filing cabinets, hoping that a bullet would at least ricochet behind the desk. They did nothing but puncture the metal, and make Hargreaves yell in fright.

'*Now!*' yelled Pearce from the corner of the room.

'Get the army here and save me, and *then* I'll push the button.'

All I need to do is keep him panicking...

'I hear gunfire,' said Pearce. 'You don't have that long left.'

'I might…'

Kate tried to think of something she could shout into the room to influence the conversation, but no words came to mind. Besides, knowing her, she would say something wrong and persuade Hargreaves to raise the shield after all.

'Jonathan,' said Pearce, who unlike Kate knew precisely what to say, 'do you know why all our families have luxury accommodation in New London's walls?'

'Because otherwise nobody would agree to work with you?'

'Wrong. It's so that every employee has something to lose. In your case, it's Louise, Michael and Jessica. *Turn the bloody shield on.*'

The line cut out. It was a cold and cruel tactic which Pearce must have known would work: remove the other person's chance to speak, show that you don't value their words, and the other person won't value them either. People had done that to Kate all the time back in the old world.

'Jonathan,' she yelled to the man inside, hoping the first-name approach would help, 'he said something about the Harpenden squad being a mile away? You know they won't let you live, right? If we die, you die with us.'

'I'll be keeping my family safe,' the man muttered, barely audible. 'That's all the consolation I need.'

'Safe from Grant, Marshall and Pearce? These guys are threatening your family and you're siding with *them*?'

'Makes no difference now…'

Kate's jaw dropped. She had heard the futility in the man's voice, so blatant that even a girl like Kate could identify it.

'You've already pressed it, haven't you?'

No answer.

Try not to panic. You're going to worry, you're going to get anxious, but try not to panic.

'But we haven't seen a flash or anything,' she continued, 'so it must take a minute to charge up. How long have we got?'

'If you escape Oakenfold, my family gets thrown into the Inner City.'

'*How long?*'

'Less with every second.'

There was a disturbance in the light behind the office's back window. Kate jumped at the sudden appearance of Mark, who lifted his hands into view: a handgun butt in one, and a grenade in the other.

Kate was shocked, but understood that the laptop needed to be destroyed even if the shield couldn't be stopped. Nonetheless, she felt guilty for reminding Mark about the grenade in his belt before he had run. Mark smashed the glass with his rifle butt, pulled the grenade pin and dropped it through the empty window. It bounced on the floor to the sound of a shriek from Hargreaves before it exploded, ripping him and his laptop to pieces.

Kate was thrown to the back wall of the corridor by the force of the explosion. Suffering from instant sensory overload, she could not tell whether the word 'sorry' from Mark in her radio was real or psychosomatic. But as the ringing in her ears faded and the sight returned to her eyes, she heard him asking something. Whatever it was, it didn't matter. Her hand scrambled to her radio, although she screamed loud enough to be heard school-wide without it.

'*Everyone get out!*' she yelled and she rose to all fours and pushed herself onto her knees. 'Reinforcements are coming, the shield has been activated, and it's charging up right now! Get outside!'

Kate didn't hear the responses. If her friends had any sense, they wouldn't waste time replying.

What about his family? She asked herself as she tried to stand.

Yeah, came a sarcastic answer, perhaps Mark's own thoughts invading her head, *let's sacrifice six Underdogs so a bad guy's wife and kids can live in luxury. No, we're going.*

Kate staggered to her feet and jogged in an approximate straight line, picking up speed as she went. If her life weren't under threat, it might have felt liberating to run in the school corridors. Once she got into her rhythm she found herself sprinting faster than she ever had as a student. Even as a gymnast, she had never been so athletic. The new Kate Arrowsmith, hardened through a year of combat, ran so fast that her feet could barely support the shifting weight above them. It was like running downhill, except in the dark.

She reached the school's entrance. Against all common sense, and the imaginary noise of her brain screaming at her to reach safety, she grabbed the nearest fire extinguisher and used it to wedge the door wide open. The others might not have time to open the door for themselves.

Kate ran exhausted through the car park, and stumbled past the little metal objects that looked like landmines. They were starting to hum and make aggressive electrical sounds. Mark had already stopped a few metres beyond them, in a position he assumed to be safe. In the background, Gracie could be seen heading for the hill. She must have been looking for Jack.

'What will it look like?' Kate asked as she approached Mark. 'When it goes up?'

'We'll find out any second,' Mark replied.

'Maybe we should cover our eyes.'

'You can, if you want.'

Kate trembled, and realised she didn't want to look away. Rightly or wrongly, her eyes fixed themselves on the entrance and looked for signs of her friends.

There was movement, and Kate sighed with relief. Ewan was right on time. He and Simon bolted out of Oakenfold like racehorses from a gate, and made it past the boundary of metallic objects halfway through the car park.

'Everyone OK?' Ewan asked. Or at least mouthed while he caught his breath.

'The twat got me in the forearm,' said Mark. 'Otherwise, I'm OK. So are Kate and Gracie. Not heard from Jack but I assume he's fine.'

Kate's legs started to weaken, but not from the run. Seven students had come to Oakenfold, and six had walked inside.

One was missing.

Halfway between the library and the front entrance, Raj took the longest strides he could manage at top speed. He knew he had the right documents under his arm, although it had taken a lot of reading – even *after* Kate's warning to get out.

He regretted nothing. He couldn't afford to escape Oakenfold without the right documents, and he couldn't carry them all out. Not in the time he had.

The entrance was ahead, wedged open by a fire extinguisher. *That must have been Kate. Nobody else would be so thoughtful in a crisis.*

Her efforts saved Raj at least three or four seconds, at a time when every single one of them counted.

He was about twenty metres behind the metal points when they buzzed, and the shield went up.

There was a red flash, like sheet lightning up close, which vanished a moment after it came. It was replaced with a sea of crimson ripples which distorted the sight of the world outside Oakenfold, including the hill and the faces of his horrified friends.

Before the ripples lost their colour, Raj looked up. The AME shield formed a dome over the school, like a semi-spherical net pegged down by the metal points. The crimson barrier faded in silence, and their surroundings returned to normal.

Kate was screaming.

Raj said nothing. He retrieved his handgun, pulled the topside to remove a bullet, and tossed it half-heartedly towards his friends.

The bullet hit the shield and exploded violently, causing Raj's bladder to weaken. Around the area the bullet had hit, a set of furious lightning shards buzzed across a metre-wide canvas of crimson ripples, before they all faded again into nothingness.

'Raj!' shouted Ewan, running as close to the shield as he could get away with. There was anger rather than sorrow in his eyes. 'What the bloody hell took you so long?!'

He's not angry at me personally. It's his way of grieving the loss of a friend.

'These did,' Raj replied with a hiccup, lifting the files he had seized from the library. 'I can't pass the folder through because it's got metal rings, but I can give you the paper.'

He opened the folder and removed its contents, concentrating hard enough on the task to ignore the enormity of what was happening to him. But that became difficult when he passed the pile through the shield, and saw the air calmly ripple around the papers as they went through. Ewan's hand took them at the other side and passed them to Jack, who had made his way down the hill.

'It tells you which parts of New London deal with AME,' Raj said, his voice quaking. 'I know because... because I read it.'

Jack and Ewan's eyebrows lifted in surprise.

'...I *read it*, guys,' Raj repeated for the satisfaction. He may have been a dead body in waiting, but he had kept their hopes in the war alive. And he had done it by reading.

'The way they've set it up in New London is similar to here,' he said, hoping that Ewan would take time away from his anger and listen to him. 'There's a computer that controls the shield, filled with coordinates for these metal things. They're border points of some kind... Grant probably has a posh name for them.'

Raj pointed to the nearest mine-shaped object. Ewan took one glance, and then fired a stream of bullets towards it – perhaps in the hope of making a hole in the shield's coordinate field or something. To Raj's horror, the border point seemed to have its own miniature shield too.

There was a shriek on his right. Mark was physically holding Kate back as she screamed.

'But destroying a computer won't be enough,' he continued, doing his best to sound brave. 'You've got to wipe out all their research too. Get into their files and delete anything that mentions Atmospheric Metallurgic Excitation, and blow up their physical archives too. Do that, and they'll have to start over. It could take years for them to get it right again. And don't worry about here... I set fire to the library before I left it, and the fire should spread. I'm sorry, Ewan... but like you said, stop **AME** even if it means...'

'You did the right thing, Raj,' Ewan said. 'Now find a way out.'

'What, through the shield? Sorry Ewan, I'm screwed.'

Raj had noticed how casual Ewan's voice sounded, like he was refusing to accept the hopelessness of the situation. Raj did not have that luxury: his dyslexia-driven ability to see to the core of a problem told him exactly what his situation was, and his ability to come up with off-the-wall unexpected ideas would have helped if there were any kind of way out. But Raj knew that searching for one would be like trying to avoid a one-move checkmate.

'Dig underground,' Ewan said, trying to hide his growing desperation. 'Get to one of the grassy areas, and—'

'The brains that came up with AME must have thought of someone tunnelling,' said Raj, his first tears emerging. 'And besides, how much time do you think I have? Reinforcements are minutes away.'

'Then strip,' said Jack in his usual matter-of-fact manner. 'Leave your weapons, and remove any clothes that have traces of metal. We only need your body to get through.'

'I'm sorry,' Raj replied. 'I had a spinal operation when I was twelve, remember? I told you when McCormick and Lorraine were arguing. There's metal all down my back. Even if I were naked, the shield would blow my spine out.'

Kate finally got past Mark by punching his jaw and kneeing him in the groin. She reached Ewan and Jack and stared at her boyfriend through the invisible barrier that would cost him his life. And with her panic-stricken eyes gazing into his, she opened her mouth but no words came out.

Raj understood. He had absolutely no idea what to say to her either.

'But actually,' he breathed, 'getting my spine blown out might be the best option.'

'What the hell's that supposed to mean?' barked Ewan.

'I mean not getting captured. You know why, Kate.'

He looked at his wordless girlfriend, who had lost her wailing anger and replaced it with stunned silence. Raj closed his eyes, and confessed.

'I know the name of our village, guys. I always have done.'

Ewan turned his back and swore at the top of his voice, looking for the nearest large object to kick repeatedly.

'So if you're taken alive,' muttered Mark as he approached, 'we're all dead.'

'Yeah,' Raj replied with unashamed fear. 'Remember Daniel,

who gave away our names? He was a tough lad. I'm not. If they interrogate me they'll... they'll find what they're after. If I stay behind this shield, Spitfire's Rise gets found, we lose the war and Grant kills me anyway. Either I run through and live, or I run through and die. Both are better options than staying here.'

His six friends did not make a sound between them. But Kate was shaking her head in baseless denial.

'Jack, you're the logical one,' Raj said. 'Tell me I'm wrong.'

All eyes fell on Jack, who seemed aghast at the thought of being responsible for good ideas at a moment like this.

'I'm serious, Jack,' Raj continued. '*Please* give me a reason why it's a bad idea. Because I'm bloody terrified here.'

Jack kept up his silence, and Raj looked at his remaining friends: Mark, who rarely let humanitarian issues get in the way of solving a problem. Ewan, who was no stranger to making dreadful decisions in no-win situations. Gracie and Simon, who were all too willing to admit defeat. The only one who needed convincing was Kate.

'Y-you're religious,' she gasped approximately. 'Isn't there... isn't there a no-suicide rule or, or something?'

'This isn't suicide, it's sacrifice,' said Raj, removing his helmet and taking his first of many steps back. 'Giving my life for yours. There are religious figures who saw the value in that, trust me.'

He kept walking back, and nobody but Kate objected. They were horrified, but compliant. Some stepped out of the blast radius his body was about to create.

God, please let me be right about you. Please see this as saving my friends.

I spent almost a year shooting clones for these friends, and for millions of innocents. Please forgive me if that counted as killing.

Forgive me if I was wrong in anything I did. Every shot I fired this year was to save human lives…

'Ewan, Jack, get Kate to the bottom of the hill. Simon, Gracie, follow them. Mark, stay here. If the explosion only half-kills me, shoot me in the head.'

It was the only moment in a year of warfare when everyone unanimously listened to him. Everyone except Kate. There was no sensitive, heartfelt goodbye from his girlfriend as she was manhandled across the car park. But that was OK. They could each have died in a hundred ways in the war against Nicholas Grant, and almost none of the others would have held decent farewells either.

The last of Oakenfold's free students gathered a hundred metres away from the shield, staring back at their friend while they still could. Not too far away, Mark was in place.

They're not going to leave me. Reinforcements are heading right this way to kill them, and they still won't leave.

I have to do this right now.

Raj had stepped back far enough.

The view before him looked completely normal. As if he were just leaving school in the dark. He looked at the metal border points, and judged the distance.

God, I love you but I'm terrified. Please… just please…

His brain ran out of thoughts, and for the first time in fifteen years he surrendered to his impulses.

Raj Singh took a long run-up, and leapt through the shield.

Chapter 8

Ewan heard a rumbling *boom* from the distant shield. Raj was backlit with a red curtain of air as the metal supports in his spine exploded and ripped open his back. Smaller explosions went off around his body wherever metal could be found on his clothes, with a sizeable fireball on his right wrist. Ewan couldn't see whether his metal watch had blown his hand off, but it made little difference. Raj's misshapen body landed on the tarmac of the car park, the top half of his torso at a right angle to his abdomen. After the shield faded, Ewan could make out a blood-coloured mist hanging over him. Mark bent down, took one look at Raj's face, and turned around to walk away. No extra bullets would be required.

'You're going to hate me for this,' said Jack, 'but we have to run, and we all know it.'

Ewan *did* hate him for it. But at that moment he hated everyone and everything, including himself and anything that was good about him. Twelve Underdogs had become eleven, seven Oakenfold students had become six, Britain's last army had lost every advantage that Raj had brought to it, and Kate was becoming too much to handle.

'What the hell are we still doing here?' asked Mark when he arrived back.

'Splitting up,' Ewan muttered, disgusted that people were turning to him for leadership while a devastating cocktail of bereavement and PDA clouded his judgement. 'We've got about a minute before clones start arriving, and we can't all be in the same place. Mark, you take Kate and Simon. I'll take Jack and Gracie.'

'Why?'

'Because I said so,' Ewan grunted, knowing but ignoring that it was the worst reason a leader could possibly give. 'You go through Harpenden, we'll take the fields. Whatever you do, don't head home the way we came. You'll be followed. Get lost in the countryside if you need to, and use the north star tomorrow night. However you do it, just lose them.'

'Got it,' said Mark. 'Simon, Kate, with me.'

Simon followed as soon as Mark began to jog, but the silent shell of Kate Arrowsmith barely even looked in the right direction.

'I'm sorry, Kate,' said Ewan, saying the words but feeling nothing but rage, 'but you have to go. Mark will look after you, and he needs you to look after him. Go.'

Mark shot an offended glare, but said nothing. He must have worked out that Ewan's words were to encourage (or manipulate) Kate rather than belittle him. Mark ran for the school driveway, one arm around Kate's shoulder and the other pushing Simon forward. His journey home would be slow as well as long.

Ewan was left at the foot of the hill with Jack and Gracie. Behind them, Raj's unapologetic body lay just outside the invisible shield, daring to still be dead.

'Let's go,' he muttered, and made his way up the hill. He paused at the top to wait for his teammates at the spot where he had once hidden for a whole afternoon, back when his world had been marginally easier. He took one last look at Oakenfold Special School, protected by an invisible AME shield, not knowing how the hell they would ever take it back – if they ever did.

There was a fire spreading, as Raj had promised, from the burning library. Torchlight emerged from the distant forests. Raj had been right about not having time to dig under the shield. Ewan picked up the pace whilst stuffing the New London papers into his shirt, wondering how detailed the Outer City map would have to be for Raj's sacrifice to be worth it.

They half-walked, half-jogged for a mile before Ewan felt it was safe to slow down and speak his mind.

'Gracie, I put you with Raj...'

'Not now, Ewan.'

'Shut up, Jack. Gracie, you two were supposed to stay together...'

Ewan deliberately avoided her gaze, and kept his eyes on the darkened grass beneath his feet. Jack and Gracie were behind him, right where they belonged.

'I've got metal fillings!' Gracie wailed, far too loud. 'If I'd stayed with him I'd have died too!'

'If you'd made *him* stay with *you*, you'd both be alive.'

'He chose to stay!'

'You chose to leave him.'

'Ewan,' Jack interrupted, 'I know you're not in the mood, but Raj couldn't have got the New London stuff without staying and searching.'

'*Shut up*, Jack. She could have stayed with him and searched quicker.'

'When Mark tells you to run, you run. It'd take a very resilient—'

'*Shut up, Jack!*'

For about five seconds, Jack took his advice. The silence was welcome, and for a moment Ewan felt the cold breeze, and the wet grass wiping against his boots. If he cared enough to look upwards, he could have seen the sky lit up with stars, and remembered that all his worldly troubles were just a tiny speck on the vast expanse of reality, or some crap like that.

Apparently, five seconds was enough for Jack.

'You need to stop being nasty to me, Ewan. If you didn't want that chat about your parents earlier you could have just said so, rather than hate me for the rest of the night. Take a moment to yourself, and leave Gracie alone. I'll call comms and break the news to Alex and Shannon.'

Ewan's PDA came right to the surface, and Jack's set of commands made his fists clench in a reflex action. The breath caught in his throat as his sense of control – the very last of it – vanished from his mind. But by the time he turned around, Jack already had his phone in front of his face. Ewan couldn't start a fight while Jack was calling comms. Not with Shannon watching via video call.

Screw you, Jack… screw you and your advice and your dinosaur obsession and your love of machines and…

You're right. But screw you anyway.

It had been the comment about his parents that hurt the most. Because Jack had been right about them too.

When Ewan made an effort to remember his mother, he had fond memories of who she had been. But his memory of her personality and his memory of their relationship were different things, and his strongest memories of their time together were best avoided. The good parts of his formative years had been spent with Dad, and the bad parts with Mum.

They had split their parental responsibilities pretty well, right down to Dad having the military job and Mum doing the housework. It seemed like an old-fashioned family set-up, but it was Ewan's fault she had become a stay-at-home mum. His mainstream head teachers had dragged her into school so many times that it was easier to just sit at home and wait for the phone to ring, rather than take every afternoon off work and run out of holiday leave.

But the split went beyond household roles. Dad had been the parent who taught Ewan the skills he would need for adulthood, physically and mentally. He'd taught him the foundations of what being a man would one day be like, and gave him the best chance he could at preventing his neurology from screwing up his chances. Major George West had been a good man, and a good father. But he had only been effective on Ewan's good days. It was Mum who had dealt with the bad ones.

She had always been there when something caused him to stumble. Exclusions from primary school were dealt with by tearful cuddles on the sofa. Post-meltdown evenings as a teenager had been solved with movies and homemade shepherd's pie. She had provided the consistency and stability that a troubled boy desperately needed, and she had done it to perfection. But it had come to define their relationship: a priceless mother-and-son bond that was built entirely upon the things that went wrong.

Ewan had spent his happiest days with Dad. Mum had been there on the sidelines, silent, non-judgemental, waiting for her turn to be needed again. And each time she had picked him off the floor, hugged him better and sent him on his way, the young Ewan had gone back to his usual habit of avoiding her. Unless she was right there on a day when he needed fixing, it was easier not to associate with someone who so firmly reminded him of his bad moments.

When Ewan thought about it, he treated the memory of Mum exactly how he had treated the real woman when she was alive. Nearly a year on from Mum and Dad being gunned down inside their barricaded house, Ewan still couldn't think of her without digging up his worst times.

It was nothing personal. Ewan had loved her. But enduring the pain of those memories wouldn't bring her back. She was dead. Dad was dead. His aunt and uncle and eight-year-old Alfie were dead, along with Raj and Charlie and all the others on that bloody Memorial Wall.

The pain of missing someone is always worth it for the joy of having known them, said a wise man's voice in his head.

Shut up, McCormick, Ewan's mind said back.

'Ewan,' came a voice behind him.

The breeze came back into existence. As did the rest of the world around him. They weren't far from the edge of the field now, and a tree line that would give them cover.

The stream of tears across his face became real too.

'Ewan,' Jack repeated, 'I gave comms the news, and told them not to expect us back for a while. Shannon... Shannon passes on her best wishes.'

Ewan didn't answer. Shannon's company would have been welcome at that moment.

'And I told them we're splitting up even further,' Jack continued. 'You can go on your own, and me and Gracie will stick together. We'll meet up at the house in Lemsford – the one we slept in last time. Might take a whole day to get there, but it's better than getting followed to Spitfire's Rise.'

Ewan grunted, but didn't turn around. Jack's unwelcome fingers landed on his shoulder.

'I told them we were splitting up to lose anyone chasing us. And because it'd make us all faster. I didn't tell them the third reason. Figured you'd need some time alone.'

Screw you, Jack, Ewan thought again. *Screw you for knowing me so well. For knowing where I'm weak, and…*

…And for being my friend.

Chapter 9

Kate twitched in fright as Mark's brick smashed her geography teacher's car window. To their left, Simon shook his head frantically.

'You're making me do this,' Mark growled as he opened the door from the inside. 'You're both slow as hell, and the clones are coming. Either I break the no cars rule, or I leave you both behind.'

You had no problem leaving my brother behind...

'Get bloody running, they're not worth it', you said. You had no idea how much James was worth.

One day, when I'm my better self, I'll confront you about it. Not today, but one day, Mark.

They had stumbled for about a hundred metres before Mark had realised the hopelessness of escaping on foot. Before Kate knew what was going on, he had ordered them back to Oakenfold where he had picked out Stuart Lincoln's car: the one which just happened to be the newest in the car park, and perhaps the most reliable.

Mark reached somewhere behind the steering wheel. A crunch sounded, and a couple of wires appeared. Kate didn't understand what happened next, nor how Mark knew the science of hot-wiring a car, but it didn't surprise her. A few moments later, she heard the rev of a car engine for the first time in a year.

'You getting in?'

Kate started to move. Simon, rather tellingly, headed straight for the back seats as if he weren't allowed to sit in the front. Once Kate was in the passenger seat with the door half-closed, Mark pulled away. Her door flung open again and bashed against the first car they passed, and the resulting *bang* sent some much-needed adrenalin through Kate's veins. She closed the door properly on the second attempt, and glanced through the window as something moved in the early morning light.

They were clones. *Angry* clones, and they were running.

'Mark!' she shouted, her first and only word since her boyfriend had blown himself to pieces.

'Heads down!' he yelled back as the car accelerated. Kate obeyed, and squeezed her eyes shut too. It would not shield her from bullets, but would help with the sensory overload that would surely come. Mark must have ducked his own head, as the car's path became wonkier and more chaotic. A short spray of bullets attacked the car, hitting nothing but its metal back. Mercifully, the tyres were unaffected. Simon did not follow Mark's command, showing unexpected independence by sticking his head out of the window and firing back at the distant clones. Kate did not look back to see whether he hit any.

Mark turned a corner, and the clones' gunfire fell into silence. But it did nothing to help Kate calm down. The engine was still roaring, the floor still shook beneath her, and Raj was still dead. Two more corners later she opened her eyes, if only to keep an eye out for more hunters.

The urban drive felt like a ride on a post-apocalyptic ghost train. Some buildings were burned-out shells. Some shops had been looted by bands of survivors following Takeover Day. The blood on the tarmac had long faded, but the occasional skeleton in faded clothes still occupied a space on the pavement. The meat had long been picked clean from their bones: perhaps the crows above Harpenden had developed a taste for human flesh.

That's what lies in wait for Raj…

'My house was down the M1,' Mark shouted, 'I used to take this route every day to Oakenfold.'

You barely came to Oakenfold. You vanished for a year after you got sentenced, and after that you only turned up when you felt like it.

'Of course, if we hit the Takeover Day traffic jams on the M1, we'll be waiting a bloody long time for the traffic to clear. But it's better than getting shot to death here.'

Kate felt something warm on the back of her neck. Simon was panting behind her, the whole of his body frozen except his lungs, which took rapid, erratic breaths. His panic and Kate's overload left Mark as the only truly active member of the team.

When they arrived at Britain's oldest motorway – the birthplace of their country's worst traffic jams – they discovered the M1 had ended its life with the worst blockage of all. Vehicles were strewn across the road as if a toddler had thrown their toy cars across a fabric floor map, forming a metal hedge maze of vans and people carriers and articulated lorries. Regardless, Mark found a way to manoeuvre through the vehicles whose owners had tried in vain to escape the clones almost a year ago. Kate's seat rocked beneath her whenever he moved onto the grass, and her fingers twitched in discomfort each time her door scraped along a neighbouring car.

They must have travelled nearly a mile before the explosion.

Every window in their car – and the cars surrounding them – shattered with piercing shrieks. The rusted Astra three cars ahead flew out from the flames, knocked aside like a golf ball from its tee by the raging fireball at its side. The ground trembled so much that Kate was sure their own wheels left the tarmac. She watched the Astra smack the line of trees at the side of the motorway; it had landed behind their car, suggesting the explosion had happened in front of them. The smoke mirage faded from the crater ahead, and she saw what had fired the shell. It was half a mile beyond the overhead bridge in front of them, crunching its way over the dead vehicles in its path.

'Bloody hell,' yelled Mark, 'that's an actual bloody tank!'

It's a Challenger 2. Ewan was in my English class, and did tanks for his Speaking and Listening presentation.

It had been the only presentation delivered with any enthusiasm, so it was the only one that stuck in Kate's memory. She mainly remembered the worst parts: that it could kill from up to five miles away, and that the only thing ever to destroy a Challenger 2 had been friendly fire from another Challenger 2.

'How the hell did Marshall get his hands on one of *them*?' asked Mark.

'I don't think anyone tried to stop him,' she whispered.

Mark seemed to not hear her answer – or more likely did not care – as he found a way around the crater and continued their path along the M1, straight towards the tank.

Simon made a yelling noise in the back seat.

'Yes, we're going *towards* it,' Mark muttered. 'If we retreat it'll get us for sure, or chase us back to Harpenden. If we go towards it, there might be a one per cent chance we'll get inside its range.'

Kate didn't mind the odds being against her survival. Not at that moment. Her intellect told her she could still contribute to this war, but the rest of her brain told her she had nothing left to offer.

'And yes,' Mark muttered, 'I know about its secondary weapon. But I'd take my chances with the chain gun over those shells.'

Ahead, the tank surged over another row of cars. Kate watched as the first car – a large black people-carrier – crumbled and flattened in submission. Her parents' lawnmower had never cut grass as efficiently as the Challenger 2 mowed its way over a carriageway of vehicles.

The tank fired a second shot, which smashed into the brow of the bridge above before it could reach its intended target. Half a tonne of concrete left the bridge, flew through the sky and tumbled its way into the nearest caravan, which exploded over all four lanes like a wood and metal supernova.

The remainder of the damaged bridge collapsed into the road, leaving just one gap underneath the part blown away by the tank. Mark bit his lip as he found a way through the dust, squeezing through a gap between two cars, a gamble which cost them both wing mirrors. There was an even tighter gap ten metres ahead, between a painter's van and a petroleum tanker.

The gap between them and the Challenger was closing. Kate gasped as she finally realised the flaw in Mark's plan: that even if they got close enough to escape its long-range weaponry, and even if the chain gun operator were a useless shot, the tank could just crush them underneath its tracks. In fact, the clones inside might find the experience more satisfying.

The third blast roared from the barrel, but the humans' lives were saved by bad timing. The tank reached the end of the set of cars underneath it, and dipped forwards. The barrel sank by about ten degrees, sending the third shell several hundred metres too short.

If they'd fired correctly, we'd be dead. A shell anywhere close to the tanker would have done the job.

'OK, their sight is blocked by the dust cloud,' Mark said. 'Get out.'

Simon obeyed as expected. Kate wanted to follow, but her body wouldn't let her. Mark leapt out of the driver's seat, and took the time to stare back into the car before closing the door.

'Kate,' he said, 'I'm sorry Raj is dead. He was a nice lad. And I wish we had time for you to go through your I'm-so-sad-my-life-is-over phase. But we don't. The tank is coming *now*, so I've got this plan and I really hope you can pull yourself together quick enough to be part of it.'

Pull yourself together... that's what the teachers back in mainstream used to say.

Mental health issues don't just 'pull themselves together' Mark, you bloody numpty. You don't stop grieving by 'pulling yourself together'. Even now, I don't know how people do it.

She felt angry, an emotion she had not had the energy for all night. It squeezed itself between her fatigue and her misery, and motivated her to move herself. She huffed as loudly as she could manage, and opened the passenger door.

For a split-second, a small but important realisation entered her brain. One of her therapists had once talked about humans' 'fight or flight' instincts: that when a situation got too much for them, a person would either face it head-on or get the hell out of there.

Last time someone had told Kate to 'pull herself together', she had not left her bed all day. It had been better to waste a whole day than approach something that scared her, especially for the sake of a person who didn't know how anxiety worked. That morning, on the abandoned M1 in the midst of her grief, she was taking action just by getting out of the car.

The war against Nicholas Grant had changed her instincts.

A year ago she chose 'flight' every time without fail. Nowadays she could fight, even after losing somebody she cared about.

Kate stepped out of the car into the morning light, and followed Simon to the grass bank. Mark stayed at the car for a few moments, busying himself with the petrol cap.

She followed Simon until they reached the other side of the bank. Now on foot, they could get to some proper shelter: even the best aim from a tank wouldn't kill them if they hid behind a small hill.

Next to the car, Mark had removed his shirt. He produced his bottle of whisky from somewhere – the same whisky that had spent a year in his Oakenfold locker awaiting his return – doused the lower half of his shirt with it and stuffed the dry half into the petrol tank.

Kate had expected Mark to reach for his lighter without incident, but he leapt suddenly at the sound of a horrifying *ptat-ptat-ptat*, followed by what looked like miniature fireless explosions spreading across the cars around him. The muzzle flash behind the dust cloud revealed that the Challenger's chain gun was firing blindly, and its huge bullets were ripping apart the abandoned cars.

Mark – crouched low, for all the good it would do against chain gun bullets – tore the pocket fabric out of his trousers, brought out his lighter, and turned the bottle of whisky into a Molotov cocktail which he hurled straight at the tank.

The tank got through the dust cloud not one moment before its sight was lost again, as the bottle struck not far from its visor and spread flames and smoke across their field of vision. Mark used the distraction to run from the car, out of the way of the random path of chain gun bullets, and arrived behind the peak of the grass bank alongside Kate and Simon. He even found the time to put his hoodie back on along the way.

Kate focused her eyes on the petrol tank, as if trying to force the flames to do their work by willpower alone.

An exploding car won't be enough to destroy a Challenger 2. Even if it goes off right next—

Their vehicle blew itself apart, spreading its burning shrapnel across the M1 and flames over its injured chassis. The tank, still fifty metres away, was unaffected. A white cloud burst from the visor, as one of the crew took care of the whisky fire with an extinguisher.

'Do we run?' she managed to whisper. Mark shook his head. The tank headed straight for the burning car, perhaps looking for their victim's burned remains. Their colleagues across Hertfordshire would want to know when to stop hunting survivors.

When ten metres remained between the tank and the burning vehicle, Mark leapt to his feet.

'You numpties cost me my whisky…'

It had been so long since they had used their firearms that Kate had forgotten about the assault rifle hanging from Mark's shoulder. He pointed it straight towards the tanker behind the car and emptied the rest of his magazine into its side. A dozen leaks sprung from the side of the tanker, and Kate buried her face into the grass as the flurry of petrol spilled onto the carriageway and spread towards the flames.

Unlike the car explosion, miniature by comparison, the shockwave of the exploding tanker threw all three of their bodies down the side of the bank.

Mark later said that her sensory overload had lasted several minutes. All Kate remembered was coming to her senses as if waking up from some kind of empty hallucination, and staggering to the top of the bank. Once she was lucid again, she noticed that the tank lay motionless, in flames but undamaged.

'It's not destroyed…' she mumbled.

'We didn't need to kill the tank,' answered Mark, 'just the clones inside. They either burned to death or lost all their oxygen. Don't know which, don't care either. Now let's run home.'

Kate followed as instructed, too tired and deep in grief to appreciate the brilliance of Mark's achievement. Maybe someday she would care that an eighteen-year-old youth offender had become the second person ever to destroy a Challenger 2, but it would not be that day. And, most likely, not for as long as she mourned Raj.

Chapter 10

As he passed the welcome sign into Lemsford, Jack checked his watch. Four in the afternoon. Their strike on Oakenfold had started thirteen hours ago, and he had barely stopped moving since.

Gracie, to her credit, was only five steps behind. She had slowed on their approach to the village, but despite her worries about this place she had never been to, she had kept up.

'Where now?' she whispered.

'The Hunters' house. Eighteen, School Lane. Follow me.'

'You remember the way?!'

'I was here less than a month ago. And I have the memory thing. Now come on.'

Jack was thankful that Gracie didn't offer a response. In the old days, any discussion about his Asperger's traits – positive or negative – usually resulted in the other person giving some kind of belittling response, such as 'you don't *look* autistic', or 'oh, I'm so sorry'. At that moment, the predictable response would have been 'oh, but I can remember directions too! That's not an autism thing!'

They would never be able to see what the memory of the house looked like inside Jack's head: the well-mapped, in-depth and painfully specific details of each minor event. Kate's conversation with McCormick to tell him they had arrived. Alex taking little Matthew's room and sleeping under dinosaur bedsheets. (Everything related to dinosaurs stuck in Jack's head like the intro to 'The Final Countdown', while most people wouldn't have even remembered the little boy was called Matthew.) That joke he had made about Dawn Hunter, asking if she was some kind of vampire assassin, and nobody getting it. Charlie saying 'the last time he kissed a woman he still called her "Mummy"', and everyone laughing.

It wasn't the joy or the pain that made the night memorable. Jack Hopper simply didn't get a choice in what he remembered. Once a memory was in his brain it stayed there like a fly stuck to insect paper, never to leave. Sometimes it meant memorising fifty-eight species of sauropod at the age of six. Sometimes it meant remembering number plates of random cars on long journeys, whether he wanted to or not.

To Gracie at that moment, it just meant knowing his way around a village. Jack found his way to School Lane, and the Hunters' house was there as promised.

A little part of Jack had expected the house to look welcoming, perhaps for the grass to be more colourful than he remembered or the windows to look cleaner. But nothing special awaited them. The two-storey building looked as dulled and silent as before, indifferent to the return of an old visitor. Jack walked up the garden path and pushed the front door open, holding his breath to avoid choking on the dust.

Dust. Unless Ewan had used a different entrance, he had not arrived yet.

Eighty per cent of dust is human skin. Maybe some of this is ours.
Maybe a part of Charlie still exists here.

'You OK, Jack?' Gracie whispered.

Apparently he hadn't hidden his misery as well as he had thought.

'Charlie spent his last night on Earth here,' he answered.

'I thought he made it to New London?' she asked. 'And died three days later?'

'I don't count that as Earth.'

Jack made his way to the living room, and his eyes met the spot on the floor that had been his bed three weeks earlier. He wondered what Ewan's reaction would be once he arrived, whether his own memories would be as specific, and his emotions just as provoked. It took Jack a moment to remember that he was supposed to check the house for clones, rather than taking a trip down Crap Memory Lane.

'Can I ask you a question?' asked Gracie.

'You just did.'

She sighed behind him.

'Why do you always do things like that?'

'Is that your real question, or another supplementary one?'

Gracie's next sigh was more of a snarl. Jack closed his eyes, realising that it wasn't the best time for his brand of humour.

'Sorry,' he said. 'Go ahead.'

'Did you know Charlie well?' asked Gracie.

'I did towards the end.'

'Was he nice?'

Jack sighed. Eleven months had passed between Takeover Day and Charlie Coleman's death, and even after spending so much time in such cramped conditions, there were still people in Spitfire's Rise he hadn't got to know.

'He was Charlie, I guess.'

'But was he nice?'

'He was… endearing. I don't think "nice" was the best word to describe him. But he had his good sides, even if you had to look for them.'

Gracie sat down on the faded sofa, her face indecipherable.

'I didn't speak to him. Not once.'

'He was a decent guy,' said Jack. 'It's a shame you two didn't get to know each other.'

Gracie shrugged, and gave her response in a low, subdued tone.

'I don't think either of us missed out on much.'

Jack wasn't prepared for that kind of answer. He took a deep breath, and then coughed out a mouthful of dust.

Gracie was sad about herself, and Jack wasn't sure why. He was an expert at being kind and caring, but knew nothing about *how* to show kindness and care. Sometimes when people were sad they wanted to talk about it, and sometimes they wanted to be left alone. And whichever Jack gambled on, he always seemed to get it wrong. It was a heartbreaking position to be in: wanting so deeply to help people in need, but constantly being scorned for trying and failing. Jack could follow any instruction manual to perfection, but people were more difficult than machines.

In the end, he put a hand on Gracie's shoulder and gave what he thought was a sympathetic smile. It seemed like the action least likely to be offensive.

'I'm going to check upstairs, and keep watch on the street,' he said. 'Ewan shouldn't be far away. Stay down here and have a rest if you like. You deserve it.'

Gracie said nothing, and Jack couldn't tell whether his response had been the right one. But either way, the house needed guarding. And he had to admit, he was anxious about why Ewan hadn't reached the house first.

Five o'clock came and went, and Ewan was nowhere to be seen.

Half past five came and went, and daylight began to fade.

Six o'clock came, and Jack made a phone call to comms to check if they had heard anything. The call did nothing but make Shannon scared. Even Alex's voice seemed to lose its cool.

By half past six, Jack's nerves had turned to clear and simple panic.

Ewan remembered the way, didn't he? He just needs to find a familiar road and take the same route as before.

Was he in a fit state to agree when I told him the plan?

Is he deliberately taking his time? Does he need the cool-off period that badly?

There was a creak at the top of the stairs behind him. Jack didn't worry: the footstep was so loud that it couldn't have been made by someone sneaking up on him. He turned around and saw Gracie, her hands trembling and eyes pointed at the carpet.

'Jack?'

'You OK, Gracie?'

At first she gave no answer. But just before Jack turned his head back to guard the approach to the house again, she spluttered her words out.

'Did I kill Raj?'

Jack stared back in confusion.

'What?'

'Did Ewan mean it? Is it my fault he died?'

Jack gave a long sigh.

'Ewan was angry because he'd just lost a friend. He was saying it out of hurt, nothing more.'

'But he's right… if I'd brought Raj out with me, we'd *all* be alive.'

'You're assuming you could have made Raj give up and run. He was a stubborn guy.'

'But I could have…'

Gracie began to sniff, and Jack gritted his teeth. Situations like these were beyond his social understanding, according to the many people who had made him feel bad over the years. And from a logical perspective, it was difficult to argue with her. If Gracie had been more forceful, maybe it really would have saved Raj's life.

But maybe it wouldn't have.

It would be so easy, pretending to know what he'd have done in the same situation. But Gracie had been the one inside Oakenfold, not him. And he had spent many years enduring those who had judged him without knowing his background, so he would never judge others in the same way. Gracie would spend the rest of her days wondering about the what-ifs, being judged by other people who *definitely* would have done this or that in her position. Jack refused to become one of them.

'You did what you needed to do, Gracie,' he finished. 'If you'd stayed, you could have both got trapped.'

Before he could turn to face the street again, Gracie was hugging him. He did not know whether it was a friendship hug or a romantic hug, whatever the latter was. But it lasted longer than most of the hugs he endured.

Back at Spitfire's Rise, his friends had spent months joking about the possibility of him and Gracie getting together. The joke had been made so many times that he had wondered whether it was a joke at all. Unfortunately for the crowd, Jack wasn't attracted to Gracie. He was just the only person her age who made time for her: the one who never called her Lazy Gracie, or underestimated her because of her habit of blending in with the crowd.

Then again, that probably mattered to her.

The hug continued, as if she was after something that Jack could not give – and did not even know how to give. Not only did he have zero experience in the field of romance, but he had no motivation either. Jack Hopper felt no attraction to girls. He felt no attraction to boys either. He didn't feel it for anything.

There was probably a word for it somewhere, but he had been too afraid to check. Life as a teenage boy without physical attraction was difficult – especially in a world where he was expected to go after the ladies, as if it were his civic duty as a male. His lack of sexuality had been one of the many factors that had led to him heading to his room with a bottle of pills on two different nights. Just one more thorn in his side, alongside his dead mother and years of relentless bullying...

Gracie squeezed, and Jack squeezed back. It seemed polite. But inside he was struggling with the morals of the situation: was it OK to let Gracie think there was a chance at all? Would it be better to tell her the truth? Which option would hurt her less in the long run? He may not have felt any attraction to Gracie, but he cared about her. And he didn't want her to get hurt by something beyond her control.

A third option appeared in his mind, and he used it without thinking.

'Are you hungry?' he asked.

'Hmm?' came a voice from the face buried in his combat uniform.

'It's getting dark soon. I can get some food for us, if you don't mind guarding for me.'

Gracie nodded, and Jack escaped the hug. He took his first steps towards the staircase, but felt the need to do something nice before he left.

'If it makes it easier, you can borrow my rifle while you're up here. Two automatic weapons are better than one.'

'What about you?'

'I've got a loaded handgun,' he said, surrendering his assault rifle. 'I'm fine. See you in a bit.'

Going by Gracie's reaction, he had not done badly. He doubled-checked his pocket for the handgun before creeping downstairs, and his thoughts drifted to a frightening question: how long could they afford to stay in Lemsford before heading home without Ewan?

There was a thump somewhere on the ground floor.

Jack froze, but smiled. Perhaps Ewan had been his usual stealthy self and arrived without them noticing.

Well, we spent a whole minute hugging with our eyes away from the window. A parade of clowns could have wandered through the front door, as long as they weren't too noisy.

All the same, it was better to be careful. The thump could have been nothing, like the half-dozen thumps at Spitfire's Rise each night. Or it could have been *something*.

Jack reached the foot of the stairs, which joined on to the living room. He crept across towards the doorway to the hall and poked his head around. After a long, tense silence, Jack was relieved when he saw a familiar figure walk out from the kitchen. After almost a year living under the same roof, he recognised his companion immediately.

But…

What the hell is Alex doing here?

The clear and obvious figure of Alex Ginelli, tall, black and muscular, edged into the hallway with slow, calculating steps. He peered around with hawk eyes and a bad-tempered expression, his submachine gun held in a way that did not suggest self-defence.

Jack didn't know the correct response, but he knew it had to be an instant one. Alex was a friend, but something seemed wrong with him – even without the obvious question of why he had abandoned his post at comms. Unwilling to raise his weapon and uncomfortable with breaking his silence, Jack withdrew his head from the corridor and looked for a place to shelter. He slipped towards the back wall of the living room to duck behind the television. It seemed like a decent place to keep an eye on things.

Alex stepped into the living room and took a look around. He seemed focused on learning where the entrances and exits were.

It didn't seem right. Alex knew this house just as well as Jack: he had been here that same night, and slept upstairs in little Matthew's bed.

Then a second Alex Ginelli followed him into the room.

What the everloving crap in a handbasket...

The two Alexes walked into the most well-lit part of the living room, and Jack noticed the navy blue shade on their uniform.

The obvious question entered Jack's mind, but there was no time to think about how the hell Alex had been cloned. A third Alex entered the living room, a third submachine gun in his hands.

Jack, sheltered in the dark with his feet tangled in the snake-pit of television wires, would not jump up and shoot. He had given his assault rifle to Gracie out of social awkwardness, and his handgun was semiautomatic: one bullet per trigger pull. One moment of hesitation or one bad shot, and three submachine guns would answer back. He would have to wait until they turned their backs on him.

The first Alex cast his gaze up the stairs.

No, no, no. Just assume there's nobody up there. Nobody has to die for this...

Alex One, as Jack had subconsciously named him, took his first step onto the staircase. Alex Two started to follow. Gracie would have her gaze pointed out of the front window, and assume any noise to be Jack – who couldn't afford to call out and draw the clones' attention—

'Hey,' came Gracie's voice from upstairs, loud and joyful, 'I think that's Ewan heading up the road!'

All three Alexes leapt in surprise, with the same shocked expression that the real Alex wore whenever Thomas jumpscared him for fun. The shock faded a moment later, and all three faces turned angry. Their war modes had been activated.

Alex One accelerated up the stairs.

'Gracie, you numpty…'

The whisper was loud enough.

Alex Two turned to investigate the darkness. When he found nothing visible he opened fire indiscriminately, his bullets riddling the walls, the mounted lights, the DVD rack and the television. Jack ignored the strobe light of the muzzle flash, flung himself to the carpet and fired all eight of his handgun bullets. Two of them flew towards the staircase, and pierced Alex One in the shoulder blade and kidney. One of the others hit Alex Three in the chest and sent him dead to the floor. The rest struck nothing but the painting next to Alex Two.

Alex One toppled to the staircase, alive but in tremendous pain. But even then, there was fury in his twisted facial expression rather than fear. Gracie's voice sounded from upstairs, asking if Jack was OK. Alex Two looked at his colleagues in surprise, giving Jack enough time to cast his empty handgun to one side, leap to his feet and reach for his hunting knife. He threw it towards Alex Two but it missed pathetically, bounced off the wall and drew the clone's attention to where he stood. In desperation, he grabbed a glass pot of boiled sweets on the mantelpiece. He charged across the room, his enemy too angered and confused to aim with any

117

accuracy, and raised the glass pot over his head. He brought it crashing into Alex Two's face, where it shattered upon impact.

Jack did not feel the sting, nor the warm trickle of his blood as it spilled from his hand. The clone before him was in agony, his eyes closed and his hands picking glass shards from his cheeks. Jack grabbed the clone's submachine gun in one hand and used the other to deliver his strongest punch to his enemy's nose.

Jack realised the hopelessness of his situation. The real Alex Ginelli was twice as strong as Jack Hopper, and the clone versions were no different. They may not have been grown with Alex's taekwondo skills, but they shared his muscular form. That, and Jack had *never* seen that kind of ferocity in Alex's eyes.

Before Alex Two could steady himself, Jack's best idea was a head-butt to the face – his helmet cracking into the clone's forehead – and then throwing the weight of his whole body against the clone until it slammed against the wall.

To his right, the wounded Alex One batted his hand around the stairs in search of his dropped submachine gun.

'Gracie! Bloody help me!'

Jack wrapped one arm around Alex Two's neck, ignoring the punches to every part of him the clone could reach, and tried to seize his weapon with desperate fingers. The angry clone wrestled back with both hands, a struggle Jack would definitely lose. Jack checked for a clear run to his left, forced all of his strength into the arm wrapped around his enemy's throat, and charged towards the window.

Alex Two's forehead shattered the glass, and formed several jagged edges that scoured the face that followed. There were no screams from the clone's missing vocal cords, but his mouth opened wide and the rest of his body twitched in pain. Before his adrenalin peaked, Jack used his newfound strength to hold the injured clone in place. Alex Two fought with all his power to bring his head back into the living room, but could not stop Jack from squeezing his fingers into his collar and carving his neck back and forth against the broken glass.

The wall beneath the window painted itself red, and the clone's resistance grew weak. Jack turned just in time to see Alex One's submachine gun pointed in his direction, before his last enemy was shot dead by a flurry of bullets from Gracie above.

'Are you alright?' she asked from the top of the stairs.

'Yeah,' said Jack as Alex One toppled down the staircase, 'peachy, thanks.'

Jack double-checked each of the three bodies in turn to make sure they were dead, and found that against the odds, he and Gracie really had won.

'And I thought sharing a house with *one* Alex was difficult,' he muttered, as he tended to the cuts in his forehead. Head-butting a clone with glass wounds to its face had *not* been his brightest idea.

'What do we do now?' asked Gracie.

'We call comms, describe everything we've seen, and tell the real Alex he's no longer special and unique. After that, we get out of here. Hundreds of thousands of houses between Oakenfold and New London, and *this* is where they searched.'

'Just our luck,' said Gracie.

'It's never luck,' came a voice at the front door.

Gracie's announcement had been right. After two and a half hours of waiting, Ewan had finally found his way to Lemsford.

'You've got a theory?' Jack asked him.

'You're the logical one,' Ewan answered, looking across the bodies on the floor. 'Three clones found their way to this particular house, and all three of them were modelled on someone who's been there before. What's the most likely explanation?'

'That they share some of Alex's memories.'

Ewan's eyes stared piercingly into Jack's, filled with anger.

'So *where else* do they know the way to?'

Chapter 11

By the time Ewan reached Spitfire's Rise, it was breakfast time on May 18th. Less than forty-eight hours until Nicholas Grant's birthday, the anniversary of Takeover Day, the rise of the AME shield, and the end of their chances of winning the war.

Jack and Gracie followed him through the trapdoor, and endured the silent journey through the tunnel to the armoury.

In my head, I'd hoped all seven of us would return together.

Oh, who am I kidding? The whole thing was a trap from the start. We were always going to end up separated. Even Raj's death wasn't that surprising when you think about it. Bloody tragic, but not surprising.

When he opened the door into the armoury, Thomas was sat next to the Memorial Wall.

On most days, opening the door to Thomas was like coming home to an overexcited Labrador. But that morning the boy rose to his feet like a tired old man, the excitement gone from him.

Does he already know about Raj? Or is this about something else?

What happened on the operating table?

Thomas ambled up to Ewan and gave him a soft hug, followed by Jack and even Gracie in turn.

'You OK, Thomas?' asked Jack.

The boy shrugged.

'Is McCormick alive?' Ewan asked.

'He's OK,' Thomas replied, offering no further details.

Ewan glanced at the Memorial Wall, and found the name of Raj Singh already chiselled beneath Charlie's. That may have explained Thomas' mood, but Ewan's patience was too low for uncertainties. He headed for the steps up to the house, and was met on the ground floor by Mark and Simon on the living room sofas.

'Where's Kate?' he asked.

'Don't worry, we all lived,' replied Mark. 'She won't be leaving her room for a while though.'

'Mc—'

He didn't have time to finish the word, as the man had already heard his voice and walked in from the kitchen. Joseph McCormick was alive, well, and smiling.

'Ewan!' he said with a wavy, uncharacteristically emotional voice, 'I can't tell you how glad I am to see you again.'

'Me too, sir,' Ewan gasped.

'No hugs I'm afraid. My abdomen's been cauterised together by a soldering iron, so I'd rather not go squishing things around. Nonetheless,' he finished, holding out one hand in a shaking position, 'it's good to have you home.'

Ewan shook McCormick's hand, but avoided the warm smile on his face. There were already too many troubled thoughts running through his mind, and the joy of seeing his surrogate grandfather's smile would cause enough internal conflict for tears to flow.

'How's Lorraine?'

'She needs time,' McCormick answered, reaching into his

pocket and drawing out a small plastic bag. 'Now, want to see something disgusting?'

'Well I've not slept since I watched Raj get his spine blown out, and his body land on the school car park in a thousand pieces. But sure, impress me.'

Ewan was trying so hard to hide his disgust at McCormick's actions: the risks the man had put himself through, and his plan to put himself at even more risk by joining the next strike team. But even when Ewan tried to mask his emotions, he was transparent. McCormick apologised for his clumsy language, with genuine regret in his voice, and held out the plastic bag. An ugly whitish-reddish sac lay inside, about half the size of Ewan's thumb. The large cyst that had kept McCormick safe in Spitfire's Rise was now outside his body, like a leash that had been unclipped from an irresponsible dog.

Clearly he didn't learn his lesson in December. The cyst wasn't the only reason he struggled in New London the first time.

'Any damage to your stomach?'

'Abdomen. Here it is.'

Jack, Gracie and Thomas walked into the living room just as McCormick raised his shirt. Gracie slapped her hands over her face, the idea of a grown man's belly just too much for her.

The mark wasn't quite as horrible as Ewan had predicted. It was certainly bigger – spread across more than half his abdomen – but it made sense that the cut would have to be bigger than the cyst itself. The burn marks from the soldering iron had left a canyon of thickened red mess: skin that looked hard to the touch, like overdone beef.

'And how are you actually feeling?' asked Jack.

'Surprisingly good after a day in bed,' McCormick answered. 'And I've got at least twelve hours more before I need to do any exercise.'

Crap. It's already the eighteenth. The New London mission starts tonight.

'Has Ewan told you about Alex?' asked Gracie.

McCormick's puzzled face revealed his answer.

Ewan stood in the armoury with his arms folded, his eyes focused on the door to the exit tunnel. The comms team had been faithful in duty, waiting for confirmation that all six soldiers were home before leaving their post. But Ewan suspected Alex had other reasons for delaying his journey.

Everyone was in the armoury, watching the exit like Thomas had. Even Lorraine and Kate were halfway down the steps, not daring to miss the scene that would follow.

Ewan watched Shannon as she arrived first through the tunnel door. She gazed at the crowd as she entered, looking concerned but unsurprised. Somehow, Ewan could read her feelings better than other people's.

Her first reaction was to walk past him, her hand brushing deliberately along his fingers. It was a nonverbal, discreet way of saying 'I'm happy you're safe – we'll talk later, when we're alone.' Shannon headed to Kate on the stairs, and whispered something that included the words 'sorry' and 'Raj'. She offered Kate a hug, which she accepted.

Alex wandered into the armoury, uniting all eleven surviving Underdogs in the same room, and let out a huff towards the crowd.

'We need to talk,' said McCormick.

'Fine, thanks. How was your morning?'

Sarcasm, thought Ewan. *Predictable response.*

'Now, Alex,' McCormick said.

'Alright,' Alex began, removing his weapons and placing them back on their shelves as if to pretend the crowd weren't there. 'Number one, I'm not a clone. Number two, I have never been through a cloning machine or anything. So I can't help you much, really.'

'But you *were* cloned, Alex,' said Ewan, twice as loud as normal. 'With or without your permission, Nathaniel Pearce grew three copies of you. And probably a thousand more. If you're not willing to talk about this—'

'There's nothing to talk about,' said Alex, dumping his knife onto its regular shelf and leaning against the wall unarmed. 'I've had a lot of time to think about this in comms, and the more I think about it the less I have to offer you.'

'Then you must have seen this question coming,' came Mark's voice. 'Someone's got to ask, so it might as well be me. How do we *know* you're not a clone yourself?'

Alex rolled his eyes, and pointed to his lips.

'Words. Duh.'

Ewan looked across the crowd, as a reminder for him to keep his temper under control – for his own sake and for everyone else's. A day earlier, Alex's argument would have been good enough. That morning, an extra layer of paranoia got in the way.

Jack spoke first.

'Do you really think Pearce is incapable of making a clone with functioning vocal cords?' he asked.

'We've not seen one so far,' spat Alex.

'He'll have his own reasons,' Jack answered, stimming his fingers to help him concentrate. 'Probably to control his minions. But he *must* be able to make speaking clones. I'll ask again – do you *really* think Nathaniel Pearce can grow a clone with a complete digestive system, nervous system, circulatory system and a full set of organs, and a brain that enables them to operate radios and basic computers, but somehow find *vocal cords* too tricky? Shannon, back me up here.'

Ewan turned around, and saw Shannon jump in surprise at the foot of the stairs. Almost like a deer in headlights.

'What?'

'You know your dad better than the rest of us. I think Grant ordered Pearce to leave his clones mute so they'd always be inferior to real humans. What do you think, am I right?'

Shannon paused, as if the thought of reading her father's mind filled her with existential dread.

Knowing her upbringing, Ewan thought, *it probably does.*

'...Everything he ever did was about control. M-maybe you're right.'

'And if he truly wanted to give his clones the power of speech – to spy on his enemies or something – he'd be able to do it, right?'

She paused again.

'Yes. He would.'

'And he could even remove the war and peace settings in their mind, to make them act like regular people?'

'...Yes.'

'OK,' said Jack, 'then I propose a blood test.'

He pointed at Alex's face and made fierce eye contact. Ewan was impressed at his friend's directness: it was as if the experience of killing cloned versions of Alex had given Jack a newfound confidence around him.

'We take some of Alex's blood,' Jack continued, 'and put it in a petri dish or something to see how quickly it ages. In three hours' time we look at it and check if it's started turning to jelly. If it hasn't, we know he's telling the truth.'

There were nods of agreement all around the armoury, including from Ewan, but no words. Nobody in the group had anything to add to Jack's logic, except for Alex.

'For the sake of fairness,' he spat, 'how about all ten of you go through the same thing? OK, so Grant must have taken my DNA from somewhere. Most of us have been to New London. Even McCormick's been once before! And if they took it from *me*, they could have taken it from anyone who's been in the Outer City and bled on the floor, or spat, or sneezed, or picked their nose and wiped it on the wall!'

'You're wrong, Alex,' Ewan said. 'They didn't take it from your DNA. Not unless your DNA has a memory. Shannon, do you think clones can be made with attached memories? If Pearce scans the previous model's brain or something?'

'...Yes.'

Alex snorted, and thumped an angry fist against the wall behind him. Ewan spoke again.

'What are the chances of those clones finding their way to Lemsford?' he asked. 'What are the chances of all three of them being grown from your model? There's a one in a million chance of it all being coincidence, so the other nine hundred thousand must be the chance of them remembering.'

'You really do have learning difficulties, don't you?'

'They can't get your memories from snot wiped on the wall,' Ewan replied, ignoring the blatant insult. 'At some point, your brain must have been scanned. It's time to stop lying.'

'*I'm not f—*'

'Sorry, Ewan,' McCormick interrupted, with a soft voice that silenced the cellar, 'but we have to consider all possibilities. We don't know anything about Pearce's technology, so it's still possible for Alex to be the victim without being aware. Nonetheless, Jack's suggestion of a blood test is a good one. Alex, I'm sure you understand.'

'I'll do it,' said Ewan, his head pointed at the wooden door to the neighbouring house. 'In the farm next door, out of everyone's way. Mark, I'll need a second guy – and some rope, a chair and a plate.'

Mark nodded, and headed up the stairs. Ewan turned to McCormick, and whispered to him with eyes of sympathy and sorrow.

'You know what else this means, don't you?'

McCormick nodded, visibly saddened.

'Tell them, Ewan.'

Ewan turned to the crowd, hesitating before giving his command.

'The rest of you,' he finished, 'pack up your things. If those clones remembered the way to Lemsford, they'll remember their way here. Take whatever food and weapons you can carry. When the strike team leaves tonight, you're all leaving here too.'

'But—'

'No buts, Thomas. Tonight, we're leaving Spitfire's Rise.'

A solemn silence fell over the crowd. Moving house had been difficult enough in the old days, but his surviving friends were faced with the task of doing so with one day's notice and nothing more than two handfuls of belongings.

Grow some guts, all of you, Ewan thought. *We all did exactly the same thing on Takeover Day.*

'Alex,' he muttered with a hand on the wooden door, 'come with me.'

Ewan took no pleasure in tying Alex to a chair, although a part of him felt like he should have done. Alex had served the Underdogs well over the past year, but if it weren't for the urgency of the situation it would have been nice to see the overconfident show-off put in his place. Mark had sat himself down on the floorboards, poking his fingers through the soil and uprooting the occasional carrot. The farm would be useless in a matter of hours anyway.

'Alex,' Ewan began, drawing out the hunting knife from its sheath, 'I hope you understand, but I won't be apologising for this.'

'You never were good at basic manners.'

Ewan smirked. Alex wasn't wrong, to be fair.

'Before we do this,' he said, bending over just slightly to look Alex in the face, 'I need you to be completely honest. And I mean *completely* honest. Put your pride behind you, for the sake of all of us.'

'Yeah, cos I'm a compulsive liar.'

'I mean it mate. Don't try being defiant. You're talking to the pathological *king* of defiance here, so it's better not to compete. You couldn't have been cloned without knowing anything about it.'

'Ewan,' Alex growled like a jaded schoolteacher towards the end of a bitter career, 'for the last time – I'm *not* being defiant, I'm *not* being dishonest – I just literally *do not know anything* about how they could have cloned me. End of discussion.'

'Well let's not give up yet,' said Ewan. He did his best to use McCormick's approach to disagreements: discussing them rather than arguing over them. It was difficult when emotions were high, especially with his PDA-inspired need for control kicking in, but it was still the best way into Alex's brain.

'One way or another,' Ewan continued, 'the cloning happened. Let's at least find out *when* it could have been.'

Alex closed his eyes. Perhaps he found it easier to be straightforward when he couldn't see the people he was accountable to.

'I've not been anywhere interesting in a year,' he said, 'except New London. Last time I was there we destroyed the clone factory. Well, you guys did – I saw the place, took a bullet to the shoulder and spent the next three days in a bungalow. Either way, my clones must have been grown there before you blew the place up.'

'And when did you see New London before that?'

'The day Ben Christie died. *Months* ago.'

'OK,' said Ewan, 'so it must have happened when… on the clone factory mission.'

'When Charlie died'. I almost let that sentence slip out.

'I was pretty crap, to be fair,' said Alex with a bitter laugh. 'Didn't last an hour before getting shot. By the afternoon I was wrapping my shoulder in someone's shirts, trying to stop the blood.'

Ewan couldn't help but offer a well-humoured smile. Alex never talked about his failures, so it was only polite to avoid rubbing them in when he did.

'The next three days were the most boring of my life,' Alex continued. 'Or they would have been, if I hadn't spent them worrying about you guys.'

'Flattery will get you nowhere,' grunted Mark through a mouthful of carrot.

'No, I actually mean it,' said Alex. 'That was the whole adventure for me, except for going upstairs with Kate, getting shot and going downstairs again.'

Kate was with him for the start of that day, and she never reported anything unusual…

Then he was on his own. Cornered in the clone factory's alpha control room with no witnesses.

'Alex… what happened once you were trapped in that control room?'

'I got out and reached the bungalow.'

'Take me step by step. How did it happen?'

'I took a rifle from one of the dead clones, shot my way free, then got out and reached the bungalow.'

Ewan's eyes widened. He looked over to Mark, who had also noticed the vagueness in his answer.

'*Step by step*, Alex. Start from when you shot your way free.'

Alex opened his mouth, and nothing came out.

'You got out from the control room, and...'

Nothing.

'...Alex?'

'I... I don't remember.'

'Bingo,' said Mark.

Ewan watched Alex's expression turn from puzzlement to fear to abject horror. It was a mood he had never seen in the man's face before.

'I mean, I literally have no memory,' Alex continued, his eyes to the floor and his head shaking rapidly in disbelief. 'I escaped the control room, and reached the bungalow. I don't remember anything that happened in between. But I... I don't even remember *not remembering*, you know? I didn't even realise there was a gap in my memory until right now... it was like I've tried to avoid thinking about it, but not realised...'

More words came out of Alex's mouth, but none of them helped Ewan understand him any better. All he knew was that there was a blind spot in Alex's memory, during which Grant and his allies could have effectively done *anything* with no witnesses.

'Ewan,' said Mark, 'the sooner you take his blood, the sooner we can end the experiment and evacuate. The sooner you can get some sleep too.'

Ewan clawed his fingers into his head, reluctant to admit Mark was right. Drawing a knife over Alex's skin would have been unpleasant enough at the best of times, but somehow it was worse when the man was tied to a chair, vulnerable to the point of tears, and trying to imagine what the hell Nicholas Grant had done to him without him even remembering.

Nonetheless, Ewan raised his knife.

'I'm sorry, Alex.'

'You said you wouldn't apologise...'

Ewan picked up the plate at the side of the chair, and leaned forward towards Alex's cheek.

'Wha-wait... the face? Seriously? You can't take blood from my arm or somewhere?'

'You didn't tell him, Mark?'

'Your show, not mine.'

Ewan took a deep breath. Less than a foot in front of him, the whole of Alex's restrained body twitched in fear.

'There could be thousands of your clones running around. The only way we'll feel safe is if we make you look different to the rest of them.'

'You're scarring my face...'

'We're protecting you. From us. Because we're scared too.'

'Scared?' Alex gasped. 'You have all your memories. No blank spaces where unknown bad stuff might have happened. You don't even know what scared means...'

Ewan grimaced, and lay the hunting knife against Alex's right cheek.

Chapter 12

Oliver Roth lumbered down the Floor A corridor, exhausted from his all-night journey back to the Citadel. It was rare that he saw grass or sunlight these days, but he realised how little he had missed them. New London held everything he was truly interested in, and he had no idea how the rebels could live such unluxurious lives in the countryside.

Well, the ones that are left anyway, he thought, as his prize rolled and thumped around in his backpack.

Despite Roth's tiredness, his enthusiasm remained. He had walked from Harpenden to Floor A without even sitting down along the fifteen-mile journey, kept on his feet by the thought of later boasting about the achievement, and his allies awaited him behind the next door for a meeting that apparently couldn't be delayed any longer. Rather than being demotivated, Roth was consumed with excitement.

Through the glass wall of the office, he could see Marshall and Pearce sitting at opposite sides of the long table, predictably distant from each other. At the front of the room, a large screen displayed the same countdown as every other spare screen on Floor A at that moment.

34:01:21

34:01:20
34:01:19

The numbers were digital-shaped and bright red, like the countdowns on those bombs from the movies. It seemed a childish choice, but nobody was going to offer that feedback to Nicholas Grant. Certainly not the dull-mannered duo sitting at the elongated table.

At one end, Iain Marshall sat hunched in his seat with a face like a smacked arse. At the opposite end, Nathaniel Pearce was tucking in to his brunch, his little-too-happy smile visible even with his mouth full. The sight of cheese and jalapeños forced an involuntary rolling of Roth's eyes: there could have been a whole food laboratory growing those jalapeño peppers for Pearce, and Roth didn't trust the common sense of a man who guzzled spicy food before midday.

Then again, of all the reasons we have to distrust Nat, his jalapeños are pretty bloody far down the list.

Marshall had told him everything. Back in Roth's training days, when Marshall hadn't seen his twelve-year-old apprentice as a possible future threat, the man had spent a lot of time ranting about his colleague and former best friend.

After a dozen years in the armed forces and eight as an international arms dealer, Marshall had thought it better to quit the latter profession while he was still alive. He had told Roth that it was a sensible, calculated decision, like every decision that needed to be made during combat. But Roth had seen through him, and he knew that weak arms dealers didn't merely lose money when their influence started to wane. Marshall had left his exciting war zones and fled back to regular boring Britain, got himself married to a regular boring woman, and started a regular boring job at a private defence contractor with a regular boring name: 'Marshall Contractors'.

Roth couldn't remember the technical details and didn't care about them either, but he remembered that 'Marshall Contractors' became 'Marshall–Pearce Solutions' when his boss' old university roommate failed at his own business. Pearce's pharmaceutical company had been a casualty of Britain's worst economic downturn in thirty years (although his terrible business sense hadn't helped either, according to a ranting Marshall). Marshall had created a senior staff position for his old friend, allowing the near-bankrupted Pearce to desert his sinking ship two months before the rest of his company collapsed into dust.

It had gone well for a while, until a man called Nicholas Grant wandered in and bought their company in a day. It was—

'Well, here's Oliver,' came Marshall's voice from the other side of the thin glass. Roth brought himself back to reality and scanned his keycard against the door. He scurried through as it opened, making his remaining energy as visible to his superiors as he could.

'Made it with… fifty-five seconds to go,' said Pearce.

'Adults always start their meetings late,' Roth said, dumping his rucksack on the floor next to his chair. 'Besides, you may be three minutes from your bedroom but I had to walk here from Harpenden. Made it without sitting down along the way, you know.'

Before Roth could check their faces for reactions, the countdown on the television flickered off. The screen turned pure white, and a monotone buzz of blank noise suggested Grant's microphone was on.

He's not showing his face. For all we know he could be sitting at his desk in his underwear, playing chess against himself or something. Or maybe he thinks a blank screen is more imposing.

Roth understood. Reputation was far scarier than a visible face. Marshall had once taught him that.

'Let us begin,' came the voice of Nicholas Grant.

'Great timing,' said Roth, 'I've just arrived! But of course you knew that, didn't you?'

'Perceptive boy. Yes, I was watching.'

Roth tried to look around for wherever the camera was, without it being obvious he was searching. He felt more comfortable knowing which part of his head was being watched by the world's most controlling dictator.

'Hungry, Nathaniel?' asked Grant. Roth's glance landed on Pearce as he swallowed his mouthful of cheese and jalapeños.

'I've got to eat here,' he said, 'hope you don't mind. Struggling to find time for nourishment with the AME project where it is.'

'Lose the sandwich, Nathaniel,' Grant boomed. 'What you're doing is a transparent attempt to impress me with how busy you are, and I'm not gullible enough to fall for it. Unless you think I am?'

'No sir,' Pearce answered, 'I don't.'

Pearce's trademark smile collapsed at the edges, and he placed the cheese and jalapeño sandwich on the table.

'*Bin*, Nathaniel.'

There was a moment of beautifully awkward silence, as Pearce's smile dropped even further. At the other end of the table, Marshall wore his poker face to conceal how amusing he must have found the telling-off. Roth didn't bother, and openly snorted with laughter. Nathaniel Pearce, pharmaceuticals genius and creator of the clone soldier, picked up his sandwich and walked over to the corner bin like a naughty primary school child. With his brunch thrown away he sauntered back to the table and sat down, trying not to look too embarrassed.

'Now,' said Roth in his most jovial voice, 'where were we?'

'First things first,' said Grant's voice, 'talk to me about the results from the AME test centre.'

Otherwise known as Oakenfold Retard School.

'Things are looking rather positive,' said Pearce.

'You've had a day and a half to sift through your results,' said Grant. 'I want more than "rather positive".'

'Based on the performance of Atmospheric Metallurgic Excitation at the test location, I can confirm a near one hundred per cent likelihood of success when we apply the same technology on a larger scale – to an area the size of New London Citadel, for example.'

Pearce continued with scientific terms that Roth did not understand. And the longer the Chief Scientist's monologue, the more sour the expression on Marshall's face. Roth thought back once again to those rants of old, about how Iain Marshall's best mate from university had stopped existing under the leadership of Nicholas Grant, replaced by a creepy smiler who used big words to impress important people. A man who had vanished into the lab for days on end, stopped heading to the Red Lion for a pint at the weekends, and even ignored Marshall's social calls.

Roth wondered whether they could have been reconciled when Grant finally sat them down and told them about his plans for Great Britain. But Marshall had screwed it up catastrophically, and Roth was glad—

'Iain,' said Grant. 'Anything to add?'

Roth looked to the ceiling, and found the camera. At his side, Marshall was still searching, as subtly as he could.

'No,' Marshall replied, 'I think Nat covered it neatly. If I may talk for a moment about the rebels—'

'I don't care about them. They're thirty-five hours from being irrelevant.'

You do care about them, thought Roth. *Otherwise you wouldn't have hosted the AME tests at Oakenfold.*

Oh, and there's also the Ginelli Project.

And your daughter.

Looking at Marshall's face, he had clearly had the same thought.

'Shannon's still with them, sir,' Marshall said. 'The destruction of the clone factory proves it. They used Lambourne's technology, which they could only have got from her—'

'And how many of them are left, exactly? It was your idea to lure them to the test centre. Did it work?'

'Hargreaves and Simmonds died as expected,' Marshall finished, 'but I'm led to believe we got one of them. The clone teams further afield reported no further kills. Oliver?'

Roth grinned. Time to shine. He reached into the rucksack next to his chair as he spoke.

'Yep,' he started, 'another one down. I arrived at the test centre last night and confirmed it myself. If you want to see how effective the AME shield is, take a look at this.'

Roth brought his hand out from his rucksack and dumped a thick, red-stained forensic evidence bag onto the table. Marshall's eyebrows rose to the top of his head. Even Pearce, no stranger to gore in the laboratory, opened his mouth so wide that Roth could smell the jalapeños.

The head inside the evidence bag was of Indian descent. It had young skin, and eyes that were squeezed shut. Roth was looking forward to researching the dead kid's name once the meeting ended.

'Bloody hell, Oliver…' came Marshall's voice.

'As you can see,' Roth said, 'the shield works. This lad had metal implants in his spine… or I'm guessing he did, given the state of his remains.'

'You realise,' said Grant's voice with a low chuckle, 'that mutilating the deceased is against the Geneva Convention? And that includes decapitation.'

'Decapitation? There was only a flap of skin holding it on when I found it. Now the best part is, the rest of his crew might have been watching when this happened. This guy's body will be one hell of a deterrent for them. Raising the AME shield won't just stop them from getting in. It'll stop them from even *thinking* about it.'

Roth inspected the head on the table next to him. The jaw was broken, suggesting that it may have had metal teeth fillings too. A forensic analyst could have had so much fun looking at his remains.

'Bringing a severed head to a meeting,' said Marshall. 'This is a new one, Oliver.'

'You're not grossed out, are you?'

'No, just worried about your well-being.'

'I'm doing better than him, don't worry.'

Roth's grin was not returned. Not even by Pearce.

'Oliver,' replied Marshall, 'there's no point in having unbridled enthusiasm if it's counteracted by an enormous lack of judgement. A soldier must be objective and rational, and not waste time delighting in personal pleasures. And could you please stop drumming your fingers on Raj's head while I'm talking to you?!'

Raj! So that was his name.

Roth stared at Marshall in the eyes, his expression an unwavering vision of confidence. As predicted, Marshall pushed the conversation no further.

It was a wonderful skill, his ability to shut up his boss whenever he wanted. The beautiful part was that the reason behind this ability was never spoken aloud, but always on both their minds.

Marshall and Pearce must have been in that very same meeting room the day Grant had shared his ultimate plan. Marshall, thinking of his young family in the Derbyshire Dales (or so the story went), had been horrified. Inspired by the risk to Hannah and his twin daughters (apparently), who would be doomed to grow up and grow old on New London's upper floors (as if that would be a bad thing), Marshall had reached into the company's private army training programme and pulled out a red-haired teenager.

Oliver Gabriel Roth, then aged twelve, was set to burst out of comprehensive school four years later with a fine assortment of high grades. He had planned to enter the military, but a place in the British Armed Forces didn't offer half as much money as a private defence contractor. And to a young man with unsupportive parents, money mattered.

Roth remembered Marshall's reasons for choosing him. Apparently he had seen 'a battling attitude, raw unbridled enthusiasm, and a total reliance on victory for his sense of self-worth', according to an email on his computer that Roth hadn't been meant to look at.

Despite Roth's young age and lack of experience, Marshall was convinced there was nobody on his payroll more suitable for the assassination of Nicholas Grant.

From the beginning, Roth had known the reasons for his promotion. He had even met his target face to face and shook him by the hand. The private education promised to the authorities was a lie, replaced by intensive military training. By his thirteenth birthday, he had been going to bed each night twirling the childproofed bottle of cyanide tablets between his fingers, waiting with growing impatience for the signal to slip them into Grant's morning coffee.

The signal never came. Marshall had never admitted it, but Roth knew his boss had accepted that his own fate relied on the success of Nicholas Grant. But by calling off Grant's assassination, Marshall had surrendered his fate to a teenage boy too.

Roth had never blackmailed him aloud, and he had never needed to. Even that day, with Britain subdued and the war nearly won, a cheeky smile on his face told Marshall everything he needed to know. To buy his silence, Oliver Roth had been swept into a life of luxury on Floor A, and total freedom from authority.

One year on from Takeover Day, the relationship between the Big Four was complicated. Each one of them was hated by each of the others, but their animosity was rarely committed to words. There was an unspoken wobbly tension between them, like a wooden raft tied with loose rope, but they depended on one another for survival.

Roth drummed his fingers on the top of the forensic bag one more time, and smiled at Marshall.

'If Iain's finished being offended,' said Grant, 'we need to discuss the tasks that need completing outside of New London. After that, I believe we're done here. What needs doing, gentlemen?'

'How about the external backups I've been requesting?' asked Marshall. 'The sooner this technology is sent to other Citadels, the safer we'll be.'

'You'll have them,' answered Grant, 'but not tonight. And we've already been through why.'

'Why?' asked Roth, not content with being out of the loop.

'Because you're talking about whole chambers full of very large pieces of equipment, and data so complex it can't simply be emailed. The sheer volume of it all can only be transported across two lanes of empty motorway, which we no longer have anywhere on this island, or via huge freight trains, which are no longer powered. We'll be able to fit it all on the *Sheila*, but she won't be ready for another few weeks.'

Roth smiled at the thought of the *Sheila* coming into use. It would be a long while after this day had ended, but it was sure to be beautiful once she embarked upon her maiden voyage.

'In the meantime,' said Pearce, 'there are still resources from the test centre that need bringing here. Research papers, computers and the like.'

'Sorry to break it to you,' Roth said, his sympathy clearly limited, 'but a quarter of the retard school was burnt to a crisp when I arrived. A bunch of that stuff will be gone. This guy must have started a fire before he killed himself,' he finished, patting the top of Raj's head and looking to Marshall for a reaction.

'Then we'll search through the other three quarters,' answered Pearce.

'The school's safely trapped behind a shield,' said Roth. 'Why spend time and resources getting anything back?'

'Because,' Pearce said with an irritated sigh, 'someone in their crew might only need to remove their metal earrings to have free access to any surviving research. Some of the paperwork may have been destroyed in the fire, but I want everything else brought back here.'

'Fine,' Marshall butted in, 'I'll send out some transport. I'll need to bring the shield down though.'

'You can do that remotely from the AME computer in your office,' said Pearce. 'I'll tell you when.'

'Sort it out between you,' said Grant. 'Anything else that needs doing outside these walls?'

Roth shrugged, and hoped his colleagues would do the same. There was a bed in his room not far away that awaited his attention.

'There's a weapons cache out towards Beaconsfield,' said Marshall, 'left over from the days of using quarries as drop-off points between Citadels. Better to bring those weapons inside so they don't fall into rebel hands.'

'Start right away.'

'It'll take until tomorrow evening, but I'll start as soon as this meeting is over.'

'Then it's over. Keep in touch.'

The white screen reverted back to its countdown, and the background noise from Grant's microphone fell silent. The meeting was over, and not a moment too soon. Pearce wasted no time in heading to the door, and Roth caught the man's eyes gazing forlornly at the bin as he passed it.

'Right,' said Roth, grabbing the forensic bag in one hand and stuffing it back into his rucksack, 'it's been a lovely morning, but I need some sleep. Wake me up when something interesting happens.'

'Oliver,' said Marshall, 'a word, please.'

'Twat. That's a word.'

'Out in the corridor, now.'

Roth rose to his feet and laughed.

'Why not in here? Because you're afraid Nick's still listening? And hi Nick, if you are.'

Marshall didn't say another word. He walked to the door, grabbing Roth by the shoulder as he passed – tight enough to show his impatience but not tight enough to make it seem aggressive. He took Roth out of the office, found an empty stretch of corridor, and stood him against the wall.

'Sadism, severed heads and cavalier bad judgement. Not cool, Oliver.'

'Do you have any idea how much I cringe when an adult tries to use the word "cool"?'

'My language is not the problem here, Oliver. An

experienced war veteran is giving you combat advice, and you should bloody well listen to it.'

'Go on then. Advise me.'

'However much you hate an enemy, you can't veer from your military training. That's how they win. Even if you despise them with all the passion in your whole being, you still dispatch them with tactical cunning and ruthless rationality. What you *don't* do is give in to mindless impulses which tell you to indulge in sadism and self-entertainment, like carving off a dead enemy's head just for a trophy.'

Marshall took a step back. Until then, Roth had neither noticed nor cared how close Marshall had been to his face. His boss' words had been predictable: Roth had spent many meetings listening to Marshall's lectures about logical approaches and strategic brutality. But brutality wrapped in logic was still brutality, and Roth felt that his personal investment in his work added to his effectiveness rather than dulled it.

'The younger version of you used to know all that,' Marshall continued. 'This last year, you've started to lose the sensible, measured determination I used to admire in you. You're on dangerous ground, and you can't even blame it on puberty hitting you like a tonne of bricks. This—'

'No, I can't,' Roth interrupted. 'I'm blaming it on *you.*'

While Marshall took time to react, Roth took the opportunity to steal the initiative.

'If you think I'm a monster, I'm a monster you created. I still played Pokémon when I was twelve. And if you hadn't promoted me as quick as you did, *for the reasons you had*, maybe I'd still be that friendly ambitious kid now and still be playing bloody Pokémon.'

It was the closest Roth had ever come to directly referencing Marshall's extinct assassination plan. He would go no further.

Not today. There was a momentary twinge of fear in Marshall's face before he replaced it with predictable anger.

'Nobody goes through what I did without becoming what I've become,' Roth finished. '*You* made sure of that.'

'You're wrong, Oliver. Everything you became is what you *wanted* to become.'

'Did you *want* to be a miserable authoritarian moron then? Or a failed arms dealer?'

'I made my own choices and I know who I am. Do you know who *you* really are, Oliver?'

'Well I'm sure you're going to enlighten me either way, so stop wasting my time and go ahead.'

Marshall's top lip began to quiver and his face turned red. There was just a little part of him that seemed tempted to lose control: a sub-personality within him that looked like it wanted to throw his own advice out of the window.

'Oliver,' he began, 'you are the result of a perfect storm of bad circumstances. Apathetic parents, enormous opportunity, and a complete lack of boundaries. And those circumstances have tricked you into thinking that no matter how little self-discipline you have, the world will just accommodate your errors of judgement. You are the school bully who never grew up to learn that the real world doesn't care how cool you were as a teenager. You are the one person on Earth who has been given *everything* he ever wanted, and it has destroyed any possibility of you growing up to be a good man. But at the very bloody least, Oliver, be a decent soldier.'

Oliver Gabriel Roth might have been impacted by that little speech, if he had not had the defence barriers up in his mind. He gave no reaction.

'Don't you have a wife you're pretending to care about back

in your apartment?' he asked. 'I'm sure she misses you, and is pretending to care about you too.'

Marshall rolled his eyes and turned away. Roth knew, alongside so many other details about his boss' life, that his relationship with Hannah and the kids had gone cold long ago. Still, he imagined that coldness was more comforting than the searing hot hatred of his colleagues.

As his boss and former mentor walked back towards his apartment, Roth checked up and down the corridor for witnesses. Since there were none, neither Iain Marshall nor anyone else saw the double middle fingers pointed towards his back as he walked.

Chapter 13

Even when Spitfire's Rise had been crowded, Ewan's bedroom had always been his sanctuary. It would not remain that way for much longer. Once he walked out of the bedroom he would never return to it – regardless of whether or not they won.

Ewan could not remember the last time he'd felt so frustrated and insecure inside Spitfire's Rise. It was probably back in the early days, during a Temper Twin incident with Charlie. Or maybe even on Takeover Day itself, when he was frightened enough to shoot—

'Ewan?' came a friendly voice from outside the bedroom. Ewan turned his head to the door and found Shannon poking her face inside. Once she saw that the bedroom was unoccupied except for him, she walked in and sat down beside him on the bed.

'You alright?' Ewan asked.

'Yeah, I'm no stranger to this,' Shannon replied, her face to the floor. 'This is the third time I've had to run away in the last month. Abandoning New London with Anthony Lambourne... getting taken from the clinic by Keith Tylor...

and now fleeing Spitfire's Rise. Pretty much my whole life has involved running away from things.'

Ewan sighed. Shannon had only been with them for three weeks, and the house already meant as much to her as it did to him. Normally, that would annoy him: how could her mere three weeks of attachment possibly compare to his year-minus-two-days? But somehow, Ewan was fine with her sharing his feelings.

'Are you busy?' she asked. 'I thought you were packing, or…'

'Just pretending to be,' Ewan answered. 'Needed some time to myself. I'm fine with you being here though.'

'Are you OK?'

'No.'

'…Can I help?'

'No.'

'Do you mean that, or are you just frustrated?'

Ewan paused. His second 'no' had been automatic, and she had caught him out. He was sitting next to the best possible person to help – the only Underdog who had ever seen the uppermost floors of New London.

'Well,' he answered, 'I suppose if you have any tips for getting past Floor F, I'm listening.'

Floor F was the highest accessible storey from regular stairwells. According to the stolen schematics, the stairwells only connected neighbouring floors after that: one stairwell from F to E, a separate one from E to D, and so on. And according to the papers Raj had found at Oakenfold, some of the AME technology was kept as high as Floor B.

'Make sure you have keycards ready,' Shannon answered. 'Human keycards. Clones can't go higher than F unless humans *let* them up there.'

Ewan held his face and swore into his hands. Humans were

rarely found *below* Floor F, which complicated things even further.

'And don't make anything personal,' she added. 'You'll want to, but don't. If my father or Oliver Roth is right in front of you, don't waste any time thinking about your dead family. Just keep calm and take the shot, no matter how much they try to wind you up.'

Oliver Roth's pretty good at winding me up. The way I fought him after Charlie died, I'm amazed he didn't kill me.

'Thanks, Shannon,' he said. 'I think that'll help—'

She leaned in for what Ewan thought was a hug, but she ended up heading for his face. Before Ewan could react, he was being kissed.

Ewan had never kissed anyone and meant it. During his younger teenage years he had had casual girlfriends who he had kissed because he was supposed to, but none of them cared like Shannon did. This was a kiss that had real affection in it, from a girl who truly liked him.

It felt like it lasted for ten whole seconds, but it could have been twenty, or one. It was difficult to tell. When Shannon pulled away again, her face was red.

'Sorry,' she said. 'I shouldn't have done that.'

Wow, thanks.

'…Why not?'

'Things are… complicated,' she answered, rising to her feet. 'That's all.'

'Yeah, you just snogged the guy who's leading the charge against your dad. I thought you'd enjoy doing that!'

'I did! I just…'

Whatever the true reason was for her reluctance, she wasn't planning to say it. But Ewan could guess.

'You're afraid that once I go to New London, I won't come back. Or we'll lose and the war will be over.'

Shannon didn't say a word.

'For what it's worth,' he continued, 'it terrifies me too. And I'm not going to lie, success isn't likely. If there's a single mission in the history of the Underdogs we're likely to fail, it's this one.'

Shannon headed for the bedroom door and yanked it open.

'You need to brush up on your comforting skills,' she said as she stormed out. 'You'll need them for when you get a girlfriend one day.'

'Girlf—'

The door slammed shut.

Ewan decided not to waste time trying to decipher what Shannon meant. He had already avoided the downstairs gathering for too long. After waiting long enough for Shannon to have a decent head start, Ewan left his bedroom for the final time, and headed for the living room.

All of his housemates were present, but he was struck by how empty the room felt. The eleven of them were only a third of the house's wartime residents.

Not long after Takeover Day, McCormick had stood in the same spot and delivered a rousing speech to more than thirty people, who had all cheered and whooped at the idea of fighting back against Nicholas Grant and his million clones. Most of that crowd had since died: many in combat, some through illness, and poor Mike Ambrose had killed himself. The remaining Underdogs – six special needs students, an old man, an ageing nurse, a child, the dictator's daughter and a man who had since been cloned – were a pathetic army by comparison.

Ewan found Alex in the corner of the room, with the right-hand side of his face concealed against the wall. It would take him a while to get used to his three-inch scar. But he was in the cellar with everybody else, and nobody seemed to avoid him. Presumably they'd all been told the result of the test: that Alex's blood had coagulated normally, which meant he was as human as everyone else in the room.

'Ah, Ewan,' said McCormick, 'we were just sharing our favourite memories of this house. I thought it'd be a nice way of ending things before we leave. Why don't you join us?'

'Save it,' Ewan answered. 'If we're leaving we'd better do it now rather than later.'

'We can wait until nightfall. Come on, share your own.'

Ewan wanted to respond with something that would kill the mood. Maybe the time he and Jack got drunk in the cellar, after Oliver Roth had murdered David and Val Riley. Or stumbling across Mike Ambrose's body in the generator room. Or anything else involving friends who had suffered horrible deaths.

But he restrained himself. McCormick's own emotions must have been unsteady: this house meant more to him than anyone else. It may legally have been Polly Jones' place, but for years it had been McCormick's home too.

Ewan knew what his favourite memory was, but it wasn't one he could declare aloud. It was his favourite moment for strategic reasons rather than blind sentiment.

It had been on Takeover Day, when the clones had come to raid Spitfire's Rise, burst through the door and left without incident. He and McCormick had sheltered upstairs, having seen the platoon approach from a distance. The soldiers had entered, seen Polly Jones' dead body, and left with the assumption that the house had already been raided. Not long afterwards, the clones had left the village altogether, allowing Ewan to leave the house and tell his friends about the shelter he had found.

In all the time that had passed since then, none of the Underdogs had been told that McCormick had been a resident at the house all along. Or that Polly existed.

I guess he won't have to keep it a secret much longer. Once we're gone from here, we can afford to let people know the truth. Then he can be thanked properly for taking us in.

Then again, maybe not. Once the secret's out, we lose the chance to ever use this place again.

'My favourite thing,' said Thomas, presumably for the fifth time in the conversation, 'was when Mum told off McCormick for farting at dinner, and he just answered her with another fart!'

Ewan leaned against the wall, and gave a reluctant smile. If the conversation gave Thomas a chance to talk about his dead mother and laugh, perhaps it wasn't such a bad idea.

'Rosanne was nice,' said Jack, referring to a lady in her seventies who had passed away long ago. 'She gave a "nice old lady" vibe to the place which I don't think we've had since. No offence, Lorraine.'

The room went 'ooooh' and gave nervous laughs in response. Lorraine, aged only fifty-two, clouted him round the back of the head.

'OK,' said Jack, 'let's move on quickly. What's yours, McCormick?'

'Honestly,' McCormick replied, 'I think mine might be the night Shannon arrived.'

Shannon, sitting on the floor next to Thomas, widened her eyes.

'I hope you don't mind me saying it,' McCormick continued, 'but it revealed a lot about what kind of community we are. This war had taken a toll on all of us, but we remained the type of people who would welcome a stranger and do our best to make her comfortable.'

'You did a better job than I was expecting,' said Shannon, a comment which raised a few smiles. Then she offered a moment of eye contact with Ewan, and a discreet grin. Perhaps all was well.

An hour passed before McCormick brought the conversation to a close. He took a step forward, deeper into the crowd, and straightened his back. And just like that, the group knew the discussion was over.

'Half an hour from now,' he began, 'we'll be leaving Spitfire's Rise. Before we say our final goodbyes to the house, we should establish who will be going where. My route into New London has space for four people. I need three of you on comms, and that leaves the other four to find us a new home.'

Simon held up three fingers, a confused expression on his face.

'Yes,' replied McCormick, 'three on comms. Two to communicate and one to guard. This house isn't the only place those clones might remember, but we can't move all our resources from the comms unit in time for this mission. For better or worse, the comms team will be stuck there. Now,' he said, with his arms spread wide across the room, 'I'm about to ask for strike team volunteers. Before I do, make no mistake – this is by far the riskiest mission we have ever undertaken. We're going to several locations across the northern wall of New London, some of which are on *Floor B*. To date, we've never been higher than Floor F. The mathematician in me says the odds are stacked overwhelmingly against us, even though the human in me still has faith. So before volunteering, you should know there's no shame in wanting to sit this one out. If I had a choice, I would.'

You do have a choice, you stupid old man, Ewan thought,

feeling immediately guilty for the insult crossing his mind. *It's your own stubbornness that's telling you to charge your sixty-four-year-old body into a war zone, just for the sake of 'leading from the front'.*

Ewan was one of five people to raise his hand. Lorraine, Thomas, Shannon, Simon and Gracie kept theirs down, to the surprise of no one. Jack, Mark and Alex had their hands up; the latter highest of all. Kate, who had avoided the whole discussion as far as Ewan could tell, raised hers too.

'OK,' began McCormick, 'Ewan, the two of us are certainties. Mark, I want you to be the one guarding comms. If the clones come, I honestly believe you'd put up the best defence.'

'Thanks, sir,' said Mark with a very deliberate huff.

'Alex, I'm assuming you're volunteering in order to get revenge. That's not a good idea.'

'It's strategy,' Alex replied, 'I'm not a complete numpty. Unless they get up close, nobody will even know I'm human. And thanks to Ewan's bad shaving, I'm safe from you guys shooting me too.'

McCormick left a pause, his faint nods giving away his answer in advance.

'Alright, I won't argue. And Jack, if you're up for it you're in. Sorry Kate, but I think you need more time to—'

'To get over Raj?' Kate barked, as if McCormick had brought her suddenly and painfully to life. 'Just to make this clear, I will *never* get over Raj. Just like I never got over what's happened to James or my parents. Just like none of us have got over *anything*! My hand is up because Raj died to make this mission happen. We're using the information he gave his life for, and I won't insult him by sitting out.'

It was difficult to read the reaction on McCormick's face, but the length of his pause spoke volumes.

'In all fairness,' added Jack, 'if you want to find a suitable home, you'll need an analytical person with close attention to detail. I'm cut out for that, and Kate's probably better than me in combat anyway. If she really wants it, I'll stand aside.'

'Thanks Jack,' said Kate before McCormick could give his own answer. The man shrugged, and gave a small nod of his head.

'Fine,' he answered. 'Shannon, Lorraine, I want you two on comms with Mark guarding. Shannon's got the best knowledge of Grant's upper floor, and Lorraine… well, you know why. The rest of you, follow Jack as he searches for a new home. Try to find one with comfy beds, OK?'

McCormick's last joke fell on deaf ears. The remaining Underdogs rose to their feet, and prepared to evacuate.

Ten minutes to departure. McCormick dragged his legs behind him into the attic. It was time to say goodbye to Barbara again, this time probably for good. Even if he were lucky enough to survive tomorrow's hellfire, it wouldn't be Polly's house he'd come back to.

He rose to his knees, and found his box of memories straight ahead next to the boiler. But, first things first, there was something in the attic that would have to go wherever the Underdogs went. He reached to his left, opened the thin box of sealed envelopes, and started to flip through them.

'Jack… Mark… Simon… Gracie… Shannon…'

The sixth envelope in the pile, the one he had flipped through to find, sank his heart.

'…Raj.'

McCormick took the envelope in both hands, and tore it to

pieces. The information inside had been for Raj's eyes only, now to be left unread forever. He stuffed the remains into the pocket of his combat uniform, planning to dispose of them somewhere along the journey. The River Lea would churn them up well.

With one less envelope in the thin box, he crawled over to his favourite part of Spitfire's Rise. When he removed the aged photo frame from his memory box, Barbara McCormick's smile seemed to have grown.

'This isn't goodbye, Barbara,' he began. 'I'm just moving house again. Like I did from Durham. Only this time, my physical memories won't be joining me.'

McCormick smiled at the realisation that he was talking to a photo. But that was OK. He had spent three years not minding.

'Tomorrow I'll be heading to New London. Only the second time I've ever been. And you know what, Barbara? There's a chance I might actually come back. I'm prepared for the worst, but I'm hoping for the best. I don't think my work's done yet.'

There was a moment of heartbreak as McCormick thought about what 'his work' truly meant. He had used a lifetime of experience to build up his housemates to be the best versions of themselves they could be, and he had also led two thirds of them to their deaths.

Then again, he could have just let them stay at home and wait to die, like the group Shannon and Lieutenant Lambourne had found in the clinic.

'But either way,' he finished, 'I hope you know about your part in all this. I was never leadership material. It took the most wonderful woman in the world to turn this adult male into a man. And I hope I'm living my life in a way that honours what you did. You deserve my best, and I hope I'm giving it.'

'McCormick?' came a child's laugh from the top of the ladder.

McCormick bit his lip.

'Hello, Thomas.'

'They're waiting for you downstairs.'

'I'm coming. How much did you hear?'

'Something about you needing a woman to make you a man. What does that even mean?'

McCormick smiled, mainly with relief.

'I was just talking to myself,' he answered. 'About my wife. She turned me into the person I am. Before I met her, I was just a kid in an adult's body.'

There was a laugh, followed by a noise on the floorboard beside him. Thomas, uninvited, had joined him in the attic.

'Even though she died too early,' he continued, 'her influence lives on in the people she loved. And she changed me for the better, little by little, all the way up to the day she died.'

'She sounds awesome.'

'She was!' answered McCormick with a hearty laugh. 'Really, really awesome.'

'I hope…'

Thomas' voice trailed off. When McCormick looked over at him, he had sealed his mouth shut.

'You hope what?'

'Nothing.'

'It wasn't nothing, Thomas.'

'OK…' Thomas started, his voice trembling. He seemed to already feel guilty for the words that would come. 'I was about to say that I hope… I hope Mum did that to Dad before they split up. I know they hated each other by the end, but… I hope she changed *him* for the better too.'

Thomas began to shake, and McCormick knew why. He had known Beth well enough to know why. Thomas knew he had said something good, but his upbringing had restricted his freedom of thought. He was not supposed to talk about his parents' break-up, and it must have been drilled into him from before Takeover Day. His mother had even complained about their last name still being Foster: if the divorce lawyers had been quicker, her son would have started the war with his 'real name'.

Nonetheless, Beth's overprotection had never stopped her son from saying kind words.

'That's a very mature thing to say, Thomas.'

'Really?' the boy asked with genuine surprise.

'Yes. And you know what? I'm going to trust you with something.'

Brushing his memory box out of Thomas' line of sight, he drew the boy's attention to the thin box of envelopes. He pushed them over, and lay a soft hand on Thomas' shoulder.

'Wherever our new home is, take these with you.'

McCormick watched Thomas' face as he stood among the crowd in the cellar, at the front so he could see the Memorial Wall one last time. The boy had been uncomfortable with the reason behind McCormick's instructions, but he had understood.

'We'll never be properly home unless we take the whole family with us,' said Jack.

'You're welcome to carry it if you want,' replied Mark.

McCormick adjusted his helmet for the fourth time that minute. It had been a long time since he had last needed to wear one, and it would take the whole evening before he acclimatised to the feel of it again. He stood in place in front of the Memorial Wall, and held out his hands.

'Everyone ready for this?'

Wordless, the Underdogs linked hands, and McCormick began.

'To honour those who gave everything they had, we will give everything *we* have. To honour the dead we will free the living, united by our differences.'

'*United*,' answered the group. McCormick had expected a subdued, saddened response, but instead his friends were *loud*. Evidently, they were taking the opportunity to make their last meeting before the Memorial Wall mean something.

One by one, the crowd started to leave. Some were carrying weapons, others were carrying food. Nobody could carry the generator, so they had left behind everything that would require electricity. Their standard of living was set to dip dramatically. Before Jack walked out with a rucksack full of batteries, McCormick noticed the thermal blocker in his hand: the miniature-football-sized object which kept their body heat off any scans Grant could perform. Ewan's father had stolen it from his barracks on Takeover Day, and that impulsive act had kept them alive for a year. It was by far the most important piece of luggage carried by any of the crew – including all their weapons combined.

McCormick kept himself at the back of the group, and was the last person to leave Spitfire's Rise.

'Thank you, Polly,' he whispered into the air, before he walked into the tunnel, took a final look at the Memorial Wall, and closed the door behind him.

Chapter 14

Kate had been close to the same house forty-eight hours earlier. She had been sitting on a patch of grass less than half a mile away, at the top of a hill next to her boyfriend and their five fellow students.

If she'd known McCormick would bring her back to Oakenfold, perhaps she wouldn't have volunteered after all. The man lay next to her on the sofa at that moment, catching some sleep while he could. It was already gone midnight.

Oakenfold Special School lay at the end of the street, silent and empty. Not even a buzz to suggest there was an active shield surrounding it. It was the perfect trap: invisible, indestructible, and already proven to be fatal.

Two men in dark navy uniforms appeared not far from the house. Kate retrieved her weapon, but on closer inspection they were just who she had hoped. Ewan and Alex had returned from their search for clone uniforms.

'OK,' Ewan whispered as he walked through the front door and passed around another two sets of clothes. 'There's yours, there's McCormick's... I think we're set.'

'Do we seriously think this'll work?' asked Kate, looking down at the uniform being handed to her. It must have belonged to one of the clones Simon had shot during their escape. Not that the disguise would serve much purpose, since Nicholas Grant had never produced a female clone before.

'We've at least got a chance,' answered Alex. 'Besides, it's May nineteenth now. Twenty-four hours from the AME shield going up, any risks are acceptable.'

It wasn't quite the answer Kate wanted. But she could hardly choose to not accept it.

'Did you see Raj?'

Ewan looked at Alex. They were both noticeably uncomfortable.

'There's not much left to see,' said Ewan. 'I wouldn't bother. Won't do you any good.'

That *was* the answer Kate had wanted. She had needed to ask the question to stop it bouncing around in her skull, and now she knew there was no need to go to the entrance and look for herself. She lay down on the living room floor and rested a blanket over herself.

'The shield's still up,' Alex said to her. 'So if you were thinking of stealing some more research…'

Kate shook her head. In front of her, Ewan was doing the same.

'They're not going to bring the shield down unless they absolutely have to,' Ewan said. 'Which they will, once they start hauling the research back to New London. Anyway, any idea how much sleep we're likely to get?'

Not that any of us will actually sleep.

'Literally no idea at all,' said McCormick, who seemed to have awoken out of nowhere. 'The supply trucks could arrive at any time. Safe to say they'll be gone before the evening though.'

'Even with all the machines they'll be loading?' Kate asked.

'No, they won't be transporting much besides paper. The

only bits of hardware here are the border points, which are useless without the laptop Mark destroyed. And the electricity generators in the sports hall are just normal generators, nothing to do with AME research. It won't take long to pack up everything and transport it to New London.'

'Or to some mystery location away from New London where their secret backup is,' Alex mumbled.

'The research we stole made no mention of *off-site* backups,' McCormick said. 'Which means they either think New London's secure enough by itself, or there's something physically stopping them. In my opinion, it's clearly the latter. But either way it's good news for us. Everything's in New London.'

'And once we get there we've got... what, five targets?' asked Ewan, who must have already known the answer but wanted the reassurance of knowing he was right.

'Yes,' replied McCormick, 'five. The Central Research Headquarters on Floor F, for starters. Also the data servers on Floor P, since they'll have all their internal backups, and the paper archive on Floor R. There's also the experiment chamber, also on Floor F, which will hold their last physical traces of research. And... Iain Marshall's computer. On Floor B.'

The silence that followed was painful. Kate could hear the soft wind blowing outside, and even that felt haunting.

'And you chose this particular mission to be your first visit to New London since before Christmas?' said Alex. 'You didn't even *do* much the other time you were there!'

'I did more than you think.'

'Oh,' Alex continued, 'and one really important bit of advice. Make sure you listen to this. If you come up against an enemy, don't try to convert them, right? Don't try to see the good in them or bring them under your wing or win them over with love or—'

'Shut up, Alex,' Kate said.

'Nah, he needs to hear this. Everyone in the building, from Oliver Roth to clone number one-million-and-whatever, will be trying to kill you to death!'

'Ah, Oliver Roth,' muttered Ewan as he knelt down and prepared his own blanket. 'Bumping into that ginger git will be the icing on the cake.'

'Yeah, well wait until *after* we've won, OK? If you're looking forward to getting killed, get the timing right.'

'Oh, it'll be *me* killing *him*. He's got it coming. It's karma.'

'Ah yes, "karma",' said McCormick. 'Lots of people say they believe in karma. Most of them just believe in revenge. Anyway, I think it's time for a change of subject. Serious conversation please.'

Kate felt relief and concern at the same time. As much as she welcomed the change of subject, McCormick never used the word 'serious' unless he meant it.

McCormick rolled over on his sofa and reached into Ewan's rucksack of gadgets. When his hand emerged, it held a cigar-shaped metal casing. It was difficult to see much of it in the darkness, but Kate could tell it was elaborate enough to have been stolen from the British military. Perhaps it had been one of those devices they had stolen from the barracks and kept in Spitfire's Rise unnoticed for a year. McCormick pressed a button that opened the casing and revealed a screen that displayed six blank digits, along with a miniature numbered keypad and a large clear button at the top.

'Let me guess,' started Ewan, 'you brought along some plastic explosives and you want us to plant them somewhere important, then use that as a remote detonator.'

'Almost.'

'We're out of plastic explosives, sir. I checked today before we started packing.'

McCormick smiled.

'Mine were planted several months ago.'

Kate, Ewan and Alex looked around at each other, as if seeking guidance on how to react.

'Where?' asked Kate.

'Well, I can't tell you where,' McCormick answered, 'because this could change the course of the war. We cannot let the information fall into the wrong hands. Knowledge of its location is restricted to myself and Lorraine, since someone at comms needs to be in the loop.'

'Why not Shannon?' asked Ewan.

'Because Lorraine was on comms when I planted them in December. Like I said, I did more than you think last time I went to New London. While Mark, Sally and Rachael were sabotaging the munitions factory, I was laying explosives in a nice sensitive place. It would cripple Grant's empire for a good couple of weeks if it ever detonated.'

'Hold on,' said Alex with a mocking laugh, 'so *nobody* noticed you carrying a man-sized pile of explosives to the Citadel?"

'I only needed a fistful. I used NPN8.'

Another hush fell over the strike team.

Seriously? NPN8? Whatever he's planning, it had better be worth it.

NPN8 was by far the most powerful plastic explosive available to the military. Kate remembered how Ewan had once described it to her in just two sentences: 'use C4 if you want to blow the lock off a door. Use NPN8 if you want the room to stop existing.'

'So it's small enough not to be noticed,' finished McCormick. 'I have no doubt that half a year on, it's in the same place as I left it.'

'Why haven't you detonated it before now, just to be safe?' Kate asked.

'That's the problem with explosives – you only get to use them once. I've been waiting for an occasion like this, one on which the whole war depends. Now, I need a volunteer. And with apologies for being frank, it should be the one among you who's likely to live the longest.'

How diplomatic, thought Kate.

'Well, I grew up eating my greens and not smoking,' said Alex. 'My life expectancy's probably still in its eighties.'

'Be sensible, Alex. And your life expectancy will be a lot lower if you're planning to go off on your own again—'

'Alright. I vote Kate.'

She sat up straight, alarmed.

'Why?' she asked.

'Because Ewan will have half of New London after him, and I'm screwed the moment they realise I'm not a clone. I'm guessing McCormick wants the volunteer to hold on to the detonator and only use it when absolutely necessary, and let's face it – you're the most careful one of us.'

'No,' said McCormick, 'I don't want Kate holding this.'

Kate gasped, conflicting thoughts fighting inside her mind. On the one hand, a scary responsibility would no longer be hers. On the other, why the hell would McCormick deny her the opportunity? The man had spent his whole life using responsibility as a tool to build up young people, so it seemed out of character for him.

'Why not?' she asked, a little too loud.

'Because you might end up having to use it. Just trust me.'

'I vote Kate too,' said Ewan.

Kate began to wonder whether she was truly opposed to the responsibility. Her friends' encouragement seemed to be changing her mind. And at her side, McCormick's resistance was fading.

'I'll be giving you the most powerful explosive device this war has ever known,' he said weakly.

'It's a good job you trust me then, isn't it?'

McCormick let out a long sigh: the kind of sigh people resorted to when they knew they were beaten.

'If our situation becomes unsalvageable,' he said, 'I'll give you the six-digit code. Ideally, this won't happen. The plan is to get inside, destroy the shield's control system, wipe out every single bit of research down to the last Post-it Note, and – if possible – get out and go home—'

'Wherever home ends up being,' said Alex.

'Get out and go home… and if we can do all that without needing a big explosion, we'll save this weapon for another time. You'll give me the detonator back and we'll never speak of this again. But if I *do* give you the code – if our strike goes so badly that we need to take this kind of action – you must follow my instructions to the letter. Because this is the one weapon in our arsenal that we absolutely can't afford to waste.'

'OK,' muttered Kate, 'I get it.'

McCormick nodded and sighed as he tucked the detonator back into the rucksack.

'When we get inside,' he finished, 'take it out of here, and look after it well.'

Even with the limited light available, Kate could see the sadness in McCormick's face. There had never been a figure in her life who had held as much faith in her as McCormick, but just for once it felt like he didn't believe in her. Not for this task, anyway.

Not that it matters, she thought. *I'd be surprised if even one of us survives tomorrow. McCormick's an old man. Alex has had Grant messing around inside his head. I've got Raj's death affecting my judgement. And Ewan claims to be strong-minded and independent, but he's useless without support from people he cares about.*

Between the four of us, I don't see any potential survivors.

It was Shannon's third consecutive night in the Boys' Brigade attic, having had only a daytime's break between the Oakenfold mission ending and New London beginning. She had become used to the dark and dingy nature of the Underdogs' comms unit, and this time the company wasn't much brighter. Mark was stood downstairs near the entrance, using a tiny window on the front wall as a vantage point to watch for possible invaders. And next to her in the attic, Lorraine sat unsmiling next to a cold mug of tea.

Lorraine had changed over the course of the week. Or maybe hidden parts of her personality were becoming visible as times became more desperate. The uncompromising but loving nurse who had greeted her at Spitfire's Rise three weeks earlier had become a harsh, openly wounded figure. By operating on McCormick, perhaps she had altered something inside herself too.

Shannon didn't know whether Lorraine would allow a well-meaning conversation or dismiss it hurtfully, but it was worth a try. The silence in the attic was nothing short of painful.

'Did I ever thank you?' asked Shannon. 'For taking care of me when I arrived?'

'I didn't do it to be thanked.'

Her voice was gruff, but not unkind.

'Well… thank you anyway.'

'You're welcome.'

The answer might have been genuine. Shannon didn't get the impression that Lorraine was trying to shut her up. But she was uncomfortable with the unenthused, generic responses, which suggested that Lorraine didn't value her own place in the group as much as she deserved to.

'You're allowed to be proud of what you do, you know…'

Lorraine shot her a glance that was halfway between disbelief and offence.

'And what makes you think I'd be proud?'

'You save lives. Remember the last trip to New London? You treated Alex and Kate's gunshot wounds, and even Ewan would be dead from infection if you hadn't—'

'I know the importance of what I do,' Lorraine answered in a condescending voice. 'But pride isn't something I'm into. I do what I do out of duty, not to feel good about myself.'

Lorraine's tone gave Shannon the temptation to drop the subject altogether. But she couldn't.

'Can't you at least be *happy* that you save lives?'

'Happiness doesn't come into it either.'

Shannon had seen miserable people. There had not been one happy human in the whole of New London's Outer City, including herself. But even so, she felt hurt by Lorraine's refusal to even consider positive thought.

'How can you think like that?' she asked.

Lorraine paused, and took a sip of her cold tea. For a moment it was unclear whether she would respond at all, but eventually she did.

'Shannon,' she asked, 'do you believe the world is a beautiful place?'

Shannon paused.

'No,' she answered, honestly.

'People get to know me and assume I'm the same. The truth is, I *do* believe the world is beautiful. And I thank God every day for what we do have.'

Shannon looked at her, confused.

'Yes,' Lorraine continued, 'I'm a believer. I'm not a shout-it-from-the-rooftops believer like Raj was, although I used to be. These days though, it's difficult for me to talk about religious faith when I see the world's ugliness more than anything else.'

'But you just said—'

'That the world is beautiful. And it is. But I don't see that beauty the way I used to.'

Shannon looked around the attic, and imagined the remains of Great Britain beyond it. When she thought about it, Lorraine's words were unsurprising.

'I was a teaching assistant once,' Lorraine said, 'before my twenty years as a nurse. Worked with eleven-year-olds, mostly. Towards the end, I worked one-to-one with a boy called Joey Shetland. He had the kind of childhood that involved social workers. And the police, once in a while. He didn't have the best start to life, and worst of all he *knew* that he hadn't. Even as a child, he hated himself.'

Shannon nodded. She understood.

'But there was an extra layer of self-loathing, backed up by his parents. His mum told him he'd grow up to be useless like his dad, and his dad told him he'd grow up to be evil like his mum. So obediently, he believed them.'

Lorraine paused, either for dramatic effect or to prepare herself for the rest of the story. Shannon suspected the latter.

'I did some great things for Joey. And yes, I was happy about it. I was even proud. But halfway through Year Six he started talking about killing himself. Imagine it, Shannon, wanting death at the age of eleven.'

I know, right? I was at least fourteen.

'It wasn't truly death that he wanted. He just wanted the bad thoughts gone from his head. Long story short, I helped him deal with his issues. He reached the end of the year in one piece, and when he finished juniors his family moved away.'

Shannon breathed a sigh of relief, but Lorraine interrupted her mid-smile.

'Within three months Joey was dead. A week after his twelfth birthday. I won't tell you how.'

Lorraine's breathing pattern changed, as if fighting back tears.

'He wrote... wrote two suicide notes. One to his family, telling them everything they had done wrong to him. The other was for me, of all people. My head teacher gave me the day off for his funeral, and that's where Joey's mother passed me the letter. It was still sealed, so she hadn't peeked. Come to think about it, that was probably the only decent decision I remember her making. I read it at home... he didn't even try to explain why. He only wrote two sentences. "I'm so sorry Mrs Shepherd. I just couldn't do it".'

A bunch of Shannon's own memories resurfaced in her mind. Hearing Joey's story whilst dealing with her own background was no easy task.

'It taught me the hardest lesson I've ever had to learn,' Lorraine continued. 'You can move Heaven and Earth to help people, but some things are beyond your power. I couldn't save Joey because I couldn't change his decisions. The only way to help people is if they let you. And not everyone will.'

Lorraine let out a cough, and took a moment to steady her breathing. Shannon had no idea what to say, if anything at all, but it seemed like the hardest part of the story was over.

'I couldn't go back to the classroom after that,' Lorraine continued. 'Then I figured if I was in the lifesaving industry, I might as well go the whole hog and train as a nurse. A twelve-year-old's death dragged me into a world where people died around me all the time, however hard I tried. The work was difficult, my husband and daughter had to suffer my moods when I came home at night, but I did a lot of good for a lot of people. So in my head, it was worth it.'

By the end of Lorraine's monologue, most of Shannon's words had vanished from her mind. Only one sentence remained, and she spoke it.

'Why are you telling me this?'

'Because God may have created a beautiful world, but we've made it bloody ugly. The way we treat each other, the things we do to ourselves, the way we neglect the sick and needy – human actions make *everything* ugly. So to be honest, I don't have high standards for happiness anymore. I'm not here to make the world a beautiful place, Shannon. It's already beautiful when we stop hurting ourselves and each other. I'm here to reduce this world's ugliness, not increase its beauty.'

Shannon had no words in response. Lorraine picked up her mug and drank the rest of her tea all in one.

'And by allowing McCormick to go to New London,' she finished, 'I'm afraid that I might have added to the world's ugliness.'

Chapter 15

Jack stood in the hallway of his new house – Spitfire's Rise Mark 2, unless he could come up with a better name – and decided that, all things considered, it would be a suitable building. It didn't have the fancy wallpaper or the nice furniture or the cleanliness that came from a year of being looked after, but there was a grandfather clock that looked nice and plenty of unexpired food in the cupboards.

It had taken them until midnight to choose an acceptable village, but by one in the morning Jack had already found a house there that would suit the Underdogs' needs. He hadn't expected success that quickly, or even by the end of the night.

Well, that was weird and unplanned, he thought as he nodded to himself in satisfaction. *Just like me, I guess.*

As predicted, Jack had done most of the work himself. Thomas had plenty of ideas but none that were practical, Gracie had shied away from contributing at all, and whereas Simon was not to be underestimated, he had seemed content to follow the group that night. Or more specifically, to follow Jack.

Jack marched back down the stairs and reopened the front door to the trio awaiting him in the front garden, their rucksacks and boxes of belongings rested on the driveway. Shannon, Lorraine and Mark would have more at comms, but even then it was a pitiful amount to have brought from home.

I just called Spitfire's Rise 'home'. Even now.

'Guys,' he said, 'I think I just found us a new house.'

'Are the beds comfy?' asked Gracie.

'Wasn't testing them, oddly enough. Come on, let's start unpacking.'

Gracie, Thomas and Simon in turn passed him, and walked into the building they were supposed to accept as their new hideout. But most of Jack's brain was telling him to think of this as just another stop-off on the way to a mission, like Lemsford had been, and that after a night here they would be heading home tomorrow.

In fact, how the hell are we going to keep this place a secret like we did with Spitfire's Rise? I've already seen the name of this village. Even if I take down all the signs myself before anyone else sees them, the moment I get captured…

Jack shuddered. He pretended to himself that it was from the cold night breeze, rather than the memory of what Raj had done to himself to keep his knowledge a secret.

Jack had searched in the most logical way he had known how to, of course. North of the original Spitfire's Rise, to avoid any invading force from New London passing the new house along the way to the old. But not too far north, otherwise hours and hours would be added to every trip to New London. Out in the countryside to avoid the diseases of the cities. And most importantly, just the right balance between being an unlikely place for Grant to search but not being *so* unlikely that it would paradoxically become the most obvious place for them to hide.

Jack hoped he had got everything right. The Underdogs

were dead if he had made a mistake. And as a seventeen-year-old who was accustomed to the world telling him he was wrong about most things, he had a lot to overcome in order to feel confident.

He turned to the front door and entered his new home, trying in vain to wipe the village's name from his memory. With a memory like his, he wasn't going to manage it. And with a village name like Tea Green – the most stereotypically English name a village could possibly have – it was already buried in his brain forever.

He walked back into the darkened house, and switched his torch back on. This house was going to be intimidating and claustrophobic without the lights their petrol generator could have powered.

'I don't like it,' came Gracie's voice from somewhere on the ground floor.

As was so often the case back in the old world, even Jack's absolute best was not good enough.

'Well, let's see if the beds really *are* comfy,' he answered, in a voice he made to sound confident. He fumbled his way up the stairs towards the closest bedroom. Ten seconds of this house being his home and he already needed a time-out. He started climbing through the dark; first one step at a time, and then two steps, and then jumps rather than steps. Just like how people found themselves needing the toilet more urgently the closer they got to it, Jack's need for shelter became stronger with every step towards the bedroom.

One of his quivering hands brushed against a living person that his torchlight had not detected. Both Jack and the small figure jumped in fright.

'Sorry…' said Thomas in the darkness. 'Where do you think McCormick would want these?'

Jack looked down at a collection of envelopes in Thomas'

hands. Jack loved Thomas as much as any decent person would, but at that moment he reached for the most dismissive answer possible.

'Depends what's in them,' he said. 'If it's private, under his mattress.'

'…Which one's his?'

'You get to choose.'

Jack didn't hang around for a reply. He slipped into the bedroom, closed the door behind him and plunged himself into the pitch black. He found the bed, and collapsed onto it with such force that the dust on the duvet leapt into the air like a swarm of disturbed flies.

This isn't home. It's unfamiliar. It's dark. It's cold. It's missing all the little things that made life in the abandoned countryside tolerable, like electronic games and chessboards and our own little farm. Even the right people aren't here. Most of them are dead and we don't even have a Memorial Wall for them here.

And on top of all that, this is one of the things in my life that I absolutely cannot afford to get even the slightest bit wrong…

I'm scared here. I always will be.

Before Jack knew it, he was in tears. He was not expecting actual tears – just the below-the-surface bubbling of emotions clawing their way towards his eyes – but the tears came regardless.

It was absolutely the wrong moment for the silhouette of Gracie to walk through the door, but she did anyway.

Two interruptions in less than a minute. Almost like the universe did not want him to rest.

'I'm cold, Jack,' she said.

'Me too.'

There was a hint in her voice that she wanted something

else, but Jack couldn't translate it. After a momentary silence, she spoke again.

'Could we... warm each other up?'

Oh bloody hell Gracie, don't put me in this position...

'You know? With... kissing?'

I took the hint, Gracie. Even I'm perceptive enough for that one.

In one of the most awkward and uncomfortable moments of Jack's adolescence, Gracie sat down on the bed next to him. The touch of her hand felt like a miniature electric shock; one which he felt guilty for feeling.

He had spent much of the last year avoiding Gracie's advances. But in Lemsford they had spent an afternoon alone, which had started with them making some kind of connection and had ended with them saving each other's lives. Jack had since been wrestling with the idea of telling her the truth, and the hand against his side persuaded him the problem was not going away. It was better to get it over with, and that moment was the best opportunity to do so: not least because he had reached his full mental capacity for sadness anyway, so the ordeal wouldn't make him feel any worse.

'I'm not going to kiss you, Gracie.'

'Why not?'

'I can't. And not *after* today either.'

'I can teach you how it works if you like—'

'*No*, Gracie. I'm sorry, I really am, but the answer's no. I...'

He took a deep breath, then finished his sentence after coughing out the dust that invaded his lungs.

'...I can't be who you want me to be.'

At first, she gave no response. She probably hadn't expected that answer. Maybe the thought of rejection hadn't even crossed her mind, and in her own planned version of the conversation Jack was supposed to say yes. They were close friends after all, weren't they?

'What do you mean?' she asked, not quite offended but certainly hurt.

'I'll never have a girlfriend, Gracie. Or a boyfriend. Or anyone. It's my fault, not yours. There's something up with my brain, and not just autism. It means I can't find people attractive. Even pretty people… or people I really care about. And I do care about you. Honestly, I do. But if you can't have me as just a friend then you can't have me at all. I'm sorry… I don't get to have a say in this. It's my brain. My soul truly cares about you, but my brain doesn't… well, you know. I'm sorry.'

Gracie gave no words in return. Her breathing got louder and more erratic, and the mattress rose underneath Jack, revealing that she had stood up. One creak of the door later, the room fell silent.

Well bloody played, Jack. The one person who will ever want to go out with a weird kid like you, and you broke her heart as punishment for asking.

Then again, thought the other side of his brain, *not telling her would have hurt her more in the long run. Whichever way I chose it was going to be wrong, but at least I chose the lesser evil.*

It was the type of thought train that could have occupied his brain for the entire night if he had not been interrupted. But a moment later, Simon completed the set of interrupters by bursting into the room.

Finally, after holding himself together so well through the evening, Jack ran out of patience.

'Oh, bloody burning balls of crap,' Jack snarled, far too loudly, 'is there anyone else behind you in the bloody queue, Simon? A hedgehog with a poorly foot that only *I* can look after? Or a fox wanting career advice or something? Do I have to declare "base" before people respect that my day is over and *I'm in bed now?!*'

The silence was predictable, and horrible.

But it was quiet enough for a different voice to enter Jack's head: one he had not heard in its physical form since he was twelve.

Jack, said a voice in his mind that reminded him of his mother, if that had truly been what she had sounded like. *It's because they rely on you. Don't you get it? You're valued here, and sometimes being valued is hard.*

Jack squeezed his eyes shut. It made little difference to his vision, but it helped him to focus the chaos in his head.

There's no easy way of living, is there? Thought Jack's own voice.

No, came the answer. *If you're lonely it's hard. If people depend on you it's hard. That's the truth of it, and I wish it were easier.*

'I'm sorry, Simon,' Jack said, before the voice in his mind could say anything else. Somewhere in the silence, Jack was sure he heard a whisper.

'OK?' it said.

At first Jack thought he had invented the noise himself. Simon had never spoken to him with words before.

'I'll be alright, Simon. I'm sorry I got frustrated. It's been a long night. What did you want me for?'

There was a pause, and Simon's whisper came again.

'OK?'

'Yes, I'm sure I'm fine. What can I do for you?'

'...OK?'

The penny dropped. If that was the right phrase. Jack looked in the direction of the whisper.

'Is that what you came here for, Simon? To ask me if I was OK?'

'Ye…'

Jack was overcome with a whole different range of emotions. It was a wonderful compliment, but it came with searing guilt. Simon had come to check up on his friend, and been ranted at in return – by a friend who almost never ranted at anyone.

But beyond the emotional struggle, it was an opportunity Jack did not get very often: someone offering to listen to how he felt rather than ask for his advice. And it was an opportunity worth taking.

'Well, I guess my secrets are safe with you,' Jack said, swinging his legs off the bed and switching on his torch. A moment later, he realised how the sentence had sounded.

'Wait,' he blurted, 'I didn't mean because of you not talking much. It's because I know I can trust you. Sorry if it… well, anyway…'

Simon sat on the bed at his side, and patted him on the shoulder. Jack pretended not to hate it. Simon was being his own kind of supportive, and discouraging a selective mute from nonverbal communication would be a dreadful idea.

'Simon,' Jack said, 'I think I've just worked out why I'm still alive.'

He shone the torchlight vaguely towards Simon: enough to see the confusion on his face.

'I don't know if you know this, but I tried to kill myself a couple of times. Back in the old world. I've not tried since Takeover Day. Never even come close. And tonight, just now, I think I've worked out why. It's because people depend on me.'

Jack thought he could feel another tear, but he had stopped being bothered about them.

'I mean, I started crying when I collapsed on this bed. And when you think about it, that was the moment nobody needed me to be OK. A whole night of looking for a house in the dead of night and I was fine. Ten seconds of everyone being OK and I fell apart. You know what that means, Simon?'

Simon huffed. Jack could not decipher what kind of huff it was.

'It means I value the rest of you more than I value myself. So I keep myself alive and well for you all. And alright, yeah, it's a crap reason to keep yourself going. But if it works it works, right?'

Simon huffed again, and even Jack could tell it was a huff of despondence.

'I'll be OK, Simon. You don't need to worry about me.'

Jack wasn't sure how true that was, but it seemed like the right thing to say. Simon patted him on the shoulder again, and Jack forced himself not to flinch in case it hurt Simon's feelings. They were much more important than his, after all.

'Thanks for the chat, Simon,' Jack said. 'At least *someone* asked if I was alright.'

Simon smiled in the torchlight, and rose to his feet. The conversation ended there and then as Simon walked out of the door and left Jack to his own devices. Jack lay himself flat on the bed, without getting undressed or even covering himself with the duvet. It took him several hours of inactivity, but he eventually fell asleep from exhaustion.

He awoke in daylight, with his watch telling him he had slept until mid-morning. But a whole night's sleep had not rid the conversation with Simon from his mind.

As he looked out of his bedroom window at the unfamiliar street, his thoughts turned to Ewan and the others. In a sense, they were keeping themselves alive for other people too, so maybe Jack was nothing special after all. He just hoped that by the time it struck midnight that evening and it became May 20th, his friends in New London would still have lives to keep.

Ewan was impressed with himself, which wasn't a feeling he experienced often. He hadn't thought he could spend a whole day walking around Oakenfold surrounded by clones without a single emotion appearing on his face.

Then again, most of his life had been spent masking his feelings for the convenience of others. Sixteen years of practice had led to him putting on a stellar performance that day.

Ignoring the sensory assault of his navy blue clone uniform, he took the last box of papers from the makeshift shelf and handed it to Alex, who stood beside him, equally emotionless. Alex had been given a few funny looks from clones who were not yet familiar with the new clone model, but nobody had made a fuss or even bothered to question his scar. Even Ewan's appearance had not been questioned: perhaps they assumed him to be one of the reinforcement models from New Reading.

It was late afternoon, the day's brightness showing warning signs of fading through the windows, and their job was nearly done.

'This *is* the last of them, right?' Alex whispered, as faintly as he could and after double-checking that they were alone.

'*Shh,*' Ewan replied anyway.

'But it is, right?'

Ewan rolled his eyes and nodded. Thanks to Raj's efforts in the library, there had been less paperwork to carry to the transports. He walked towards the sports hall's exit, Alex close behind with the box in both hands.

'We've spent the whole day helping the enemy, you know.'

Ewan grew impatient enough to whisper back.

'The sooner we're finished packing, the sooner they start the journey to New London. Besides, we'll be burning all this stuff once it reaches the paper archive anyway.'

'Why am I carrying the last box?'

'Because you were daft enough to take it from me.'

'Ewan, if I had a free hand, guess what I'd be doing with my middle finger?'

'Picking your nose. Now shut up.'

Ewan and Alex walked out of the school entrance towards the convoy of transport vehicles in the car park. For what must have been the twentieth time that day, they walked past Raj.

His headless body had been horrifying enough the previous night, without the details being revealed in broad daylight. Of all the reasons for Ewan to struggle with keeping a straight face, the repeated sight of his friend's exploded body was by far the most challenging.

Ewan reached their van and opened the back doors. Alex placed the final box of papers on top of the pile, and slammed the doors shut before any onlookers could see what else lay inside. The two young men in clone uniforms headed for the driver and passenger seats, Alex driving of course, and waited for the convoy to start moving in front of them.

The journey to New London Citadel, when it finally began, was a dull and joyless one. As the gargantuan northern walls came into view, Ewan's biggest emotional response was relief from his boredom. Somewhere up ahead, the first van in the convoy slowed as it approached the wire fence. There was a faint buzz in Ewan's ears as they passed: he had never been close enough to the fence to know it was electric, but had often suspected it to be.

'This place looks familiar,' Alex muttered as they approached the concrete guard post ahead. Ewan looked to its side, and found a semi-cylindrical tunnel that looked familiar to him too.

'You were here when we broke out of New London last time.'

'When I broke you out, yeah. Which means we're just about to hear the dullest voice known to man—'

'Soldiers in Vehicles 131 to 137,' came a monotonous voice through the driver's radio, 'this is Arnold Salter, deployment director for Vehicle Port Three. Once cleared by security, park in your vehicle's assigned bay and assist guards with inventory checks. All vehicles, please acknowledge.'

Ewan pressed the communication button on his clone radio, and produced a long beep.

'Wow,' said Alex, 'three weeks since I last heard him speak, and only for a few sentences, *and* I was busy being an action hero at the time. But I still remember every boring inflection of Salter's stupid voice.'

Ewan did not comment. After two minutes of waiting for the traffic to move, Alex began to trundle the van along the mile-long road to the vehicle port. The entrance became visible inside the enormous shade of New London, a tiny mouse hole compared to the concrete walls that surrounded it.

Their van drove into the port and they were ensnared by the flurry of clone soldiers running to and fro, transporting the inbound equipment on giant trolleys. Alex found his allocated spot and pulled up his handbrake.

Ewan thought it better to act while the inspection guards were busy with the neighbouring vehicle. He swung his side door open and stepped onto the tarmac, fixing his unbothered expression back in place, and once again masked all fear of the plan going wrong. He met Alex at the van's rear, where they threw open the back doors.

Ewan and Alex leapt in pretend shock – the kind of shock a clone would feel if the two stowaways among their equipment really had been unexpected.

One of the stowaways was an old man. The other was a young woman. Ewan reached for the pistol in his holster.

His shower of bullets caught the attention of every clone in the vehicle port, and the inspection guards pelted in their direction. By the time they arrived the gunfire had ceased, leaving two blood-spattered bodies among the boxes of paper.

Ewan looked to his right as the flustered lead inspector switched to war mode, and squeezed his radio's panic button as if trying to crack a walnut with his fingers. Arnold Salter's reply was so quick that his opening words were lost under the beep.

'—uards, report situation.'

The main inspector, still deep in war mode with his face reddening and hand muscles tensed, typed something with the communication button on his radio. He was using the clones' best method of communication – a simplified form of Morse code – but Ewan could not identify what was being said.

'I'll report this to Grant immediately,' came Salter's voice, which had lost its bored monotony. 'Vehicle staff, confirm that the rebels actually *are* deceased, then advance to Office 35 near Stairwell 15X for a formal identification. I will meet you there.'

Alex leapt into the van to check Kate and McCormick's pulses, and gave a thumbs down to the guards. Ewan climbed inside, and they took one body each. With a nod to the inspection guards, their interaction was over.

'Other vehicles,' Salter's voice continued through the radio, 'be vigilant. There has never been an attack by only two rogue humans. There may be more hidden in the convoy, and they might have heard you shooting their teammates.'

Ewan smiled as discreetly as he could at Salter's words, as he slung Kate's body over his shoulder. Alex was unable to complain about being left with the heavier body, and followed with McCormick on his back. They climbed out of the van, leaving the dozen heavy boxes of paper for someone else to sort out.

Ewan had expected an intense, dangerous amount of interest from other clone soldiers in the vehicle port. He was surprised when they turned back to their vehicles and continued their job as if nothing had happened.

Well, I guess Underdogs are less interesting when they're dead.

Ewan and Alex made their way through the vehicle port exit and the heavy door slammed behind them, leaving them and the bodies on their shoulders isolated in the corridors of Floor Z.

'Thank bloody hell for that,' said Alex with a laugh as he lowered McCormick from his shoulders. Ewan lowered Kate to the floor with a relieved smile across his face.

'And you all doubted me,' said McCormick, resting a hand against the wall and straightening his back. 'I told you, didn't I? If we can't sneak in unnoticed, we might as well *be* noticed and not be seen as a threat.'

'Good job the clone blood lasted all the way through the journey,' added Kate, double and triple-checking the rucksack to ensure nothing had fallen out while she had been carried. 'We'd have been less convincing covered in powdery blood.'

Ewan shrugged, not entirely surprised. The blood had been fresh when they had killed the driver and passenger at Oakenfold – with nice, silent stab wounds – and daubed the blood across Kate and McCormick's stolen uniforms. The blood had jellied a little, but the powdering stage usually didn't happen until after a day.

'Guys,' he said, 'are we *really* going to stand here chatting in clone uniform? We just pulled off something brilliant. Let's not ruin it now.'

'Fair enough,' said Alex. 'What's the plan?'

'Well,' answered McCormick, stretching his legs and readying himself for a jog, 'Arnold Salter is on his way to

Office 35 on Floor X, preparing to meet us and identify our bodies. Let's make his acquaintance.'

Chapter 16

Office 35, Floor X. Hardly deserving of the title of 'office'.

Ewan only needed to look around him to recognise what the room was for. Even if it hadn't had a plaque stuck on its entrance that read 'Identification Chamber', its interior felt like some kind of operating theatre or a morgue, with sinks and hygiene equipment like gloves and waste bags, walls lined with desks covered with test tubes, syringes and obscure DNA analysis machines or whatever, and a central table for dead bodies.

How many of my friends have lain dead on that table? Ewan asked himself, picturing Nicholas Grant personally standing at the entrance crossing names off that list of rebels. He imagined that just about all of the Underdogs who had died inside New London would have been brought to this room. He gave a shudder at the thought of Beth Foster, Thomas' mother, lying dead on the table he was staring at. Or David and Val Riley after Roth had forced one to kill the other. Or Miles, Tim, Ben, or any of the others. Daniel Amopoulos had probably missed the chance to see this room, since they already knew his identity before torturing him to death for information. Charlie, however...

Ewan felt anger – genuine, three-dimensional anger – as he stood in the same room where the dead bodies of his allies, friends and classmates must have been dropped onto that table and autopsied.

'You alright, Ewan?' asked McCormick.

Perhaps it was a question that wasn't a question. Adults loved asking those. McCormick would have seen the expression on Ewan's transparent face and detected his mood.

'Yeah, fine,' Ewan answered, giving the response that adults seemed to love too. 'You know, if you and Kate are dead you'd better get on the table before Salter arrives.'

'Ah yes, good point,' said McCormick, heading to the edge of the makeshift operating table. He rested himself against it, leaned backwards with the slow, creaking precision of a construction crane, and swung his legs into position at a speed that made Ewan wonder how long the man would last if chased by roving clones. Kate followed suit, the concern in her face so visible that even Ewan could detect it.

Alex, however, seemed as unaffected by everything as usual.

'I know we're trying to make Salter talk,' he said, 'but let's not encourage him too enthusiastically, OK?'

'Our priority is to destroy the AME shield,' McCormick answered from his morgue table, 'and it's likely to involve people getting hurt. I'm planning to be far more merciful to this man than most people would think he deserves. Remember who we're dealing with, Alex: Arnold Salter would have had his minions kill all four of us if he'd had his chance. And when you command people to murder, you're doing the equivalent of pulling the trigger yourself. No one in that position gets to claim the moral high ground.'

'Oh, it wasn't that,' Alex answered with a grin. 'Trust me, you don't want to hear too much of his voice.'

'Speaking of not hearing voices,' said Ewan, 'everyone be quiet. We're clones, and you're dead.'

Alex obeyed, and the identification chamber fell quiet. Five long minutes passed in dull, lifeless silence, Ewan's fingers fidgeting in anticipation, before a beep sounded at the door. Ewan took a deep breath, and lowered his hands to his hips.

The door opened, and a short man with a face like a turtle ambled into Office 35. He was flanked on one side by the tall blonde clone model, and on the other by a clone of Japanese origin. Ewan did not recognise him. He must have been an import.

He and Alex, as agreed ten minutes earlier, waited until the precise moment the door closed and locked itself before they drew their pistols and shot both clones dead.

The clones fell lifeless to the floor. Between the two corpses, Arnold Salter wore an expression of clueless horror. His jaw hung open, but he was as wordless as the two dead clones. The whites of his eyes began to stand out more than the rest of his face.

'You must be Arnold Salter,' Ewan said. 'Good to meet you face to face.'

Salter looked to his left, and let out an audible gasp as Kate and McCormick's bodies rose from the examination table. To Salter, it must have been like watching zombies rising from their graves.

'You may have gathered, but—'

Salter, seemingly fuelled by impulse (or perhaps fear of what Grant would do to him if he put up no resistance), reached for his holster to draw out a little pistol. Before he could do so, Alex fired a bullet, which popped through his right hand and tore through most of its tendons. Salter stumbled around in agony, producing a sound that Ewan almost didn't recognise as human. It certainly wasn't monotonous anymore.

'Didn't have to do that, did you?' Alex said to him as he and Ewan grabbed his arms.

Salter's body did the only thing it knew how to do under the circumstances, and a small pool of vomit spilled over his bottom row of teeth. Most of Ewan froze in disgust, except for his feet which shuffled away from the floor beneath Salter's mouth. He looked at the man in disbelief as he choked on the thin trickle that hadn't quite made it to the top.

'Really?' he asked, forcing Salter towards the centre of the room and bundling him onto the table with an Underdog at each corner.

Not all monsters look fearsome, Ewan thought to himself as he stared at Salter's face. *Some monsters hide away in their offices signing death warrants. Some monsters wear suits or sit at computer desks. Some vomit in fright when they're caught.*

Kate returned from seizing the automatic weapons from the dead guards, dumped them onto the desk and gripped Salter's right wrist. Alex removed the man's firearm from its holster and lay a forceful hand against his forehead, pressing the back of his skull against the table. Ewan inspected the man's face, tracking where his eyes went in case they revealed his intentions. His gaze seemed to land on McCormick.

'You're him,' Salter gasped with widening eyes. 'You're actually him… you're Joseph McCormick!'

McCormick chuckled, and raised his hands in fake astonishment.

'Wow, this identification chamber really *does* work!' he said with a laugh. Ewan tried not to smile, but it was difficult to resist the ageing man's wit. McCormick walked to the clones and picked up their radios, before leaning directly over Salter's face. Ewan had never seen Dr Joseph McCormick as an imposing figure – authoritative, maybe, but not imposing.

Perhaps he was seeing what the man had once been like with his university students when they needed a serious talking-to.

'We don't have much time,' started McCormick. 'It's a quarter past eight, and we need to be done by midnight. You must be clever enough to know what we're doing here.'

'The AME shield,' Salter gasped. 'You want me to stop it going up, otherwise you'll kill me... if killing is your modus operandi...'

'Our what?' asked Kate.

'Our way of doing things,' answered McCormick.

Ewan gave no reaction, glad that Kate had been the one to ask the question. He had spent enough of his life looking like the stupid one in large groups.

'I know you've killed hundreds of clones between you,' Salter said with a panicked squirm, 'but clones are clones, here today and gone tomorrow. Could you really bring yourself to slaughter a human being? One who can look you in the eyes and speak in your own language?'

Ewan trembled at the memory of the real humans who had died by his hands. Salter was wrong in assuming he couldn't kill humans, but the words affected him anyway.

But still, Ewan could use his history to his advantage.

'Remember Steven Elcott?' he asked. 'Fat guy, worked in the officers' sector on Floor S, died last month?'

Salter's eyes widened as they met Ewan's, which alone answered the question.

'Yeah, that was me. He was my third human. Strictly speaking, I've been a human-killer since Takeover Day.'

'Who the hell did you kill on Takeover Day?' asked Alex with a curious laugh.

'Shut up, that's who,' Ewan replied.

Ewan turned his eyes away from the inevitable hurt in McCormick's face, and hoped he didn't look so guilty that

Salter picked it up. But either way, their captive must have had other things on his mind.

'You still remember Steven's name,' Salter whispered. 'He must still haunt you.'

Ewan's mouth dropped open, and his blinking increased. Salter, despite his helpless situation, had struck him where it hurt: right in the conscience. But Salter said no more, perhaps aware that the strategy of hurting his captors would not help him escape his situation.

'I can't stop the AME shield from being raised,' Salter continued, 'and no matter wh—'

'Oh, we know,' said Alex. 'For all your sins, and despite all the horrific things you've said yes to during your employment with Grant, you're still a generic nothing-special vehicle port officer. We're not expecting you to help that much. We *do* need your keycard though.'

'It's in my left pocket. Take it.'

Kate's hand rummaged through Salter's left trouser pocket and emerged with his keycard. Salter began to gasp in even more erratic, panicked breaths, and Ewan understood why. Without that card, Salter was no different to a clone soldier, or even one of the rebels. His life in the upper floors of New London was over.

'OK,' Salter said, tears emerging in his eyes, 'make it quick.'

'Oh, we don't like killing humans,' answered McCormick. 'Unless it results in saving the lives of *more* humans. And we don't need to kill you, so we won't.'

'Sir,' said Alex, 'not to contradict you in front of the enemy, but—'

'He won't give us away. He's dead the moment he speaks. He's let rebels into New London and given them access to the higher floors. Grant won't let him live.'

McCormick's right, Ewan thought. *If one bit of information spills out from Salter's lips, Grant will probably save him for Oliver Roth.*

'But I can offer you a deal,' McCormick continued. 'It involves us staying undetected, and you staying alive. Win-win, I'd say.'

'I'm listening,' Salter gasped. Ewan was astonished at how quickly this man complied with their every demand. For a man with no good options, Salter seemed to instinctively know where his best chances of survival lay.

'You leave this room,' McCormick began, 'unarmed and without your keycard. Carrying nothing but your radio, and the radios from the two clones on the floor. You use the authority you still have in Vehicle Port Three, take a van of your choice and leave New London, sheltering in a nearby village away from Grant's forces but within radio range.'

'I can actually recommend a nice little bungalow—' said Alex, before Ewan shushed him.

'In return,' McCormick continued, 'you keep all three radios by your side and check in whenever commanded.'

'Which is every fifteen minutes tonight,' said Ewan. 'I took the dead clones' radios at Oakenfold so they wouldn't detect them missing. Had to check in so many times on the way to New London, I almost wish I hadn't bothered.'

'Once the night is over,' finished McCormick, 'you can live out the rest of your days in the English countryside, away from Grant's brave new world. How does that sound?'

Salter nodded.

'Wait,' said Kate, 'you're just going by *trust*? How do you know he won't give us away the moment he's out of sight?'

'Because,' Ewan said, 'when Grant finds out what he's done, he's dead. What do you think, Arnold? Is it worth giving your life to reveal our presence?'

'No. Now please, just let me get out quickly.'

The soldiers backed off, and McCormick passed the dead clones' radios to Salter. Even unrestrained, Salter didn't move a muscle, perhaps magnetised to the table through fear.

'Here,' said Alex, tossing a little green box towards him. 'Have a med-kit for your hand. No hard feelings, mate.'

Salter tried to catch it, but it slipped through the remains of his wounded hand.

'Right,' said Ewan, 'let's head off. The Central Research Headquarters and the Experiment Chamber are both on Floor F. Alex and I will take that.'

'Wait—'

'And no, Alex, you're *not* doing your lone wolf thing again. We can't afford the risk. Sir, you and Kate can take the data servers and the paper archive, since Floors P and R are next to each other.'

'Learn the alphabet, Ewan,' said Alex.

Ewan didn't waste time checking whether Alex was right. It would do him no good.

'One thing I've been meaning to ask,' said Kate. 'Even if we destroy all those things, won't all the border points still be around the Citadel? Can't they get something back from them?'

'Border points don't contain software,' answered McCormick, 'they just respond to a remote computer. Trust me, Grant trying to extract data from a border point would be like looking for files inside a printer that just printed them.'

Ewan nodded, pretending to understand. At his side, Alex opened the exit door and wandered straight into the corridor without checking for enemies.

'Alex!' snapped McCormick. 'Where's your concentration?'

Alex looked up and down the corridor. Once he knew the coast was clear, he rolled his eyes at his allies.

'I'm a clone, remember? Why would I need to be careful

walking around my own corridors? I don't even know we've got intruders yet. Come on, Ewan.'

Ewan fought his way past the blatant demand from Alex, and forced himself to hold his tongue since Salter was listening in. McCormick passed him the rucksack, after reaching inside to remove the cigar-shaped little detonator which he passed to Kate.

'Salter,' said McCormick, 'aren't you supposed to be going somewhere?'

Ewan looked back at Salter, who hadn't moved a millimetre from his position on the table.

'Yeah, get out of New London,' said Alex, as Salter's legs woke up and slid off the table towards the floor. 'And quick, before you throw up again.'

Salter obeyed. He tucked the two clone radios into his pockets, double-checked that he still held his own, and left Office 35 to flee for his life.

With the enemy no longer watching, Ewan's emotions ran straight to the front of his mind. He stared at McCormick, finally coming to terms with the fact that they were separating.

He must have looked openly afraid. There was fear in McCormick's eyes too. Fear and love.

'Take care, my boys,' McCormick said with a smile on his face and in his voice. At the door, Ewan smiled back like he had once done to his father.

'You too, sir,' Ewan answered. 'Don't do anything I wouldn't do.'

'There's nothing you wouldn't do for the British people, Ewan. So I can assure you I won't.'

Alex walked further down the corridor, blank-faced and confident once again. It hurried Ewan and McCormick's goodbye, and Ewan briefly hated him for it.

Nonetheless, Alex's haste was necessary. And all being well,

Ewan would see his mentor again at the end of the night anyway.

All being well? He thought to himself as he left McCormick and Kate to chase Alex down the corridor. *We've got to avoid losing a war tonight. All being well is a bloody tall order.*

Chapter 17

'We're taking the lift?' said Alex. 'Seriously?'

Ewan stood up straight, self-assured and confident. It was an act and he knew it, but it was what non-autistic people did all the time in moments of self-doubt.

'We'll be fine,' he said. 'If we were going to be caught, we'd have been caught in the vehicle port when everyone was looking. Besides, it's half eight. Time's a factor here.'

The lift arrived and Ewan marched inside. As Alex joined him he pressed the button for Floor F: the highest available button, and the floor where their first targets lay. Ewan could not be bothered to work out how many floors lay between F and X, but—

Ewan's heart was thrown into his stomach. After a year without using an elevator, he was unprepared for the seasickness when the lift rose at the speed of an accelerating car. To his side, Alex gripped the side rail with tightening fingers. Twenty seconds later the lift slowed to a halt as if a driver had slammed on the brakes. The two young men, supposedly toughened through a year of battle, glanced at one another and shared a nervous laugh.

They fell silent as the doors slid open. It was time to become clones again.

The Central Research Headquarters was a fifteen-minute walk from the lift, with the Outer City monorail several floors away. But the walk was anything but boring. Ewan had to stop his eyes from widening as he gazed at his fancy surroundings, a world apart from the bland yet haunting atmosphere of the lower floors. Floor F looked like a serious attempt at a laboratory complex: the walls had white paint, and the floor was textured with the flat, patterned material found on the hospital wards of old. There were metal labels on every door from security offices to store cupboards, and the whole atmosphere had an air of quality. Ewan had not felt so amazed at man-made beauty since his brief visit to the officers' sector three weeks earlier.

It's not the beauty I remember about that visit though, he thought, with Charlie on his mind.

Wait, Alex was on Floor F for that same mission, at the clone factory. Why is he looking as fascinated as me?

Alex, Jack and Kate had all seen Floor F, but none of them had told Ewan what it looked like. It had been a minor detail compared to everything else that had happened that week. But Alex's face – as much as he tried to disguise it and as difficult as Ewan found it to read – suggested he was seeing it for the first time.

Do you even remember this place?

At the end of their fifteen-minute journey, there was no mistaking the door to the Central Research Headquarters. The set-up of the surrounding area had based itself around that one chamber: octagonal, wide, and placed mid-crossroads between four approaching corridors. Ewan walked to the windowless entrance and swiped Arnold Salter's keycard through the slot.

Chris Bonnello

When the LED flickered from red to green, he pushed through the door looking as unexcited as he could.

The chamber's interior looked just as he had predicted. Its walls were lined with computer desks and monitors, an air conditioning unit rumbled loudly on the ceiling, and a trolley of spare laptops lay by the door. A security camera hung from one of the top corners.

However, Ewan had not imagined he and Alex would be the room's only occupants.

'Empty?' he whispered, his lips facing away from the security camera. 'The Central Research Headquarters can't really be unattended?'

As Ewan glanced around the room, Alex walked to the computer furthest to their left. There were no blind spots in the octagonal chamber, but he picked a chair that would face away from the lens of the spying CCTV camera.

'Why not?' Alex answered. 'The AME project is complete now. How much else do you think they need to do here?'

Ewan followed his teammate to the furthest edge of the room and sat himself at the neighbouring computer. It gave him access to every delicious scrap of information an Underdog could want to get their hands on. He just needed to locate them.

'Fair enough,' he answered. 'Looking for the research files now.'

'You do that. I've got something personal to search for.'

Ewan shot Alex a surprised glance.

'Personal? Like, your dad or something?'

'Yeah,' said Alex with blatant sarcasm, 'my taekwondo coach stuck down in New Brighton prison, who they're definitely keeping an eye on because he's such a fascinating guy. No, you numpty. I've got missing memories to find.'

Ewan felt a little pool of rage bubbling up inside him at

199

Alex's insult, but he took a deep breath and composed himself. The insult must have been based on hurt, and he knew better than to take things personally when they were said by a teammate going through a rough time.

For a moment, Ewan wondered whether those thoughts were truly his own, or planted there by his experiences among other Oakenfold students. Or even by McCormick, during his year of positive influence.

Then, without his permission, his fingers twitched and he slammed a hand on the table.

'You OK there?' asked Alex.

'Not exactly.'

'Worried about the old man?'

'…Yeah.'

Ewan opened the first of many folders he was set to search through, and found himself lost like a child in a busy shopping centre. He would not be finished in a hurry.

'It's not like the other missions,' he continued to Alex, if only for the sake of expressing his thoughts out loud. 'Every mission for the last year, all I've needed to do to see him again is avoid dying and get back to Spitfire's Rise. But when I said goodbye to him tonight, it hit me. *He's* in danger here. I could do everything right tonight, complete this mission and head home unscathed, and *still* never see him again.'

Alex took a break from his own search and looked towards Ewan, although the camera prevented him from turning far enough to make his lips visible.

'Kate will look after him,' he said in a rare, compassionate voice. 'And if he goes off on his own, he won't do anything stupid.'

'You're sure about that? He knows what's at stake.'

'Well let's be frank. If he were to do something to put himself in danger, it wouldn't be out of stupidity. It'd be for something *worth* putting himself in danger for. He's an adult – a real adult, I mean – and a mathematician too. He doesn't have the reckless impulsive side that the rest of us have. He's too calculating for it.'

He's right, I guess, Ewan thought. *The two of us are at far more risk than him. If death is coming for anyone tonight, it's me or Alex.*

Ewan blinked himself back to his senses. The AME research was somewhere in front of him to be found and deleted, and it was time to regain focus. Once he did, it didn't take him long to realise that even once he found the data, deleting it would not be simple. He would need special clearance or admin access or something.

There was only one person he knew who had experienced Nicholas Grant's technology from the inside. And thankfully, she was sitting in comms at that moment. The sound of her voice would be welcome too. Ewan removed his phone from his pocket, lay it at the front of his desk and put it on speakerphone before dialling.

'Wow, subtle,' said Alex as it started to ring.

'Should I put it next to my ear for the CCTV cameras?' Ewan asked with matching sarcasm. 'And tell them a mute soldier is talking on the phone?'

'Hello?' interrupted a voice on the desk.

'Shannon! It's Ewan. Don't worry, everything's fine. But... I need to ask you something.'

Ewan's voice began to waver. Discussing Shannon's ex-boyfriend would have been tricky in the normal world too. But especially so now, since the guy was dead and the conversation was time-sensitive.

'You know how you and Anthony Lambourne did all that tech work with the clone factory virus?' he asked. 'Does that mean Lambourne had access to important files?'

'Yeah, why?'

'Because I think I need clearance to delete—'

'Really?' said Alex. 'You don't think they *might* have deleted Lambourne's account after slashing his throat?'

Bloody hell, Alex, Shannon's right here listening.

'I don't think he'd have been stupid enough to use his own account,' Ewan answered. 'I just need to know—'

'You're right,' came Shannon's voice – annoyed, hurt, but fiercely determined – a voice infused with her unmistakeable personality. 'Whenever we did something that broke the rules, we used Richard Unsworth's account.'

'Who the hell's Richard Unsworth?'

'One of Pearce's underlings. High enough to have access to loads of stuff, but not high enough for people to bother checking where he was logging in. Let me know when you have the login screen up.'

Ewan clicked a box in the corner of the screen.

'Yep, ready.'

'Username is Richard, dot, Unsworth. Password, all in capitals, is K, R, B—'

'One second. Let me process it.'

'Oh yeah. Sorry.'

Ewan's mind was drawn back to Luton Retail Centre, and his outburst at Shannon after she had said the GPS coordinates too fast. It seemed so long ago now.

At that moment, he found himself being much more patient with her. Being that far apart, he wanted every word between them to be pleasant.

'Ready?' she asked.

'KRB?'

'Yeah, K, R, B, 4, H, 9, 7, D, W, 1. After he found it out, Lambourne made me memorise it in case he ever got caught...'

Ewan pressed the 'OK' button and the computer accepted the password.

'OK, logged in as him. Thanks a lot. And I'm sorry I brought up your ex.'

'He'd have wanted you to do this. Trust me.'

'Fair enough. You doing alright?'

'I'm fine. Lorraine is too. Stay safe, Ewan.'

'Yeah, I will. Take care.'

'Bye.'

Ewan hung up the phone and took a long breath.

'That wasn't a *moment*, was it?' Alex asked at his side. Ewan wasn't sure whether it was a real observation or just general Alex mockery, so he didn't bother with a response. He put his phone back in his pocket, as subtly as he could with the CCTV camera watching, and got to work as Richard Unsworth.

The folders had odd labels, mostly named after dates, odd scientific terminology or staff members. They probably made sense to science-minded people, but not to Ewan. He performed a database search for the phrase 'Atmospheric Metallurgic Excitation', grateful to himself that he'd managed to memorise the words, and hoped for the best.

The search yielded disappointing results. Ewan clicked the only file with a decipherable title, and found the central report into the development of AME. It was a ten-page summary of the entire project from beginning to end. Not useful in the scheme of things, but it was his best starting point.

The entrance door swung open without warning. Ewan's instincts told him to pounce forward and retrieve his assault rifle from the desk, but Alex remained quiet and kept working as if nothing was unusual. Ewan noticed his friend's strategy just in time, and got back to work as the five clone soldiers marched inside. Ignorant to the humans in their lair, they occupied one computer terminal each and started clicking away.

Ewan would never know what the group cared about so

much that it took all five of them to work on it, but their work was not his priority. Just as long as none of them peeked over his shoulder.

Ten minutes passed in the crowded room. Nine o'clock on May 19th.

Ewan had been the worst student in his drama class – with the sole exception of Jack, who had never known how to act like anyone but himself (or perhaps a range of dinosaurs as a child) – but he and Alex were doing a good enough job of pretending to be clones. Good enough to still be alive, anyway.

The ten-page report had been the first stepping stone in a digital paper trail, which had led him to the correct region of Grant's information atlas. The summary report had contained the name of one particular human scientist – Richard Unsworth, curiously enough – who had been tasked with collecting and analysing the research. Nathaniel Pearce had been the primary researcher, and the man who had watched the explosions and blood fireworks, but Unsworth had dealt with the boring paperwork side of his abhorrent experiments.

Unsworth's personal section held enough files and subfolders to fill an average civilian's computer, but Ewan felt he was close to the needle in his data haystack. He had narrowed his search down to three folders, all of which were labelled with nerdy sciencey names that sounded too clever for him.

The clone two desks away moved and the back of his head twitched. Ewan almost leapt to his feet, but calmed himself when he discovered the clone had only stood up to stretch. Ewan was closer to Grant's bedroom and the brain of New London than ever before, and his nerves were showing.

He got another shock a moment later, when the printer behind him pierced the silence of the chamber. Zip-whirr, zip-whirr, zip-whirr. Alex stood up from his seat and walked to the back of the room.

Ewan shook his head as discreetly as he could. While he was stuck in his seat, drawing as little attention to himself as possible, Alex had no problem walking across a roomful of clones towards the noisiest object in the chamber.

But is that confidence or desperation? If I had gaps in my memory, I'd probably throw caution to the wind too.

Whatever 'caution to the wind' is supposed to mean.

Wait… did I just find what I'm looking for?

Inside the penultimate folder of his search lay an average scientist's lifetime of work, and the bulk of Pearce's research over the last six months – from the opening preamble and theoretical principles, through a thousand spreadsheets of experimental data, to the final preparations for coordinate tracing and mapping. Ewan didn't understand a word, but he knew it all needed deleting.

Pearce and Unsworth had proved that even the world's cleverest scientists were not always smart people. They had made the same mistake that the Oakenfold staff once had with their students' behaviour records, and kept all of their files in one place to be found and destroyed by the first rogue teenager who had the chance.

Two other clones rose to their feet. Ewan moved his eyes, and noticed that the stretching clone had not sat down again.

He highlighted every file in the magic folder, and planted his forefinger on the delete button. His heart skipped a beat, then his actions were met with the most annoying safety net in human history: the double-checking dialog box.

```
Are you sure you want to delete the
selected item(s)?
```

No, I'm joking. Numpty.

Before he could press 'enter', Alex laid his papers down on the desk and pinched him on the arm.

A pinch. It was an odd way of getting his attention. Ewan turned to find Alex pointing his eyes towards a neighbouring computer screen.

As a fourth clone stood up, Ewan kept his head still but moved his eyes, and read the alert message that had caught Alex's attention.

```
RED ALERT - FOR URGENT ATTENTION OF
SOLDIERS IN THE CENTRAL RESEARCH
HEADQUARTERS

The occupants of Stations 3 and 4 are
highly dangerous armed insurgents and must
be neutralised immediately. A discreet
surround-and-shoot method is advised. Do
not make them aware of an attack before
you have shot them dead.

Marshall
```

The last clone rose to his feet. Ewan stopped breathing.

Chapter 18

We can't defend ourselves with bullets. If a gun goes off, every clone within half a mile will head this way.

There wasn't even a split-second to hit the 'enter' key before Alex tore his knife from its sheath, spun around at the nearest body and ripped the blade across its throat. The stunned clone had not even touched his holstered weapon before the shock took over his body and sent him to the floor.

Ewan was so quick to jump to his feet that his brain had not quite realised what was happening, and for the opening seconds of combat it felt like someone else was controlling him. He gripped his assault rifle in both hands and picked out his first opponent, as it raised its own rifle to fire.

He leapt forwards to within whispering distance of his target, and killed with one blow for the first time in his life. He swung the butt of his rifle upwards into the clone's nose, sending bone fragments into his brain, and the open-eyed dead soldier fell backwards into the arms of his ally behind him.

The unexpected body was enough of a distraction to allow Ewan to leap again and attempt the same trick twice, but he was faced with the largest clone model in Grant's army – and an enemy who saw what was coming. The clone's dodge put

Ewan off balance, and a knee thundered into the bony part of his thigh. Ewan staggered in pain, for a moment not even realising that his assault rifle had fallen from his hands. The large clone threw his dead ally's body away from him, but could not aim his rifle before Ewan's clawing hands snatched out for it.

Ewan was losing the wrestle. The clone's hands were stronger, and had a much more secure grip on the weapon. Desperate, Ewan looked to the other side of the room to call out to Alex, but his teammate had problems of his own.

Alex was up against both the other surviving clones, keeping them in single file ahead of him like a hostile game of piggy-in-the-middle. The soldier in front of him had a chance to fire his handgun, but when Alex seized the barrel and twisted the muzzle towards the clone's own chest, his enemy decided it wasn't such a good idea. Alex released one of his hands from the gun – the hand which still held his knife – and plunged it into the centre of the clone's chest.

A punch to Ewan's cheek knocked out his sense of direction, and he drew his gaze away from Alex. He kept both his hands in a tight grip on his rifle, but his huge enemy lifted it upwards. Unwilling to let go, Ewan's feet were separated from the floor, and the clone charged across the chamber and rammed the base of his spine against the computer desk.

Ewan let out a yelp, his back muscles screaming at him as the top half of his body was stretched across the desk. His own weapon lay half a room away, beyond the focus of his blurred vision. The clone's rifle was the only firearm within reach, but he released one of his hands from it anyway.

With two hands against one, the clone seized his chance and jumped backwards. The rifle was torn from Ewan's one-handed grip, but the clone was too horrified to open fire. He had seen what Ewan had done with his spare hand: his forefinger had reached over the keyboard beneath it and smashed onto the enter key.

He had just said 'yes' to the dialog box.

Ewan did not see the screen as the entirety of Pearce's AME research began to disappear into nothingness, but the look on the clone's face told him everything. The distraction was all Ewan needed as he pounced forward, grabbed the giant's shoulders in both hands and sent both knees into his stomach, the force of his body weight forcing the clone backwards until he tripped over the body of his partner. Ewan held on for dear life, as if to a falling tree, and the clone tumbled to the floor and landed on his back. The shock was enough for the clone to release his grip, and Ewan seized the assault rifle from his hands and smashed the butt repeatedly into his face. After the fifth strike, the clone stopped moving.

Dizzy and in pain, Ewan hopped to his feet to see Alex and the final clone wrestling over a handgun. The clone's sweaty fingers crept towards the trigger, his plan obvious. It would not matter where the bullet went. It would be a distress signal to every clone within half a mile of the chamber.

Ewan staggered into position behind the clone, secured both hands around his victim's head, and snapped his neck.

The Central Research Headquarters fell back into silence as the fifth and final body collapsed to the floor. For the first time since his work had been interrupted, Ewan took a glance around. In what must have been under a minute, the scene had changed from seven uniformed men working at computer desks, to two men standing among a collection of dead bodies on the bloodied floor. Alex rested a hand against the nearest desk and gasped a sentence.

'Five kills, no bullets, no scratches,' he said.

'Speak for yourself,' Ewan grunted. 'My leg and back are—'

'Whatever. You win, mate. Three to two... lucky boy.'

'It's never luck.'

Alex's laugh came with a wheezy cough.

'*Never* luck? Good job one of us saw the alert before they could open fire!'

Ewan ignored Alex's compliment-fishing, and ran back to his workstation. The progress bar had barely travelled across the screen. Perhaps a quarter of the files had been deleted, maybe fewer.

To the left of the entrance, a telephone started to ring.

Ewan's eyes perked. The sight of a landline phone was rare enough, but the timing couldn't possibly have been a coincidence.

'So... are we answering it?' asked Alex. 'I mean, Marshall knows we're here anyway.'

'Well volunteered, Alex.'

Alex rolled his eyes, stumbled over to the entrance and picked up the headset.

'McCormick and Sons Family Butchers, good quality meat-carving since Year Zero. How can I help?'

Alex fell silent for a couple of seconds, rolled his eyes again, and held out the phone towards Ewan.

'He wants you, not me. Story of my life.'

'Who is it?'

'Iain Marshall.'

Ewan gritted his teeth, and cast a frown towards the CCTV camera above him. He took the phone from Alex, and began to snarl.

'I'm listening.'

'Ewan West, I believe?' said the voice.

'I'm listening.'

'Good. My name's Iain Marshall, Head of Military Division. I'm guessing you've heard of me?'

'Actually yeah,' Ewan said with a grin towards the camera.

'You used to be important before Nicholas Grant took your security company from you. But he decided to keep you instead of killing you. For a failed businessman you've done fairly well for yourself.'

Alex sprinted to fetch his assault rifle, and stood guard against the door.

More clones have been called, and all three of us know it. But we can't leave before the files finish deleting. One push of a button could cancel all our work.

'You've done fairly well too,' answered Marshall. 'Leading the charge against an innumerable army, in the face of autism, Pathological Demand Avoidance, intense behavioural issues, exclusion from six different schools, and just generally being a twat.'

'So you've read up on me. Oh, I'm so scared.'

'Yes, I have. You look a lot different from the passport photo I've been looking at.'

'Yeah, I was a lot sexier back then. War does horrible things to people, doesn't it?'

Ewan glanced at the screen. Halfway done.

'So,' he continued, 'did you call to talk about something, or are you just keeping us here long enough for reinforcements to arrive? In fact, if you *knew* we were up here, why didn't you kill us ten minutes ago? You left two rats chewing at your computer wires for ages. I've had a great time rummaging through Unsworth's things.'

'Because of a little incident we just had at a checkpoint near Vehicle Port Three. Does the name Arnold Salter ring any bells?'

Alex's eyes widened too. Clearly, Marshall spoke so enthusiastically that his voice could be heard across the room.

'Twenty minutes ago I received an alert that the vehicle

port's deployment director was seen trying to leave New London. He got as far as the security booth at the electric fence, but was unable to provide any reason for his departure, or even identification. One of the guards called his line manager and Salter tried to speed away. Of course, the armed guards didn't let him get far.'

Poor guy. The vomiting wonder barely lasted a minute outside New London. Good job he was on their side and not ours.

'After a little research,' Marshall finished, 'it turned out he'd used his keycard to check himself into the Central Research Headquarters, at exactly the same time as he was abandoning his post. It didn't take a genius.'

Ewan let out a huff, which must have sounded down the phone.

'Frustrated?' asked Marshall. 'Then you're going to *hate* this next bit. Because I have to ask… how exactly are you planning on destroying everything related to Atmospheric Metallurgic Excitation in the whole Citadel, fight your way up to Floor B and destroy my computer, all in the space of half an hour?'

Ewan checked his watch. Midnight was nearly three hours away. What the hell was Marshall talking about?

'Half an hour?' he asked.

'Give or take,' Marshall answered. 'You thought we would launch at midnight, didn't you?'

Some heavy object froze inside Ewan, restricting his muscles and paralysing his chest.

'It's the kind of thing Grant would do,' he whispered, unable to hide his nerves.

'Wrong, Ewan. It's the kind of thing he'd want you to *believe* he'd do. What his daughter would believe he'd do, and what she'd tell her allies. In reality, there's a weapons cache in Beaconsfield that needs emptying, and a steady stream of transports are bringing the stock back here. Grant's switching the shield on as soon as the last vehicle makes it past the border, and they've been given a deadline of nine thirty. He's had countdowns to nine thirty on his office walls and everything, and once the countdown ended he was going to launch the shield, deliberately reduce security and watch you walk straight through... with your metal weapons, ammo, watches, belts and so on. You would have looked spectacular as you'd blown up like your other friend.'

Ewan's fingers began to twiddle with the phone cord, for whatever anxiety relief it would bring. The game had changed, without warning or mercy. *Everything* had changed. Marshall's computer destroyed by half nine? He and his friends had never even been to Floor B. A thirty-minute time limit wasn't enough. It was lunacy.

'Why are you telling us?' he asked in a meek whisper.

'Because I'd rather you knew. You're far more likely to lose a gunfight if you know you've already lost the war. Psychological warfare, Ewan. Now I've put that knowledge into your head it's going to stay there, bouncing around in your thick little skull. If the Taliban had used that kind of genius against Major George West, they might have actually won and you'd never have been born. They'd have improved the world in one way, at least.'

'Did you ever fight the Taliban?' Ewan spat, the mention of his father restoring some of his energy. 'They were smarter than the cavemen everyone thought they were. Dad told me the stories. I grew up with them.'

'Afghanistan was a playground, Ewan. You think that barren, mountainous country is hard work? Try selling anti-tank rockets to two West African militia leaders, each of whom is trying to commit genocide against the other. Money and firearms are all you have, and they're all your clients care about.

Have you ever looked into the eyes of an ally who values the clip of bullets in your hand more than he values *you*?'

'Maybe you're just crap at making friends.'

Ewan glanced to the computer once more. Only a fraction of the data remained. The promise of progress both energised him and frightened him. According to Alex's face, Ewan was not alone in his stress.

'That's fine talk, coming from you,' said Marshall. 'Your father may have been a decent soldier, but he couldn't turn you into a decent person.'

The phone trembled in Ewan's hands. Not through fear, but anger.

'My dad was more than a decent soldier. He was everything to me.'

'And now he's a decomposed skeleton scattered across your living room floor. Along with your useless mum. And your aunt, and your uncle, and eight-year-old Alfie. Still, it was nice that we kept the whole family in one place after we killed them.'

'Not the whole family,' snarled Ewan. 'You should have killed one more.'

'Oh dear. We missed the retard.'

'Yeah. And don't you regret it now?'

He turned around, expecting Alex to be grinning. Instead, he was worried.

'Only for the next few minutes,' said Marshall. 'Because that's the thing with rats who chew at computer wires. They're too stupid to know when they've spent too much time chewing. And one flash later, they're dead.'

Ewan heard running footsteps.

'Any last words I can pass on to Grant?' asked Marshall with a laugh.

'Yeah,' said Ewan with his eyes pointed at the CCTV camera. 'Tell him his daughter's a great kisser.'

Ewan hung up the phone, grabbed his assault rifle, and ran to the nearest clone's body. He plucked the keycard from its pocket, assuming Salter's to have been deactivated. Then he ran to the computer screen. So close. *So* close.

'A great kisser?' said Alex. 'Seriously?'

'I shouldn't have said that. It was disrespectful to talk about her that way.'

'You mean you and Shannon are—'

'When we leave,' Ewan interrupted, 'we split up. Whichever one of us reaches the experiment chamber first, burn it to the ground.'

A dozen pairs of footsteps grew louder.

The progress bar vanished, replaced with the shape of a little green tick.

Half an hour to bring down an empire. Starting right now.

'Go!' he screamed at Alex, who picked up his printed papers and charged for the exit. The two Underdogs fled the Central Research Headquarters like murderers from a crime scene, with five clone bodies in their wake.

We don't stand a chance.

But I'm fighting anyway. We didn't survive the last year by respecting the odds.

Chapter 19

Kate's night had been boring. Under normal circumstances, boring missions were good. Less action meant fewer people got hurt.

But not tonight. Things needed to happen tonight.

She understood why McCormick insisted on walking up the stairwell rather than running. But she felt like a child wanting to run towards an ice cream van, tethered to a grandparent who couldn't run along with her.

She stood at the exit to Floor S, her handgun pointed towards the door handle just in case. After a short while McCormick arrived behind her, and it was time for his next mission: ascending the steps to Floor R.

Will we even reach Floor B by midnight?

Alongside her annoyance, Kate couldn't help but feel enormous admiration. McCormick clung hard to his forced habit of never, ever losing hope, and his attitude towards each set of stairs never worsened or became less enthusiastic.

Kate ran up to Floor R, and guarded the exit as before. When McCormick was halfway up, Ewan's voice screamed out of her waist pocket.

'Guys, big trouble!'

McCormick took the shouting as an excuse to rest against the wall, and caught some breath as he retrieved his radio.

'Talk to me, Ewan.'

'We don't have until midnight! Grant's pushing the button at *half nine*!'

The panic in Ewan's voice spread to Kate like an airborne disease, and her body froze in place.

'Do you have any evidence of this?' asked McCormick from half a floor below.

'The words of Iain Marshall himself. The shield was supposed to kill us when we arrived, but we got inside before the last transport vehicles made it from some weapons cache somewhere. Unless we can do *everything* in the next *thirty minutes*, Grant's going to win the war. There'll be no way for us to get out, or for the others to break in with weapons *ever* again!'

Kate commanded her body to stop panicking, but it wouldn't obey. Her brain was congested with so many thoughts that she couldn't pin down a single one.

'Looks like we're doing it in half an hour then,' said McCormick, having ascended the stairs and rested next to her. 'How's it looking on your floor?'

'Part way there,' answered Ewan between gasps. 'We wiped the files and we're heading to the Experiment Chamber. But they know we're here – Salter's dead. What about down there?'

'We're on Floor R,' answered McCormick, 'the right place for the paper archive and two floors away from the backup servers. Leave it to us – you and Alex destroy that chamber and fight your way to Floor B.'

'Yeah, nice and simple,' said Ewan. 'See you later, sir.'

The radio fell silent as Ewan resumed his sprinting. Kate's

eyes sank to the floor as the enormity of their task settled in her brain.

Five objectives, and we've still got four left.

Destroy the Experiment Chamber. Destroy their backup system. Destroy the paper archive. Destroy Marshall's computer.

All in thirty minutes.

'I'll phone comms and ask for directions,' McCormick said, his breath mostly steadied. 'You go for the archive, I'll go for the backup servers.'

'Actually,' said Kate with a quiver in her voice, 'I've got a better idea…'

Years of experience told her she had done the wrong thing by speaking out, and should prepare for her opinions to be corrected. She knew that McCormick was an approachable adult, but her instincts had been burned into her brain by countless adults and peers who had loved telling her she was wrong.

To her relief, McCormick listened.

'Those battlements on the roof,' she continued, 'where the snipers hide to watch over the countryside. Is it just me, or are there lower battlements too?'

'Floor L, if I remember rightly.'

'I can buy us some time. I'll go to Floor L, you go for the paper archive, and whoever finishes first goes for the data servers.'

Even then, it'll only work if Ewan and Alex reach Floor B. But it's our best shot.

'Sounds good,' said McCormick, as he fumbled around in his pocket for his phone and battery. For the first time since they had started their climb, there was a moment of silence in the stairwell.

'No need to wait,' said McCormick. 'I'll radio you any directions you need.'

'Sir,' she answered, 'I'm not going to start running without a goodbye.'

'Then say it quickly. I enjoy your company, but time's not on our side.'

Kate marched across to McCormick, and demanded his eye contact. Painful as it was – and McCormick would know how painful she found it – the eye contact was worth it to make her point.

'*Be careful,*' she said, in the most commanding voice she dared use. 'The rest of the Underdogs will slaughter me if they find out I left you alone. If you get caught or killed while I'm away, I'm taking it personally.'

'No, you will *not* take it personally,' McCormick said in his calmest voice. 'I don't want anything clouding your judgement tonight.'

Kate stared at him, open-jawed, as he powered up his phone.

You don't really think it's that simple, do you?

She began to quicken her breaths, the expression in her face a dangerous cocktail of protective love and anger.

'I know your week's been horrible, Kate,' McCormick said to her. 'And I'm not going to try telling you to get over it. But if there's one thing on Earth that Kate Arrowsmith is good at, it's facing her fears. Without your anxiety, you wouldn't be half as brave as you are – and all you need to do tonight is use the bravery you've always had. And that includes overriding whatever fears you have about me.'

A stray tear fell from Kate's eye. McCormick smiled and laid a hand on her shoulder.

'Run upstairs, and buy the boys their extra time. If I need a hand I'll give you a shout.'

Kate nodded. No words came to her. She turned and ran up

the stairs towards Floor L as McCormick began to dial. One floor up, she stopped to eavesdrop on her leader's conversation.

'Lorraine, it's me,' McCormick began, followed by a brief pause. 'Yeah, not bad. I'm on Floor R and can find my way to the paper archive. Have you got directions to the data servers yet?'

There was a brief silence. Kate could not hear Lorraine's words, but they were easy to work out.

'*Nothing's* beyond my reach. Not tonight.'

I don't like the sound of this.

'No, not even the HPFC. Tell me where to go.'

Kate gasped, hopefully not loud enough for McCormick to hear. She had not heard the High Priority Functional Cluster even mentioned through most of the war. And there was a good reason for that.

But time was running out, and Floor L was high above. With gritted teeth and a sense of powerlessness over McCormick, Kate looked up the stairwell and ran.

As far as Ewan could tell, his sense of direction had not let him down. Distractions were everywhere, but he was pretty sure his route was the correct one.

The biggest clue was that the clone patrols were getting heavier. Ewan thought it might have been the perfect opportunity for them to blow him apart with speed mines, but clearly they didn't want to damage any rooms important enough to be on Floor F.

He took a peek around the next corner, and was spotted by six biorifle soldiers.

Bringing in the big guns now. Literally.

Marshall wants me to run out of ammo. He's using the soldiers with weapons built into their arms – guns I can't steal once they're dead.

His first spray of bullets took down four of the soldiers. Despite their advanced weaponry, the remaining two did not last much longer. Ewan double-checked the corridor and ran over to the bodies, and found that some of their other weapons could be stolen.

By far the most interesting weapon was the belt of incendiary grenades. Four of them. Ewan grinned. He couldn't have asked for a more suitable weapon to bring to the Experiment Chamber. He seized the whole belt for himself, and astonishingly found the room he was looking for three doors later.

About time we had something good thrown our way. Right, let's do this.

He used the seized keycard against the door, and it worked. He wouldn't have long until someone noticed a dead clone checking into the Experiment Chamber, but fifteen minutes between check-ins would be more than enough.

Come to think of it, Ewan was surprised they hadn't locked down the chamber altogether. But it had been out of action since the research was completed, and would never be needed again unless all their research mysteriously vanished.

Ewan walked inside. The Experiment Chamber was far from what he had expected. He found himself in a small, caravan-sized control room lined with computers, swivel-chairs, microphones and telephones, bordered by a wall of glass that separated him from the main body of the chamber. Small adhesive signs had been stuck to the corners of every glass panel, reading 'DANGER: no metal or metallic products inside the chamber'. Beyond the glass, the chamber contained very little – just a large pile of metallic objects in one corner that included weights, empty weapons and clothing with metal attachments. Meanwhile its tiled floor had been half-cleaned of powdery bloodstains: clone blood that had come to rest between two stone pillars.

Ewan checked the porthole-shaped window on the door. No sign of Alex approaching. He hoped his teammate was OK, wherever he was. Or at least alive.

'Alex,' he whispered into his radio, 'updates?'

Silence.

'*Alex.*'

'Still far away,' came Alex's voice, tired and gasping. 'Got chased the wrong way down the corridor by a load of biorifles.'

'OK,' answered Ewan. 'I'm here now, so no worries. Head to the nearest stairwell and get as close to Floor B as you can. I'll meet you up there.'

'Got it.'

The radio went silent. Ewan was on his own, but the work could easily be done alone. And it started with making sure he was in the right place.

He looked back at the desk, trying to guess the uses of the several dozen buttons and levers across the control panel. The red button next to the microphone was obvious, and the palm-sized button on the wall labelled 'kill switch' must have been there to stop experiments before someone important got killed. The dial at the far right seemed to control the lighting for some reason, and for all he knew the brown lever delivered fresh coffee or something.

There was another red button, protected beneath a translucent panel of plastic so nobody would use it by accident. Ewan's instincts, fuelled by a whole childhood of toying with anything that looked interesting, commanded him to push it.

When he did, there was a brightly-coloured burst of light on the other side of the glass, like a red camera flash. Ewan looked up, and lost his breath.

Between the stone pillars, he saw the same type of shield his team had watched light up the skies around Harpenden. The same type of shield that had surrounded Oakenfold, and killed Raj. He stared in hatred at the crimson waves that flowed between the pillars like vertical water, and the little lightning bolts that leapt out from the metal 'border points' – or whatever Raj had called them before he killed himself. After a brief squall of excitement, the shield faded into invisibility.

Ewan could barely feel the organs inside his chest. Adolf Hitler with atomic weapons would have been less dangerous than a dictator with this technology. If Grant had his way, the same kind of shield would surround the whole of New London, and in time his other Citadels too, rendering him invincible forever.

Ewan reached for his assault rifle.

He released a flurry of bullets into the glass wall. The glass did not shatter, and the bullets only produced a couple of spider-web-shaped cracks. Clearly the chamber's glass was bulletproof.

Bullet resistant, not bulletproof, Ewan corrected himself. *No glass is perfectly bulletproof. You just have to get creative.*

Ewan put his brain into gear. When it came to non-academic tasks, his brain was a formidable weapon. At that moment, it was remembering a school trip to the Roman walls at St Albans, back when he had been allowed on mainstream school trips. The tour guide had shown him a legionary's sword – a gladius, if he remembered right – which had a little steel stub at the end of the handle. It was for braining enemies who got too close, by thumping the handle onto their head where the tiny stub would crack through their skull. The full force of a Roman's arm would be concentrated into a square centimetre, and the results would be devastating.

The glass could be broken. Ewan just needed a gladius.

The butt of his rifle made a fine handle, with a flat enough surface to attach some kind of stub. He reached to the corner of the nearest window pane and peeled off the adhesive warning sticker, rolled it backwards over itself to make it sticky on both sides, and placed it across the rifle butt.

On the desk at his side, some smart-arse scientist had left his coffee mug behind – one that literally read 'smart-arse and proud of it'. He grinned, and wondered whether that scientist had been smart enough to know a little fact that Ewan had learned via YouTube: that ceramics were great for smashing windows. He threw the mug to the floor, and picked through its shattered remains. He stuck a promising-looking piece to the butt of his rifle, and after three hits from his makeshift gladius the entire pane of glass shattered.

The scary side of the Experiment Chamber lay open before him, and Ewan engaged in a one-man war against the horrors of military science. He released his first incendiary grenade, which landed at the base of the first metal pillar. It exploded with a furious vomit of fire, which spread across the tiled floor and spilled up the pillar towards its border points. Ewan threw a second grenade at the other pillar, and a third at the collection of metal objects in the corner. They both exploded with equal ferocity, and through squinted eyes Ewan could see the objects in the pile begin to alter their shapes, and then melt. The border points, however, were holding on for longer.

With three nearby fires burning at over 2,000 degrees Celsius, Ewan's skin prickled with sweat. He turned his rifle the right way round, and fired his bullets into the control panel. The gun clicked before he thought it would, and he threw his assault rifle to one side with a snarl. He would have to approach Floor B with nothing but his handgun.

The Experiment Chamber was all but destroyed, with one incendiary grenade remaining. But Ewan's head was turning woozy. The fires around him began to moan and shout. The chamber had no flammable objects inside, but it was drenched in roaring flames regardless as the incendiary grenades burned on their own fuel. The thermite reactions would continue until they got bored of destruction, eating away at their surroundings and choking up the atmosphere.

It was time to quit while he was ahead. Ewan staggered towards the door and reached for the handle, just in time to hear the click-clack of the door locking itself. Ewan pulled, but nothing happened. He swiped his stolen keycard, and was met with a red LED.

He was trapped inside the burning chamber, and the smoke was descending around him.

Ewan looked out of the porthole-shaped window. The grinning young assassin on the other side had fiery ginger hair.

Chapter 20

Oliver Roth waved a friendly hand through the porthole window. Then he turned it round and stuck up a middle finger.

Ewan did not respond. His brain was split between two tasks: searching for an idea that would give him the slightest chance of survival, and outstaring his enemy. He pointed his nastiest expression towards the fourteen-year-old assassin who had killed eight of McCormick's army – soon to become nine – and hoped that just for those couple of seconds, Roth would see in Ewan's eyes just how much he *hated* him.

Ewan heard a buzz from the edge of the door. Roth had pressed the security intercom. With no better ideas, Ewan pressed the talk button and let his enemy's voice into the room.

'Surprise, retard,' said Roth happily. 'Long time, no see.'

'Yeah,' Ewan snarled into his side of the intercom, 'it's been a few weeks. How's your broken nose?'

'Good as new – it healed in less than a fortnight. How's Charlie? Did *he* get better?'

Ewan felt a surge of boiled anger through his arteries. Whether it was his temper or the approaching fires, he couldn't tell.

'Oh,' said Roth. 'Still dead then.'

'You killed him on his birthday.'

'Who gives a crap?'

'Me. And I'm amazed you even remember his name.'

'Well, yeah!' said Roth with an enthusiastic grin pointed through the glass. 'I love learning about the people I've killed! Beth Foster... Miles Ashford... Tim Carson... the Rileys... and another three, including Charlie. You can poke fun at my broken nose until you burn to death in there, but I've caused you more pain than you could *ever* cause me.'

'Why not open the door and put that to the test?'

'Nah, I'm alright thanks.'

Something horrible got into Ewan's throat and sent him into a coughing fit. He had spent the conversation racking his brain for ideas on how to escape a burning room with a locked entrance, and had come up with nothing. Roth was watching his every move. The heat was increasing, the oxygen running low. And Alex was on his way to the nearest stairwell, clueless about Ewan's troubles and too far away to rescue him anyway.

'Looks like you took those incendiary grenades from the biorifle soldiers,' Roth laughed. 'Aren't you happy I left them for you? I figured you'd use them to set up your own death trap.'

'You *wanted* me to kill a biorifle platoon, just so I could take their weapons?'

'Unless they killed you first. Either way I'd have been happy. Besides, they're just clones.'

Ewan's eyes, watery from the advancing smoke, gazed at the burning floor at the stone pillars. The powdered remains of clone blood between them, long burned away, had proved Grant and Roth's attitude to their own soldiers.

At that moment, Ewan realised.

That clone was let into the chamber somehow. He didn't smash the glass like I did.

There must be a second door somewhere.

'You alright, Ewan? Not dying on me, are you?'

Ewan didn't answer. He turned his head, spotted a cupboard with red and white tape, and figured it might have held some emergency equipment. He ran from the entrance, jerked open the cupboard door and found a gas mask. It wouldn't filter all the smoke, but it was better than nothing. He removed his helmet, rested the mask halfway over his forehead, then returned to the door and pushed the intercom again.

'I'd love to stay and chat, but I just had my ears talked off by Marshall.'

'Irritating, isn't he?'

'The worst, except for you. Anyway, I'm heading for the other exit – the one inside the chamber. Feel free to chase me.'

Oliver Roth's face lost its overconfident grin, and his eyebrows started to rise. Clearly the thought of a second exit had passed over his head too.

'It'll be locked,' he replied. 'It'll be for nothing. You're going to *burn* in there.'

'Fine,' finished Ewan. 'Stay here and explain to Grant how you failed to get me again. Bye.'

At just the right moment, Ewan had remembered how to be manipulative. He secured the gas mask around his face, hoping he could get out of the room before it melted to his head, and leapt through the empty pane of the shattered window.

Bloody hell! How can one room contain so much heat?

Ewan tap-danced his way across the Experiment Chamber, avoiding puddles of burning thermite on the floor, praying his clothes wouldn't catch fire. Even the large melting pile of metal objects, presumably there to test the shield during experiments, had started to emanate its own heat. Ewan slammed himself at the nearest wall, edging around the room in an effort to find the concealed door.

He felt woozy, as if drunk, drowning and burning all at once. He knelt down to search for a richer pool of oxygen. The walls, so clean and white when he had arrived, were covered with enraged reds and oranges. At the top, but creeping down with each second, they were charring black with smoke.

Ewan found the second exit.

It was locked.

He didn't waste his breath on shouting or swearing. Grant must have only built fire escapes for his human staff, not for those on the wrong side of the Experiment Chamber glass. He was locked in the room on both sides, and he was going to die.

Somewhere under the sound of the roaring flames, Ewan heard a buzz. He lifted his head towards the control room, and saw Oliver Roth bursting through the entrance. Perhaps he didn't know the second exit was locked, or perhaps he wasn't willing to gamble.

Ewan pulled the pin from the final incendiary grenade, and launched it through the empty window frame. It bounced off the control panel, and landed on the floor beneath Roth's feet.

Roth made it through the window frame and into the chamber just before the grenade went off, releasing a set of fireballs that attacked every remaining computer, console, button, lever and filing cabinet.

Ewan West and Oliver Roth shared the same burning room, and both were armed. Unfortunately, Roth had brought a shotgun to the fight.

Ewan did not have time to draw out his handgun. Roth's first shot barely missed him as he took shelter behind the large pile of melting test objects.

'Your choice, Ewan!' Roth yelled between coughs. 'Stay low

to the ground and choke slowly, or pop your head up and have your suffering ended by a nice quick gunshot!'

Ewan did not offer a response. He looked to the floor and found that a bunch of odds and ends had fallen away from the pile before him. Some were everyday objects such as phones and watches, and others were half-kilogram weights made of different metals.

Ewan grabbed hold of the nearest weight, ignored the searing heat against his hand, and lobbed it as hard as he could towards Oliver Roth.

Roth did not look bothered. Not until the weight passed between the two stone pillars. He had not witnessed Ewan switching on the AME shield.

The weight detonated against the shield, causing violent red ripples and a fiery explosion that threw Roth from his feet. As the assassin fell against the wall, Ewan jumped upright, leaned around the pillars and shot him four times in the chest.

As satisfying as it would have been, Ewan did not hang around to watch Roth collapse to the hot ground. He leapt back through the empty window frame, took a running jump over the burning control panel, and tore off his gas mask as he landed in front of the open door. Wheezing, weakened, but alive, Ewan stumbled back into the Floor F corridor, slamming the door closed behind him just to be certain.

He shot his tired gaze down the corridor, and found himself to be safe. There were no clones waiting for him. Oliver Roth had acted alone, and lost.

There's no way I should still be alive after all that.

It's almost enough to make me believe in luck. Almost.

With surprisingly little guidance from Lorraine and Shannon, Kate had found the lower battlements of Floor L. The corridor looked different to anywhere else she had seen in New London.

Her corridor stretched in a straight line as far as her eyes could see: a mile or two, at the very least. Most Outer City corridors had turns at least once in a while, accounting for the different-shaped rooms they passed, but not this one. Kate was fairly sure she could fire a bullet each way down the corridor and hit both the eastern and western Citadel walls. Every hundred metres there lay a door on her left, unlabelled and cream-coloured. She picked one at random, took a deep breath, and swiped her latest stolen keycard.

There was no buzz. Snipers didn't like to be distracted by sudden noises.

She opened the door, slowly and silently, and found what must have been the smallest type of room in the whole Citadel. There was enough space for a small man to lie down on its inbuilt mattress, but little more. At the front end, a square hole in the concrete wall pointed diagonally downward, through a widening tunnel to the cool air of the outside.

The floor was occupied by a sniper, who lay on his front with both hands wrapped around a rifle that had been fixed in position. When Kate looked at his short mattress, she discovered why Grant could afford to design the rooms so small.

She was looking at half a clone. Its body ended at its waist, with a perfectly formed head, shoulders and arms, and a torso large enough to contain its vital organs. Clearly, Nathaniel Pearce had decided not to waste resources on legs they would never use. The clone model was built for the specific purpose of sniper duty, and the design of their bodies – like the absence of vocal cords – must have made them easier for Grant and Pearce to control.

Kate used her childhood gymnastics experience to walk lightly on her toes, ensuring her approach was silent.

She almost felt sorry for the half-clone; she could only imagine how long the sniper had laid there, or how his attention span had coped with continuous, unrelenting sniper duty. But nonetheless, this clone would be as determined to kill her as any other. Kate slid her knife from its sheath, held her breath and bent over the clone on the mattress like a sinister tooth fairy.

'Guys!' Ewan's voice yelled from her radio. 'Good news!'

Kate leapt in horror. The clone on his mattress rolled over with panic across his face. He fumbled for the handgun on the belt around his stumped abdomen, but his vision was obscured after hours of having one eye closed and the other through a telescope. Kate fell to the mattress knife first, and stabbed it into the front of her victim's neck.

'Is this important?' she whispered. 'I'm... busy.'

The clone's eyes rolled up towards his brain, and Kate watched his face for fading signs of life. She noticed how little she regretted her actions, or even felt anxious about killing a clone from inches away, given the urgency of the night's mission. She was proud and alarmed in equal measure.

'Two targets down, three to go!' Ewan screamed, thankfully after Kate had turned the volume low. 'I just destroyed the Experiment Chamber!'

'Make that *three* targets down,' answered McCormick's voice. 'The archive was closer than I thought.'

'It's gone already?'

'Paper burns very quickly. There are no more written records of AME left in existence. Just the backup server to go now, then we can storm Marshall's office and put an end to AME forever.'

'Oh,' said Ewan, 'and just while we're talking… I killed Oliver Roth.'

Kate froze in disbelief.

'Oliver Roth?' said Alex. 'You've got to be kidding.'

'Four bullets in the torso, then I locked him in a burning room. I'm *pretty* sure we can go home tonight and declare once and for all that he's dead!'

Kate felt two stone lighter. Somehow, the absence of one teenage monster made the whole Citadel feel less frightening. She pushed the dead clone from beneath her, and took his spot on the bloodstained mattress.

'Wonderful news,' answered McCormick, albeit with a humane twinge of guilt, 'but I'm afraid he's only bonus points. If the shield goes up, we still lose. It's twenty past nine—'

'Leave it to me, sir,' Kate interrupted. 'Go as fast as you can, but don't do anything stupid. You'll have more time than you think.'

She focused one eye through the sniper's scope. Through the lens of a telescopic sight, the whole world looked different. And not just because of the occasional tremble of focus, or the blur around the scope's edges. Through a sniper rifle, every detail on the ground looked like something to be inspected rather than seen.

She was thankful the wall faced north. The glow of the sunset was on her left, rather than in her eye. Plenty of twilight remained – twenty past nine wasn't so dark in May – but she didn't have long before the awkward part of dusk when it was too dark for plain sights, but too bright for night-vision.

Her search began. She knew exactly what a border point looked like, having seen them up far too close at Oakenfold. A little part of her brain, which had been suffering from enormous anxiety at the moment the memory was made, remembered that each border point had its own miniature shield. Perhaps that meant that the loss of any single coordinate would bring down the whole network.

Now, without the shields raised, the border points would *not* be impervious to bullets. Or at least, Kate hoped not.

She found a landmine-shaped lump of metal in the grass within the first two minutes of her search. She fired a bullet straight into it, and in the dimmed light she saw a glimmer of metal somersaulting through the evening air like a tossed pancake.

Kate smiled. It had been her first smile since the day she and Raj had watched the missiles over New London. Maybe, just for tonight, she was going to be OK.

The border point had landed the right way up, but the LED was blank. It was out of action. In ten minutes' time, Grant would push the magic button to a fanfare in his head, and be sorely disappointed. It could take hours for that point to be located and replaced.

'Ewan,' she said to the radio, 'you can scrap the time limit. I don't know how long we've got, but it's more than ten minutes now.'

'Prove it.'

'I just shot a border point with a good quality sniper rifle. The shield won't activate unless every link in the chain is working. We've got loads of time before they replace it.'

Ewan didn't answer, suggesting he was satisfied.

'Lovely,' answered McCormick. 'I'm almost at the HPFC. Don't bother chasing me, Kate. I'll be done by the time you get here.'

Kate snarled. McCormick was most likely right, and there was no point denying it.

'Fine, you do that,' she whispered. 'When I'm done here I'll meet the others on Floor F and we'll head upstairs together. That OK, boys?'

234

'Not without me, you won't,' McCormick butted in before Ewan or Alex could answer.

Stuff that. If I can't put myself at risk for you, I'm not letting you do the same for us. Sorry sir.

'We'll be far above you,' she answered. 'We can't afford to hang around for you to catch up, and then spend another half an hour waiting for you to recover. When you're done with the backup server, find a safe place to hide and we'll meet you on the way down.'

'You're trying to keep me safe. That's not what I'm doing here.'

'Sorry sir,' came Ewan's voice, 'but Kate's right. And we're not just being protective. We *literally* can't wait for you. Just trust us to do the right thing while we're up here.'

'Oh, I know you'll do the right thing,' answered McCormick with misery in his voice, 'that I don't doubt.'

His feelings were clear without the need to see his face. The mission had been his first direct action against Grant since before Christmas. He had endured Lorraine's ugly surgery to earn the right to take part, risked his life on a gamble in the vehicle port and exhausted himself with the stairwell, only to be denied the opportunity to see it through to the end. The final showdown would involve the other members of his family – the adoptive sons and daughter – but not the father. It almost made Kate feel guilty, but she knew better.

'Good luck down there sir,' she finished. 'We'll be in touch.'

Oliver Roth's keycard still worked against the Experiment Chamber exit. He took a long breath of fresh air and tore the Kevlar away from his chest, moments before the thermite fire chewed its way to his skin. He staggered into the Floor F corridor and collapsed from physical exhaustion, crying tears of real pain. Stripping to his bare chest and crawling on all fours, he reached a fire extinguisher outside the neighbouring room and sprayed its water all over himself in an effort to remove the heat from his body.

I was so stupid! If he'd got me in my head or neck, I'd be dead!

Why did I follow him in there when he was almost certain to die? Would the other exit even have worked?

Roth lay topless on the cool tiled floor, looking down at the burn marks that were forming across his muscular frame. The thermite itself may not have touched his skin, but the heat alone had been damaging enough. There would be ugly misshapen scars across his chest for the rest of his life.

As the minutes passed, the throbbing began to fade but his tears did not. Oliver Roth came to realise that he was no longer crying through physical pain, but through emotion. It was a level he had not sunk to since he was a young child, and he felt ashamed of himself. Lying half-naked on a corridor floor with burn marks that even a whole fire extinguisher could not sort out, crying because an older boy had outwitted him, Roth wondered what his bosses would have thought if they could see him at that moment.

At least I had enough common sense to wear the Kevlar…

As he spread his twitching arms and legs, his tired brain came to realise the unspoken benefits of a bulletproof vest.

It hadn't just saved his life. It had given Ewan every reason to think he was dead. And no doubt he would be showing off to his pathetic teammates.

'Oliver,' barked a voice on the other end of his radio.

Roth looked down, surprised. Other than a few melted parts to its casing, his radio was undamaged. He sat himself upright, and took some time before answering. Iain Marshall could wait until he had steadied himself.

'*Oliver.*'

Roth wiped his tears from his eyes, and breathed slowly enough for the wobbling to vanish from his voice.

'Yeah…'

'You sound miserable. Did your trap work?'

The tears almost returned, but he fought them off.

'No, but—'

'And the Experiment Chamber?'

'Up in smoke. But on the plus side—'

Going by Marshall's yells, which Roth didn't bother listening to, he was not in the mood for silver linings.

'…On the plus side,' Roth said once Marshall had finished yelling, 'the rebels think I'm dead. Ewan ran off thinking he killed me. Sorry sir, got to go.'

Roth switched off the radio before his voice crumbled, and he collapsed to the floor again. The redness in his torso had not faded, but it had started to feel numb. He wasn't sure whether that was good or bad.

Either way, Oliver Roth relaxed his muscles, and smiled through his own tears. 'Missing, presumed dead' was a powerful position to be in.

Chapter 21

Alex was struggling to navigate along his improvised route, thanks to too many clone platoons blocking his original path. Lorraine and Shannon had done their best to redirect him, but with limited success.

Thankfully, there was something familiar about the path he was on.

Nothing about Floor F had been familiar, despite him having been there before. It was a gap in his memory, just like everything that had happened between being trapped in the clone factory control room and resurfacing in a bungalow somewhere.

Nonetheless, *something* was familiar about the corridor he jogged down.

It didn't take him long to work out what it was. The clone factory control room was dead ahead.

Alex's common sense conflicted with his instincts. One told him to investigate; to gain clues about the gaps in his memory. The other told him to get the hell away from there.

He went inside.

His decision was helped by Kate's assurance that time was no longer a factor. That, and he would probably never get another opportunity to revisit the place where his memory ended. The door was unlocked: there had been no reason to secure a door to a disused room.

The Alpha Control Room was similar to how Alex remembered, as much as he *could* remember it. The layout of the control panels and diagonally downward windows all matched the picture in his head. The view past the windows, however, was entirely different.

The clone factory was a metallic wasteland. Steel and glass lined the floors, with raised pads that had once been the bases of the clone pods dotted approximately across the factory floor. Chemical pipes that had been ripped apart still lay in place like gutted snakes. The monorail carriage stood at the station, charred and useless. But most striking of all was the silence: even behind the glass, the constant hums and hubbub of the factory floor had made it to Alex's ears. It had since been replaced with deathly silence.

Alex became aware of a feeling that had subtly entered his head without his permission. It was loss, anger, and panic rolled into one – and the image of Dean Ginelli lay under it all.

Dad? Why am I thinking of Dad?

Alex was no stranger to negative feelings about his father. But why they nagged him so strongly in New London's clone factory, he had no idea.

However, the papers in his left hand would give him some clues.

Alex had almost forgotten about the report from the Central Research Headquarters. The half nine deadline was so firm in his mind that reading it had been an impossibility. He sat down in one of the swivel-chairs, kept one hand on his assault rifle, and started to read.

Executive Summary Report: The Ginelli
Project

Last updated May 18th, Year One

They were working on this yesterday!

This document provides information
relating to the following:

• The cloning of insurgent Alex Ginelli
from <u>Terrorist Faction 001</u>;

• Events concerning the deal made between
Alex Ginelli and New London Complex staff
on April 25th;

• Cross-references to the early
experimental stages of Acceleration (<u>see
separate report</u>);

• Subsequent attempts to locate the
insurgents' base of operations (referred
to by Ginelli as 'Spitfire's Rise').

By the end of the opening paragraph, Alex was so engrossed
that he had forgotten he was in the midst of a battlefield.

Deal? What kind of deal did I make?

And why don't I remember it?

…What will I tell the others, once I find out what I did?

A song tried to enter Alex's head, but he managed to keep it
out.

Wait, what was that about?

He read on, his heart thumping against his chest as if trying to make him stop.

On April 25th, Year One, an intrusion was
made by five members of Terrorist Faction
001: Alex Ginelli, Ewan West, Kate
Arrowsmith, Jack Hopper, and Charlie
Coleman (deceased). Ginelli was separated
from his group and trapped inside the
Clone Factory Alpha Control Room, and the
decision was made to involve Dr Gwen
Crossland (psychiatrist/experimental
hypnotherapist).

There was a whisper in Alex's memory about a woman called Gwen, but no more. However, the mention of 'experimental hypnotherapy' frightened him.

Dr Crossland's previous interactions with
insurgents had yielded no positive
results, despite her unparalleled
expertise. Her previous test case, Daniel
Amopoulos (deceased) was unable to offer
details about Dr Joseph McCormick or
'Spitfire's Rise' due to his own lack of
knowledge. He also did not consent to the
cloning process before his death.

And I did?

In contrast, Ginelli's resilience was soon
worn down, and he was amenable to a deal

```
whereby he would provide a new clone model
- and information about his group's
whereabouts - in exchange for his own
safety.
```

Alex's stomach started to disagree with him. Nothing in these words sounded like the person he believed himself to be. The real Alex Ginelli would last longer than Daniel, surely? Why did he volunteer himself to be cloned? How was his resilience 'worn down'? And how could he give away the location of Spitfire's Rise without knowing it himself?

None of it made sense. Grant's staff would not offer him a survival deal and actually keep him alive at the end of it. And Alex was smart enough to know that, so he would never have accepted such a deal.

A song tried to enter his head again, and he dismissed it. He scanned through the document to get to the part where he was manipulated.

```
Dr Crossland was instructed to use her
experimental 'two-track mind' therapy to
create two different memory streams: one
where Ginelli would remember the entirety
of his experience with us, and one where
he would remember none of it. Ginelli
would be forcefully switched between each
memory stream depending on our purposes.

Dr Crossland was able to glean Alex's
vulnerabilities using data from his old
social media accounts. Two songs were
chosen as triggers to switch Ginelli
between his typical state of ignorance and
```

```
his state of full awareness. His full
memory would be switched on and off
respectively by:

1) Smoke on the Water (Deep Purple, 1972)

2) Barbie Girl (Aqua, 1997)
```

'Barbie Girl'?! Seriously?

It made sense. Just two lines of that song made him want to shut down his whole brain, and he had probably told that to Facebook at some point.

But he had found out how to get his memory back.

'Smoke on the Water'. It was the same song he had spent the last few minutes trying to keep out of his head. He had known his brain was fighting against it, but not consciously realised what it was doing – in the same way that he had known about his memory gap for three weeks, but his brain had avoided thinking about it, so he had never realised.

All he needed to do to switch his memory back on was sing 'Smoke on the Water'.

The prospect terrified him. It crossed his mind that he might prefer to live in ignorance rather than learn what he had done. But the situation was bigger than him. His friends would suffer if he didn't do this.

They may have suffered already because of me. But screw it, let's see what happens.

'Duh duh duuuh, duh duh *duduuuh*, duh duh duuuh, duh duh…'

To an outsider, the scene would have looked ridiculous: a grown man sat on a swivel-chair, in an abandoned room above a burned-out clone factory, singing to himself whilst reading and balancing an assault rifle on his lap.

But as the song entered his head, a sleeping part of Alex Ginelli woke up. He was met with the greatest headache of his whole life, as if he had absorbed an entire encyclopaedia in less than a second, and his brain switched over to its other memory stream.

Kate had better get out, he had thought to himself as he had clutched his sticky shoulder wound. *Otherwise I got trapped here for nothing.*

He had not known what had become of Ewan and Charlie. Ewan had aborted the mission and told them to return to Floor Z where Jack was guarding the exit.

A miniature army of clones had surrounded the door of the Alpha Control Room, and his only weapons had been rifles from the control room's dead clones and their limited ammunition. But twenty minutes had passed, and the army outside had done nothing but wait.

Alex had worked out that his fate would be similar to Daniel's. If they wanted him dead immediately, they could have invaded and shot him.

The phone mounted to the wall had rung, and Alex had swallowed his fear and answered. 'Smoke on the Water' had been the first sound he had heard, and then a soft, soothing voice spoke over it.

'Alex Ginelli,' she had said, 'my name is Gwen Crossland. Listen very carefully. Your life depends on what you do next.'

'Tell Grant no deal,' Alex had answered. '*Ever.*'

*

The clone factory had been so much louder on the inside. And bigger too: from the Alpha Control Room, still visible to Alex somewhere in the distance, it had looked enormous. From the factory floor, it looked unending.

'Are you ready for this, Alex?' the soft voice of Gwen Crossland had said.

Alex had looked sideways at Crossland, a four-foot-something, grey-haired old hag with a wicked smile and the demeanour of a nearly-retired headmistress. She was forceful without being loud, although the hundred clones behind her had helped.

'You won't remember it,' she said, almost whispering. 'You won't even remember consenting to the deal.'

Consent, Alex had thought, *consent doesn't count if it's forced. Why the hell did I even say yes?*

It had been the pain, of course. Crossland had barked at him down the phone while the large clone model stamped on his shoulder wound, accurate and devastating like a surgeon with a hammer. Crossland's idea had been simple: keep up the pain until he either agreed to the deal, or died from his wounds. Unfortunately the wound had not been deadly, so death would have taken hours. The word 'yes' would be instantaneous – and he always had the option later of running away and getting himself shot to death nice and quickly.

He had not taken that option. The cloning pod was dead ahead.

'Will my clones remember what I did?' he had asked.

Crossland had given a sweet smile.

'We grow our clones without their models' memories.'

'So they're not perfect copies after all.'

'Oh, don't get me wrong, we have the technology! Just like we could give them vocal cords if we wanted. But Grant and Pearce agree it would be a bad idea. The closer a clone becomes to a human, the more tempted we'd be to treat it as such. Besides, the memory transfer process would take a whole week of open-cranial brain analysis. The model would have to die first, and we'd rather it didn't come to that. Plan A requires you to stay alive, even if Plan B does not.'

My clones won't know who I am, where I've been, what I've agreed to...

...or where I live.

'Now,' Crossland had continued, 'it may have occurred to you to make a run for it rather than fulfil your end of the deal. But bear in mind we have no reason to kill you once we're done. As a matter of fact, we *need* you to escape New London so your friends know you're unharmed.'

'How very kind of you.'

Crossland had laughed.

'If you spend several days in the Outer City walls, it will be obvious something happened to you here. If your friends think you're dead and you later turn up alive, it'll be suspicious. Your escape to the countryside will be a nice, peaceful way of keeping your friends' anxiety at bay without affecting our deal. Now, off you pop.'

Alex had given her a dirty look, and recognised his own powerlessness. There would be a chance to win, but it would not be then. Not that day.

He had stepped into the cloning pod, and the door had sealed shut behind him.

He had been held against his will in the bungalow for two days. Although most of the time, he had not been aware of being imprisoned.

In his regular state, the one in which he knew nothing about his capture, he had refused to leave the bungalow. He had believed himself to be acting on his own free will, staying in place like the loyal teammate he was, until the teenagers found their chance to escape.

Each time he entered his fully aware state, he realised it was Crossland's doing. Conditional thought, she had called it. Every thought that passed his mind about leaving the bungalow had been met with an instruction that had been planted there: 'I will stay here until the teenagers need me.'

The teenagers must have been dead, of course, but Crossland's work would force him to stay put. It had been torture without a torture chamber. A prison where the prisoner believed he was choosing to stay.

Forty-eight hours after his imprisonment, 'Smoke on the Water' sounded yet again.

It had been speakers fixed to the top of the approaching vehicle, as normal. The memories had come flooding back to Alex: the memories of what he was *really* doing at the bungalow.

Crossland had strolled through the front door as if she lived there, flanked by two clones on each side, and greeted Alex like a rebellious teenage son.

'I have a treat for you today,' she had said, producing a twelve-inch laptop from a pink and purple pouch.

'A video of my clone children growing up?'

'No,' she had answered, '*you* are the child in this scenario. When was the last time you spoke to your father?'

His birthday. Six months before Takeover Day.

'The population of New Brighton has been declining for a while,' Crossland had said, 'some kind of disease did most of the work. Among the survivors, your father was easy to find.'

'...You're using my dad as leverage against me.'

'That's the sad thing,' Crossland had said in a voice of genuine pity, 'we can't do any physical harm to you, otherwise when you revert to your ignorant state you'll wonder where the cuts and bruises came from. We even had to give you the telescopic handgun you dropped in the corridor, simply because you *would* have taken it if you'd escaped independently. So we'll have to use a different means of extracting information.'

She had sat down at the dining room table, beckoning Alex to follow. There, she had powered up her miniature laptop.

'Your father is up to speed on the situation, so don't worry about explaining.'

He knows I'm fighting against Nicholas Grant. That's something, at least.

And suddenly, Dean Ginelli was on the screen. Alex had felt his insides shrink, as if he were a small child in front of his taekwondo instructor once again.

'Alex,' his father had said.

'Hi Dad.'

No more words had been spoken.

The video background had been a blank wall. There were no clues about where in New Brighton he was being held. Not that it would have mattered.

Gwen Crossland had stood up, invited Alex into the chair, and towered over him as high as her short body was able to.

'Your friend Daniel couldn't tell us anything useful, but maybe you can. Tell us the location of Spitfire's Rise, or your father gets shot in the head. You have one minute.'

This exact scenario had occurred to Alex. It was their most obvious move. But two days in the bungalow had given him almost zero time to think of ideas, as he had spent most of it unaware his father was even in danger. As far as he could remember, this was only the third time they had woken him up.

'Don't you dare, Alex,' his father had said.

'My decision, Dad, not yours,' Alex had replied, just for the power trip.

'Fifty seconds,' Crossland had said.

Alex had stayed silent. It was interesting watching his father's reaction: stuck between determination to stay alive, and determination for Alex to not give in. He had seemed to want life and death at the same time.

'Twenty seconds.'

The New Brighton clone, out of shot, had cocked his gun, and the barrel came into view, pointing at the side of Dean's head.

The power is all mine now. Everything that happens is my decision, not his. In another world, this might have been rewarding.

'Ten.'

What if I saved him and didn't betray my friends?

'Nine.'

I could lie. Why does nobody think of that in interrogations?

'Eight.'

If I lie and get away with it, they'll either keep him alive or shoot him, depending on what they were planning all along.

'Seven.'

Of course, one day they'll learn I was lying and kill him anyway.

'Six.'

But even then, better that than losing the war.

'Five.'

Screw it, let's do this.

'Four—'

'Stop!' Alex had yelled, to the horror and relief of his father.

Crossland closed her mouth and smiled.

'...Lemsford,' Alex had said, remembering Matthew's room and the dinosaur bedsheets. 'Spitfire's Rise is in Lemsford. But you don't have to kill them! Just make them surrender—'

'Which house in Lemsford?'

'I don't know. School Lane or something, I think? We never need to remember road names…'

Gwen Crossland had given him a pat on the back, and said no more.

'Hey. Woman.'

Dean Ginelli's voice had power, even from the other side of a small laptop screen. Crossland had given him her attention.

'You don't need to use me as leverage anymore,' Alex's father had said with a crestfallen voice. 'I no longer consider him my son.'

Before Alex could respond, Crossland had powered down the laptop.

'Thank you, Alex,' she had finished. 'We will keep your father in a safe place until we have visited Lemsford and determined whether your answer was accurate. If it was not accurate, then—'

'Then my father is dead, I know.'

'That too. But we'll also initiate Plan B. We'll take you back to New London and open your skull, and spend the next week transferring your memories to a new clone model. There's no guarantee they will lead us accurately to Spitfire's Rise, of course – science offers no guarantees about anything – hence why we tried the *living* method first, but it's more likely to work than listening to more lies. Good day, Alex.'

Within two minutes she and her clone entourage had left the house, and driven away with 'Barbie Girl' blasting out of the speakers. Then Alex had gone back to his dutiful clueless self, guarding the bungalow and waiting for his friends to escape New London.

*

Back in the disused Alpha Control Room, Alex staggered to his feet, lay a hand against the diagonal windows and suppressed the contents of his stomach as they threatened to rise. The memory blast had provided the physical pain, and the betrayal of his father had provided the emotional pain.

He checked his watch. It had felt like several days had passed, but it wasn't yet ten o'clock. There would be plenty of time before Grant replaced the border point and booted up the AME shield.

'Guys,' came Ewan's voice from the radio, 'I'm on Floor E. I found a stairwell. Anyone need directions?'

'Not yet,' said Kate.

'Yeah,' said Alex.

Ewan told him the route, but he only paid as much attention as he had to. Once he had memorised the directions, he skipped to the end of the report in his hands. Before moving forward with the night's mission, he had to find out what had happened.

Alex Ginelli was able to leave his designated post upon the escape of his allies, rendering Crossland's backup plan of memory transfer unworkable. In the aftermath of the destruction of New London's clone factory, the inspection of Lemsford was delayed until staffing issues had been resolved. A failed trap at Oakenfold Special School forced an end to this delay, and on 17th May, Year One, a scouting team of Ginelli clones reached Lemsford and searched for the insurgents' headquarters.

They found Jack and Gracie…

They were killed during their search of
School Lane, and therefore a larger force
was dispatched later that night.

The village of Lemsford has since been
searched with the most intrusive methods
available, and subsequently destroyed
through a series of air strikes. The
search found no evidence supporting Alex
Ginelli's claim.

Therefore, at the conclusion of the
search, Dean Ginelli was executed in New
Brighton Citadel.

Alex did not know how to react. The text in the document
didn't make it seem real, but he believed it. His father had died
two days ago, and he hadn't had any idea.

It wouldn't have been such a bad thought – most of the
Underdogs would have lost relatives by now without knowing
– but he had *caused* his father's death and not even realised.

Alex and his father had not been on good terms since his
teenage years. But in different circumstances, Alex would have
fought like hell to protect him. Perhaps Dad would have fought
for him too.

There was only one silver lining, and Alex clung onto it as if
it justified him betraying his father. He picked out his phone,
and called comms.

It was Shannon who answered.

'Hello?'

'Shannon, it's Alex.'

'You OK?'

'I'm alive and uninjured… tell me, have the others found a new shelter?'

'They had Jack leading them. He found a good place before the night was even over.'

'Tell Mark to fetch them home. We can return to Spitfire's Rise. Grant doesn't have a clue where we live.'

There was a moment of quiet, as Shannon tried to process the information. In the background, Lorraine mumbled something about proof.

'Are you sure, Alex? I mean, absolutely *certain*?'

A tear fell from Alex's eye as he decided it was better to tell them the truth. He did well to spill all the details in his three-minute time limit, especially in his emotional state.

There were only two details he missed out: the names of the two songs that changed his memory state, and any mention of his father.

Shannon and Lorraine were compassionate and understanding, although Alex wondered whether that would remain the case once he came home. The conversation ended, and Alex removed the battery from his phone.

All the relevant information had been shared with those who needed to know. There was no need for him to keep the memories himself. He left the Alpha Control Room, abandoning the papers to avoid tempting himself to go down the same route again. Once the clone factory was no longer visible, he started to sing 'Barbie Girl' – the only time in his life he had ever done so voluntarily – and wiped away all memory of his father's death.

At least I'll still believe I have someone to fight for, came his last thought before it all faded.

Then Alex blinked, and looked around the corridor. Where the hell was he going again?

'Ewan,' he said into the radio, 'what's the latest?'

'Still on Floor E waiting for you,' Ewan replied. 'Are you at the stairwell yet?'

'No, where is it?'

'You can't remember? I told you about a minute ago!'

'Sorry,' said Alex, nursing his head, which ached for some reason. 'I must have zoned out.'

Chapter 22

McCormick knew how much depended on him. If he failed to destroy the data servers, then the others could reach Floor B, destroy Marshall's computer, stop the shield from going up and still lose the war. Ewan and Alex may have deleted the data in the Central Research Headquarters, but if the backups lived through the night then Grant would have everything he needed to just build another shield.

Unfortunately, the data servers were located in the most dangerous spot on Floor P. McCormick found himself wishing he still had the body of a teenager. Or at the very least that he had not come to the HPFC alone.

As vast as New London's Outer City was, the upper floors couldn't hold every room that mattered. According to the maps they kept at comms, Floor A was reserved for the residential quarters of high-ranking staff, Floors B–D were where missions were planned and executed from, and Floors E–G contained scientific and military research and development. There were a load of rooms essential to running an empire that could not fit at the top, so a full square mile of Floor P had been built, guarded and reinforced as a high-security complex.

The High Priority Functional Cluster had one entrance, and

McCormick was just around the corner. In his way stood a thin empty pathway, devoid of doorways, side corridors, upward pipes or shelter points of any kind. Three clone guards stood on the outside of the Cluster, with three more on the inside, the two groups separated by a titanium door that would only open for those with the correct fingerprints, retinas and eight-figure passcodes.

Beyond that, if their maps were to be believed, lay a maze of silver corridors, twisted and claustrophobic enough to make a carrier pigeon reach for its compass.

If Theseus had been trapped in this labyrinth, the minotaur would have won.

But he didn't have Lorraine and Shannon navigating for him.

'I'm almost here,' he whispered into his phone. It was an audio call rather than a video call, of course. The fewer visual distractions he had, the safer he would be. 'Take me through the directions one more time.'

'Once you're inside,' answered Lorraine, 'you'll, er, reach a crossroads fairly quickly. Take the right-hand corridor, go past the Nutrition Farm, and follow a curve around when you reach the Special Weapons Storage Facility, which should take you right— no, left...'

'And how can I tell which rooms are the Nutrition Farm or the Special Weapons place?'

'Well either way, once you've taken the curve to the left... I'm not— wait, yes— you keep going...'

Moments away from storming a one-floor fortress, McCormick came to realise the damage he had inflicted on Lorraine Shepherd. She was exhausted – physically, mentally and emotionally – and almost all of it had been his own fault. He had been too demanding of her, and her limits were finally beginning to show.

McCormick heard the sound of hands against Lorraine's phone, and after a moment of quiet, Shannon started to talk.

'McCormick,' she began, 'walk to the crossroads and turn right. When the path curves to the left, follow it to the next crossroads and go right again. Then left, left again, and it's the second door on the right. Did you get that?'

'Fairly sure.'

'Then say it back to me. Now, before you forget.'

McCormick smiled. Shannon's fiery nature had given her an uncompromising personality too. But even though this war was more personal to her than anyone else in the Underdogs, she was uncompromising in a productive way rather than a vengeful way.

'Right at the crossroads,' McCormick answered, 'round the curve and right at the second crossroads. Then left, left, and second door on the right.'

'Correct. If you find yourself at the Central Power Generator, you've gone a door too far.'

Nicholas Grant had put lots of his golden eggs in one basket: his main power source, his army's food supply, his armoury for advanced weapons and the backup for all his data, all within a square mile. It spoke volumes about Grant's faith in the security of the HPFC.

'Thanks, Shannon. I'll let you know if I get out.'

'*If* you get out?' asked Shannon. Lorraine seized the phone.

'If *you* get out?' she yelled. 'You're doing this alone?!'

'I'm the only one close by, and the other three are fighting their way to Marshall's office. It's the only strategy we have.'

'You won't even get past the entrance on your own! And how do you plan to get out again?'

McCormick held out his dental mirror around the corner with trembling fingers, and took a long sigh.

'Getting out's not an essential part of the plan. You know that. Like Oliver Roth, safety is just bonus points.'

'Don't you dare—'

'Lorraine, this is why the plan will work. When Grant designed this place, he assumed it would be attacked by people who planned to get out. And I *hope* I'll get out. But I know where my priorities lie.'

'Joseph, *promise* me—'

In the dental mirror, McCormick saw a flash of green light and a guard's head turning. Something had unlocked the titanium door, and his time had come. With no time to lose on politeness, he hung up his phone and raised his assault rifle.

If Barbara could see him now, she would not recognise him. She would look at him with terrified eyes and see another person.

But that was OK, in the grand scheme of things.

Or perhaps not OK. Just necessary.

The titanium door slid open, and McCormick leapt around the corner. His first spray of bullets killed two of the outdoor guards, injured the third in his shoulder, and caught the clone in the doorway straight in the forehead. Dr Joseph McCormick, the oldest and frailest soldier in Great Britain, had forced a breach point in the High Priority Functional Cluster.

The third guard had no time to inspect his shoulder wound before McCormick's second spray killed him too. The three inside guards were busy pulling the jammed bodies away from the entrance in an attempt to lock McCormick out, so there was plenty of time for the man to begin his charge. He sprinted at a speed far too unhealthy for a man his age, and found himself five metres away when the bodies were cleared. He did not have much time.

McCormick knew he would not have the strength to keep a sliding door open against the pull of six hands, so he had to find another blockage. He slammed his body against the entrance, clutched the hair of the Asian clone on the other side, and dragged his head into the hallway. The other two clones hauled the door closed anyway, snapping the bones in their colleague's neck. The door rebounded open, far enough for McCormick to reach through the gap with his assault rifle, and finish off the final two guards.

Seven young clone soldiers, wiped out by a man nearly old enough for a free bus pass. It pays to be far too ambitious!

McCormick stumbled over the bodies and began his jog. There was panic in the HPFC now, among soldiers who could not possibly have expected an invader.

He reached the crossroads, rained ammunition down the right-hand corridor, and continued his charge against the desperate wishes of his ageing body. Lorraine had muttered something about a Special Weapons Storage Facility next to the curve in the path, and McCormick was keen to find a weapon that would speed up his job. He pulled open the door and shot a bullet into the room's single occupant.

McCormick tore through the wooden crates before him, and scowled in disgust at the range of advanced weaponry. Cluster-rocket launchers. Napalm mines. And a box which read 'Acid grenades: for use on civilians'.

He stuffed his pockets with acid grenades, for the inevitable moment his bullets would run dry, and then found a weapon that fitted his needs perfectly.

The hand warhead. Iain Marshall's nifty name for a handheld weapon the shape and size of a traditional hand grenade, but filled with NPN8. Its warning label included, bold and capitalised, 'NEVER USE WITHOUT A FULL SURROUND OF SHELTER', suggesting that its blast radius would reach further than it could be thrown. McCormick took two in his left hand and a third in his teeth, leaving his heavy assault rifle in the grip of four tired fingers.

He burst back into the corridors and ran to the next crossroads, gunning down another clone as he ran to his right. Two left turns later, having followed Shannon's instructions to perfection, he found himself one door away from the final resting place of Nathaniel Pearce's hallowed research.

McCormick jerked open the door to the data servers and found a thin chamber the length of a train carriage, filled from front to back with caged hard drives and enough flickering lights to fill a disco. The heat was intense; even the groaning fans that lined the ceiling were locked in a constant battle against the temperature of the computers.

Someone opened fire from down the path. McCormick sheltered behind the open door, and decided enough was enough. One of those bullets could have killed him stone dead, and wiped out any chance of him fulfilling his mission. He couldn't afford to die, not when he was so close to destroying their fourth target out of five.

Are we really that close to surviving the night? I honestly thought we'd be dead before we got three.

McCormick shook his head and took a deep breath. The sooner he did this, the better.

He pulled the pin on the first hand warhead, and launched it to the far end of the chamber. He aimed the second at the halfway spot on the metal floor, and sent the final one a distance he thought he might just survive from. He took his rifle in both hands, leapt back into the open corridor, and killed a clone who had not thought an old man could jump so fast.

McCormick slammed the data server door shut with half a second to spare, as the hand warheads detonated. Like the sound of a sprinting giant, the thunderous explosions leapt closer and closer and sent the HPFC rocking with the force of an earthquake. McCormick was thrown against the back wall. He fell to the floor, double-checked that the impact had not broken his spine, and scrambled to his feet as Floor P began to steady itself.

He smiled as the gravity of his actions dawned on him. The AME files would be left to starve in cyberspace, never to be found again. And after a visit to Floor B, Pearce would be naked of knowledge altogether. All McCormick needed was to find a way out of the HPFC alive, before his adrenalin ran out and he remembered how afraid he was.

'He's down here!' came a raging young voice. 'Follow the explosions!'

It was a human's voice, of course, but one which McCormick did not recognise. Whoever it was, he was coming along McCormick's escape route, leaving him with a choice between running for his life or finding a good place to hide.

He would lose a running race. But he remembered Shannon's words about a Central Power Generator. It was one door away, and the best hiding place he could hope to find.

McCormick stumbled through the entrance to the neighbouring room, and closed the door moments before the angry soldier could storm around the corner. He switched off the lights and ran to the generator, a cylindrical casing filled with a mess of turbines and loud noises, and positioned himself behind it for his last stand.

A set of loud footsteps came to a halt outside the door. McCormick's sense of adventure began to falter, and he finally admitted that he was alone in the dark, trapped and terrified.

'You're finished, you sad coffin-dodger!' came a scream. 'Come out and get yourself a peaceful death before I come in there and make it slow!'

An all-or-nothing strike had felt like such a good idea at

the time. But there was no way out for McCormick anymore. His rational mathematician's mind kept him from panic for just long enough to reach for his radio. It was time to play his last, most desperate move.

'Kate!' he yelled. 'The code to the detonator is one-nine-two, double-three-seven!'

He scrambled for the acid grenades in his pockets, lay them on the top of the generator, and began to pull pins. After he had finished, he ran to cower in the furthest corner of the room.

'McCormick?' came Kate's quivering voice.

'One-nine-two, double-three-seven! Set it off at *exactly* half past ten, no questions asked, and phone comms the *moment* you've done it! And if I don't get out of this... I love all three of you. So, so much.'

'No—'

The door was booted open to reveal the soldier's silhouette, and he pointed his rifle straight at McCormick's face. With tears falling from his eyes, McCormick spoke his final words into the radio.

'They got me. But the data server's gone. You know what you need to do. *One-nine-two, double-three-seven*, at *half past ten.* Win this war, my friends.'

The human switched on the light. He was younger than McCormick had imagined. He signalled for McCormick to drop his assault rifle and radio, an order which he obeyed. The assassin shot the radio to the sound of Kate's screams, breathed in to bark a command, but his voice was lost in the following explosions. The three acid grenades spilled their fizzling payload over the hull of the generator. Before his captor knew what had happened, the room around them, the whole of Floor P, and the entire Citadel were plunged into darkness.

'Bonus points…' McCormick whispered to himself.

In the dark, it was easier for him to imagine the scene across the rest of New London. Everything from their munitions factories to their clone training facilities would have shut down in an instant. The vehicle port they had entered through would only have been lit by the dim sky outside. Clones in computer rooms might have watched their screens go blank a split-second before the lightbulbs followed. High-ranking human officers on Floor A would have felt under threat for the first time in a year.

The fizzling noises stopped at McCormick's side. The acid had burned itself out.

'You know,' the boy hissed, coming into view again as he flicked the switch on his rifle torch. 'I was going to kill you, doctor. I was going to spread the guts of the great Joseph McCormick all across this room, and stick your miserable head on the spike of an electric fence for all your pansy little friends to see.'

'I'm sure you'll get your chance.'

'You're damned right I will. Make no mistake, you old fart – the only reason you're still breathing is that code I heard you mention. I want answers.'

Of course that's why I'm alive. Why do you think I shouted it loud enough for you to hear?

An angry voice yelled through the soldier's battery-powered radio.

'Oliver! The whole of Floor A just lost its electricity! What the hell's going on?'

'Good news and bad news, Nick… the data servers *and* the power room have gone to hardware heaven. But I've got you a prize that'll make it more than worth it.'

'You killed McCormick.'

McCormick took the optimism in Nicholas Grant's voice as a huge compliment.

'Not yet. He was shouting a code into his radio for some kind of detonator. He doesn't get to die until I know what it means.'

'Outstanding. Bring him to me so I can extract the answers myself.'

The assassin gasped in fury, like a child denied a packet of sweets.

'Yes, sir,' the boy snarled. 'Will be there in ten.'

Grant called him 'Oliver'. And while the lights were on, I noticed he was a young redhead.

The others are in grave danger and they don't even know it.

With the assassin's rifle barrel pointed to his face, McCormick raised his arms and let out a surprised gasp.

'You're Oliver Roth,' he breathed.

The boy nodded.

'Alive and well.'

Chapter 23

In one short radio conversation, Ewan had lost five years' worth of behaviour management lessons. He screamed and swore at the top of his voice, not caring how many clones heard and came running, thrusting his assault rifle through every window he passed in the darkness. He hit the tears away from his face instead of wiping them, and kicked against the walls as if trying to tear New London to the ground piece by piece.

He had wasted his second-to-last clip of ammunition on a dead clone, who lay at his feet with eight handgun bullets to his chest.

'What the hell just happened?' shouted Alex through his radio.

'What the hell do you think?' Ewan spat in response. 'McCormick took out the backup place and died anyway! He came to New London to babysit us and got himself bloody killed!'

The words sounded unbelievable, even though they came from his own mouth. The great Joseph McCormick, father of the Underdogs, the head of Britain's last army, and Ewan's surrogate grandfather, was almost certain to be dead.

If felt so wrong, the thought of outliving McCormick. He was supposed to survive the longest. He deserved to.

Out of the thousand thoughts that raced through Ewan's head, there was one that made him inconsolably guilty: the hope that McCormick really *had* died rather than get himself captured. If Grant made McCormick talk, the war was over.

The corridor around him was pitch black. How McCormick had thought a power cut would help them reach Floor B, he would never know. He had been halfway to a stairwell up to Floor D when the lights had gone out and rendered the map in his head useless.

'I shouldn't have left him alone,' Kate wailed through the radio, 'it's my fault! This all happened because of *me!*'

Ewan wanted to tell her she was right. He wanted Kate to blame herself, but he knew it would only be to reduce his own guilt. Besides, he only had three quarters of his team left. And one way or another, a computer still needed destroying.

'Kate,' he snarled reluctantly, 'you left him so you could kill a border point and buy us more time. If you'd stayed with McCormick we'd have lost the war already.'

There was no response through the radio, except the faint crackle of sobbing.

'I… I just wish we could push the reset button… go back to before he collapsed and do things differently…'

Ewan shivered. His mentor's collapse at Spitfire's Rise felt like a month ago.

'We screwed up the whole week!' Kate wailed. 'Raj is dead, Alex has been cloned, Lorraine's almost worked herself to death and now we've lost McCormick! And unless we get to Floor B, it'll all be for *nothing!*'

'All the more reason to get up there and finish this,' came Alex's voice, both through the radio and somewhere in the audible distance. He was close. 'By all rights we should be dead by now. And if Raj were here, he'd say there's a God-given reason we're still alive. Let's prove him right, OK?'

'Alex,' Ewan called out across the corridor. Stumbling noises came from a small distance away, and they spent the next thirty seconds ignoring Kate's cries and bringing themselves towards each other, using their voices to navigate through the dark.

'Good to see you again, mate,' said Alex once he came close.

'Alex, you can't even see me.'

Alex dared to laugh, and tried to pat Ewan on the shoulder. Instead, he hit Ewan's head.

'Missing your helmet?'

'Lost it in the Experiment Chamber. Traded it for a gas mask.'

'Huh, well done. Whereabouts is K—'

Alex was interrupted by a message that echoed through every radio in the Citadel, including the bodies spread across their Floor E corridor.

'Calling all soldiers,' said Iain Marshall, 'there is a special guard priority in place for the next fifteen minutes, along the stairwell from 58F to 58P. *All* nearby units must abandon their posts and guard all stairwell entrances and exits. That's 58F to 58P. Do so now.'

Alex let out a delighted laugh.

'McCormick's alive!'

'That's a bloody quick conclusion to jump to.'

'No, think about it. What's so special about Floors F and P? The stairwells go up to F, and McCormick was captured on P!'

It sounded realistic enough. Ewan nodded, although Alex would not see it in the dark.

'And if you don't believe me,' Alex finished, 'call Lorraine and Shannon. I bet Stairwell 58 is right next to that place he was attacking! He's being taken up to the big guns... probably because of Kate's detonator.'

McCormick – helpless, unarmed, and exhausted after the long climb – was half a storey away from Floor F. His only consolation had been enjoyment at keeping Oliver Roth behind him like a car stuck behind a tractor.

At the top of the stairwell, waiting for the prisoner who had led a war against them for a year, wiped out every scrap of AME research and reduced New London to torchlight, stood Iain Marshall and Nathaniel Pearce. Their faces were difficult to read in the shallow light beams, but they weren't happy.

Back in the days of television, McCormick had seen Marshall and Pearce on the news once or twice. Not quite as often as Nicholas Grant, but he still remembered what they had looked like with their posh suits and professional haircuts. The casual clothes and bitter scowls had not been part of their onscreen personas.

'*This* is him?' sneered Marshall.

'Yeah,' answered Roth. 'Disappointing, right?'

McCormick wasn't insulted. He knew what he looked like. But it was quite a compliment that they had expected him to be something more.

'Don't underestimate him,' said Pearce. 'Before he takes one more step towards Floor B, he's getting a full search.'

'Volunteering, are you?'

'*You're* performing the search, sunshine,' Marshall growled towards Roth with fierce eyes, 'because this is your fault. If you'd got to him *three seconds earlier* you'd have saved the Citadel's power, and we could have just marched him through the X-ray on Floor D! Cover every millimetre from head to toe, because there's no way he's coming to my office without a full search for weapons.'

'*Your* office?' laughed Roth. 'The one with the computer he's trying to destroy?'

'Trust me, there's a plan. You know about the bomb, don't you?'

Roth threw a glare towards his prisoner. McCormick could not see it in the darkness, but felt it.

'Actually, yeah,' Roth answered. 'I believe it was me who called it in.'

McCormick held his firmest poker face, amused that he had been right. The people at the top of Grant's empire really *did* hate each other. He had predicted as much: power-hungry people never truly liked their colleagues.

'Good,' finished Marshall. 'Now McCormick, there's a spare storage room over there. Would you kindly go inside and strip down?'

The exhausted McCormick ambled away towards the spare room, Roth's assault rifle poking his back. He walked inside, and Roth closed the door behind him rather than follow.

It always made McCormick smile, how people assumed they could not be heard on the other side of a closed door. Especially people with Roth's level of overconfidence.

'You mentioned a plan?' he asked. 'One that involves moving a live prisoner to Iain's office?'

'Nick's orders,' answered Marshall's voice. 'Until we know where the bomb is, he doesn't want us spread out.'

'We'll be one big target.'

'That's right – one big target, right next to a man who knows exactly where the bomb is. My office is almost certainly outside the blast radius, but if it's not, we'll wait for McCormick to start sweating. Then we'll evacuate to the other end of the Citadel and get someone to find and defuse it.'

'You don't get it, Iain. Tonight I saw that man storm his way through the HPFC, blowing up rooms and slaughtering clones, and even when I had him at gunpoint he kept talking over his radio! This guy's not afraid to die.'

'Everyone's afraid to die, Oliver,' laughed Pearce, 'even you.'

'Some people love victory more than their own lives. I give you my word, if that man had to choose between survival and victory, he'd choose victory.'

That's not admiration in his voice, is it?

'And he'd *still* be afraid, and it'd *still* show,' finished Marshall. 'You don't survive as a face-to-face arms dealer without learning how to read people, my boy. Now go, your prisoner's waiting.'

McCormick heard the sound of Roth's assault rifle clattering to the floor, almost as if it had been thrown down in frustration. Then the door opened, and Roth readied his hands for work.

Oliver Roth and Joseph McCormick – two titans of the Great British Civil War – found themselves alone in a small room, lit with the glow of two portable lights. And for the first time that evening, McCormick was able to take a proper look at the assassin, without the distraction of a firearm being pointed at his face.

The fourteen-year-old boy in front of him looked just like that: a fourteen-year-old boy, except in military uniform. There was even a handsomeness to Oliver Roth that McCormick had not imagined before meeting him: an endearing spread of freckles and a rusty, deepened shade of red in his hair – the type of shade that protected boys from ginger jokes, and gave them Norse warrior-like appeal once they grew up. McCormick also noticed a keen, inquisitive default expression on the boy's face, as if once upon a time he had been enthusiastic about learning for learning's sake, and a pair of eyes beneath stern eyebrows that held an expression of confidence usually reserved for those wiser than their years.

McCormick had seen the same expressions, mannerisms and character in several young people he had once known and loved – teenagers who had never been corrupted like the person before him. In another world, or a world inhabited by fewer negative role models, Oliver Roth could have made a fine young man.

McCormick interlocked his fingers behind the back of his head, and failed to suppress his nervous hiccups.

'Clothes off,' commanded Roth, 'down to your underwear.'

'You're not afraid of seeing an old man's body?'

'I've seen messier sights. And this is your own fault, you know. You could have just wandered through a friendly X-ray machine, like one of those old airport scanners, and then been on your way. But now you're getting humiliated.'

McCormick checked his watch as he removed it. It was almost five past ten.

I only need to go twenty-five minutes without breaking and telling them. I can do this.

McCormick took off his helmet, then began to remove his clothes. Layer by layer he shivered a little more, and item by item the expression on Roth's face grew more and more disgusted. Clothes disguised a lot, and McCormick must have looked surprisingly fat.

'What the hell happened to your stomach?' Roth barked as McCormick reached his underwear.

McCormick glanced downward at the cauterised wounds across his abdomen. The cyst that kept him out of combat was gone forever, but the procedure hadn't been without cost. Third degree burns were spread across his body, like a scale model of the Grand Canyon made from human flesh.

'Let's just say I've had a very difficult life lately,' he said with a pensive voice, 'especially these last few years.'

'Well it's not far from over now.'

McCormick sealed his eyes shut as Roth poked around his feet and gradually up his shins.

'So besides the obvious,' Roth continued, 'what's made your life so tough? Did your cat die or something?'

'No, my wife. I thought you'd know that, with Grant's background research.'

'I'm only interested in my enemies once I've killed them.'

'That's a shame,' replied McCormick, daring to smile. 'We're an interesting bunch. But to answer your question... when you get to my age, your whole generation starts to fall apart. There are the unlucky ones who get cancer in their forties, followed by those with unhealthy lifestyles who barely make it past sixty. By then you start wondering whether you'll be the next to go, or whether you'll have the pleasure of living the longest. The best case scenario is living long enough to watch all your friends drop off the perch before you.'

'Huh. At least now your friends get to die younger,' said Roth with a savage grin. 'What's the youngest? Fifteen?'

'Thirteen. A boy called Callum. Ran out of insulin within a week of surviving Takeover Day.'

'Survival of the fittest, mate.'

McCormick shuddered as Roth's fingers pushed into the gaps between his ribs, as if expecting to find a hidden clip of bullets.

'There comes a day for most of us when the funerals start to outnumber the weddings,' McCormick continued, 'but if you look to the younger generation, the world always feels alive. It wasn't what I planned when I set out to build people up to be the best they can be, but it's a happy side effect. I tried to guide those who needed guiding. Sometimes it worked, sometimes it didn't. But it was always worth it, and it was always the right thing to do. I may not have had the easiest life, but I've lived it well.'

As Roth lay his fingers around the base of McCormick's neck, their eyes met.

'And what about you, Oliver? Where do you see *your* life going after this war?'

Roth spat a laugh, and took a defensive step backwards.

'Oh, no. *No.* You're not using your magical love powers on me. Eight of your friends were murdered by these hands. You of all people should know I'm unreachable.'

'Nobody's unreachable,' McCormick answered. 'You wouldn't believe the kind of people I've had the honour of turning round. The world is full of young people who think their futures are already decided – that they're *supposed* to be this kind of screw-up or that kind of failure, just because they've been told to believe it by the people around them. But once they've had someone tell them the truth, the realisation can be literally life-changing.'

'And what is that truth?'

'That even though we don't get to decide what happens to us, we *do* get to choose how we respond. And even if people tell you your future is predestined, you have more control over your personality than you think.'

McCormick was expecting Oliver Roth to laugh. He wouldn't even have minded: he was sure to go through worse that night. But instead, the teenager gave a curious nod. Perhaps his prisoner was offering him conversation that Grant, Marshall and Pearce could never hope to provide.

'Is that what you've been telling your retard army?' asked Roth. 'Was it you who turned Ewan West from a school-hopping violent-minded moron to the sweet little do-gooder who thinks he killed me?'

'Hey, you leave Ewan alone. He's a good lad.'

Roth gave a confused face, as if wondering whether to laugh

or fall silent. McCormick smirked, aware that he'd just tried to break up the war's bitterest rivalry with a fatherly voice of reason, as if it were a playground argument between two young children.

'Whatever,' said Roth, 'let's be honest here. You don't seriously believe people like *me* – the kind of guy you pray your kids don't turn into – can be turned by anything you say? Do you honestly believe bad people can turn good?'

'Why not? It's as easy as good people turning bad.'

Roth smiled: a reaction McCormick did not expect.

'It's far easier for someone to turn bad than turn good,' said Roth. 'It's human nature. We're all crap people deep down.'

'That's just your own experience with corrupted people.'

'No, it's my experience with humans. Nobody's truly good. If you don't believe me, spend half an hour in rush hour traffic and watch how people act. Or even better, put a million of them in a giant walled prison and see what they're like a year later.'

McCormick looked to the floor, unable and unwilling to hide the sadness in his face. It was difficult to argue against Oliver Roth, even taking his own helplessness out of the equation.

His sadness appeared to spread to Roth. When the teenager spoke again, he spoke in a sombre voice.

'One second,' he muttered, 'I just need to do your face and then we're done.'

Roth took a step forward, and only then did McCormick realise how long had passed in conversation. For much of their time together, Roth had not even been searching him.

Roth started to run his fingers around McCormick's head, obviously just going through the motions rather than performing a genuine search. With the top of his body reached, McCormick knew how little time he had to complete his own personal mission.

'All those youngsters from difficult backgrounds who I've helped over the years,' he said, 'most of them had something in common. It was their expression. Their eyes. Something in their brains showed in their faces – depression, self-pity, isolation… they all held something in their eyes that other people didn't. But you know what's strange, Oliver? I don't see it in you. I see nothing negative in your face at all. Maybe you weren't affected by your background, but experience tells me that's impossible. I think you've grown used to hiding the hurt in order to look normal, and can pull off Oscar-worthy performances when important people are around.'

McCormick held his breath. All he had done was describe the Oakenfold students' habit of masking their difficulties, but he wondered whether he had struck a hidden, vulnerable nerve with Oliver Roth. He had momentary visions of Roth losing his cool, and storming outside to grab a gun and shoot him in the head.

Instead, Roth did not react. He withdrew his fingers from McCormick's head, his inspection over.

'Actually,' came his answer, 'my upbringing was fine. Boring, actually. No hidden childhood abuse, no teenage depression, nothing. I had a good education, I was the smartest guy in school, and had a nice secure family life. But thanks for assuming I'm some kind of screw-up who went off the rails.'

A few minutes ago you were boasting about how many of my friends you've killed. But let's ignore that for now.

'You say you had an average upbringing,' McCormick answered, 'but something has always been missing from your life. You've never placed your trust in anyone, have you?'

Roth could have sent McCormick's nose through the back of

his head. Instead he maintained eye contact, and held a worried expression on his face.

'You may never have been abused, Oliver, but you weren't loved either. That's why you don't have the expression I was talking about. It's not carefully hidden fear. It's *nothing*.'

McCormick imagined that Roth had spent very little of his life in tears, of pain *or* joy. The teenager would not know how to deal with the sudden tightening of his throat, or the rippling of his exhaling lungs.

I'm the leader of this boy's arch–enemies, and in one conversation I must have offered him more compassion than any of the men he fights for.

'You taught yourself that look of indifference,' McCormick continued, 'and you kept yourself cold and emotionless until you didn't know anything different. But there's help out there. You just need to start hanging with the right crowd.'

The portable lamps on the floor began to dim. There would not be much more time for conversation.

'You must think I'm a terrible person,' Roth muttered.

'Terrible does not mean unreachable, Oliver. The only thing that could ever make you unreachable is your own *choice* to never be reached.'

Roth looked away from McCormick, as if he had been staring into the sun. McCormick was surprised when his captor picked his shirt and trousers off the floor, and offered them back to him. He had imagined being led to Floor B in his underwear, but perhaps this was Roth's way of showing sympathy or respect.

'You can put these back on if you like,' said Roth. 'We're ready.'

McCormick slipped on his shirt and his trousers in turn, and when he looked up again he saw Roth's fingers on the door handle.

'You're a fine man, McCormick,' he said. 'One of the best I've ever known. But if you tell anyone I said that, I'll gut you myself.'

McCormick laughed, as if his captor were joking, and followed him back to Marshall and Pearce.

Chapter 24

As he was led through the security door on the stairwell between Floor C and B, McCormick wondered how his friends could ever hope to reach the higher floors themselves. Even if all their enemies vanished into thin air, the mazy corridors and security provisions would make it virtually impossible.

Nonetheless, the others were coming. Ewan, Kate and Alex would not abandon him, nor would they be able to rescue him. McCormick's biggest hope was that they just didn't get themselves killed.

At the top at the stairwell, he was met with an electromagnetically sealed door. It was secured shut; his power cut had not disabled the magnet or made the door slide open like in the movies.

'You use fail-*secure* locking devices?' McCormick asked Pearce at his side. 'Not fail-safe?'

'What's the difference?' asked Roth.

'Fail-safe electromagnetic seals unlock themselves in a power cut. Fail-*secure* ones don't. You've chosen the dangerous one.'

'So?' spat Pearce.

'What happens if you need to evacuate?'

'What happens if a feral old man cuts the power?'

They value security over their own safety. That would surprise me, if I still had any expectations of these people.

Marshall had his gold-coloured keycard ready for the moment the power cut was sorted, and when the lights flickered on McCormick sneaked a look at Pearce's watch. Twelve minutes past ten.

'You didn't think melting the generator would keep us in the dark forever, did you?' asked Pearce.

'No.'

'Well, Grant's a big fan of renewable energy sources. You wouldn't think it – the son of Francis Grant abandoning his family's obsession with fossil fuels. But we had a whole spring's worth of solar power stored in industrial batteries, just waiting to be connected to the main grid.'

McCormick did not respond. Marshall swiped his keycard and revealed the carpeted corridor that led to his office. Pearce's handgun prodded McCormick in the base of his spine, and forced him to tiptoe bare-footed into the bright and colourful Floor B. One level down from the villains' bedrooms, this was as close as the Citadel got to a relaxed, cultured environment. McCormick had often wondered how Ewan and Charlie had felt inside that officers' sector with its leather sofas, sky-blue wallpaper and fluffy carpets, but it must have paled in comparison to this corridor. He even spotted a recreation room, complete with table football and videogame consoles, and...

Wait – is that a real Monet painting? Seized from the National Gallery in Trafalgar Square?

McCormick was dragged into a wide, spacious room that dwarfed any of his university offices. One of Marshall's walls was overloaded with a fancy collection of war photography, as well as a large television screen. The mahogany desk displayed good quality model fighter jets, a photo of his daughters, and another of his wife in a lesser quality frame. Hannah Marshall, if McCormick remembered right. Shannon had told him about some of the people she had known on Floor A, and there had been a little less venom in her voice whenever she had talked about Hannah. Perhaps Iain Marshall's wife didn't share his nature.

Turning around, McCormick could see why the nearest wall was so heavily decorated. The other three were filled from floor to ceiling with the biggest and brightest computer system he had ever laid eyes on. The AME computer was secured against Iain Marshall's own office walls, each panel a foot thick and filled with a storm of circuit boards, LEDs, transistors, capacitors and other odds and ends that McCormick vaguely remembered from his old electronics classes. The whole three-walled computer seemed to be inside its own huge glass aquarium, filled with a blue liquid that McCormick assumed to be a cooling system. Any computer big enough to power such a feat of technological futurism was bound to need a lot of coolant, and McCormick was embarrassed that the thought hadn't occurred to him before that moment.

Behind him, Pearce was laughing.

'Bet you thought you could just come up here, find Iain's desktop computer and put a bullet through the hard drive,' he sneered. 'Unfortunately, the computer for the AME shield is rather big. And protected with bullet-resistant glass.'

The final piece of the puzzle is right here in front of me. We may have done well tonight, but unless this behemoth of a computer is destroyed, we lose.

Once Pearce had stopped talking McCormick could hear faint gurgling sounds, which must have been the coolant liquids in the walls. If Marshall's hearing was as good as his own, that gurgling must have been hell to work with, unless the impact was softened by the music that came from the speakers.

It didn't seem like the kind of music that Iain Marshall would enjoy, given how well the rest of his office illustrated his personality. When Marshall spoke, he confirmed McCormick's suspicions.

'Great,' Marshall snarled, as he joined Pearce and Roth in the middle of the room. 'He's playing Bach, in *my* office.'

'Nothing wrong with a bit of Bach,' came a heavy but lively voice from the entrance behind them, 'he was the original father of harmony. Beethoven's words, not mine.'

McCormick had heard the man's voice before. Less than an hour earlier, on the other side of Roth's radio. He knew the man's identity without needing to turn around.

'I'd have thought Bach was a bit churchy for your taste,' McCormick replied.

A hand grabbed the bone of McCormick's shoulder and turned him around, and he was met with the formidable sight of the most hated man on Earth. Dressed in the smartest of tailor-made suits, with a full head of shoulder-length white hair, the face McCormick had only seen on television had found its way into real life. The man greeted him with an entertained smile, his body giving off the enthusiastic energy of a televangelist. He clamped McCormick's hand in a vigorous handshake, releasing him moments before cracking his finger bones.

'My name is Nicholas Grant.'

'...Dr Joseph McCormick.'

A discomforting smirk settled on Grant's face as he glanced up and down his prisoner's body. His head and shoulders swayed back and forth, as if he were a snake readying himself for a strike. After a judgemental shake of his head, his voice rose to a piercing bellow.

'*This* is the man I got dressed up to meet?' he asked. 'I waited a full *year* to make contact with the great Joseph McCormick – the leader of the only rebel faction in Britain – the man who united thirty-two people on Takeover Day and turned them into an actual miniature army – the man whose soldiers spent a year burning and sabotaging their way through New London – the man who even convinced my *daughter* to live among him and his minions... and this is who I end up meeting? An exhausted man in torn clothing, gasping for his final breaths after a simple walk up the stairs, aged in his mid-sixties but with the stench of death already buzzing round him. And on top of that, the good doctor happens to be really fat.'

Wow. I'm glad he didn't do my best man speech.

Grant dipped his head to meet his enemy's. McCormick was tall compared to most people he knew, and he hadn't met anyone taller than him in over a year, but Grant stretched towards seven feet. For the first time since completing his doctorate, McCormick stood before someone who made him feel insignificant. Not just in stature, but in authority.

'This suit cost me three thousand pounds,' Grant continued, 'back in the days of the good old British pound, of course. Way back from my father's last days in charge of his oil company. I haven't worn it since his funeral. Tonight was my chance to take off my shirt and jeans and... well, dress to kill. What a let-down this is.'

'You look like the kind of man who loves a good suit,' answered McCormick. 'Fancy offices for your staff, Bach over the speakers... I bet you get suited up daily, just to look good in front of your subordinates.'

The domineering figure spat a laugh.

'I'm Nicholas bloody Grant. I don't have to impress anyone.'

McCormick could have smiled, were it not for the terrible truth behind Grant's words. With the exception of Shannon, none of his friends had ever laid eyes on Grant in the flesh. For a year his friends had waged war against a name: an invisible figure with a larger-than-life reputation. Like gravity, or oxygen, or perhaps even the work of God, nobody saw Nicholas Grant in his physical form, but his impact was everywhere.

'We don't have much in common,' Grant continued, 'but I have to appreciate *your* drive to not impress people either. Your name will be forgotten the moment your friends are found and destroyed, but that doesn't seem to discourage you. I like that.'

'Oh, don't try finding common ground between us,' said McCormick wryly, 'I'm sure I couldn't possibly measure up to you.'

'What do you mean?' asked Grant with a smile. 'You mow down your enemies with the same mentality as me. You have only one goal, and anything and any*one* is expendable in order to reach it. Isn't that right? You must have known the death sentence you gave to Arnold Salter the moment you took his keycard, even if you released him to ease the weight on your conscience. And now his young ones will be cast into the Inner City. Always happens when a staff member dies. You must have known that too, but you took his keycard anyway. He had three kids, you know. And his wife died two years ago. His children only had a father to rely on.'

McCormick dipped his head.

I won't let him make me feel guilty. He won't trick me into thinking our side is as morally wrong as his.

'Tragic, right?' said Grant, seizing McCormick by a clump of his remaining hair and demanding further eye contact. 'You see yourself as the deliverer of all things good, and the saviour of suffering people, but you and your servants tear apart the lives of the innocent just like I do. Leadership... isn't it lonely?'

'I've lived my life around friends... I could never be lonely. Not like you.'

'Your friends are dying out!' Grant shouted, half laughing. 'Raj Singh lies dead and decapitated outside his old school. Last month Oliver took away Charlie Coleman. Before that we tortured Daniel Amopoulos to death, before that we found Rachael Watts' body in the wreckage of a car, and before *that* Ben Christie—'

'*I get the point.*'

He made me raise my voice. Nicholas Grant is getting to me.

'Spitfire's Rise gets lonelier with every failed mission,' Grant whispered into his ear. 'Your shining stars are flickering out one by one, as if they *know* their universe is dying. The sky is getting dark, and your house is growing quiet. How long until the last star goes out?'

The first tear ran down McCormick's cheek, as if it were trying to flee the conversation.

'Doctor?' asked Grant. 'You do have something to say, right?'

McCormick wiped his fingers over his face, and gasped a sentence.

'The pain of missing someone is always worth it for the joy of having known them. Always.'

'What the hell is that supposed to mean?'

'It means that even though I miss the friends you killed, I can look back on a year that was far less lonely than yours.'

McCormick had never taken a punch before. Grant's closed fist struck against his chin, and his head keeled to one side as his brain tried to work out how to balance itself. Grant was yelling something, but no words registered in his mind.

When his sight found its way to the door, two of the three faces were smiling. The odd one out, curiously, was Oliver Roth.

'You can hit me all you want,' McCormick rasped, 'but it won't change the facts. My friends and I practically took down your empire tonight. Four against infinity, and *we're winning.*'

'And it'll all be for nothing in a matter of seconds. A circuit-break alert sounded the moment your little girl fired that sniper bullet, and it even indicated where the break came from. Last I heard, my men were about three minutes away from replacing the Perimeter Point she shot. I don't know what you think your bomb's going to do, if it even exists, but it'll go off ten minutes too late.'

Perimeter Point… Raj was close, calling them 'border points'.

Raj… another shining star that flickered out under my leadership.

McCormick felt his body falling to the side, but steadied himself just in time. Nicholas Grant packed a serious punch. The white-haired dictator wandered to Marshall's mahogany desk with a little joy in his step, removed a key from a drawer, and unlocked the plastic covering that surrounded a black switch on the giant computer. McCormick's eyes followed Grant's to the digital clock on the wall, which he had not noticed before that moment. It read '10:16:23 p.m., 19/05/ 0001'.

Thirteen and a half minutes without breaking. Easy peasy.

'That "Kate" you were talking to over the radio,' Grant started. 'Kate Arrowsmith, if I remember right. How accurate's her watch?'

'Set to Big Ben. Remember that thing?'

'Collateral damage. But it's good to know that our clocks are synchronised. I want to know exactly how long I have to deal with her threat.'

You and me both.

'So I have a few questions to ask,' Grant continued. 'Iain, is Gwen nearly here?'

'She tells me she is,' Marshall muttered from the entrance. McCormick detected resentment in Marshall's voice; presumably he despised his office being occupied by his colleagues.

'You'll like Gwen Crossland,' Grant said to McCormick. 'She's *very* persuasive.'

'I didn't spend my last Christmas running around and planting bombs just to give the game away with thirteen minutes to go.'

'We'll let her be the judge of that. And it's not just the bomb I'm interested in. How *did* you shelter so many people in the depths of England, against all my satellites, thermal imaging technology and random clone searches? More importantly, where the hell *are* you sheltering? Once my shield's up and we're done with your little weapon, I'll want some answers to those questions too.'

McCormick's breath held itself inside his throat.

He doesn't know where Spitfire's Rise is. Alex didn't give it away after all.

But that's not the point here. Grant won't need to go after us once he's raised the shield. He'd be hunting us for revenge, not strategy.

'Ah,' chuckled Grant with a slow nod, '*now* you're nervous. Which reminds me. Iain, Nathaniel, how anxious has the good doctor been since his capture?'

'No more than you'd expect,' answered Pearce from the back of the room. 'Actually, his mood's the same as when we first met him on Floor F.'

'So if his nerves haven't changed, it's fair to say we haven't walked into the blast radius by coming here?'

Pearce shrugged.

'If it were me, I'd take him on a tour of Floor B and watch for a change of expression.'

'Give me a break,' McCormick answered with a limp cough. 'It's late at night, and I've done a year's worth of jogging today. I'm tired.'

Grant smiled.

'Iain,' he said, 'get on the phone to every section officer in New London and order them to inspect their areas *fast*. I want the HPFC searched, I want every room the rebels have ever visited to be turned upside-down, I want vehicle ports torn apart and *every* officers' sector gone over inch by inch. Nathaniel, load up some security files and find out which of our rooms were targeted around Christmastime.' He flashed a proud pair of shiny blue eyes towards his twitching prisoner. 'And thanks for giving that part away, you old fool.'

A phone rang on Marshall's desk. Marshall jogged across his office and answered. Sadly, the conversation did not take much time.

'Nick,' said Marshall, 'the Perimeter Point has been replaced.'

Nicholas Grant laughed, lifted the plastic cover at his side and rested his fingers on the black computer switch.

'Dr McCormick,' he said, 'it's a beautiful coincidence that you're here to watch my empire become utterly invincible – and all before your secret weapon had any chance to make a difference. Iain, turn on your TV. I want to see a security feed to the outside of the Citadel. It's a shame we'll be indoors for the man-made northern lights, but watching my victory on television will have to do.'

Marshall obeyed, and flicked around with his remote control until he found a video feed from the upper battlements. The view stretched across the English countryside, soon to be as isolated from New London as Sydney Opera House.

McCormick looked back at Nicholas Grant, just in time to see him flick the switch and activate the AME shield.

Chapter 25

McCormick had never been keen on videogames, but he had seen the 'undeserved death face' in plenty of children whose characters had unexpectedly got shot or fallen from high platforms. When the switch was flipped and nothing changed on Marshall's enormous computer, Grant mirrored those children's expressions perfectly.

'*What the hell do you mean "coordination error"?!*' he screamed, droplets of saliva landing on the offending screen. '*I just bloody replaced the Perimeter Point!*'

McCormick could not hide his smile. Grant started to pace around the borders of the room, looking for something on his three-walled computer that would make everything right again. Unsuccessful, he glared at McCormick, his neck and shoulders trembling. McCormick decided to speak before somebody forced him to.

'I may be a mathematician,' he said, 'but I know a thing or two about physics. And it looks like you organised your circuits in series instead of parallel. Maybe you had to, given the nature of the shield and how it depends on every single coordinate working. But it means your Perimeter Points are like Christmas tree lights: once the circuit's broken, *you can't tell how many are faulty at the same time.* I imagine you've worked out where I'm going with this.'

Grant thumped his fist onto Marshall's desk with so much force that he almost sent mahogany splinters into his muscles.

'Long story short,' McCormick finished, 'you don't really think my "little girl" fought her way to the battlements to shoot *one* of them, do you? Your field must be littered with dozens of broken Perimeter Points.'

Grant had stopped listening. He stomped his way across the carpet to shout at his allies.

'Iain,' he began, 'the borders are *your* responsibility. Get every one of those things along the northern wall looked at and replaced.'

'That'll take a good hour or two.'

'I don't give a flying rat's arse. *Do it.*'

Marshall rolled his eyes the moment Grant looked away.

What's it like being you, Iain Marshall? Taking orders from a boss who consumed your company and used it to shape world history? How do you feel working for a tyrant who made you build an army and conquer a nation, while he put his feet up and listened to Bach?

'If you're interested,' Pearce said to Grant, 'while you were busy shouting at the computer I got a message from Adam King.'

'Who?'

'Archives manager. He found where the Christmastime raids were targeted. They were spread all across Floor Z.'

'Well, that's helpful,' spat Grant, throwing his head upward in disgust.

'Maybe it's more helpful than you think. He compiled a list of the targeted rooms and mapped them out – turns out they make an approximately straight line, all the way from the outer walls to the border of Inner City.'

Grant froze in place, and glared at Pearce as if he were the man responsible.

'Every one of those rooms needs inspecting, Nathaniel. Get people on it *now*. I've got a bad feeling there are explosives in every single one of them.'

'Really?'

'From one end of Outer City to the other? In a straight line? Engage your bloody brain. He wants to blow a tunnel through the walls for the prisoners to escape!'

Poker face... poker face...

Grant began to laugh, and McCormick tried to turn his head away from his enemies. The dictator barked a tirade of commands, sending every clone on Floor Z to the stretch of rooms on King's list. McCormick looked at the clock, and found eleven minutes remaining. When he looked forward again, Grant was staring into his face.

'Game over,' Grant said with a beaming smile. 'Either my clones find your explosives and defuse them, or they go off and you create a death tunnel for tens of thousands of escapees to get shot in. A pretty awful plan if I may say so, but I suppose you couldn't do much better on the lower floors.'

McCormick sighed.

'So I guess you have a little time to spare,' he said. 'Do you offer last requests?'

'Not normally, no.'

'But in my case?'

'You're welcome to ask.'

McCormick looked at Grant's face, and used a voice that made his plea sound as gentlemanly as possible.

'Before I die, I'd like to know what this war is truly about.'

Grant began to laugh, longer and louder than he had all evening.

'You think we're opponents in a *war*?' he asked. 'You're

nothing more than civil unrest! An unwelcome brawl! A minor inconvenience from dead men walking! For you, it must look like the biggest war humanity has ever fought. But from my perspective—'

'Answer my question. Now, please.'

Grant smiled, almost entertained by McCormick's attempt at a command.

'I'm going to miss you, Joseph. May I call you Joseph? It's a shame we'll only ever get this one chance to talk.'

'Then let's make it count. Is this about world domination? Is that your master plan?'

'World domination,' Grant repeated with childlike laughter. 'I dislike that phrase. I don't want to dominate the world. I just want to subdue it.'

'But *why*?'

McCormick was not expecting an answer. When Grant gave one, his heart stood still.

'Simple. To cull the human population.'

The breath caught in McCormick's throat, and he could not ask for details. But Grant sensed the question.

'Nine billion people live in this world. That's about six billion too many. Everyone goes on about wanting to "save the world", but the world looked after itself just fine before humans came along. If it needs saving, it needs saving from *us*.'

McCormick found himself muted. Just when he thought nothing else could surprise him about life on the upper floors, the great Nicholas Grant – son of an oil tycoon – had revealed himself to be an eco-warrior. But not the progressive, philanthropic type, like those who had protested government inaction on climate change before Takeover Day. A rich, powerful, *genocidal* eco-warrior.

'Once the power of humans has withered, it'll give the planet some time. Rainforests will grow back. Polar ice caps will stop melting. Nature will have its oceans back. And once there are too few humans left to wreck the world again, we'll close down the Citadels across the globe, purge the clones and allow the survivors to rebuild. But that'll be generations from now. I don't suppose I'll live long enough to see the world safe again.'

'What you're suggesting is monstrous…' McCormick said as he found his voice again.

'Monstrous? Consider this, doctor. The end of every geological era – Triassic, Jurassic and so on – is marked by a mass extinction. The meteor that killed the dinosaurs was the Cretaceous–Paleogene extinction event, which killed three quarters of all animal species. The Permian–Triassic extinction event killed ninety-six per cent of *everything*. But those extinctions took place over thousands, maybe millions of years.'

Grant walked to within a metre of McCormick, so he could lower his face to finish his point.

'We're in the middle of a man-made extinction event *right now*. Up to ten thousand species vanish every year – that's *thousands* of times higher than the natural rate. And this is just over a couple of hundred years. Just imagine what we'd do over the course of a million!'

McCormick made the mistake of looking into Grant's eyes, and saw his unbridled enthusiasm. He believed every word, and worst of all, he knew that science backed him up.

McCormick dipped his eyes away from Grant's stare. At least a dozen people in his life had been part of the climate change protests before Takeover Day. If they were still alive they were now being kept in the Citadels, due to be killed off by a rich man in the glorious name of 'saving the world' – as if *they* were the people the world needed saving from.

'This is the first time in the known history of the Earth,' Grant continued, 'that a mass extinction has been caused by one of its own species. If it were any other species, we'd wipe them out and call it saving the world. So tell me... who are the *real* monsters?'

McCormick raised his head again.

'The real monsters,' he answered, 'are those who force whole families into concrete prisons, then collect the bodies of their starved children.'

At the back of the room, Marshall took the opportunity to interrupt.

'Radio message, Nick,' he said. 'Kate Arrowsmith got six Perimeter Points.'

McCormick's broken face lit up just a little. Grant's culling of the human race was not a certainty just yet.

'Six? How long will it take to—'

'An hour. Maybe more.'

Grant gave McCormick his deepest head teacher stare, before turning and heading for the exit.

'Well sod it, then,' he shouted, 'I'm staying in my quarters until the show's ready. Or at least until this bomb scare is sorted.'

'You're not watching the prisoner?' asked Roth.

'No. We're leaving him with Iain.'

'We?' asked Pearce.

'Yes. Nathaniel, you're going to your own office. Oliver, you're going downstairs to hunt rebels. Try not to get killed again. Iain, you stay here. And when Gwen Crossland arrives, tell her she's a slow cow. Stay close to your phones, gentlemen.'

As Grant passed through the exit, McCormick shouted after him.

'Hey Nick,' he yelled. 'May I call you Nick?'

Grant did not turn around.

'Sorry,' he answered, 'did I just hear a dead man talking?'

'Probably. But you're forgetting one thing about the human race.'

'And what's that?'

McCormick gave a proud smile.

'It's made up of people like Ewan and Kate.'

Grant abandoned McCormick without another word. With a shrug, Pearce walked out and made his way towards his own office.

Marshall stepped further inside. At first, Roth refused to leave.

'I know what you're thinking,' Roth snapped at his boss, 'and don't be stupid. Grant will string you up if you torture him for information.'

'Why, what would you do? Because I know what I'd do in *your* position.'

'What's that?'

'Get the hell downstairs like you've been commanded, and clear up the other three. *Now.*'

Roth hesitated, but ultimately obeyed, as Marshall drew out his handgun. McCormick and Marshall were left alone long enough for a quick glance at the clock, which revealed eight minutes remaining. Not one second later, Gwen Crossland walked into the room.

'How can I help you, gentlemen?' she asked softly.

McCormick bit his lip. This tiny ageing woman looked like the opposite of a typical villain, but there was a little something in her facial expression that told him she was a perfect fit on the inside.

'Nick says you're a slow cow,' said Marshall.

Crossland gave a discreet smile with the corners of her lips, but no further response.

'We need your help extracting information from this man,' Marshall continued.

'The location of a mysterious weapon, if I heard right.'

'No, we found that. My soldiers are disarming it as we speak. He has other information we need.'

'The location of his headquarters,' said Crossland, adjusting the top button of her cardigan. 'Well, you won't get that in eight minutes. I could perhaps get you a precise address by the end of the week.'

'A precise address? Like you managed with Daniel Amopoulos? Or Alex Ginelli?'

Daniel... Alex... two of my boys. Will I ever know what you did to them?

'Neither of them had the address we needed to extract,' Crossland continued. 'This man will have a much higher likelihood of knowing. And if your traditional methods fail, call your friend Nathaniel and clone this person. We haven't used the memory transfer technology since...'

Marshall turned to her with a transparent look of surprise.

'Well,' Crossland said, 'I probably shouldn't talk in front of a patient as if he's not in the room.'

She pursed her lips, and turned to face the exit.

'I'll be in my lower office, on Floor G,' she finished, 'setting up my equipment. If you could dispatch a team of clones to escort him down Stairwell 32, I'll be happy to meet them there.'

Floor G, Stairwell 32, thought McCormick, *far, far away from the luxury of Marshall's office. Right next to the satellite control room, if I've memorised the maps right.*

The thought filled him with uninhibited dread.

When the time comes, should I tell her we'll both be in the blast radius?

Before Crossland could leave the room, a string of buzzes sounded on Marshall's radio. He held out a flat hand to stop her in her tracks, and brought the radio to his ear.

McCormick had not learned the clones' coded language, but a translation became visible on Marshall's horrified face. He turned a shade of maroon, and his quivering gun hand pointed his pistol at McCormick's head.

'Nothing found on Floor Z,' he snarled. '*Nothing*.'

McCormick did not move a muscle. Not even in his face. Especially not in his face.

'Six minutes until half past, and the bomb is nowhere to be found. Gwen... better get to work now.'

Gwen Crossland shook her head.

'I've told you before,' she said with the slow voice of a playschool leader to a three-year-old. 'Just like I told Nicholas when we had Ginelli. My work is not fast food. It takes time and precision. I can promise results that are accurate and trustworthy. But I cannot produce them at the speed that you and all the other impatient men want me to. If you have six minutes, my methods can't help you with any reliable accuracy.'

She walked away from Marshall's office, and her faint footsteps didn't take long to leave McCormick's earshot.

'For the record,' McCormick said to Marshall, 'I don't think six minutes is long enough either.'

'You'd be amazed what I can do in six minutes,' Marshall answered. 'Gwen can spout whatever crap she wants about her precious methods, but I've got methods of my own.'

Marshall lowered his handgun just a little, and squeezed the trigger. A horrible *bang* sounded, and the bullet struck McCormick in the shinbone.

Chapter 26

'Guys!' Kate screamed into the radio. 'Talk to me! Where are you?'

Her eyesight was blurred with tears. The Floor D corridors were a mess of unfamiliar sights and the layout was barely navigable.

'About half a corridor from the stairwell to Floor C,' came Ewan's voice. 'If a miracle happens we can make it.'

Raj used to believe in miracles. I don't think I ever did.

Her whole world was racing through her mind. The thought of her grandfather figure, trapped in a mystery location somewhere on the upper floors. Marshall's computer not far above her. Mum and Dad in New London. The possibility of James still being alive. Her dead boyfriend. But more than anything else, the cigar-shaped detonator in her left hand.

She had dialled in the code the moment McCormick had revealed it, not trusting her panicked memory to remember it later. His secret weapon had been armed for what had felt like several hours, with the top cover closed to prevent her pressing the button by accident.

Kate didn't know what the world would look like once she pressed the button. She only knew that the closer she was to Floor B when it happened, the easier it would be to reach Marshall's computer while everyone was distracted.

'Kate,' came Alex's voice, 'we need a favour.'

'What is it?'

'We found the stairwell to Floor C. The security door is humans only, and the keycard we stole has been cancelled already.'

Kate wiped her face, leaned against the nearest wall and let out a moan. She knew what was coming.

'If you find a human, kill them and take their keycard. Ewan and I didn't find anybody on the way here.'

10:26 P.M.

Shannon had not been frightened at first. Not until Lorraine had burst into tears. Her cries had been loud enough to hear halfway down the street, but she didn't seem to care. The attic's tiny size amplified the volume as the sounds echoed off the walls.

'Do you want me to be in charge of the phone?' Shannon asked.

'Not a chance,' Lorraine replied.

Shannon knew better than to argue. Perhaps Lorraine blamed herself for McCormick's capture. And, in all likelihood, his eventual death once Dad was finished with him.

Shannon had vivid memories of Daniel Amopoulos' torture, which she had kept to herself. Nobody in Spitfire's Rise needed to know that her father had made her watch. Or how it had ended for Daniel, and what probably lay in store for McCormick too.

Unless, of course, his bomb helped the others rescue him.

'Lorraine,' she said, 'I don't know what's happening in four minutes, but if you're not up to talking then I have to be. Tell me everything I need to know—'

'Maybe it'll mean we win the battle, but not the war. Or maybe we won't win either. But once it goes off, *everything* changes.'

Lorraine lay her head in her cupped hands, and rested her elbows on the table to support its weight.

'I told you about Joey Shetland tonight,' she said, 'and my twenty years of trying to make the world less ugly.'

'It was brave of you to tell me. Come to think of it, your whole life's been an act of bravery.'

Lorraine ignored the compliment.

'Nursing taught me that sometimes, ugliness can't be avoided. And combat has taught me that sometimes you have to *cause* ugliness to make the world better.'

Shannon took a moment to remember Keith Tylor, Grant's number two assassin, who she had stabbed to death the night she first met the Underdogs. That had been ugly enough, and it had made the world better. But she wasn't sure it was the type of ugliness Lorraine meant.

'McCormick's bomb will make the world ugly?' asked Shannon.

Lorraine nodded, but offered no details.

'In a few minutes' time,' Shannon continued, 'you'll be explaining the whole thing to Ewan. If it'll make it easier, you can practice with me right now.'

Lorraine gave Shannon a vicious eye, but turned her seat in her direction. Apparently she thought it was a good idea.

'Lorraine,' asked Shannon, 'where did McCormick plant the bomb?'

10:27 P.M.

The return to Spitfire's Rise should have felt warm and welcome. Instead, Jack felt embarrassed. He had found that replacement home at a speed that had impressed everyone, only for everyone to wonder why they'd bothered once Mark had called them with the good news.

Jack laid his box of weapons on the grass before he opened the trapdoor and leapt inside, and tried his best not to feel ungrateful. They were back in Spitfire's Rise, a place that had become more of a home to him than any of the houses from his previous life. In fact, his time away from the house had reminded him exactly how much he both loved it and depended on it.

I did my duty and served the others well, he thought to himself, *and ultimately it was all for nothing.*

Then again, that's what to expect when you live your life for the sake of others. Unrewarded servitude.

Jack bit his lip and let out the quietest sigh he could. Reward or not, it had still been the right thing to do. And if Spitfire's Rise were ever in danger of being exposed again, he would take the same actions again. His personal preferences had no right to enter into it.

But serving others did not mean they would like you. Gracie had been colder to him than frostbite ever since he had told her the truth. She and Simon followed him into the tunnel, and Thomas brought up the rear with a small box of food. Once they reached the entrance, Mark was waiting next to the Memorial Wall.

'That's everything, is it?' he muttered.

301

'Yeah,' answered Jack. 'What's that in your hand?'

Mark lifted up the bottle of wine, and Jack read the label closely.

'Crémant de-something-or-other-Frenchie,' he said. 'You shouldn't be offering that to underage teens, you know.'

'I think we need a bottle,' Mark answered as Simon and Gracie dumped their boxes of weapons, and Thomas carried his food in the direction of the farm. 'One way or another, we're writing history tonight. Either we lose this war forever, and we'll drink to the death of Great Britain. Or the guys will return victorious, and we'll drink until we believe it.'

Gracie crept up close and brought her eyes level with the bottle's label.

'Be careful with that,' she said. 'It looks like strong stuff. It's... seven hundred and fifty ml.'

Jack opened his mouth to correct her, but shut it again when he remembered he was her least favourite person in the world.

There was an odd sound at the door to the farm, like falling paper. Jack turned around. Thomas had dropped something from underneath his box of food whilst trying to open the tunnel door.

At the boy's feet were a bunch of envelopes – the ones Jack had told him to hide under McCormick's mattress and given no second thought to ever since. A look of fright appeared on Thomas' face as the envelopes landed face-up. The top one read 'Mark'.

The young man stormed over, ignoring Thomas' desperate protests, and ripped the envelope open.

'...I promised McCormick...'

Mark brushed Thomas to the side, and started to read. Jack ran over to look.

Dear Mark, the paper began.

10:28 P.M.

Ewan checked his watch, and swore.

He and Alex had been trapped in the stairwell to Floor C since they had arrived. So near to Marshall's computer, yet so far.

The lower door burst open, too fast for either of them to ready their weapons. Thankfully the intruder was Kate, with a golden keycard in one hand and her detonator in the other.

'You found a human then,' said Alex.

'Yeah,' said Kate. '...I knocked him out.'

Ewan looked at her face. It reminded him of his own face on Takeover Day, right after he realised he had made his first kill.

'Right,' said Alex, 'let's get going.'

'No,' said Ewan. 'Not for another minute and a half.'

His friends glared at him as if he had personally insulted them.

'Whatever that detonator does, I'd rather get my breath back now and take Floor C by surprise after it goes off.'

He didn't know whether Kate and Alex agreed with his strategy, but the suggestion of catching their breath was well-received. Kate climbed to the top step and sat down in front of the door.

She was afraid. Afraid enough for the detonator to tremble in both hands as she brought it close to her face. Ewan remembered McCormick's sadness when Kate had volunteered for the task. He had never been one to underestimate his soldiers, but he must have had his reasons.

There was only one decent thing to do. Ewan climbed to the top of the stairwell and sat down next to her.

'Alex,' he said, 'sit there.'

Alex rolled his eyes, but knew there was no time to argue. He sat down on Kate's other side as commanded. Between

303

them, Ewan could sense Kate's chaotic breathing through the rising and falling of her ribs.

'Kate,' he said, 'flip it open.'

Kate took several seconds to do so. Partly because of anxiety, striking at the most predictable but least convenient time, and partly because it was difficult to operate her twitching fingers.

But she did so, and the metal casing sprung open to reveal a solitary, harmless-looking clear button that would change the face of the war.

Ewan stuck out a thumb and aligned it next to Kate's. He glanced at Alex, who got the message and did the same.

'When the time comes,' said Ewan as their three thumbs lined up, 'you won't have to push it alone. None of us should feel alone right now.'

He had no doubt that Kate would have pushed the button herself either way. She didn't even know how to fail when it came to facing her fears. But this wasn't about *whether* she would do her duty. The trembling in her hand slowed down, and her breathing steadied.

'You guys are the best of friends,' she said.

Ewan smiled.

'United by our differences, guys,' he said.

'United.'

10:29 P.M.

McCormick was flat on his back, his shirt dampening in a growing pool of his own blood. But it didn't matter. Despite his blurred vision, he could see the time.

Fifty seconds.

Iain Marshall was no longer recognisable as the war veteran and arms dealer he had once been. He was panicked, and there was nothing more dangerous than a panicked man with a gun.

As demonstrated by the second and third bullets Marshall had fired: one into McCormick's shoulder and the other into his left hand.

'Tell me,' Marshall snarled. '*Tell me where you planted it.*'

McCormick swallowed, and dared to smile.

'In a minute.'

Marshall did not take the joke well. Grant's Head of Military was a man without control, utterly clueless about the war-changing event moments away, and McCormick could sense how much it scared him.

His fourth bullet struck McCormick in his lower thigh, a few inches above his knee. It hurt twice as much as the others, resting inside a big bunch of his nerves. McCormick yelled out, tears streaming down his face.

Forty seconds remained. Talking would occupy some time, and perhaps result in fewer bullets.

'The bombs are… are spread across Floor Z,' McCormick said. 'Exactly where Adam King told you.'

'They are *not!*' Marshall yelled. 'Even *you're* not stupid enough to have that kind of plan! The explosions would kill more civilians than they would save! Hundreds around the Inner City borders would die. Thousands would crush each other to death inside the corridors. My laser cannons and speed mines would start a massacre, and any survivors would get sniper bullets to the backs of their heads as they ran for the electric fences!'

'Oh,' McCormick answered with the friendliest face he could manage. 'We'll be sure to cross that idea off the list then.'

With twenty seconds remaining, Marshall was using up the last of his cool. He pushed a foot down against McCormick's wounded thigh, and pointed his handgun straight down.

'Tell me the truth,' he said, 'or I will shoot you at *point-blank range in the chest.*'

McCormick raised his hand – the one that had not yet been shot – and twirled a weak finger around the centre of his ribcage.

'This is my heart. Let's see how well you can aim.'

Marshall's aim was perfect. His fifth bullet struck McCormick exactly where he had pointed, and sheared through the muscles of his heart.

McCormick felt like the centre of his chest had been hit by a car. All strength left his body – his torso did not even bother to tremble – and the sensations in his nervous system began to fade. His time on Earth would only last as long as the oxygen in his brain, which his halted bloodstream would not refresh.

This is it... no going back now.

A voice echoed in his ears. Marshall, stomping back and forth after his moment of madness, was yelling.

'Whatever your plan is,' he screamed, with globs of saliva flying from his angry mouth, 'it won't do anything! Your war will be lost when the shield goes up, no matter how much of the Citadel you destroy! Don't you get it? However many labs and archives you burn to the ground, the computer around you will *still* be active. It's the *only* computer that has *any* control of the shield, and *nobody* in your team has *ever* come within *half a mile* of it!'

He's almost right.

None of them except me.

Even though his brain was running dry, McCormick was astonished by how much information could pass through it.

His first wave of memories focused on the final week of his life. He remembered his guilt at the pack of lies he had told his friends outside Oakenfold. No bombs had been planted on his visit before Christmas.

He remembered his delight as he had snatched the acid grenades in the HPFC, and how his destruction of the Central Power Generator had allowed him to pass to Floor B with nothing but a physical search. The X-ray machine on Floor D would have cost them the war.

He remembered how he had spent a whole night arguing with Lorraine Shepherd about the true nature of his operation.

His seizure at Spitfire's Rise had looked convincing enough. The cyst had been a convenient excuse for an operation, and one he could provide evidence for. But the only woman capable of operating had *hated* the idea of sealing their supply of NPN8 plastic explosives inside his abdomen.

Grant had called him fat the moment he had laid eyes on him. McCormick had hidden the extra weight from his friends under several layers of clothing, and carried the NPN8 inside his body for three days like his own destructive baby. Not long ago, the world's most powerful dictator had stood two feet away from a bellyful of high explosives.

The plan had always been to get out alive, and perhaps even reverse the operation. But McCormick was dead the moment Roth found him, and he had been smart enough to know it.

He hoped that Kate would one day forgive him for telling her the code, and asking her to kill him.

McCormick's head fell to the side, but he could not feel the carpet against his cheek. When he realised he could no longer read the time on the clock, he said goodbye to the world and closed his eyes.

In his last moments of brain activity, he thought of his years in the 3rd Durham Boys' Brigade, his holidays to Whitby with his long-gone parents, and the day he started university. He thought of the generations of students who had come and gone over the decades, and his honeymoon in Anglesey. He thought of his escape from depression. He thought of Ewan West, the closest lad he ever had to a son, and the words in the letter that awaited him at Spitfire's Rise. He thought of the thirty-nine years he had spent in marriage to Barbara, the two years Polly Jones had spent rebuilding him, and the 365 days he had spent with the best friends he had ever had.

Ewan, Kate, Lorraine, Thomas, all of you… I loved you so much. And Barbara…

Thank you, Barbara…

Not many rooms away from Joseph McCormick's body, Oliver Roth looked at his computer screen in disbelief, verging on horror. He had seen and heard every moment of the end of McCormick's life, spying on the CCTV system with the excuse of using it to find the remaining rebels.

He brought his hands to his face and clawed against his own skin. After every lesson Marshall had taught him about self-control, every lecture about strategic thinking, the same man had finished off McCormick with an impulsive gunshot to the heart.

Roth no longer knew what kind of death he had wanted for the old man, but his dream of 'sticking your head on the spike of an electric fence' had faded away during that conversation in the store room. One thing was for sure: he was overcome with a feeling that McCormick had deserved better.

Iain Marshall was right there onscreen, standing over the corpse of his greatest enemy, the furious expression on his face so stern that he must have known how much he had screwed up. Nathaniel Pearce couldn't interrogate a dead body. There would be no McCormick clone model either, like he had watched Crossland suggest over the CCTV, and no extractable memories that could reveal the location of Spitfire's Rise.

And on top of that, McCormick's bomb would not be stopped. Roth checked both the clock on his wall and the digital clock onscreen, both accurate to within a second of each other. They showed less than ten seconds until Kate Arrowsmith's watch read ten thirty.

'Iain,' he muttered to the psychotic idiot on his screen, 'Grant's going to kill you for this.'

Marshall wandered to his leather chair, but didn't have time to sit down and collect himself.

10:30:00 p.m., 19/05/0001. Somewhere below them all, a button was pressed.

The resulting explosion tore apart McCormick's body and everything within twenty metres of it, including Marshall, his entire office, and the final computer that held anything related to the AME shield. Iain Marshall had no time to react, or even notice the explosion, before he vanished into the fireball.

Roth did not see the explosion – just the sudden appearance of static on his screen and a moment's pause before the room shook horribly around him – but it was immediately obvious what had happened. Roth ran towards the exit into the Floor B corridor, jaw hung open in shock, as human staff began to scurry around in panic. Most of the way down the corridor, smoke emerged from Marshall's office.

Oliver Roth had never felt so saddened to be right. Given the choice between survival and victory, Joseph McCormick really had chosen victory.

Chapter 27

For the first few moments after they pressed the button, Ewan heard nothing. Just as he began to wonder whether the detonator had worked at all, the shockwave hit the stairwell and threw all three of them off the top step.

Ewan landed halfway down, bashing his ribs against the stairs. He cursed in pain, but was distracted by a sudden realisation.

That explosion came from above.

'Did anyone else feel…'

'Yeah,' said Alex, pulling himself up using the bannister. 'That came from one of the upper floors.'

Ewan hauled himself upright, and reached his uncoordinated hands in the direction of his pockets.

'Give me a second, I'm phoning comms.'

'Now?' asked Alex. 'Why not stick with the plan, and barge upstairs to grab McCormick while they're distracted?'

'We need to find out what the hell that was.'

As he inserted the battery into his phone, his eyes landed on Kate. She sat in silence, holding up her last victim's radio. Voices were starting to yell.

'Nick! Get to the bloody radio!'

Nathaniel Pearce...

'You'd better tell me what the hell that explosion was,' bellowed Nicholas Grant. 'It felt like it came from *your* floor!'

'It did!' came Pearce's wail. 'Iain's office is gone!'

The breath halted in Ewan's throat.

'Gone?' Grant screamed.

'Yes! Literally *gone*! I'm standing here right now... there's just a pile of black debris and walls splattered with fire! It's still burning now!'

Ewan looked around, and found confused expressions that mirrored his own. It all sounded too good to be true.

'The AME computer?'

'Destroyed,' Pearce wailed, like a man who had just lost a family member. 'The rebels have won. All my technology... all the research I ever did on AME... it's gone, and the computer's in a billion pieces...'

Hold on, thought Ewan, *did we seriously just win? How the hell did we do that?*

What did McCormick do?

Alex was pumping his fists in delight. Kate looked as confused as Ewan, but nonetheless she was smiling.

Ewan's phone powered up, and he started to dial.

'What about Iain?' Grant's voice asked through the radio.

He asked about the computer before he asked about Marshall. How revealing.

'His body's in here next to the desk. At least, I'm pretty sure it's him.'

'And McCormick?'

'...Nowhere to be seen.'

'Wait wait wait,' said Alex. 'Why did he ask about McCormick? Why on Earth would *he* be in Marshall's office?'

Ewan's brain had never been particularly fast when it came

to academic subjects, but his strategic instincts operated like lightning. If McCormick had entered Marshall's office – for the first time in his life – and the computer had suddenly been destroyed, there was only one logical explanation. The bomb had been with him all along.

And if McCormick could no longer be found, despite being guarded well enough to have no chance of escape, there was only one logical explanation for that too.

Lorraine answered the phone.

'Did she push the button?' came her tight, choking voice. One sentence alone was enough to reveal her level of distress.

'Yeah,' Ewan answered. 'We all did.'

A yell, strong enough to rattle Ewan's eardrum, sounded in his earpiece. It was loud enough to catch the attention of Alex and Kate.

'Lorraine?' Ewan asked. '…What just happened?'

Shannon had tuned herself out of the conversation. Listening to Lorraine's explanation had been traumatic enough the first time, and she already knew what had happened. Marshall was dead, his office and computer destroyed, and the AME project had been utterly annihilated just hours before it would have rendered her father invincible.

And all it had cost them was the life of Joseph McCormick.

Shannon hadn't had much longer to deal with the news than the strike team. Lorraine had finished her explanation about a minute before half past, which left Shannon mourning McCormick while he was still alive.

'Just come home,' Lorraine finished. 'The mission's over, and McCormick can't come with you. Get out while everyone's still distracted.'

Shannon could hear Ewan's voice shouting in the

background, but Lorraine hung up without letting him finish. She turned to Shannon with a look in her face that was nothing short of harrowing.

'The whole world's uglier now,' Lorraine groaned.

'My father lost his shield,' Shannon replied. 'He won't be invincible after all. It could have been uglier, I guess.'

But not much uglier.

It'll be even tougher for Lorraine once she gets home, and tells the others what she did.

'I couldn't stop Joey Shetland from killing himself,' she wailed. 'I couldn't save Callum Turner when his insulin ran out. I couldn't cure Roy Wolff's stomach cancer. And now I helped McCormick engineer his own death. What kind of nurse...'

'You can't save everyone, Lorraine.'

It was the only sentence that came to Shannon's mind, and she knew it wouldn't help. Lorraine rested her weary head in one hand, and stared deep into Shannon's eyes.

'Tell me you can forgive me for what I did.'

Shannon raised her eyebrows in surprise. She knew that Lorraine wanted comfort, and that comfort from anyone would do. But forgiveness was a big word to use so soon.

'I can understand why you did it,' she answered.

'But tell me you can *forgive* me...'

Shannon's mind wandered to the McCormick she had known and loved, who had taken her in and accepted her despite her background, and done more for her in three weeks than he ever could have known. She remembered his gentle humour, and his quiet but unrelenting love. Her thoughts rested on the first night she had met him, when he had stood over her in the clinic with his unforgettable warm smile.

A smile that would never return to Spitfire's Rise.

'Shannon?'

'I can understand why you did it,' she repeated.

When Oliver Roth had learned that his enemies had escaped, his main reaction was relief.

The destruction of Marshall's office had wiped out any chance of organising Floor Z. The soldiers scouring for fictional explosives had not been told their orders had expired. The surviving insurgents were able to vanish without a trace, victorious but without their leader.

Roth was just grateful to return to his room for the night. He staggered along his Floor A corridor, the last of his energy faded after an evening that had involved a fight in a burning Experiment Chamber, a rampage through the HPFC, escorting a high-profile prisoner through the darkness, and the violent death of Iain Marshall. And Roth knew that if it weren't for his boss' orders to hunt the other rebels, he could have died in the blast too.

He walked into his messy bedroom, dropped his helmet onto the floor, sauntered to his bedside and collapsed onto his covers with an ear against his pillow, half-focusing his eyes towards his personal armoury. Even in his own sanctuary, he was surrounded by instruments of death.

When Oliver Roth looked back on his short life, he didn't see much that mattered. There were a couple of old schoolmates he had liked, but he had focused more on his bullying victims. There had been vague hobbies, but his biggest efforts went on his social media presence. There had been plenty of decent teachers, none of whom he had respected. Now every one of them – from the pleasant but useless to the unbothered and ineffective – had all ended up inside their nearest Citadel. Some may have been dead.

Meanwhile, McCormick had achieved more than that whole bunch in the five minutes they had spent alone. And somehow, McCormick's departure from Earth didn't feel like an extra Underdog scalp. It felt like the world had lost a part of itself. The only man ever to have seen Oliver Roth's vulnerable side was dead, which was both a distress and a comfort.

Without moving himself from his bed, he kicked off his boots as angrily as he could. It had been more than a year since he last went to bed before midnight, but he just wanted his brain to shut off for the night. The anger infesting his thoughts was unbearable, and it came from a perfect storm of three different sources.

First, the fact that McCormick had seen through him. Roth never *had* placed his trust in another person. He had plenty of mates at school, but no real friends. And certainly no girlfriend who would expect him to open up. He *was* neither abused nor loved, and his apathy towards the human race was probably the biggest reason he'd been able to slip so easily into his job.

The second reason for his anger was the obvious one: he had failed the night in every conceivable way. He had let Ewan out of the Experiment Chamber instead of letting him burn. He had been moments too late to stop McCormick from revealing the code to Kate. But his biggest mistake had come from a rare moment of compassion, when he had offered McCormick his shirt back. It had covered up the scar which, in hindsight, must have been where someone had inserted the bomb. Without that shirt, Iain Marshall would have been smart enough to realise what was going on.

Finally, and worst of all, he knew it was too late to change anything about himself. McCormick had tried in vain to bring him away from darkness, but he must have known that Oliver Roth could not be turned. His allies would kill him the moment he became ineffective. Maybe five years earlier, a man like McCormick could have changed him. But even at the young age of fourteen, Roth had already made the decisions that would define the rest of his life. McCormick may have talked about lives being falsely predestined, but Oliver Gabriel Roth would have to remain the murderous assassin forever.

Roth buried his face into the pillow, and took a breath deep enough to rupture a weaker man's lungs. Whichever way he looked, in his home life and his work life, as an assassin and as a person, as a potential hero and as a certain villain, he was a failure.

Chapter 28

At five o'clock in the morning on the first anniversary of Takeover Day, Ewan was alone in the basement.

My family were murdered a year ago today.

His new family at Spitfire's Rise all knew where he was. But they knew not to disturb him. Just like Lorraine, who had sealed herself in the clinic again, Ewan had found his own space and planned to keep it all morning. He sat on the concrete floor alone, with McCormick's envelope in his hand.

For the eleventh or twelfth time, Ewan read the stone tablet in front of him, and remembered a personal detail about each of the chiselled names.

UNDERDOGS MEMORIAL WALL
In loving memory of those who fought and
gave their lives in the Great British Rebellion.
Sarah Best
Callum Turner
Joe Horn
Elaine Dean
Arian Shirazi
Teymour Shirazi

Rosanne Tate
Miles Ashford
Chloe Newham
Tim Carson
Roy Wolff
Mike Ambrose
Beth Foster
David Riley
Val Riley
Sally Sharpe
Svetlana Karpov
Ben Christie
Rachael Watts
Daniel Amopoulos
Charlie Coleman
Raj Singh
Joseph McCormick

Twenty-three dead in the space of a year. It seemed almost bloodless compared to the wars of old. But of an army that had numbered thirty-three including Shannon, only ten remained. The smallest army in world history.

But they had won the night. That particular night, at least. Against odds which should have been insurmountable, they had earned the right to stay in the war. Perhaps in a month or so they would feel proud, but that morning Spitfire's Rise had transformed into a dull, sad building without atmosphere or character. The loss seemed bigger than one man.

Kate and Thomas had seized the farm for themselves, to share long hugs and wallow in understandable misery. Even with Ewan and Alex's support, Kate still blamed herself for McCormick's death. Unfairly of course, but logic and facts didn't matter in the face of guilt and heavy anxiety. Ewan now understood why McCormick had been so opposed to Kate being the one who pressed the button: it was a heavy burden for an anxiety sufferer to bear, and she would bear it for a long time.

Alex had felt awful too, but his worries were different. Something about another gap in his memory, when he had apparently proved to Lorraine and Shannon that Spitfire's Rise was safe. He had no recollection of the conversation, and the women were reluctant to give him any details. It was driving him crazy.

Ewan decided the hours had dragged for long enough. It was time to open the envelope and read McCormick's letter. He had pushed the idea to the back of his mind for as long as he could, occupying his time by reading the names on the Memorial Wall again and again. The letter would be the last communication Ewan and McCormick would ever have, and the thought of their relationship ending terrified him. As long as he refused to open the envelope, there would always be something new from his mentor to look forward to.

But he owed it to McCormick to read his dying words. Ignoring the letter would be worse than clapping his hands over his ears like an infant, and would silence the man's performance before his final curtain.

Ewan held his breath and tore open the envelope. Jack had turned the generator back on after he realised nobody was going to bed, so there was more than enough light to read.

The words were difficult to stomach.

My dear friend Ewan,

Although I take no pleasure in writing this letter – if you're reading it I must be another casualty of this war – I'm happy for the opportunity to say some important things to you. It'll be difficult to put my collection of unordered thoughts onto paper, but I'll do my best.

I know it's tragic to lose anyone from our family, but try to avoid wasting your days feeling sorry for me. I lived to a ripe old age by modern standards, and spent my years filled with joy. I lived to watch so many people grow into their best selves, and by the end of my life I became the only war leader in history to know every one of my soldiers personally. No matter how I met my death, whatever pain or despair I may have felt at the end, it cannot cancel out the wonderful years I've lived.

I hope I found the opportunity to tell you this, but either way – you and the Oakenfold students were my finest work. I remember the state we found each other in on Takeover Day – the state we were all in that day – and I compare it to the fine young adults you have become. The old Ewan West is dead, buried underneath the hero who took his place. So never let your troubled past get in the way of your self-belief. Never think that your diagnoses make you a lesser person, or 'not good enough' to be who you're meant to be. And never feel guilty about what the old Ewan West did to Polly. Regardless of what happened, regardless of how much I've missed her and Barbara, I haven't cried for them in almost a year. I've been too busy watching you all with a proud smile.

It won't surprise you that I'm naming you as my successor. I want you to be the soldier who leads Britain in the charge against Nicholas Grant. I know you'll lead the Underdogs well, in your own special style that I could never have imitated, and I know that our friends will follow you. It may be a big task, but it's a task with your name written all over it.

And since I've spent most of this letter telling you what not to do, I'll spend some time giving you a little leadership advice.

First, listen to people. If your soldiers feel valued they'll support you forever. You don't have to let them control your decisions, but their thoughts are always worth listening to.

Second, make sure you know your soldiers' strengths. Know the right person for the right job. And make sure they know their own strengths too. It's easy to forget them when times are difficult.

Third, recognise that you will make mistakes. I made plenty. But the last person who never made a mistake never made anything.

And finally, love your soldiers. Even if they're a pain in the arse, love them.

We might actually win this war, Ewan. Grant may see it as impossible, and once in a while you will be tempted to think so too, but it's not beyond us. And the reason is simple: we are the Underdogs, and history has shown us that the one thing dictators have to fear is underdogs. They are the ones who start revolutions, win civil wars, and show off the incredible strength hidden inside regular people. If you win this war – if this small, untrained militia of less than a dozen brings down Nicholas Grant – if a group of teenagers from a special school defeats an army of millions – it will prove the might of underdogs, once and forever.

We are Britain's last line of defence – outnumbered, outgunned, but not outwitted. We are the people who will bring civilisation back, who history will remember for a thousand years. We are the Underdogs of Spitfire's Rise.

Do me proud, my boy. You don't need someone like me for this.

With love,

Dr Joseph McCormick.

PS – the pain of missing someone is always worth it for the joy of having known them. Always.

And with that, McCormick's friendship with Ewan was over.

But a part of him lived on in Ewan, clear and inextinguishable. That was something, at least.

Ewan felt a throbbing in the back of his head: his usual doubting reaction when someone told him they trusted him. McCormick's kind of trust could change anyone's life, but the inevitable question lingered in Ewan's mind.

'Am I worth it?' he breathed to himself, unaware that he had spoken.

The Memorial Wall did not answer him, and the words on the letter did not change. McCormick had said everything he was ever going to say, and the questions from then on would be Ewan's to answer.

'Worth what?' came a friend's wounded voice from the stairs. Ewan closed his eyes.

'Nothing, Shannon.'

She reached the basement, wandered over to the Memorial Wall and sat down on the floor next to him. Ewan was surprised when she leaned against him and rested her head against his chin. But he accepted, and placed an arm around her shoulder.

Ewan lay his letter on the ground, face down.

'I know you're not OK,' said Shannon, 'so I won't ask. Just remember that you're not alone.'

'What did yours say?'

Shannon seemed surprised at the bluntness of his question. Or maybe the fact he had even asked. The letters had been private, after all.

But Ewan's prediction was right. Shannon didn't mind sharing.

'He told me he was proud of me,' she said, 'and how great it was that I chose the good of humanity instead of a life of luxury with my dad. He told me I was just what the team needed – the right balance of fiery determination and lucid self-control, if I got his words right.'

Ewan smiled, fighting back tears. It sounded enough like McCormick.

'He also said I'll need to prepare myself for New London,' Shannon continued. 'I can't go on forever just doing missions in the countryside. Before this war ends, I'll have to go back and face him.'

She lifted her head from Ewan, so she could turn and face him.

'And he told me to look after you,' she finished. 'When times get tough, you'll need the support of your girlfriend.'

McCormick worked it out? He knew what was going on between us?

Hell, he probably worked it out before we did.

'So what about you?' she asked. 'What did he say?'

Ewan looked at the face-down paper, and decided to tell her. She had trusted him, so it was only right to trust her back. She had earned it.

'He wants me to lead the war against your father.'

Ewan did not know what reaction to expect, but Shannon smiled.

'He gave me a bunch of leadership advice,' he continued,

'then told me not to worry because the others will follow me. I don't know what to make of that.'

'I think you *are* worth it,' said Shannon. 'Whether or not you realise it, the others look up to you.'

Ewan looked at her with blatant doubt in his eyes.

'You're usually the only one in the battlefield who knows what's going on,' she continued. 'The one who keeps fighting when others lose motivation. Someone with a chaotic background who can think straight anyway. The guy who fights tooth and nail so naturally because he's been doing it his whole life. It's enough to inspire anyone.'

Ewan started to laugh.

'Shut your mouth and listen,' said Shannon. 'Since I first met you, you've been to the Inner City and got out alive. You've gone to Oakenfold and escaped. Last night you got up to Floor C without dying. I know you don't realise, but the others are amazed by all that. If you talk to them, they'll listen. If you lead, they'll follow.'

Ewan decided not to tell Shannon she was wrong. McCormick himself had advised him to listen to his soldiers.

And incredibly, she changed his mind.

'I guess there's only one way to find out,' he said.

Shannon smiled, and rested her head against him once more. They gazed at the Memorial Wall together, their eyes fixed on the lowest name.

McCormick had passed the baton, and Ewan would pick it up and run. And with the Underdogs ripped apart by grief, the sooner he started the better.

The more he thought about it, the more Ewan realised he was up to the challenge. He had spent the first sixteen years of his life around people who had forced an identity on him, who had made him believe he was nothing more than a nasty kid with special needs and a boatload of personal issues. But now, with him at the helm of the Underdogs, it would be *his* turn to tell the world who he was.

It was time for Ewan West to take centre stage. For him to speak, for the world to listen, and for his friends to win the war.

THE

UNDERDOGS

WILL RETURN.

For the latest updates about further books
in the Underdogs series, visit
the author's website at chrisbonnello.com
or the series' Facebook page at
facebook.com/Underdogsnovel.

Read on for an extract of the third book in the series –
Underdogs: Acceleration …

Chapter 1

Oliver Roth had felt uneasy when Grant called him to Floor B. It was an unusual feeling. The great Nicholas Grant had never made him uneasy before.

He used his keycard against the door to the stairwell between Floors C and B, and took a deep breath after the door had closed behind him. The rebels' strike that morning had been their first since the death of the AME shield a month earlier, and they had all escaped New London before Roth could even make it downstairs to meet them. Grant would not be happy, but still: calling a meeting about it was a surprising response.

Roth scanned his keycard again at the entrance to Floor B and was met on the other side by Nathaniel Pearce, who had clearly been waiting.

What the hell is Grant's smarmy smart-arse Chief Scientist doing here?

'Ah, Oliver,' Pearce said with his trademark grin. 'We're going to Iain's office. Nick's already there.'

'Iain's office?' Roth laughed. 'Seriously?'

'He has his reasons. And he doesn't want me to spoil them. Come along.'

Roth followed, noticing the disdain in Pearce's voice despite his grin. That lifted his spirits a little. If something annoyed Nathaniel Pearce, it was likely to be good – or at least entertaining.

Oliver Roth had not seen the office since the night Iain Marshall had died in it: since the prisoner in the room had exploded with such force that the whole AME computer had been annihilated, along with everything else in the room including Marshall. Even after a month, Roth was surprised they'd finished scraping Joseph McCormick off the walls.

A couple of Floor B workers shot a glance at Roth as he passed. Perhaps he looked out of place with his combat boots marching across the carpeted corridor, with sweat dripping from his forehead and a loaded assault rifle instead of a suit and tie. Or maybe the stares were because of his reputation. They were in the presence of Nicholas Grant's fourteen-year-old master assassin, slaughterer of countryside rebels – and occasional punisher of staff members when required.

Marshall's office was up ahead. The floor in front of the entrance had been recarpeted, with an ever-so-slightly different colour that made it stand out awkwardly from the rest of the corridor. Roth noticed himself slowing down, enough for Pearce to glance behind him.

This room was where my life began, he thought. *The good life, anyway.*

His mind, very briefly, went back to the early meetings he used to have in that office, alone with a man he admired. Iain Marshall, war veteran of twelve years (who had not yet told him about his eight as an arms dealer), had been a rare person Roth had looked up to. At twelve years old, in a Britain that existed before the clones took over, not many people held that status in Roth's life. Their meetings had largely been theoretical training sessions, with Marshall teaching him about military strategy, weapons, and the dirtier tactics that Marshall-Pearce's youth training programme had not dared to touch.

He never talked about Oliver Roth's *real* reason for being there, of course. He was too smart to discuss it in a place which stood a one per cent chance of being bugged, in addition to having compulsory CCTV. The subject only came up during their field trips and training sessions in the forest. Once upon a time, Oliver Roth was going to prevent Takeover Day from ever happening, by assassinating Nicholas Grant himself. Clearly though, Marshall had lost his nerve and never given him the signal.

Roth felt no guilt about the little fact that he could have stopped Takeover Day before it began. It had been Marshall's decision rather than his own. It had also been perfect blackmail material – the ability to walk up to Grant and spill the beans any time he liked – but Roth had never needed to actually make any threats. Marshall had been careful enough to give him everything he ever wanted in order to buy his silence.

Oliver Roth sighed as he realised the true reason why he felt uneasy that day, and why he missed Iain Marshall. His leverage was gone; all his unspoken power vanished in that explosion. He no longer had the unquestioning support of Grant's Head of Military.

He turned into the office, and found himself in unfamiliar territory. All trace of the explosion was gone, not a charred stain in sight. It looked like the room had been rebuilt altogether rather than just redecorated.

At the new desk, placed on the opposite side of the room to where the old one had been, Nicholas Grant sat in a large leather chair.

'Oliver,' he said, in a voice that could perhaps have been called friendly, 'take a seat.'

Another leather chair had been placed on the other side of

the desk. Grant stretched out a welcoming hand. Roth knew right away that this wasn't about his failure to contain the rebels that morning.

'Do you actually need me here?' asked Pearce.

'Yes,' said Grant. 'This is a formal ceremony that should be witnessed by the most valuable people in the Citadel. Unless you don't consider yourself that valuable?'

Pearce said nothing. Roth sat down in the chair, and browsed the paper placed on the desk for him to read. It was a contract of some sort, as far as he understood.

'Formal ceremony?' he asked. 'You should have let me get changed.'

'I thought you'd feel more comfortable in your current outfit.'

He's not wrong, thought Roth.

'So what's this about?' he asked.

'You're getting promoted,' answered Grant with an enthusiastic grin. 'You're one signature away from becoming my Head of Military Division.'

Oliver Roth had a lifelong habit of not letting his emotions show on his face, but it was difficult when surprises were landed on him. His eyebrows rose to the top of his head, his mouth opened, and his eyes stared into Grant's like a man who had won the lottery and been caught in a car's headlights at the same time. His thoughts about the three escaping rebels left his mind altogether.

'I'm Iain's replacement,' he gasped.

'The youngest field marshal in history.'

'Why me?'

'There aren't many other candidates, in all fairness,' Grant replied as he leaned back in his leather chair. 'I have a few other ex-military personnel on my payroll, but none of them have modern, post-Takeover experience like you. Keith Tylor would have been perfect back in the day, before he came down with that bad case of multiple stab wounds. So that leaves either you or some colonel downstairs, and you're the one I believe in most. Besides, I'm sure Iain would have wanted it.'

You'd be surprised what Iain Marshall would have wanted.

'Do I still get to serve in the field?' Roth asked.

'Yes, you'll still get to run through the corridors killing rebels. Except now you'll do it with *real* authority. And this office will be yours once it's finished. It may be a couple more weeks, but I'm sure you understand.'

Roth flipped through the contract, pretending to understand all the legal words.

'Wait,' he asked, 'so how come we *still* haven't rebuilt the clone factory two months on, but this office can be completely fixed in a matter of weeks?'

Pearce guffawed from the entrance.

'And that sentence right there,' he said, 'is why you're Head of Military and not Chief Scientist. You clearly have no appreciation for the complexities involved with building a factory that produces armies of imitation humans.'

'That and *you're* still alive. For now.'

'Oliver,' Grant said with a discreet laugh, 'don't threaten your closest colleague.'

'Why not? Iain and Nat fought all the time. I'll sign this contract, but I'm not becoming his new best friend.'

Roth grabbed a fountain pen that Grant had left next to his papers, and found the dotted line.

Then something strange happened. He had not heard McCormick's voice for a month, and had only heard it for one evening, but he recognised it when it entered his head.

The world is full of young people who think their futures are already decided, just because they've been instructed to believe it.

It had been one of McCormick's sentences that Roth had tried to ignore. Even now, he did his best.

Even though we don't get to decide what happens to us, we do get to choose how we respond. And even if people tell you your future is predestined...

Roth shook his head, and hoped that Grant wouldn't notice.

He remembered his miniature breakdown on the night McCormick died: when he came to realise that he had already made every meaningful decision that would decide the course of his life. When he had realised that, in all likelihood, it really was too late for him.

Helplessly obedient to his boss, despite being the only person in the room with an assault rifle, Oliver Roth signed on the dotted line. And just like that, he became the second most powerful person in the whole of Great Britain.

'Ok, job done,' Pearce said, stretching his arms. 'Can I go now?'

'Has Gwen arrived?'

'Not as yet.'

'Then no, you can't.'

Roth smiled. He didn't know much about Gwen Crossland, except for her now-famous work on the Ginelli Project, but he knew to keep his distance from her. After Marshall's death, someone in Grant's health department recommended her to Roth as a psychotherapist who might help him. Roth had obviously declined: the less influence that tiny well-spoken Womble had over his brain, the better off he would be.

Suddenly, she was there. Standing in the entrance, next to Nathaniel Pearce.

Bloody hell, she even moves like a bloody poltergeist.

'Nicholas,' she said, although her lips barely moved.

'Nick,' Grant corrected her. 'Are you ready?'

'My bags are packed, and my equipment is in safe hands. But my work on Floor G is not yet complete.'

'How long, do you think?'

Roth noticed how polite Grant was being to Gwen Crossland. He could not tell whether it was genuine politeness to a lady from his own generation, or politeness inspired by fear.

'I should be done by the end of the morning,' she answered. 'I'm just waiting for Nathaniel's company. He should join me to observe the Acceleration experiment.'

'I'll tell the vehicle port operatives you'll be joining them at lunchtime then,' said Grant. 'You should make it to the transport mid-afternoon, preparation should be ready by the evening, and you'll be there before midnight. Enjoy New Oxford, both of you. It's strikingly similar to New London, except the staff are less interesting.'

'In my experience,' finished Crossland, 'it's the "interesting" people who are the most problematic. Nathaniel?'

She walked away with Nathaniel Pearce in tow, leaving Roth on his own with Nicholas Grant.

'Why are they going to New Oxford?' asked Roth.

'They're going to engineer the greatest one-day bloodbath in human history,' answered Grant. 'I'll fill you in later. In the meantime, you've got a bloodbath of your own to organise.'

Grant leaned forward, placing his elbows on his desk and interlocking his fingers. The expression on his face turned bitter.

'It's not often I admit to making mistakes, Oliver. But the biggest mistake I ever made was underestimating Joseph McCormick. He and his band of countryside wildlife were able to reach our upper floors and stop us from becoming invincible, all because I didn't think they were worth paying attention to.'

Stop making excuses, you old fart. You've been paying attention to them ever since your daughter started helping them. I mean bloody hell, you even made their old school the main AME test centre.

'So it's time to deal with them once and for all,' Grant continued. 'And I know you've focused a lot of effort on them since the Takeover. You've dispatched six of them personally, haven't you?'

'Eight.'

'Even better. Now last time I checked the list, only nine names on it belonged to people who are still alive. Ten, if you include my backstabbing daughter. I need you to make it *zero*. And from now on, we're not waiting for them to come to us.'

Oliver Roth went over Grant's sentences word by word in his mind, just to double and triple-check he had interpreted them right. But whatever way he looked at it, the message was the same: he no longer wanted Shannon alive. After losing Keith Tylor to her, and then the clone factory *and* AME shield presumably because of intelligence she had shared, evidently enough was enough. The death of his daughter was now a vital part of his vision for success.

'They still think you're dead, don't they?' asked Grant.

Roth nodded, and tried to ignore the memory of why. Ewan West had beaten him in that duel in the burning experiment chamber, shooting him four times in his invisible Kevlar and leaving him to burn. His enemies had every reason to believe he had died that night, especially since the only Underdog who had seen him after the duel had died before he could speak to his allies.

'What do you want me to do?' he asked.

'That countryside hideout they have… Spitfire's Rise, I think they call it.'

Surely he's not asking…

'Sir, there must be a million square miles of—'

'I'm going to give you until the end of the day,' Grant interrupted, 'and then you're leaving New London. Take as many soldiers as you see fit, and whatever resources you feel you need. And do not return to this Citadel until you have found Spitfire's Rise and destroyed it.'

Unbound is the world's first crowdfunding publisher, established in 2011.

We believe that wonderful things can happen when you clear a path for people who share a passion. That's why we've built a platform that brings together readers and authors to crowdfund books they believe in – and give fresh ideas that don't fit the traditional mould the chance they deserve.

This book is in your hands because readers made it possible. Everyone who pledged their support is listed at the front of the book and below. Join them by visiting unbound.com and supporting a book today.

Conaire Abrams
Angeline B Adams
Rachel Simone Alsop
Dena Annand
Darren Anscombe
Darva Arellano
Rowan Astley
James Atkinson
John Atkinson
Juli Atkinson
Suzy Atkinson
Neil Austin
Toni Austin
Sara Baggins
Rebecca Baker
Eileen Ball
Sandro Ballesteros
Alexandra Barnes
Karyn Bassick

Cairn Batchelor
Helen Bates
Kathryn Bateson
George Luke Batty
Pauline Baxter
Sari Beastall
Cherry Bedford
Sarah Benson
Dylan 'Azorath' Bentley
Leia Bergqvist
Susanna Berry
Kristy Bibby
Deirdre Blackie
Georgina Blair
Joanne Blythe
Inge Boes
Zachary Borghello
Suzanne Brady
Thomas Brevik

Amy Brian
Anna-Maria Bromley
Elena Brooke
Shawn Brooks
John Buckmaster
Ali Burns
Victoria Busuttil
Fred Byrne
Eleanor Cain
Adam Carter
Grace Caven-Atack
Sarah Chambers-Tonner
Eddie Charters
Cecelia Chittey
Shannon Christensen
Lynn Clunie
Lou Coleman
Denise Cone
Jonathan Cooper
Gina Cotterill
Emma Crabb
Rachel Cropley
Rhys Lysandra Davies
Renee Davis
Dominic DeBona
Leon and Xander Delsaint
Kris Deutch
Bette Dick
Ian Dockree
Helen Doody
Robert Dunbar
Marcus Dustin
Patrick Dwyer
Cathryn Edmonds
Elise Elderkin
Emma Ellard
Chris England
Julie Erwin
Harris Family
Caitlin Ferrence
Fiona, Travis and Patch
H Fish
Matthew Fleming
Mary Ford
Oliver Fox
Julie Gagnon

Therese Gallop
Jasmin Gibbons
Sue Goldman
Wendy Graves
Jane Gray
Kären Gray
Josephine Greenland
Lois Groat
Diane Hall
Susie Halliwell
Steve Hanlon
Anna Hardy
Becks Harper
Christiane Hart
Aaron Haynes
Bonny Hazelwood
Jane Hendricks
Tim Herman
Karren Herron
Joseph Hilton
Tracey Holland
Karen Holmes
Victoria Holtz
Michelle Hughes
Christina Hummel
Tracy Humphreys
Lucas Imaguire Kretschek
Bernadette Jaroch-Hagerman
Dawn Jeyes
Danielle Jiang
Ellyn Junfola
Sonja Kaster
Zachary Keita
Kelly Kemp
Richard Kemp-Luck
Hannah Kerr
Cleoniki Kesidis
Dan Kieran
Annie Knowles
Sigve Kolbeinson
Anna Kulczycka
Derek Landress
Jane Langdon
Kris Larsen
Ezra Law
Ben League

Jackie Leiker
Tona Loving
Archie Ludlow
Helen Lynne
Hester Lyons
Tanya Maat
Lily Mabberley
Mekki MacAulay
Kim Marie
Ben W. Martin
S.I.S. Martin
Plaxy Matthews
Andrew Maynard
Rabiyah Mazhar
Jennifer McGowan
Paige McKay
Connall Mclellan
Lesley Michalska
Louisa Middleweek
Carl Mills
Karen Mitchell
John Mitchinson
Kim Mockridge
Jorik Mol
Andrew Morris
Owen Morris
Micah Mosse
Elise Mountford
Natasha Mullan
Layla Murphy-Plant
Rhel ná DecVandé
Carlo Navato
Susie Niewand
Jenny Noakes
Suzanne Nobile
Julie Nolan
Hegedüs Norina
Becs Norman
Tara Northen
Isabel O'Brien
Alexander Ogden-McKaughan
Benas Olisauskas
Maegan Oxborrow
Jade Page
Chris Papadopoulos
Cindy Payne

Kerri-Lee Pearson
Kendra Petkau
Nye Phillips
Sally Pickard
Justin Pollard
Anya Pollock
Chris Purdum
Mona Puttick
David Quinn
Karen Ralston
Brendon Reece
Katie Rich
Clare Riley
Ewan Rizzo
Elvire Roberts
Eitan Rosa
Eileen Ross
Jessica Ruh
Heidi Ryan
Riko Ryuki
Gabby Saj
Beth Saunders
Paula Saunders
Ruth Sawyer
Joshua Schlanger
Matthew Searle
Jeffrey Segal
Karen Shephard
Michael Slater
Caryn Smith
Oliver Smith
Rohan Smith
Alexander, Xavier and Letho
Soendergaard
Kels Spencer
Kate Spry
Beth Stevic
Catriona Stewart
Richard Stumpf
Kari Stuntz
Jenny Sweeney
Jessica Szucki
Mikki Tabick
Donna Taylor
Beth Tierney
Sarah Tillman

Caddie Tkenye
Kim Tomlinson
NdiVisible Tui (invisible disability/
neurodiversity blogger)
Wilhelmina Turton
Zuleika Van Dieren
Ingrid Velasquez
Jon Vogel
Dean Wade
D Walden
Louise Walton
Mathew Ward
Madelynn Waters
Merryl Watkins
Weekes boys

Wernersville Public Library
Stacey Whitaker
Carol Anne Williams
Su Williams
George Withers
Hannah Wood
Lesley Woodall
Lydia Woodroff
C, B & G Woods
Cato Woodward
Mandy Wultsch
The Wurm Family
Lucy Yeomans
Jana Young
Sandra Zeigler